DANDELION AUDIT

THE DEBT COLLECTION
BOOK 2

ANDREW GIVLER

Editor: Crystal Watanabe
Cover Illustration: Chris McGrath
Cover Design and Interior Layout: STK•Kreations

Hardcover ISBN: 978-1-958204-06-1
Trade paperback ISBN: 978-1-958204-05-4
eBook ISBN: 978-1-958204-04-7
Worldwide Rights

THE DEBT COLLECTION SERIES:

Soul Fraud

Dandelion Audit

Star Summit

STAY UP TO DATE

Scan the code or find me on these social media platforms to stay up
to date on my upcoming projects and book releases!

Sign Up for my Newsletter by visiting andrewgivler.com

Book YouTube Channel: @GivReads

Instagram: @sigils

Twitter: @Sigils

Facebook: @andrewgivler

For MH & GH
who have inspired and encouraged me in countless ways.
None of this is their fault.

DANDELION AUDIT

THE DANDELIONS ARE following me.

I know how that sounds. I'm not crazy.

They're following me because I owe the Queen of All Fae a phone call. A year ago, I rescued a golden-eyed Faerie—that's British for Fairy—named Robin Goodfellow from a lab that was doing experiments on supernatural creatures. His boss, Gloriana, the queen I mentioned, asked to speak with me. Apparently all I needed to do to reach her was blow out one of her "candles," which are what normal people call dandelions.

Ever since then, everywhere I go, the fuzzy little flowers have been waiting for me. There's been a pair growing in the cracks of the sidewalk in front of my apartment building for the past eleven months. I've seen them rooted in the planter boxes outside my favorite restaurant. I've seen at least one growing in the bottom of an aquarium. Don't ask me how that works. I should probably answer her call at some point. In my defense, I've been a little busy.

The point is: if, for whatever reason, I ever need a dandelion in a hurry, I should be able to find one without too much sweat. I only mention my floral stalkers because I was staring at a pair of them growing out of the sidewalk of the abandoned storefront that I was lurking in front of with Alex.

The dandelions might be following me, but I was following a pack of demons.

I can explain that too.

Our boss, Orion, sent the two of us to spy on a group of fiends scurrying around Los Angeles. Orion is pretty famous. He's the guy whose belt is made up of those three bright stars in a perfect line that are impossible to miss in the night sky. Don't ask me what the rest of the constellation looks like because I've never seen it. There's too much light pollution in LA.

Anyway, the Orion in the sky is named after my Orion on the ground, not the other way around. He is the Hunter and master of the Hunt. Alex and I are his squires, his proverbial left and right hands. I'm pretty sure I'm the left one, but that's irrelevant.

Turns out, joining the Hunt makes you spend a lot of time hunting. In hindsight, I guess that should have been obvious. But it isn't duck and rabbit that are high on Orion's list—he's much more interested in incubi, succubi, and every infernal in-between. As far as he's concerned, it's *always* demon season. The denizens of Hell are not welcome in the Hunter's territory.

"They're probably not even doing anything interesting in there," my friend Alex complained in a whisper to me. He was crouched low enough that his styled blond hair was hidden behind the hood of the dingy old sedan we were squatting behind. "I bet they're like junior demons selling illegal lotto tickets or something."

I snorted quietly as I tried to peer around the side of the car into the windows of the storefront. According to the sign, it used to be a Big Pappa's Pizzeria—well, that's what I was guessing "–IG P–PP–" used to say when all the letters of the sign were still there.

"Maybe they're trying to start an infernal pizzeria," I whispered back.

"I bet their red sauce would be to die for."

The average demon isn't supposed to hang out in the mortal realm, they're not allowed. There are exceptions to the rule. Some of them have work visas that let them prowl around for specific reasons, like Dan the Demon from the sales department. Some of the big scary ones have diplomatic immunity. Other than that, there's only one way for a demon to get a ticket out of the good old fiery pit and into human territory—they have to be summoned. So when Orion picked up the trail of this group of minor demons wandering around LA unsupervised, he sent his two best squires to check it out.

We're also his only squires, but that's beside the point.

Over the last year, Alex and I have suffered under the relentless training of Orion. I lost some baby fat, gained muscle, and now have a crippling knowledge of how many different things want to eat me. But some of his teachings had rubbed off on the two of us, enough that he trusted us to run a little recon on some guppy demons sneaking into the Hunter's territory.

"Here comes another one," Alex whispered, getting lower behind the car.

"That makes five," I muttered, copying his caution. "Maybe they're meeting for Demon Scouts."

"Nah, Infernals Anonymous."

"Nice," I said, and we rapped knuckles. Camaraderie and inside jokes are the only major perks when it comes to hunting demons—we don't get medical insurance or 401(k)s.

I shifted my crouch slightly to peer past the car. The demons we had seen heading into the abandoned pizzeria were all capable of passing as mortal. They had two arms, legs, and normal proportions. If you didn't know what to look for, you might sit next to one of them on the bus and never even notice. Depending on the route in LA, you might prefer to sit next to them than some of the actual mortals on the bus. Damned they might be, but I've never smelled a demon that needed to put on deodorant. I'd take a hint of sulfur over some rank body odor any day.

"Now what do we do?" Alex whispered to me after a few long moments. "It's your turn to make the decisions and get in trouble with the boss."

"Thanks," I muttered, leaning forward to scan the building again. We couldn't see anything. That's what happens when the creatures you're trying to spy on go inside and close the door. Rude.

Technically, Orion had tasked us with tracking the demons and seeing what they were up to. He hadn't told us to pick a fight with them. Even demons that are lower on Hell's org chart, the rank-and-file employees, are hard to kill. Once you get up to the managers or executive-level demons, you need something with a lot of juju, like a fiery magic sword, as a random example.

The problem with sizing up a fight with a pack of demons is it can be hard to tell what level of demon you're dealing with, until you're in the thick of it. They don't have any convenient markings, like venomous snakes or an extra fork tine in their tails. Smart money would have us wait outside and see where they went next.

But between me being a broke college graduate with no soul and Alex technically being a freelance journalist for the *Supernatural Times* or whatever, we were collectively worth maybe twenty bucks. That's not enough money to be smart or stupid. That's barely enough to buy a sandwich and a soda in LA.

"I say we check it out," I whispered after a few moments of thought.

"You sure? He didn't say anything about us making moves."

"We came all this way," I said with a shrug. "We might as well take a quick little peek."

Alex's face split with a mischievous grin. "Traffic is probably terrible right now anyway."

"You kidding me? The 405 at this hour? Basically a parking lot."

"Might as well stick around here for a little bit until it dies down."

"Hungry?" I asked, nodding my head toward the abandoned pizzeria.

"I could eat," my friend said, narrowing his eyes at the storefront, "and I have a craving for some pizza right about now."

By silent agreement, we both began crab-walking around the abandoned car toward the pizzeria. This was a bad idea. I knew it was a bad idea. Alex knew it was a bad idea. If we asked Orion, he would tell us not to do it. But he would also understand. This was our territory. Something deep in my chest was indignant that they dared to come into it. Maybe this was how dogs felt when they smelled another dog's pee on their fire hydrant. Whatever it was, Alex felt it too. The demons were not welcome, and someone ought to make sure they knew that.

Conveniently, we just happened to be a pair of willing someones.

Alex made the sprint across the parking lot first. I watched from the safety of the front bumper as he dashed across the asphalt to the side of the building. As soon as he reached the other side, we both froze, desperately listening for any sound that the demons inside had noticed. Well, I was listening, but if there was anything to hear, Alex was more likely to pick it up thanks to his Nephilim genetics.

Alex is many generations removed from his demonic ancestor. His DNA is mostly human. If you didn't notice the slight sharp edge of his ears, you would probably never even guess that he was something more than mortal. But if you pay attention, you'll notice that some of his stats are padded. He's stronger and faster than he has any right to be. Father Time skips his birthday almost every year. Although he looks to be in his twenties, Alex is closer to two hundred years old.

It's not fair.

A few moments passed, and no demonic horrors erupted out of the decrepit pizzeria to try to eat Alex's face. He gave me a tiny wave, and I jogged my way across the lot to meet him. I did it, like, exactly as fast as he did if anyone was wondering.

I joined him in leaning on the wall, across the door from him. I held my breath, which was easy because I was in no way short of breath. Frozen, we listened to see if my crossing had raised any alarms.

The good news was the demons almost certainly did not hear us run to the building. The bad news: it was because they were distracted by a screaming woman and crying children.

"Please! Just let them go," she cried.

Alex and I traded glances. His ever-present mischievous grin was nowhere to be seen. Instead a dark fury twinkled in his blue eyes, like the rage of the deep sea. He must have seen a similar expression on my face, because simultaneously, we both reached under our jackets and drew our pistols. The demons were no longer only intruders, now they were poaching. The Hunt could not abide that.

Bullets are a funny thing in the supernatural world. They're definitely less effective than what we humans are used to. But I don't care how immortal you are, the laws of physics apply to everyone. Getting slapped around by hot lead flying at six hundred miles an hour isn't ever fun. Plus, our bullets have a special cold iron jacket that loads of supernatural creatures *hate*.

I reached my free hand into my pocket and pulled out my phone. I sent our location to Orion, a pulsing Hunter signal.

The woman screamed again, her voice cut off by a harsher male tone.

Gun held in his left hand, Alex slowly reached for the door, his eyebrows raised in a question. I reset my grip on the pistol and gave him a sharp nod.

Slowly, ever so slowly, Alex began to inch the warped metal door open. My heart raced, the familiar fear dumping adrenaline into my veins by the gallon. But the fear was controlled; it did not control me. I was not the same clueless boy who had encountered a ghoul in his living room. My eyes had been opened, and I had been watching ever since.

My hands moved automatically, guided by thousands of hours of programming that Orion had drilled into me over the last year. The door slowly widened into a six-inch gap, and I stepped to fill it, my pistol aimed into the darkness within.

The door's maw opened further, and I slipped sideways through the gap, stepping to the side to make room for Alex to follow me. Slowly, he let the door close, sealing us in the dim room.

The front of the pizzeria was abandoned. A few tables and chairs lay scattered around the room like they had been hit by a tornado. A thick layer of dust lay over the whole room, except for a disturbed path leading through the wooden door into the back.

The woman's voice was back now, speaking in a slow, choppy cadence, interrupted by the occasional sob. I couldn't make out the words, but the hairs on my neck and arms began to stand at attention like the air was charged with static electricity.

That couldn't be a good sign.

With the patience of a pair of mountain lions stalking their prey, Alex and I worked our way through the eating area of the restaurant. Each footstep chosen with extreme care. Silent as the deepest moment of the night, we glided forward, hunting.

At the next door, we repeated the process. Alex grabbed the door handle, and with the iron perseverance of an ancient tortoise, began to pull it open. The plan was to open the door without making noise, letting us ambush the demons in their lair.

Grease must have been the first thing to get cut from the budget as Big Pappa's began to go out of business. The moment Alex started pulling the door open, those hinges let out a squeal louder than the final trumpet that my grandmother says is supposed to wake the dead and start the end of the world. The woman's voice cut out in surprise, and angry growls filled the room. As far as ambushes go, it left a lot to be desired.

Fortunately for this dynamic duo, the Hunter is a thorough teacher.

Our chance at surprise ruined, Alex wrenched open the door as hard as his amped-up superhero muscles could pull. It swung wide with a squeal like someone had just murdered a bagpipe—or maybe just played a bagpipe.

I surged forward into the breach, weapon raised, finger on the trigger.

A dark woman with dark hair stood in the center of what had once been an industrial kitchen, she held a giant leatherbound book in her shaking hands. Two children sat against the wall in the corner, fear bright in their eyes. Beyond them lay a man I feared was their father, motionless on the floor, blood pooling around him, bright red on the white linoleum floor.

Five demons stood around the center of the room in a half-moon formation. They looked like men, but the dark abyss of their black eyes proclaimed them as monsters.

Drawn on the ground in front of them was something I recognized all too well from personal experience—a circle drawn in the dark red of fresh blood. Candles were evenly spaced around the ring, their flames sending shadows dancing in the low light of the kitchen.

A summoning circle.

See, one of the tricks about demons needing to be summoned to be able to get out of the basement and sneak up into the main floor of the mortal realm is that demons can't summon more demons. They don't get plus-ones to the party. Just like the old vampire stories, they have to be invited by a mortal.

These demons had snuck into the VIP area and were trying to crack the door open for their friends. This poor woman and her family were their ticket to get the rest of the foxes into the henhouse.

"If you love your children, do not stop!" growled the demon at the bottom of the circle, in line with the bottom point of the pentagram. The demon wore the body of a lean man in his forties. He had thinning brown hair and a permanently frowning mouth. His body was lean like a professional runner. He reminded me of my old neighbor Carl who ran marathons.

For a second we all froze, Hunters and demons sizing each other up like two packs of dogs encountering each other in the street. The adrenaline and rage in my body was screaming at me to start shooting, but I hesitated. They had hostages.

"Kill the interlopers," the Carl-like demon commanded to the rest of the infernal pack as the woman's hesitant voice resumed chanting, adding a creepy soundtrack to our showdown.

That was enough for me.

I snapped the sights of my pistol on the demon closest to me, hidden in the body of a short woman, and fired two 9mm rounds into her. She let out a horrified shriek as the impact of the bullets sent her flying and the cold iron burned her flesh.

Alex covered me, flowing to my left, like we had practiced a hundred times. He shot at the closest demon to my left. I turned to the right and blazed away. The demons were caught flat-footed. They hadn't been expecting to face mortals who knew what they were doing.

The demons screamed as the bullets slammed into their flesh, and the smell of sulfur and gunpowder began to be overshadowed by the stench of burning meat. Three of the demons went down in the first ten seconds. We were acolytes of the Hunter, extensions of his wrath and will, and we crashed down on them like a wave of judgment.

The fourth demon froze in place, jaw dropping as her fellow infernals sizzled on the floor.

I shot her too.

Not-Actually-Carl learned from his companions' failures. Instead of running straight at us, he spun from the summoning circle and pounced toward the corner where the two children cowered. His superpowered leap would make an Olympic long jumper jealous. He slid into a sprint and snatched up one of the kids, a girl no older than twelve, who wailed in fear.

"No!" screamed Alex, pistol pointed at the lean demon.

"Keep reading," the demon snarled at the kids' mother, his voice warped in an otherworldly command.

The woman gave me a despairing look but did as she was instructed. The book in her hands shook like a paper airplane in a hurricane, tossed about by the currents of her fear.

I didn't blame her. If my children were being held hostage by monsters, seeing two twenty-five-year-olds wielding guns rush in wouldn't fill me with a lot of confidence either.

The demon sneered, turning his black eyes on Alex and me. "One more step, mortal, and I will crack this childling's skull like an egg." His long fingers wrapped around the girl's arms as he held her in front of him like a literal shield.

I cursed, frustrated by the standoff. Time was our enemy here. If we waited too long, the summoning would be completed, and whatever they were trying to bring into our world would be here. No thank you.

To make things worse, the demons we had shot were down but far from out. Cold iron might burn them more than the fires of Hell itself, but it wasn't enough to kill them. The longer we sat here, the more likely one of them was going to get back on their feet.

But we couldn't let anything happen to the child.

A dozen terrible ideas from action movies flitted through my head. I wracked my brain for an idea. What would Orion do in this situation? *He wouldn't let himself get in this situation in the first place,* I scolded myself.

In a panic, I debated just taking the shot. If we did nothing, we were likely all going to die anyway. And not to be *totally* selfish, but if I did die, given the current status of my soul, that would only be the start of my problems.

The mother's voice rose, the Latin words seeming to take on a life of their own. Tick-tock. Tick-tock.

"Let her go," I yelled at the gangly, older demon. "Or I'll kill you like I killed Lilith."

"—*in terra est!*" she cried out, and was silent.

A familiar stillness settled over the room, like fog rolling in from the ocean. It was the weight of an Immortal stepping into mortal time and space. Gravity felt slightly skewed, as if it was being warped by a mass that did not belong.

Slowly, as though being pulled by a force beyond my control, my head turned from the demon we held at gunpoint and to the summoning circle.

The man inside the ring looked like he had just wandered off the set of his magazine cover shoot to grab a quick coffee. He wore an exquisitely tailored black suit with a white shirt that you just knew was Italian. He had dark hair and a square jaw that looked like it was carved from pure marble. His black eyes were fixed on me with the intensity of a cat hunting butterflies.

This was getting to be all too familiar.

"Not everything has to have a sequel," Alex groaned from my left.

"Good evening," he said in a mellow voice to the still room. His voice carried easily over the slight sizzling sound of the demons still suffering from their bullet wounds. "If someone would be so kind as to open the door, I would love to come in and hear more about what you have to say about my dear departed friend Lilith."

I said there were levels to demons, and that sometimes it could be hard to tell the difference between them, right? Well, sometimes it's really freaking easy too. I did my best to swallow the lump in my throat without making an audible gulp. A smile bloomed in those black eyes, telling me I was not successful in hiding my fear.

But as bad as this looked, there was still a chance. This new demon was still trapped inside the summoning circle. It was functioning essentially like an airlock between our two worlds. Until our side was opened, he couldn't completely step through the two planes. All we had to do was keep his cronies from opening the final door. I had a plan—but if it didn't work, I would never forgive myself.

Not-Carl took a step toward the circle.

"Uh-uh," I told him, stepping between him and the circle. "In your dreams, demon."

"Out of my way or the child dies," he growled, moving a hand toward her tiny neck. Heart racing, I slowly shook my head. I could not afford to feel. I needed to have a heart of stone.

"You hurt that kid and you'll die screaming for mercy while your boss watches from his front-row seat," I said. Inside my skull, my personal demons went insane, fed by the flames of fear. Anxiety raged that I couldn't handle the stress. Insecurity whispered that I wasn't strong enough to protect them. Uncertainty told me I was going to get this poor child killed. I did my best to tune them out and keep my gun steady.

I kept the barrel of my gun trained on the demon. I was not a man. I was a stone. A stone does not fear. It does not doubt. It is solid. Not-Carl turned his attention to the mother behind me.

"If you want your child to live, break the circle."

I heard her take a shuffling step behind me, and my stone heart cracked but did not break. I couldn't let her set him free.

"Alex," I murmured.

Wordlessly, my friend pulled the mother away. She screamed and swung her fists at him. He took her blows without complaint, the anger on his face growing harder with each hit.

I kept my eyes on the marathon-running demon holding the child. He gave me a wicked smile, revealing his teeth had shifted to pointy monstrosities.

"My kindred will wake eventually, human," he gloated. "When we eat you and your friends, I will make sure we leave you for last."

"I have an alternative solution," murmured the supermodel demon locked in the circle. "Let's make a deal."

ABSOLUTELY NOT," I said, risking a glance over at the contained demon. He wore a confident smile, both his hands shoved into his suit pockets like he didn't have a care in the world. "I've more than learned my lesson about that one, thanks."

"Matthew Carver," he breathed in an uncomfortably intimate way. "Yes, I am familiar with your account with us. You've secured quite the care package. But there are *always* upgrades."

Against my better judgment, I looked at the smirking demon again.

"Are you some sort of manager demon?" I asked. I tried not to feel a faint glimmer of excitement in my chest. When Alex and I had accidentally summoned Lilith last year, we had been trying to speak to someone who had the authority to give me my soul back. That hadn't gone very well, but maybe I finally had the ear of a demon who could undo what Dan had done. I didn't need another vice president, just someone in middle management.

"What if I offered you a five-year extension on your payment?" the suave demon answered.

"Listen, uh, sir, I never signed the contract. One of your salesdemons forged my signature. I was kind of hoping we could just throw it out."

"Now that is a new one." The demon chuckled. "Unfortunately, I can't offer you a termination of the contract. Our CEO is personally invested in seeing it close."

Cold fear wrapped its slimy hands around my spine. I might have been brimming with newfound confidence, but I don't care who you are, being told that the CEO of Hell, el Diablo himself, is personally invested in making sure he claims your soul is terrifying. The original monster, the Big Bad himself, wanted revenge on yours truly. I suppose that's fair; I did kill his girlfriend. In my defense, she was trying to tear me to shreds at the time. I don't get the sense that he is much of a context guy, though.

Alex let out an uncomfortable cough beside me.

"Oh," I managed to choke out, after taking a second to process the devastating threat hidden in his words. "It's nice to be such a valued customer."

The senior demon's smile widened in a way that was only predatory, like a cheerleader who sees the nerdy girl has worn a homemade dress to prom.

"Ten years," he said smugly. "A ten-year extension to your contract, giving you nineteen years, one month, and three days until your bill is due. I can give you the specific minute and second time if you like."

I'm not sure if I should be ashamed to say that I was tempted. I don't know how to explain how much it weighs on my every waking moment knowing that no matter what happens, I am going to die at a specific time. It is a truth I can never escape, hovering just over my shoulder at all times, like a shadow cast over my entire life. I feel the minutes of my life slipping through my fingers like precious diamonds. I find myself desperately trying to hoard my days like a dragon with his treasure.

There was no guarantee that I would ever get my soul back. The system, such as it was, was not set up to handle a situation like mine, and I had *very* powerful enemies who did not want to see that fixed. There was a very real chance that in nine years, one month, and three days, my little soul was going to be dragged down to the fiery pits. If it was going to happen anyway, doubling my life wouldn't be nothing.

The child in the arms of the marathon-running demon let out a whimper.

All I had to do was let Hell win and set this demon free to wander out into the world. I doubted they were here to visit Disneyland. Although based off some of the rumors I've heard, maybe they were.

I looked into the abyss-filled eyes of the demon offering me another deal and actually used my brain for a second. It was this new thing I was trying out. I took a moment to step outside of myself and think. What was the point of offering me ten extra years? Sure, demons were immortal, and I've been assuming Hell exists outside of time and space anyway. What's a little extra time compared to infinity?

But also, why was this demon so eager to get out of the circle that he was willing to make a concession to me, infernal enemy number one?

A sinister thought wormed its way into my mind. A trickle of intuition that I marveled at, because I could still remember when this angle would never have occurred to me at all. But a year of dealing with people and creatures who never have just *one* plan had taught me some painful lessons.

"Out of curiosity," I said, trying to keep my voice free of suspicion, "would I have to sign something to lock in this new offer?"

"Nothing as dramatic as the last one," the demon said with a chuckle, but something flashed in his eyes. "Just a simple addendum that would get added to the contract."

There it was. A vicious pride surged in my chest as I recognized the trap that had been expertly set before me. I was right. The offer wasn't about the demon getting out of the circle. Or it probably was, but it wasn't *only* about that. You see, the one legal leg that I had to stand on to get my soul back was that I never signed the contract.

Demons are allowed to make deals to get mortals to sell their souls. That's the whole name of the game. The entire structure of the supernatural universe was apparently built around a free market, and we are the commodities. But Dan, acting as a representative of Hell Incorporated, hadn't made a real deal with me. They had stolen my soul, not paid for it. That had serious potential to cause big drama amongst the supernatural superpowers. We're talking whatever their equivalent of a World War is. Maybe a Super World War?

Apocalypse? Yeah, that was probably it.

The best chance I had for getting my soul back was the pressure that the other supernatural organizations and nations could put on Lucifer and his infernal employees if they tried to claim my soul illegally.

But that high ground would go out the window if I signed an addendum to a contract. Maybe I hadn't signed the original, but if I signed an agreement extending it, it would basically be the same thing, wouldn't it?

"Nice try," I said, turning my focus back on Not-Carl and the girl.

The caged fiend let out a dry chuckle.

"You can't blame a demon for trying," he said, not sounding at all bothered that I had figured out his ploy. "Besides, now things get much more interesting."

"How do you figure?" Alex asked. "Having a blast locked away in your little cone of shame?"

"I wonder," the suit continued in that same dry tone, "why you feel so confident that I am the *first* being this circle summoned?"

With a flash of panic, I glanced down at the ring in the center of the floor. The wicks on the candles were not fresh; they had clearly been burning for a while. The blood used was not dry, but it wasn't as fresh as I would like. I looked at the mother standing to the side, clutching the leather book she had read from. Her fear-filled eyes met mine, and she shook her head viciously.

"Oh crap—" I started to say before the back door of the kitchen burst open, and a monster charged in.

Some demons appear like mortal men and women. Minus the creepy black eyes, you might not notice them in your grocery aisle or passing you on the street. Then some demons are like Dan and don't look human at all, more like a cartoonist's nightmare, complete with the red skin, goat's legs, and pitchfork.

This new demon definitely fell into the second category. It could have been Dan's bigger, badder brother. At least seven feet tall, it had to duck its horned head to not hit it on the doorway as it stepped into the kitchen with cloven hooves that clomped on the broken linoleum floor. Its massive red torso sported four arms, each rippling with muscles like a bodybuilder, and its black eyes were locked on Alex and me, brimming with rage.

"Oh, no thanks," Alex said as we stared at the monster. "My doctor told me to cut back on sulfites."

"I think you're getting that confused with sulfur," I said to no one in particular, my mind still reeling, trying to come up with a plan.

"Oh, well, in that case, I guess I could have a little demon."

By unspoken agreement, we both spun, turning our guns on the monster, and let loose with everything we had left in our magazines. It grunted in irritation as our bullets slammed into it but didn't even stagger under the hail of our gunfire. Then without even a shrug, it charged at us, its four arms flailing like an octopus's demented half-sibling.

Alex and I dove in different directions as it hurtled through where we had been. I rolled to a crouch and fired two more shots into its hulking back. The quadra-demon twitched, like I was shooting it with airsoft pellets instead of military-grade bullets.

Like I said earlier: there's a point on the scale where the iron bullet stops being useful.

Now would have been a really great time for my hands to decide to burst into flames, unlocking the mysterious fire powers I had used to burn down an entire lab last year. I bet those flames would pack way more of a punch than our stupid bullets. I glanced down at them and gave my hands an energetic shake, but they remained flameless. There would be no magic fire to get us out of this mess.

"Stop!" cried Not-Carl the demon, holding the girl in the corner of the room. "Not another step!"

Alex and I both froze, black despair growing in my gut like the dark mold festering in the corners of this abandoned kitchen. I was out of ideas. I didn't know how we were going to get out of this.

"Free me," the suited demon said to the monster lurking next to his circle.

The quadra-demon stomped on one of the floor tiles with enough force that I was a little worried about how close we were to the San Andreas fault. We are overdue for the Big One; we don't need any extra shaking, thanks. The tile shattered, taking a portion of the bloody circle with it, tearing a hole in the ring's barrier between the demon world and ours.

With the casual gait of a veteran commuter hopping off the subway, the suited demon stepped over the ruined summoning circle and into Los Angeles. Alex and I traded glances, and I saw my own frustration mirrored on his face. We had played all our cards and lost.

"Ahhh," the suit said, inhaling deeply, like he was in the middle of a field of wildflowers, not a rotting, abandoned building. "It is so lovely to smell something other than sulfur."

Not-Carl chuckled in gleeful agreement. The monster didn't laugh, but I was pretty sure his invitation to the demon squad was due to his extra arms and not his sensational personality.

"How about we try a new deal? Hmm?" The boss rubbed his hands together, his black eyes hungrily staring at me. I felt my stomach drop as I realized that I was in more trouble than I had even realized. I wasn't just in danger of losing my life, but also any chance of getting my soul back.

"No thank you, Mr. Demon," I said as politely as I could. "My lawyer says I'm not supposed to sign any contracts that he doesn't approve."

"Call me Zagan." He paused, as if waiting to see if we'd heard of him.

I shrugged.

He sighed in mild irritation before he continued. "You are welcome to turn down any deal I offer. My only question is how many of these lovely people will my associates have to break into little pieces before you change your mind?"

I must admit, Zagan was an infinitely more effective negotiator than Dan the Demon.

I did my best not to shudder in fear. There was only one answer to that question: zero. I would let zero people be murdered by demons in exchange for my soul. Even if I got my soul back later, I would deserve to lose it all over again.

"None," I said, stepping forward to put the mother behind me.

The three demons stood in the corner, surrounding the two children. Zagan's smile spread wide, like a very satisfied raccoon. Even though I knew what I was giving up, I felt a small surge of relief that the others would be safe.

"Excellent. But what if I still want to kill one mortal for fun?" His victorious smile curled to something cruel. "I bet you'd sign anything to protect three of these humans, wouldn't you?" He sniffed dramatically in Alex's direction, like he had caught a whiff of something unpleasant. "Well, you're basically human, aren't you, half-breed?

"Let's see, who do I think would scream the most *deliciously*?" Zagan said, turning from each of us one by one, making a show of inspecting us like cuts of meat at the butcher's counter. The mother let out a whimper of fear. I didn't blame her. Her family made up three-quarters of the potential victims.

"I won't," I said, with what little bravery I had left. "You harm a single person in this room, and I won't sign a thing."

"Liar," Zagan said with an amused smirk. "You'll beg me to let you sign it before I decide I want a second sacrifice."

"Choose me," Alex said, stepping up to stand shoulder to shoulder with me. "I promise I scream real good."

I've said it before, and I will say it again: Alex is the best of people. If this was the end of our run, then being his friend was one of the things I was most proud of.

I had just opened my mouth to tell him something like that when everything went sideways—which, since we were hurtling straight down at an alarming rate, was an improvement.

There were layers to this negotiation. Before we burst into this failed pizza joint, I had lit the Hunter signal. I wasn't casually bartering my eternity away like a cheap trinket—it was bait.

A blazing sword, burning with the fiery fury of judgment, punched through the wall in the corner, its pointy tip cutting through the drywall like paper Orion drove his sword forward, stabbing into the back of Not-Carl, who was still holding the little girl hostage. The Immortal-killing blade bit into the demon's spine, and the infernal dropped bonelessly to the floor.

Zagan's mocking smile vanished.

The flaming sword drew back, disappearing to the other side of the wall. All that remained was a charred hole at neck height. I saw a flurry of motion through the crack, then in a cloud of drywall and dust, Orion the Hunter burst through the rotting wall like a wrecking ball.

"Ooooh yeah!" cheered Alex.

I felt my own spirits rise. Now they would pay.

Orion is tall, too tall. His arms and legs are also too long. He looks like he should have been swimming in the Olympics instead of fighting demons. His dark hair was cropped short and tight, which made his pointed ears even more prevalent. The flame of his sword danced in the reflection of his black eyes as he moved toward Zagan and his cronies.

Terrifying as Orion was, the scions of Hell still had a few tricks up their sleeves.

"Rise," snarled Zagan with a furious tone of command. At his word, the demons that Alex and I had incapacitated with iron bullets began to stir around the room. Whatever juice was backing Zagan's command gave them the willpower to overcome the cold iron. "Kill the Hunter and his pups."

The multi-armed behemoth wasted no time and charged Orion. The Hunter dove to the side, avoiding the grasping hands, rolling to his feet in a perfect dodge. I didn't blame him for being evasive; the demon was hurtling at him like a freight train. Stabbing a locomotive with a sword won't stop it from running you over, no matter how sharp it is. The monster smashed into the wall with so much force that it shook dust from the ceiling onto all of us like we were inside a snow globe.

Swift as a panther, Orion pounced on the recovering monster, carving searing wounds with his sword. The smell of brimstone grew to be overbearing.

Trusting Orion to be fine, I turned my attention to the rising demons. They weren't zombies, since we hadn't killed them, but it still felt extra creepy watching them begin to climb to their feet. You know the old saying, "All is fair in love and war?" It's also all fair when you're fighting demons and monsters. It's in the fine print. Look it up.

Alex and I didn't let them get back on their feet. I reached into my back pocket and pulled out a fresh magazine, reloading my pistol before firing two rounds into the demon who looked like a business-woman, knocking her flat. The other demon took three bullets before it collapsed again, sizzling like a sausage on a griddle.

That should have left only one.

I turned from the last downed demon, looking for the boss. Cold iron bullets might not be effective against a demon of Zagan's caliber, but I was more than happy to give him a few shots and see.

But the big bad demon was gone.

Orion slashed his burning blade several times, and the bestial demon collapsed, oozing black blood and the smell of rotten eggs. The only demons left in the room were on the ground, bleeding. We had won. My gaze fell on the still form of the children's father, an island in an ocean of his own blood.

It didn't feel like much of a victory.

The mother rushed to her two children, scooping them up with a grateful sob. Orion sprinted out of the kitchen, and Alex and I followed like eager puppies. Killing Zagan wouldn't make things right, but it would help a little.

I followed the Hunter as he charged out of the front of the piz-zeria. The supermodelesque demon couldn't have gotten far. He only had a few seconds of a head start. We burst out into the late afternoon

Los Angeles sun and screeched to a halt.

There was no one. No suit-jacketed individual sprinting away from the abandoned strip mall. It was silent, like the violence that had just occurred within hadn't made its way outside. The real world carried on, ignorant of the things lurking just out of sight. I guess that category included me now.

Orion spun in a circle, his teeth bared in a furious snarl. Alex and I glanced at each other, chests heaving, trying to catch our breath.

"That demon," Orion snarled, turning to us. "Did he say what his name was?"

"He said it was Zagan," Alex said.

"Dark Abyss," swore Orion. "I thought he was dead."

WITH THE DEMONS either dead or gone, the three of us turned to helping the victims. Alex carried the two children in his arms, his face a dark scowl of righteous rage as they both sobbed. When I first met Alex, he wanted to be a reporter, a modern-day storyteller of myth and legend. Now he walked a darker path.

I led their mother by the hand. Together we brought them out into the light. Demons aren't vampires. They don't burn to a crisp in the solar rays. But there's something innately protective about daylight. The golden eye in the sky always feels like it burns away the touch of foul and dark things. Maybe that's what vitamin D is for. I'm no doctor. However the science works, after a few minutes outside, the three of them began to calm down. The mother gathered both of her children in her arms and rocked them while sitting on the curb.

Orion remained inside and checked on their father. The Constellation was gone for a few moments, then he emerged with a grim frown on his face. The mother broke into fresh tears and her children, too innocent to understand why, joined her.

My list of enemies is long. I'm really obnoxious and don't know when to shut up. But I was more than happy to make some space right near the top for the demon model Zagan. From the look on Orion's face, I suspected I would have to get in line.

We did what we could for them.

It was less than I would have liked.

Thanks to Orion's status, the Hunt has a lot of sway in the supernatural world. People and creatures in the know give the Hunter and his squires some respect. In the mortal world, we're at best three illegally operating vigilantes. Even worse, I'm about two steps away from being a person of interest in my sister's kidnapping. Getting caught at a scene like this would have my LAPD friends, Detectives Jones and Rodgers, knocking on my door before I could blink.

We gave the family water. We gave the mother the phone number of a man named Driscoll, a Nephilim lawyer who would help her explain what had happened to the cops in a way that wouldn't get her committed to a psych ward. She certainly couldn't tell the mortal police the truth. Too much talk about demons killing her husband and the state might try to take her kids away.

We sat with her while she called the lawyer and then the cops.

Then we left.

I felt terrible. We'd caught on to the demons' plan too late to save the father. We didn't choose to sit by and let him die, and yet... he was dead, and his children would grow up without their father. That on its own was enough to crack my heart. But leaving the mother and kids sitting on the sidewalk threatened to shatter it completely. I understood why we had to do it, but it still felt like we were abandoning them.

Mathematically speaking, we saved three people. We had protected more lives than we had failed to at a three-to-one ratio. Yet the one that was lost weighed on me like infinity.

Orion hopped on his motorcycle. Alex and I piled into his ever-faithful white minivan. Together our little caravan pulled into traffic, our silence heavy and deafening.

"You know he's good, he's very good, but not even a comic-book-level superhero could have gotten to us through LA rush hour that fast," Alex said after a few minutes.

"What do you mean?"

"I mean the only way that he could have showed up that quickly from when you lit the Hunter signal was if he was already nearby."

"You think he was watching us?" I asked, realizing even as I spoke the question that of course he'd been. Orion's teaching style often felt like being thrown into the deep end to swim with the sharks, but the lifeguard was always on duty. I'm not sure if that made me feel better or worse. On the one hand, if Orion had also been there, then this wasn't *just* our fault. But being relieved about passing the blame just made me feel guilty all over again.

"Orion knew that Zagan demon," I said, changing the subject.

"Well, the demon certainly seemed to know you," Alex replied with a sigh.

"Yeah, I noticed that." An uncomfortable thought struck me. I had assumed that the demon was here for its own purposes, and that stumbling across me was an unexpected bonus. But what if that wasn't the case? "You don't think he was here for me, do you?"

"Let's see, a major-level demon being summoned to Los Angeles that Orion recognizes and was focused on securing your soul. I'm sure that's just a coincidence."

Well, when he put it that way, it did seem a little too coincidental.

I'd messed up last year. In a lot of ways, duh. But the biggest one might have been actually killing Lilith when she tried to kill me. The way I understand it, there are different levels of being "immortal." Alex, for example, has very diluted Nephilim blood in his veins. He's long-lived but not truly immortal. Orion, on the other hand, is an immortal. Father Time can't get his grubby hands on the Constellation. But being immortal doesn't mean you can't be killed, only that your light won't go out on its own. Beyond that, there are beings who are Immortals—the capital letter is important. Killing an Immortal takes something a little more special, like, say, a magic sword.

Lilith had been an Immortal. Fighting back against her was fine, the equivalent of having a petty argument. Killing her, on the other hand, was quite rude. Like double-dipping at a party or forgetting to flush at someone else's house.

She might be dead, but she had a whole host of powerful friends and... lovers who might want to do something about it. Considering her sweetie pie sort of runs the whole infernal company, he might have sent Zagan here to do something about me specifically.

"Why wouldn't Luci—" I started.

"No, no, no," Alex interrupted, giving me a glare. "Do not speak his name. You know better."

"Sure," I said, rolling my eyes. "Why would good old Luci-poo send a henchman instead of coming himself?"

Alex barked a snide laugh. "Are you offended that the very top of the food chain isn't coming for you himself?"

"I guess I always thought that he seemed like the type to take things personally," I said with a shrug. "You know, like committing the Seven Deadly Sins on me with his own bare hands."

"You better hope that doesn't happen," Alex said darkly. "You don't really know what you are asking for."

"I'm not saying I could *take* him," I protested. "I'm just surprised that he might be sending a henchman to do his dirty work."

"Believe it or not, I suspect the Prince of Lies has more on his to-do list than personally hunting down Matthew Carver—even if you did kill his girlfriend and are a potential whistleblower that could start a war targeting his company specifically." He paused for a second. "Okay, now that I say it out loud, I see why you might wonder a little."

"Thank you," I said smugly. "I'd like to think my resume speaks for itself."

"If he does come for you, that would be like America nuking an ant. Not an anthill. One single worker ant. That's you. You are the ant in this metaphor."

"Yes, I followed your complex literary device, thank you."

"Powers That Be on his level don't come to the mortal world and just waltz into a coffee shop when they feel like it. That's seen as an invasion."

"So, it's all done with proxies and duly appointed diplomats?" I asked.

"Something like that. Sending your pawns and knights to be annoying is accepted and tolerated. A few demons breaking in is just part of the game. Zagan and his cronies were just a little border skirmish. If he decided to come after you, it would be a full-blown invasion, and other nations would react."

"Can't Orion just stab him with his fiery sword?" I said, not sounding whiny at all.

"Don't tell him I said this, but I don't think Orion would even get close to You Know Who."

"He handled Lilith just fine."

"Lilith was different. She was a human who was *made* into a demon." I could practically hear Alex mentally ticking off points on his fingers. "Plus, she was just a demon. You know that's not a one-size-fits-all descriptor. He's a fallen archangel. That's like… uh…" He paused, casting about for a metaphor.

"Regretting you already used nukes as a comparison?" I asked him dryly.

He glanced over from the road to shoot me a glare. "It's the difference between the sun and a match," he said.

And this guy wanted to be a modern-day Homer. Poor writing aside, I was listening to what he was trying to tell me. Even though I had been in the supernatural scene for about a year, I still struggled with the staggering scale of power that existed between different beings. Humans fit into a very cozy little graph of what is capable. The very apex of our scale is some Olympian like Michael Phelps who can swim from point A to point B really fast. But in the cosmic sense of power, he and I are not that far removed from each other. No matter how much kale we eat, most of us will die before our one hundredth birthday. None of us can run faster than the speed of sound or leap over buildings in a single bound. It gets way worse than us out there in the dark.

"Is this one of those cases where the origin story is true?" I asked. "That You Know Who was an angel that got cast out and became our friendly neighborhood Devil?"

Alex shrugged noncommittally. "I'm not even two hundred years old," he said. "Why are you asking me about the great mysteries of the universe? You know what I always say: Just because it's real—"

"Doesn't mean it's true," I finished for him with a sigh.

"It's all marketing," he offered with another shrug. "The oldest profession of them all. However, of all the tales being spun, I've heard that one is one of the closest to also being true."

"How so?"

"He really was a bigwig, hotshot archangel. Might even have been the most important one. They did call him the Angel of Light. There really was some sort of throwdown, and he really did fall with all his cronies; together they became the first generation of demons."

"That's the 'what' of the story, but none of the 'why,'" I noted.

"Best way to tell a story about powerful people," Alex said dryly. "You never know who's listening."

I'm pretty sure that's the supernatural equivalent of "snitches get stitches."

My history lesson was cut short as we pulled into the parking lot behind the Olympus Bar and Grille. The Grille—the *E* is important, makes it fancy—was a popular hangout spot for folks in the supernatural community. From my experience, that had nothing to do with the quality of the food and everything to do with being a safe, but also dangerous, place.

It was safe because the mortal world ignored it. I don't know how many times I had passed by it when I was a regular joe without even giving it a second glance. But for someone whose eyes were open to the larger world around them, the Olympus Grille blazed like a lighthouse calling lost ships home. Maybe they used magic paint or something. I'm still not clear how it works.

It was a dangerous place because everyone walked in like a Wild West gunslinger. The supernatural world isn't as domesticated as the human one. Compared to them, we're the well-trained house cats pooping in boxes, and they are our tiger ancestors. Their world is more primal—in an eat-or-be-eaten type of way. Too many apex predators jammed into a small bar gave the place an edge. A safe edge, but still an edge, like the scissors they give kids in preschool.

If the Olympus Bar and Grille was the Wild West, then walking in with Orion was a bit like bursting into a saloon behind Billy the Kid. You can feel the entire room collectively clench up as hands start straying toward their proverbial holsters. It's cute, but they really don't need to bother. If the Hunter ever has one of them on his list, they'll know when the fiery sword casts its long shadow over them.

For his part, Orion ignored the reaction of the denizens of the room. A wolf does not deign to notice the grumbling of rodents, or something. He headed toward the restrooms in the back, leaving me and Alex to secure seating, like the good little squires we were. Alex shot me a pair of finger guns and headed to the bathroom as well. Apparently, immortal DNA doesn't increase bladder size.

Bravely, I set off on an expedition to the booths in the back corner. Brett, the grumpy bartender, leaned on the bar that ran along the right side of the room and watched me with dark eyes. He's not my biggest fan, but I roll with Orion, so he lets it slide. I'm tolerated but not accepted. It's high school all over again.

"Now," Orion said as the three of us settled into our usual booth in the back, an edge of frost hanging on his words. My intestines clenched in anticipation of the lecture. "Let's discuss why my two squires picked a fight with an executive of Hell *and* let him get away."

"When you say executive…" Alex began, his face crumpling in concern.

"They were hurting mortals," I said, forcing myself to not look away from Orion's eyes. "They were hurting kids. Besides, you were watching over us."

The Hunter stared at me for a long moment. To my credit, I didn't flinch under the weight of his judging stare. Even though Orion is my friend, it was still harder to do than I would like to admit. I got the feeling he was trying to decide if I knew he was following us the whole time. After a few heartbeats, he grunted and turned to Alex. Point for Matt.

"Zagan is an executive, prince, whatever you want to call him, of Hell," he repeated to Alex.

"You thought he was dead?" I asked, feeling that prickling sense of dread returning. Alex was right. This might have been about me. After a year of silence, I had lulled myself into a tenuous sense of security. Every day that the Devil himself didn't appear out of a portal and rip my head off made me feel I was a little safer.

That safety was starting to feel like an illusion.

"Last time I saw him, he had a different face. Apparently I didn't finish the job," Orion growled, his voice low. Alex and I both blinked in surprise. I know I sing Orion's praises often, but killing is kind of his thing. He's literally so famous for it that they named a part of the night sky after him. If he wants to kill someone, their life expectancy plummets.

"It was millennia ago," Orion said with a grunt. "There was a battle. We were on different sides."

I resisted the urge to sigh in frustration. He's the Constellation of the Hunter, not the Storyteller.

"A battle," Alex repeated in a flat, incredulous tone.

"It's largely forgotten in modern education," Orion said with an odd expression on his face. "It is sometimes called the Battle of Troyes, or Maurica, or Châlons."

Alex and I looked at each other. He cocked an eyebrow in question. I shrugged. Never heard of it, but also, I had a fake college degree, so I'm not sure that's my fault.

"Attila and his horde tried to invade Western Europe and topple the Roman Empire," Orion said with his own shrug. "We stopped him. For the most part."

"Hang on, hang on, HANG ON," I interrupted, holding up a hand while my brain rebooted. "You were in the Roman legion, and Hell was helping Attila invade?"

"Are you surprised? Think about what you've learned. Mortal wars are very profitable for civilizations that deal in souls as currency."

"It's like a fire sale," Alex breathed, a horrified look on his face.

I felt sick to my stomach. The history of the human race suddenly felt very different—manipulated and processed like a factory instead of organic and home grown.

"Attila's wars killed millions," Orion said with a nod. "Rome's did too. But Rome was a stabilizing empire for the mortals. They built roads over the graveyards they created. If Attila had broken them, Europe would have torn itself apart in fire and blood."

"Market manipulation exists on every level," Alex said with an impressed whistle.

"Okay, my brain is breaking," I complained, "but to be clear: You thought you killed this demon executive thousands of years ago when he was helping Attila the Hun invade the Roman Empire. But you didn't. He's back, and the first thing he did was try to get me to sign an updated agreement with Hell."

Orion's eyes narrowed. I guess he missed that part while he was skulking around, watching us fail our demon-scouting assignment.

He grunted. "That's not good."

Sick.

My phone rang in my pocket.

Thoroughly distracted, I pulled my phone out and glanced down at the screen to see who was calling me. I figured it was probably a spam call, since most of the people I actually talked to were sitting at this booth. The screen simply said: DNA CONTRIBUTOR—MALE. Don't look at me like that. My mom's contact name was She Who Birthed Me, but she's dead, so she doesn't call very often.

Then again, my father's calls were so rare that he might as well be dead too. We hadn't spoken in almost two years. Stunned, I answered and raised my phone to my ear. Alex's laughter in the background might have been in a different zip code for how far it felt from me. My heart pounded the drums of alarm in my ears.

"Hello?" I said tentatively.

"When were you going to tell me that your sister wasn't dead anymore?" my father asked me. He spoke in precise, furious words, each one punching into me like a staple.

My father and I were not close. Any love that he might have felt for me was the exact legal requirement and not an ounce more. He certainly didn't like me. After the accident that claimed the majority of our family, I didn't blame him.

My mother and two sisters died in a car crash a few years ago, on their way to see me for my birthday. My father had forbidden them to make the trip during heavy rain, but they knew I wasn't doing well. The women in my family were always the type who could not be stopped by Hell or high water, but when a flash flood swept them off a road and into a ditch, that attitude was put to the ultimate test. Since then, my relationship with him had turned into a blame game. Except in our version of the game, we both agreed who we should blame—me.

That alone made my father calling me odd. I didn't even get a phone call last Christmas. But that weirdness was dwarfed by the fact that he knew about Megan. No one else remembered that she was supposed to be dead. My friends Connor and Violet had been completely unfazed by her walking in the front door of our apartment. I hadn't called my father to tell him that his daughter was alive again because I had assumed he wouldn't remember she had died.

Yes, Alex and Orion knew that she had been dead, but that's different. They hadn't known her before her untimely demise, and they knew what was going on behind the curtain. It's kind of like the difference between believing in Santa Claus and seeing some guy change into the red suit in a mall parking lot. They knew too much.

A year ago, I think I would have been ecstatic if my father and I shared this knowledge. It would have felt so amazing to not be alone in this. But after the year—Hell, after the *day* I just had—I was only suspicious.

"How do you know that?" I asked, standing up to walk away from my friends. I knew how *I* knew that. I was there when Dan signed the contract that brought her back. A heavy silence settled on the call. I could feel my father processing my response, gauging it like a master woodsman looks at a tree trunk he's about to chop down. It occurred to me that he might be going through the same journey as me. Did his friends all think Megan had never died? Was he calling to see if I knew?

"What did you do?" he hissed after a moment of heavy silence.

For one eternal second, I considered telling him the whole story. Finally, there would be someone else who was stuck in the middle of everything with me. I could share this load. But I knew how it would go. Either he wouldn't believe me or he'd blame me. I wasn't in the mood to be anyone else's punching bag today.

"How did you find out?" I asked him again.

"I got a phone call from the police. Apparently after she started breathing again, she got kidnapped. That should probably have been a phone call too, by the way. Two separate phone calls."

We may not get along, but my sarcasm comes from my dad. The genes don't lie.

"She's fine," I replied. "Well, kind of."

"Detective Rodgers from the LA Police Department seems to think otherwise."

I winced at the thought of the sharp-eyed woman and her partner digging into the case further. My sister's kidnapping was technically in the freezer-like limbo that cases go into to cool down before they officially become cold cases.

If the detectives were hunting down my father, that was a bad sign. Maybe Robin's Faerie hypnotism had a limited time of effectiveness, like a car's extended warranty. I felt a sudden flutter of panic in my gut and turned toward the bar. Even before I looked, I knew what I would see—bad news. A dandelion that had *not* been there before peeked out of the top of the bouquet, like a flag planted at the peak of a mountain. All of a sudden, they were starting to feel like a threat. I suppose if you don't pay your bills, someone comes and turns off your electricity. Why wouldn't magical protection work the same?

"I know where she is," I replied. "She's being taken care of. But she's sort of in a coma."

"What?" It should not have been possible for my father's tone to become sharper, but I could feel his judgment stabbing into my guts like a hot knife.

"No one knows exactly what's going on with her. She's getting the best care possible," I explained. "It's something to do with… how she came back."

The judgmental silence echoed.

"I want to see her. You will take me to see her."

I thought about refusing, I really did. I don't care who you are, straight up telling your parent "no" is a heavier task than Atlas's of holding up the world. Obedience is carved into your bones by your shared DNA.

I wasn't sure what Lazarus was going to say about me adding to the guest list. The medical facility that Megan was being kept at didn't exactly have visiting hours. He and I had an understanding. Regular coma patients are probably incredibly expensive. The kind of expensive I could not afford to support, thanks to my unpaid Hunt internship. But Lazarus took care of her for free, just for the opportunity to observe her. That might sound like philanthropy, but I did burn down an entire state-of-the-art lab of his, so I'm not exactly sure how the ledger was being balanced.

"Okay, Dad," I half whispered, "I'll take you to see Megan." I gave him the address and time to meet me in the morning, and he hung up without another word, leaving a jagged tear in our conversation like it was a ripped piece of paper.

I

T SHOULD COME as no surprise that I didn't sleep well that night. I didn't expect to. Instead of blissful sleep, I spent the night alternating between staring at the ceiling and switching which side I was lying on, as if that would magically help me fall asleep. But no matter which side of my toasty body I buttered my bread on, sleep evaded me until the morning.

The sun's rising meant an official end to the Sleep Games, and I rolled off the lumpy couch feeling like I had just gone several rounds with the Sandman in the ring. My father had insisted we meet first thing, so I shambled into the shower and prayed the hot water would wake me up. Heat is just energy, so if I take a hot-enough shower, I should recharge, right? That seems like basic science to me.

The hot-shower-to-energy exchange didn't work. No matter how hot I turned my water, all I got was closer to being boiled. I guess I don't know that much about science after all. My fake college degree was in English Literature, so that might be part of the problem.

I pulled on some clothes I had left there before and dragged myself into the living room. With all the magical sexual tension between me and Violet, I avoided my own apartment like the plague. Her relationship with Connor was the one thing I hadn't messed up yet. Alex, an ever-faithful friend, let me crash on his couch whenever I wanted, without a word of complaint.

Alex was already awake and dressed, wearing a pair of jeans and a gray V-neck T-shirt. His laptop was in his lap, and he was clacking away, working on his supernatural blog.

"Morning, sunshine!" he said cheerily, sipping a mug of coffee. His Nephilim powers gave him the ability to not need sleep—very annoying. It's very telling that someone who is literally superhuman is a morning person. I knew all along that there was something wrong with those people.

"Hey, can you drive me to the hospital?" I mumbled, rubbing my eyes in a desperate attempt to kick-start my body.

"Oh yeah, time for that thing, huh?"

"Just another grand adventure in the life of Matt Carver," I said, giving him a little bow.

"Well, thanks for letting me be your chauffeur," he grumbled, setting his coffee mug down on the table. "I probably need to move the car to not get a ticket anyway, so why not?"

The tension in my body built steadily during the drive but skyrocketed as we pulled onto the hospital's street. My sister was kept at a very inconspicuous medical facility a little outside of downtown LA. It was a four-story brick building that could have been an office building for anything. There were no logos or neon signs announcing the work being done inside. Lazarus liked to fly under the radar.

She had been in a coma since Lilith orchestrated her kidnapping, and no one seemed to know why. Lazarus, the philanthropic head of the humbly named Lazarus Group, employed doctors, scientists, and people with less-traditional knowledge, who had all attempted to diagnose her and been stumped. In the meantime, they had been gorging themselves on studying her like an open buffet of knowledge.

As far as I could tell, the Lazarus Group was focused on one medical goal: immortality. Having the opportunity to study a living being who had returned from the dead was like getting a copy of the teacher's answer key in high school. It was quite literally cheating. If they could figure out how she was brought back… even I could understand how titanic those implications were.

My blood pressure spiked as I saw him standing by the entrance. His eyes locked on me through the windshield. My father is one of those people whose gaze has weight. It lands on you, and the pressure builds the longer he holds it. It has its own gravitational pull, like some sort of judgmental tractor beam.

"So that's the progenitor, huh?" Alex ventured as my father stared us down.

"Better let me out here," I managed through my sudden cottonmouth.

"Best of luck, soldier," Alex called as I closed the door and turned to face my father.

Damien Carver technically gave me half my genes. I get my height from him. We both hover at right about the six-foot mark. People say we share a nose, but I don't know what that means. My father had dark hair that was going gray at the temples in a majestic sort of way. His face was thinner and sharper than mine, more aristocratic. His eyes were hazel gray, almost colorless in the sunlight. The one other feature we shared was a chin dimple that my sister Megan and I both inherited. He wore dark jeans and a dark shirt under a dark-gray peacoat, which on anyone else would have looked ridiculous in LA, but on him it seemed natural. The heat never seemed to bother him.

For a moment, we just stared at each other, eye to eye, father to son. Most people would be drinking in the sight of a loved one they hadn't seen in a long time. I got the sense he was making sure he could still take me in a fight.

"You've been working out," he said. His tone was so bored he might have been ordering water with his lunch, no ice.

"A little," I replied.

"Where is Megan?"

"Right this way." I turned to the unmarked doors of the office building that housed Lazarus's hospital and lab. The door opened before I could touch it, and a woman charged out of the lobby. She slid past us without pausing, bumping me slightly as she went.

She was a short, thin woman who could have been my grandmother. Her white hair spilled down to her shoulders, and she was clearly in a hurry.

"Excuse me," I said automatically. My mother had drilled into me to be polite to the point that it was reflex. Kick me and I might apologize—I'm practically Canadian.

She turned and stared at me, a pair of rheumy brown eyes glaring above the medical mask she was wearing. She evaluated me for a moment before raising her hand and shooing me with a dismissive gesture. On her right hand she wore a golden ring with a pale-green stone the size of a quarter set in it. She said something in Mandarin that felt condescending and turned away.

I shrugged and stepped into the lobby, ignoring the pair of dandelions poking out of the grass by the door. My father didn't follow, he stood still, staring at the back of the retreating woman, his head tilted like a hawk sizing up a target. After a moment, he turned and stormed past me into the building.

The interior of the lab was less subtle than the outside. The lobby floor bore a giant seal of the Lazarus logo: a shepherd's staff with a pair of doves and sheaf of wheat on either end. Everything was modern and sleek, shiny marble and black and white surfaces everywhere. People in medical scrubs moved around at a brisk pace, and a pair of armed guards lurked in the corner of the lobby, casually carrying assault rifles. My father took all of this in with a glance, but his gaze settled on the bronze logo in the middle of the floor. He stared at it for at least five seconds, face unreadable.

I left him where he was and approached the guard's desk. The large man sitting behind it looked out of place, like a gorilla stuffed into dollhouse furniture. He dwarfed the chair and computer he sat in front of, his sunburnt bald head reflecting the bright lights of the lobby as he glowered at my approach. I didn't take his severe look personally. I think he actually likes me; he just was never taught how to smile, or to do long division.

"Hey, Bruno," I said cheerfully, my nerves spiking again. "Here to see my sister."

Lazarus was particular about his facility, I got that.

Bruno eyed my father for a moment, then grunted and held out a clipboard for me to sign. I don't know why they bothered giving him a computer; I'd never seen him use it. I think his fingers were too thick to hit a single key at a time anyway.

I wrote MATT CARVER and DAMIEN CARVER on the piece of paper and handed it back to him. This, as always, triggered a reminder of the rules. I know the rules. He knows I know the rules. But the telling of the rules is as inevitable as the sunrise.

"No phones. No photos. No souvenirs."

"Yessir," I said, giving him a salute. He didn't laugh. He never does, but one day I will make him laugh or teach him to feel an emotion.

He took my salute as agreement and waved me on to the elevators with another of his iconic grunts.

"This way," I said to my father, who was still staring at the logo in the floor. I had never seen him so taken aback. I felt a moment of pity for him. It had to be hard, not having the context that I did. All he knew was that his daughter had been dead and was now alive. Now here we were in a facility that looked like it was the movie-set version of a billionaire's secret lab. Maybe I should cut him a break. His world had to be imploding a little. Mine certainly had once or twice over the last year.

One of the guards flanking the elevator pressed a button on the wall as we approached, and the metallic doors shot open like a gaping maw ready to swallow us up. The elevator was an extra wide one, I assumed to accommodate gurneys or the occasional minotaur. But even with its cavernous space, when the doors slid shut, it felt far too small to hold me, my father, and his anger.

"I know it's a lot to take in," I said, against my better judgment. I stared at my distorted reflection in the shiny metallic doors, which accurately reflected my own emotions. I didn't bother trying to make eye contact with him. "She's going to be okay."

The oppressive silence only grew colder. The ding when we arrived at the fourth floor gave me more relief than any school bell ever had. The elevator opened into what could have been any hospital hallway. The two-toned walls framed a white linoleum floor spit-polished to a level that even the meanest drill sergeant would find acceptable.

I knew the steps to her room by heart. Suite 411, a single-occupant room with a window that gave a killer view of LA sunsets. Not that she had seen one in almost a year, but it was a nice gesture.

The sign on the door still read CARVER, M, and I pushed in on the door to find it exactly how I had left it the last time. My sister lay on a medical bed, hooked up to several machines that monitored her vitals. The steady beep of her heartbeat being recorded filled the room like an off-tune marching band.

Megan's brown hair pooled around her head like a fuzzy halo. Her face was relaxed, the ever-present smile that usually lurked on her face nowhere to be seen. She was the spitting image of Mom, her nose a little thicker and longer.

My father swept into the room behind me, and for a moment he was still. He stared at Megan with an expression I couldn't name, but I knew I had experienced it the first time she walked through my door a year ago. It's equal parts shock, confusion, desperate hope, and just a dash of fear for flavor. For a second, I thought I finally understood him. Then his eyes narrowed, his face hardened, and he spoke with the commanding voice of a father waking up a delinquent teenager who had slept past noon.

"Megan Rose Carver, *wake up.*" The authority in his voice rang like a bell. My own heart skipped a beat in memory of that voice and tone calling for me when I had been in trouble as a boy. I'm not sure what he expected to happen; it wasn't as if she was going to—

My jaw hit the floor as Megan sat straight up in bed, as if startled awake from a nap. Her bright green eyes popped open, and she took a deep breath like the Big Bad Wolf must have before blowing all those poor piggies' houses down.

She turned and looked at us, and I knew immediately something was wrong. Her eyes were glazed over, her giant pupils motionless as if she wasn't seeing out of them. Her blank gaze settled on my father, and she let out a bloodcurdling scream.

My father and I both flinched. The power of her cry was like a wave crashing into us, the volume and pitch rising to a frenzy that no human lungs should be able to do. The machines she was plugged into went haywire.

To their credit, Lazarus's army of doctors and nurses responded instantly. The door banged open, and a host of scrubbed people poured in like a horde of ants, one of them pushing a crash cart.

They swarmed over her like she was a picnic and forced her to lie back, her screams only growing in fury. One of the lights in the ceiling flickered as she reached a crescendo. I had my fingers in my ears, trying to dull the sonic assault.

"Lie back, Megan," one nurse urged.

"It's okay, honey, we're here," called another one from the other side of the bed.

"We're going to have to sedate her!" a doctor yelled from the cart. "Get me the lorazepam!"

"Matthew!" she shouted, her voice still painfully loud. "Matt!"

"I'm here! I'm right here," I shouted, pulling my fingers from my ears and rushing to her side. Nurses surrounded her, helping hold her down, and she writhed on the bed like a snake.

"Run," she said. Her unseeing eyes turned and stared right through me. "They are coming for you. THEY are coming. THEY ARE CO-MIN—"

Some doctor managed to sneak a syringe of something into her while she was trying to tell me something that I had a very bad feeling was important. I spun, my hands balling into fists. They had silenced my sister. They had put her back to sleep. I was going to make them pay.

"What happened here?" A voice from the doorway snapped me out of my violent reaction. I looked over my shoulder to find none other than the man who wanted to defeat death, Lazarus, standing in the doorway.

If you didn't know any better, you'd probably assume Lazarus was some sort of literature professor at the local university. He always wore a tweed suit, which, I don't care how rich you are, is still lame. He was a fat old man with a big bushy gray beard and a pair of oak-rimmed glasses that glinted under the harsh florescent light. Think a slightly more menacing Santa Claus. He leaned on a black cane with some sort of golden animal on the top.

But all that congenial appearance was a bit of a front. The people in the building with the guns worked for him. The monsters in basements being chopped in the name of science were suffering by his orders. I don't know if I considered him a "bad guy" compared to creatures like Lilith, but he wasn't winning the Nobel Peace Prize anytime soon.

Well, I guess if he cured death, that might probably get him one.

"She woke up," I said, taking an excited step toward him. "My father said her name and she just sat right up. I always thought that was just a thing in movies."

"It's not unheard of," Lazarus said, his gaze turning to settle on my father like an anchor coming to rest. "I am Lazarus." He held his hand out.

"Damien Carver," my father said softly. The two men shook hands and stared at each other for a moment that felt too long and too heavy.

"Lazarus has been taking care of Megan," I said, trying to defuse the weird tension. "I don't know what I would have done without his help."

"It has been an honor," Lazarus replied instantly. "A chance of a lifetime to be a part of such a special journey."

"You could have called me," my father growled at me, making sure I knew that all was not even a little forgiven. He turned back to Lazarus. "I owe you a great debt for caring for my daughter," he said flatly. "What have you discovered?"

Lazarus eyed both of us over the top of his glasses, as if deciding whether to give us the bad news or the worse news first. After a moment, he sighed and pulled his glasses from his head, then pulled a little handkerchief from one of his tweed pockets and began polishing the lenses.

"This is not the first time she was woken up," he admitted after a moment.

"What?" I snarled. "And you didn't tell me this?"

"I do not have much to tell you, and what little I do is not good."
Lazarus speared me with an almost sympathetic look before switching
to polish the other lens of his glasses. Looks like that made it hard for
me to place Lazarus on the hero-or-villain scale. I was fully aware that
he was caring for my sister because it suited his needs, but he didn't
have to act so human about it. What was further complicating things
was the fact that I could name a lot of billionaires and politicians who
were using their resources for far worse things than curing humanity
of that whole death thing.

"I have not lied to you. I've been trying to solve what exactly is
happening to your sister. Megan is not the first person I have encountered who is alive when she should be dead. However, she is by
far the most... whole in body, mind, and soul. A reanimated corpse
tends to not be the person it used to be. It's usually a different hand
inside the meat puppet. Your sister, on the other hand, is actually your
sister—or most of her."

"I'm not following," I said, holding up my hand. "Are you talking
about zombies?"

"Close enough," he said with a dismissive wave of his glasses.
"That's like asking me if I am talking about fish when I am talking
about salmon, but it's also not important. That"—he pointed at Meg's
still form—"is your sister. It just isn't all of her."

Slowly, I turned to look at the bed. It sure looked like her. But
I knew what he meant. I had noticed that there was something wrong
with her before she had fallen into a coma. Her cooking tasted like
sawdust to me, her skin felt warm and feverish. No one else seemed
to notice, but I could tell there was something... missing.

"I think I know what you mean," I said slowly.

"I believe that the part of her that is missing is calling her back.
That whatever the creature Lilith—"

My father hissed in vehement surprise at that name.

"Whatever she did to your sister when she took her is pulling her soul from her body into some sort of limbo."

I put up a hand to stop him. "This is all very technical—in a mumbo-jumbo sort of way. Is there a way you could explain this to me as if I am even more of an idiot than you think I am? What do you mean exactly by her soul is 'in limbo'?"

"She is being tortured," Lazarus said flatly. "The part of her that is still in the hands of Hell is suffering. When she's awake, the rest of her here appears to be experiencing that too, thus the screaming. We've been keeping her sedated to try to give her some sort of peace."

Lazarus's news left me feeling like I had just been tackled by a three-hundred-pound linebacker. My knees felt weak, and I didn't want to play this stupid game anymore. All I could think about was the rage that the Prince of Lies felt toward me, and my poor sister, stuck somewhere that she didn't belong, all because of me.

We didn't stay long after we got the news. Lazarus agreed to let my father visit Megan and promised to update us as he researched more. As we exited the facility, I turned to him, assuming he would need help processing what he had just witnessed.

Damien Carver didn't pause. He didn't look at me. He kept walking. He walked to his sleek black sedan, got into the driver's side, and sped out of the parking lot without even a glance in my direction, leaving me alone with my guilt, standing next to two stupid dandelions growing in the grass.

MY FAMILY REUNION going as terribly as I predicted was one of the rare times where being right didn't make me feel any better. Usually being right is one of my favorite things. But old guilt about my family's death was being blended with the new guilt of Megan being in a tortured coma, making a depression smoothie for me to choke on.

Not to imply that I have any flaws whatsoever, but if I did, one of them might be that I get reckless when I'm upset. But I had an idea how to set a trap for Zagan.

I don't see that as reckless behavior. I prefer to think of it as being *proactive*. I deserve a gold star for my initiative and absolutely no criticism, thank you. When my genius plan snared Zagan and we sent him packing back to Hell, literally everyone was welcome to pat me on the back.

I sent Alex and Orion a message with my idea. Orion replied with "OK," which for him is practically gushing with praise. Alex sent a voice recording of him sighing, which I took as even more proof that it was a good idea.

That is how I found myself standing at an empty crossroads as dusk settled on Los Angeles. I know it's not relevant, but West Coast sunsets cannot be beaten. The flaming eyeball of the furious sun began to drop behind the Pacific Ocean, painting the sky purple and gold.

The crossroads in question was an intersection of two quiet roads amongst a bunch of storage facilities and warehouses. Calling them "roads" was a little generous, though. They had been paved but not maintained. Dust and gravel filled the streets like a rocky flood. A dandelion had burst its way through the ground, towering over the tiny grass patch on the side of the asphalt. Not a soul was in sight. I include myself in that accounting, because you know, the whole soul fraud thing.

Judging that it was dusky enough for me to start, and with more hesitation than I would like to admit, I drew my pocketknife and flipped it open. Gritting my teeth, I sliced the side of my palm, being careful to keep the edge away from any part of my hand that bends or grips. With a hiss, I put my blade away and squeezed my hand a few times, pumping drops out to rain on the gravelly road at my feet.

You see, crossroads are where you go to make deals.

I don't know why. I'm not sure who decided having a meeting place right in the middle of multiple lanes of traffic was a good idea. But then again, demons are really annoying, so maybe that's part of their devilish nature.

Regardless of why demons couldn't resist a good intersection, it was apparently an established fact. It goes all the way back to the original deal taker of English literature, Mr. Faust, who stole the idea from the Romans. I know, I'm shocked I know that too.

Every story has a different way to summon a demon to make a deal. But the gang and I were confident I didn't need to do anything fancy. If Zagan was looking for me, all I had to do was make a little splash and the sharks would come swimming... or running, since we were on dry land. With that plan in mind, I watched my blood drip on the dusty road at my feet and decided to sweeten the pot a little bit.

"Let's make a deal," I whispered into the falling dusk.

"Thank you for contacting Hell's Deal Department," a woman's cool voice sounded in my ear.

I flinched in surprise.

"All of our representatives are currently making deals with mortals. Please stay in the crossroads, and our next available demon will be with you as soon as they are able."

There are no words to express how I felt about getting an automated Please Hold message from Hell. I wonder if we stole that from them or if they copied us? I'm not sure I want to know.

"While you wait, please enjoy the best works from blues legend Robert Johnson," the woman's voice continued. Suddenly the sounds of an American music pioneer shredding on harmonica and guitar played loudly in my ears. The connection felt familiar, but I couldn't quite place it; must have slept through that lecture.

The music kept going, and I had to admit, he was very good. Maybe a little too good, if you catch my drift. For a minute, I forgot I was on hold and just listened to him jam. Then the music paused, and I opened my mouth to say hello.

"After your meeting with a certified deal-making representative, please stay on the line for a short survey about your experience shopping with Hell," the woman's voice said.

I rolled my eyes. I would *love* to take their survey. I had some feedback for them, all right.

The music resumed. I held in a long sigh.

"Hey there," a familiar voice squeaked behind me, interrupting the music abruptly.

"Aha!" I shouted, spinning on my heel to face my prey.

But what I got was not what I expected. Instead of the male model in a sports suit that I was hunting, I found myself staring at a figure that was barely five feet tall. Instead of pants, it had thick black fur that coated it from the top of its hooves to its waist. The rest of its skin was a bright fire-engine red, including the pair of horns sticking out of its forehead. Its fake smile was plastered beneath a pair of ridiculously curved mustachios.

It wasn't Zagan. My carefully laid trap hadn't caught the Hell executive. It had caught Dan the Freaking Loser Demon instead.

"You," I snarled, my hands flashing to the waist of my pants, where my pistol was holstered. I took an aggressive step forward and felt a surge of vicious satisfaction as Dan leapt back in response. I stopped in my tracks, forcing myself to take a calming breath. Maybe this would work out even better for me.

"What are you doing here?" I asked, glaring daggers at the creature that was the source of most of my misery. Not all of it; he's not that competent.

"I *work* here," Dan hissed back at me, his voice barely above a whisper. "What are you doing here?"

"Didn't you hear me? I'M HERE TO MAKE A DEAL!" I shouted the last bit just in case anyone was listening on the other line. For some reason, I doubted Hell recorded calls for quality assurance. Still worth a shot.

Dan winced and made a lowering motion with his hands. "Don't you know how dangerous it is for you to call here?" he whispered.

"Why would it be dangerous?" I asked, still talking too loudly. If anyone looked out of the buildings around me, I probably looked crazy, standing in the center of a crossroads screaming. I didn't care, I was seeing red—and it wasn't just Dan's demonic flesh. "Is there some reason you don't want me talking to your bosses?"

"What do you mean? Wait, are you still yapping about the whole signature thing?" Dan asked incredulously.

"Of course I'm talking about that," I snapped. "What else would I be talking about?"

"Dude, you killed the boss's..." Dan mouthed the word *girlfriend* without actually saying it out loud. "What do you think'll happen when they get their hands on you? Word around the oil cooler is that *He* is making a brand-new circle just for you."

I know that the concept of the Devil himself personally overseeing the construction of a new circle of Hell in my honor should have been the first thing I latched on to. I won't lie—a cold sweat started beading on my forehead. But I had more important questions on my mind.

"I'm sorry did you say, 'oil cooler'?" I asked.

"What, do you think they let us drink water down there? That's a banned substance. We drink the straight crude stuff." The image of a bunch of demons gathered around a water cooler full of oil, gossiping before heading back to their cubicles, was too much for me to handle. I'd rather think about the circle of Hell thing.

"This seems like the perfect time for me to get my soul back, then," I said, clapping my hands together. "How about you do me a solid and tear up the contract and we never speak ever again?"

I may not have caught Zagan in my trap, but maybe this would work out even better.

"Dude, I *can't*," Dan said, his eyes shifting around nervously. "It was already bad, but you did the opposite of what I told you to do..."

"As I recall, your advice was to just lie down and take it," I sneered.

"You don't get it, do you?" he snapped, no longer whispering. "I couldn't undo this even when you were just an embarrassing mistake, only a potential supernatural incident. It's way worse now. You made it personal."

"I'm gonna be honest," I said dryly, "it's felt pretty personal the whole time. Just because they sent some executive named Zagan after me doesn't—"

Dan interrupted me with a squeal of terror. "Zagan? They sent Zagan after you? He isn't some 'executive,' he's the CFO of Hell. You have no idea what's coming for you. You can't even comprehend what he's capable of."

"He's quite right, you know," a second familiar voice said from behind me.

Dan went pale, which, with his skin tone, meant he turned a sort of salmon color. The guy looked like he might need to check his furry demon shorts. Once again, I spun on my heel to confront the demon I had baited into my clever, cunning trap. This time it was the one I wanted.

Zagan stood on the other side of the crossroads. Today he wore a charcoal suit with a black silk shirt that looked like it was worth more than my apartment. His black hair was molded into a perfectly professional side comb, and he wore the same small smile that didn't reach his black eyes.

"Thank you, Daniel, you may leave the call," Zagan said with a dismissive wave.

"Yes, sir, I—"

There was an audible click as Dan was cut off midsentence. The little red demon vanished. One moment he was there, the next he simply wasn't.

"Hello again, Matthew," Zagan said in a pleasant tone. "I appreciate you reaching out. It makes following up with you much easier than I thought it was going to be."

"My pleasure," I said, licking my suddenly dry lips. Now that the moment was here, I couldn't help but feel a little fear. I had to play this perfectly. "So, you're the chief financial officer of Hell, huh? I'm surprised they send you out into the field."

"Well, you are an accounting issue." Zagan's eyebrows wiggled.

"So you admit that my soul was fraudulently taken?" I asked in surprise.

"Oh, absolutely not. I could never speak on behalf of the company on such a matter." He placed a humble hand on his chest. "My role is simply to investigate an outstanding account and make sure that all bills are paid in *full*."

I hang out with some powerful beings, but that was one of the most terrifying threats I have ever heard.

"Okay, well, hear me out: you tear up the illegal contract, give me back my soul, and I promise to not make any legal trouble for your whole infernal company."

"That is quite considerate of you." Zagan's smile widened in genuine amusement.

"Surely even you guys don't want a supernatural World War," I said, flustered by his perfect calm. It felt like I was trying to argue with an ice sculpture in a walk-in freezer. He wasn't melting, but I sure was getting cold.

"A supernatural World War?" He chuckled. "Even if your soul was stolen, which I have no express knowledge of, you think the entire supernatural world would go to war over one lost soul? You've been getting advice from some dreamers, Matthew."

When he put it that way, it did sound a little far-fetched. In the mortal world, companies have poisoned entire towns by dumping toxic waste or shipped cars they knew would explode, and they're still in business. Roadkill only stops the truck that kills it if it's big enough, and compared to the monster standing before me, I felt about the size of a squirrel.

"Maybe not a war," I said with a shrug, trying to play it cool. "But I can make things an absolute, uh… heaven for you in super court."

"We could go to court," Zagan allowed, his perfect smile beaming at me.

I gotta say: there's almost nothing more dispiriting than someone reacting to your threats with the gentle amusement of a parent watching their toddler waving a stick like a sword.

"I would love to see the crack legal team that you're planning to unleash… on Hell."

My legal team currently consisted of my friend Robin the Faerie and some pocket lint, and Robin had been doing me a favor, so I wasn't even sure he would work for me again. I had been ignoring his boss's calls.

"I assure you, our legal department is quite robust. You do know where most lawyers end up, don't you?" the demon asked.

I guess that made sense. "Okay, you don't like my ideas. I get it," I said. "What do you propose?"

"I believe there's already quite a generous offer on the table from our last meeting," Zagan replied coolly. "An addendum of ten additional years. You get to live to the ripe old age of forty-four."

I know that the value of time is lost on the young, but part of me still thought that sounded ancient. The other part of me was terrified that I was going to be forty-four in nineteen years. What was I doing with my life?

"I thought your boss was in a rush to get his hands on me. Why the extra ten years?" I asked.

Zagan shrugged, unbothered. "What is a measly decade compared to eternity? Besides, that gives the contractors more time to complete renovations for your arrival."

Gulp. The idea that the Devil was personally redesigning a portion of Hell for me was getting more terrifying every time it came up.

I guess I sort of figured he wasn't the type to actually like his significant other. Turns out el Diablo has a sentimental side. Lucky me.

Negotiation was getting us nowhere. I figured that was because my new demon friend Zagan didn't respect me. That's fine. He didn't know who he was dealing with yet. Maybe after I played my trap card, he would be willing to renegotiate. You see, I wasn't the same ignorant kid who had been dragged into this supernatural crap shoot last year. I had found a wise teacher, and I had learned. This crossroads was a trap—but not for me.

In the end, it all comes down to geometry. Which is terrible. I wish it all came down to Froyo or something way more fun. Euclid, or whoever invented the triangle, ruined everything for all of us. Don't even get me started on whoever discovered the rhombus.

Those obnoxious shapes aside, the real power is in the unbroken unity of the circle. It is in the serpent eating its own tail, the reality-bending mass of the earth, or the promise bound in the confines of a wedding ring. Circles are the thing the universe is made of, or so Orion tells me. I tried to tell him it was actually carbon, but that one didn't fly.

I hate math, but a drowning man will use anything as a flotation device, so tonight the gang and I had become the kings of circles. Buried in the dust and gravel at my feet was a gray hula hoop.

I shifted my foot so that it was touching the edge of the hoop. As Orion had taught me, I defined it in my mind and commanded the inside of the circle to exist in its own space, to become my own world. The hairs on my arm did the wave, standing and dropping as something that felt like a static charge washed over me. The magic panic room was active. Supernatural beings like Zagan could not cross the border until I released my dominion over Matt World, or if the ring was broken.

The demon obviously felt my circle activate. He arched one per-fectly sculpted eyebrow at me, as if to say, *Really?* I gave him a smile that was all teeth. But inside, my heart was racing. This was it, time to spring the trap.

That was one circle. But there was another.

When Alex, Orion, and I had arrived several hours before dusk, we had done some prep work. I stood inside my small ring, safely protected from the chief financial demon, but he was standing in a larger circle. We had surrounded the entire crossroads in a ring of foam spray that hardened into a single, solid connection.

As I activated the first circle, Alex stepped out from behind a building and powered the second, trapping Zagan between the two barriers of our will. We had made a magic donut, and I was safely ensconced in its hole.

"No thanks," I said, smiling brightly at the sandwiched Zagan. "Under advisement from my legal counsel, I cannot in good conscience sign any paperwork, addendum or otherwise, with your company until the outstanding matter is resolved. Thanks for dropping by!"

Orion stepped up to the giant ring on the other side. His black eyes rested on Zagan. His face was expressionless, the cold judgment of a statue. The red ruby of his sword winked over his shoulder. If I didn't know better, I'd say that it was excited by the violent tension humming around us.

Without preamble, he started to recite in Latin. It was time to send Zagan back to the fiery depths he had crawled out of. Zagan's amused smile was gone now. Cold fury washed across his face as he stared at the Hunter.

"*Exorcizamus te*," he began.

"I would not do that if I were you," hissed the demon. For the first time, his voice wasn't smooth and in control. Rage bubbled out of his mouth like a volcano threatening to erupt. "Your meddling has been permitted for too long, pup. Azrael should never have let you keep that sword. I think it's time an adult took it back."

I suddenly remembered the last person who called Orion a child. It was Lilith, back when she was still alive. She had been a full demon, or something close to it. If the upper echelon of demons truly were fallen angels, and Zagan was a member of the C-Suite of Hell… Suddenly my trap felt a little like I had gone fishing for a salmon and hooked a whale.

Orion ignored the threats of the fallen angel and continued to recite the words. If anything, his voice grew in power as he stared at Zagan. I'm always impressed by Orion, but somehow my respect for him grew even more watching him stand at the front of the circle as one of the primal forces of the universe glared at him. He remained unbothered. Genetically, Orion only had a fraction of the power that resided in Zagan, yet there he stood with the upper hand, on top of the food chain.

All thanks to my genius plan. That felt good.

"Stop." Zagan's voice rang out with absolute authority. The power of it rang like the peal of a bell. Even inside the dominion of my circle, I felt shaken, like I was standing in the middle of a category four hurricane. But Orion did not falter. The Latin must flow.

Zagan stared at the Hunter for a long moment, something unknowable lurking in his stance. Abruptly, he tilted his head to the side, as though listening to a voice that none of us could hear.

"Very well," he mused. "It seems that this modern problem needs a modern solution." Then he cheated. I wasn't really surprised, since that's on the syllabus for Demon 101. Cheating is one thing, but I hadn't planned for the CFO of Hell to reach into his jacket and pull out a black Desert Eagle and point it at me. With one smooth motion, he cocked the hammer back and sighted down the monstrous pistol. The bore of the fifty-caliber pistol was so massive it looked like a cyclops staring at me with a single, furious eye.

Orion's chant ground to an abrupt halt.

"Now, then," Zagan said, his earlier calm back in place. "I believe you were being quite rude."

A quick guide on magic circles seems like it might come in handy right about now. They're more of an idea than a physical thing. Supernatural creatures aren't fully a part of our world. I don't know the exact calculus that goes into explaining that, but Zagan was a creature of Hell, not of Earth. The border of the circle could block him because there was a part of him that didn't belong. As I understand it, the circle is more like a magnifying glass; it focuses the idea or belief that whatever supernatural being in its embrace is trapped.

The circle being mostly an idea, however, makes it a terrible replacement for body armor. The giant lead slug loaded into his monstrous pistol was very much a thing of good old Mother Earth. It wouldn't even notice the cute little hula hoop on the ground as it shot over it and through me at the speed of sound.

An oppressive silence settled on the crossroads, like an ocean's fog sweeping in at night. The last of the sun's defiant rays stretched all of our shadows to be giant distorted parodies of ourselves.

"Well?" demanded Zagan after a few moments. "No one has an apology to make?"

I tore my gaze away from the gun's single eye and made eye contact with the demon holding it instead. There was an uncanny similarity between the empty blackness of the bore and his eyes. I gave him a tight little smile and a shrug. That was as much of an apology as he was going to get. An exasperated sigh escaped from the Fallen's lips before he shifted his stance to stare at Alex.

"Release me," he demanded.

"Sorry, bud, no can do," my friend replied with a strained smile. "This is involuntary therapy; you can't leave early."

"I'll shoot him." He gestured at me with the cannon-like pistol in his hands.

"No, you won't," I said, trying to sound confident. But that's a lot harder when you're staring down the barrel of a gun. "You can't kill me. Not for another nine years."

"I would *prefer* to not kill you, Matthew. There's a difference," he growled. "But I'm starting to think the fines and fees for ending the contract early might be worth it."

I was worried he'd say something like that. As far as I can figure, Lilith's plan had been to get me killed on my own so that Hell couldn't be accused of breaking their contract with me. Once that failed, she decided to just kill me herself and try to deal with the fallout.

If Zagan shot me dead right now and jammed my soul into some unused broom closet of Hell, what did it matter if I was supposed to be there or not? I would be forgotten soon enough. The gaping bore of the Desert Eagle seemed like the mouth of some abyssal worm, growing to swallow me whole and bear me to Hell. The promise of ten years felt about as effective as body armor as a circle drawn on the ground.

"Hey, Matt? I think he's telling the truth," Alex called.

"Yeah, I was picking up on that, thanks," I yelled back.

"No problem."

"Well, Hunter?" thundered Zagan, keeping his weapon trained on me. "Will you stand idly by while I kill one of *yours*? Are you ready to watch another generation of the Hunt go extinct?"

Uh-oh. Orion might be the greatest warrior to ever live, or at least the greatest since the major Hall of Famers, like Achilles or Leonidas. He is swift, deadly, and ruthless enough to make a great white shark in a feeding frenzy uncomfortable.

Pound for pound, I have never seen any fighter that I would even consider placing a bet on against Orion. Lilith, Vice President of Hell, had barely been able to hold a candle to him in a brawl. But if I am being honest, in the deep, dark reaches of my mind, I hold a secret thought: He is not the most cunning. He is a peerless predator, but even a tiger can be caged.

I'm not saying Orion is stupid by any stretch of the imagination—far from it! I have learned more from him than any teacher I have had in my life. But wisdom and cunning are not the same thing as strength. Lilith outfoxed us at every turn, and dead or not, the fallout of her traps was still chasing me a year later.

Like everyone, Orion has pressure points that aren't physical. If you lean on the right ones, he becomes like a bull in the ring seeing the red cape fluttering in front of him. He can't help but charge. I couldn't hear any music, but I knew that Zagan was attempting to play my boss like a fiddle.

As I've mentioned before, supernatural beings are more primal than mortals like me. They take ancient ideas like pack, hearth, and home very seriously. There's some sort of responsibility carved into the very marrow of their bones that makes it impossible for them to ignore.

All this to say that Zagan threatening to kill me wasn't about me, or at least it wasn't *just* about me. It was challenging Orion as pack leader, striking at the very core of what the Hunter was. The part of his identity that was still nursing a wound from the death of the original Hunt.

"Alex," Orion said calmly, reaching up to draw his blade. Unlike his flaming sword, the Hunter's rage burns colder than the ice caps. The sword blazed like a beacon, its light sending our shadows running for cover as dusk began to finally fall into night.

"Alex," I said in a warning tone.

"Release the circle," Orion commanded, his voice full of the same abyss that filled his dark eyes.

Alex looked at me with a helpless grimace that said *What do you want me to do?* as he raised his foot and kicked the hardened foam, breaking the circle.

"Finally!" Zagan crowed in excitement. He turned the Desert Eagle from my face and pointed it in Orion's direction. "As I recall, Hunter, I owe you for a scar from the last time we met. Let's see if the centuries have dulled your edge."

He held out his empty right hand and moved it in a lazy circle. After completing it, he reached his hand through the center of the space he outlined and pulled. A long black sword emerged from thin air. It was sharp only on one edge and curved slightly, in the tradition of a katana.

The sword looked like it had been burned in a horrific fire, charred black from tip to hilt. Black ash floated off it like a dark snowfall, but it always faded from sight before landing on the ground. The ruined blade seemed one solid hit away from shattering into a thousand pieces. The blade devoured the light around it, and the darkness suddenly felt oppressive and close, like night had taken two giant steps closer.

"An archangel might have let you keep that sword," Zagan said, tossing the Desert Eagle to the side like a used paper cup, "but I'm more than happy to take it away."

A FALLEN ANGEL WANTED to kill me and my friends. A year ago, I was just some kid whose mother and sisters had died in a car crash, whose father had disowned him, and wasn't ready to go to therapy. Life comes at you fast, that's the mortality guarantee.

Orion didn't react to Zagan's taunts. That's not his style. When push comes to shove, he's a real Teddy Roosevelt fan. You know the whole "speak softly and carry a big stick" thing. Except in his case, Orion lets his fiery sword do the talking for him.

The Hunter surged forward, his sword held casually in his right hand, the point trailing toward the ground. To an intermediate duelist like me, it looked like he had forgotten every rule of sword fighting that he had ever tried to drill into my thick skull.

But in a duel between two master swordsmen, rules are more like guidelines. They have mastered the language of the blade to a point where they don't need grammar anymore, they speak in abbreviations.

The Hunter's blade rose in a blurring diagonal slash. Zagan's fell sword rose to block Orion's angle. Orion spun to the side before their blades even connected, using the momentum to curve his slash like a sinuous line. Zagan casually sidestepped and launched an attack that Orion moved to intercept—this time the demon shifted his own attack before the swords clashed. They danced like this for another moment or two, blades leaping apart without ever even touching, whatever master calculus that was running through their minds determining the outcome of the duel before a single blow was struck, and deciding it wasn't the right move.

Despite the mind games, all of us knew this was only ever going to be resolved with violence. The two swordsmen couldn't dance forever. After a few moments, Orion committed to a strike that Zagan consented to meet. The flaming sword fell like a falling star, and the blade of devouring darkness rose to meet it. There was a sound like the ringing of a bell that was so loud the world shook in agony.

A shock wave rippled past our feet, carrying swirling dust. The hairs on the back of my neck stood at full parade attention. That felt like it meant something. I hate it when things mean something. It's never something nice like extra vacation days or free ice cream. It's always "oops, we accidentally awoke the slumbering monster in the deep."

The power behind Orion's blow was devastating, but these ancient warriors were just getting warmed up. Like a dark whisper, Zagan's curved blade slid around Orion's and tried to slice his chest.

But the Hunter is like a champion ballroom dancer—he never forgets his footwork. He sidestepped the dark seeking edge with a casual grace, bringing his own sword on the attack. Zagan was forced to retreat a step to keep his arm intact. My heart swelled a little seeing the big scary CFO of Hell back off in the face of Orion's wrath. It was his own fault; he pressed the big red button to make Orion mad. If you play stupid games, you win stupid prizes. Those are the rules.

A grim smile settled on Zagan's face, and his blade began to move faster than my eye could track, and Orion matched his tempo. It was all I could do to keep up with the blurs of light and darkness as they clashed over and over.

Despite Orion's aggression, Zagan was no slouch. The Hellish CFO was clearly a master swordsman in his own right. I'm brave but not stupid, so as the swords started swinging faster than I could think, I ran out of the circle to join Alex on the side. This was a fight that was so out of my weight class it wasn't even funny. I was Bambi, and they were both velociraptors.

The fallen angel and Nephilim circled each other in the ruined circle, sparks flying every time their swords clashed into each other and disengaged.

I glanced over at Alex to see he had his phone out, recording the legendary duel happening in front of us. I couldn't blame him. If I got the chance to see Hector and Achilles duel, I'd probably try to record it too. Besides, it wasn't like we could do anything to help.

The two of them danced their dangerous waltz, and Zagan seemed content to let Orion lead, retreating around the outer edge of my magical donut trap, slowly being forced to the middle, step by ponderous step. But for all the ground he gave, Orion never landed a blow. Their swords would lock, then disengage. Lightning-fast ripostes would seek flesh but never find it. I felt like I was on the edge of hyperventilating. This duel could literally decide the fate of my soul—no pressure or anything.

Despite not having blooded his opponent yet, the longer I watched Zagan retreat from Orion, the more I felt like it was only a matter of time. Zagan was on the defensive, his ability to keep up with the Nephilim admirable, but Orion was the Hunter. The stars have proclaimed his martial prowess every night for millennia. His victory was inevitable.

Or so I thought.

You don't get promoted to be CFO of Hell by being a pushover. Zagan retreated a step, and then another, and another. Then with a casual turn, he stepped into the smaller hula-hoop circle I had left behind when I had gotten out of the way.

That can't be good, I thought, opening my mouth to warn Orion, but I was too late. The Hunter swung his blade at the demon, but it bounced off the invisible wall of the reactivated circle with a dull thud. I blinked in surprise. I guess magic swords are on the no-fly list of a circle's borders too. Orion froze, chest heaving as he stared at the circle with a hint of shock.

Zagan's smile went from grim to wild in the space of a heartbeat. "Checkmate," he said with a smile. He knelt down and began drawing in the dusty ground in the center of the circle with one long finger. Not a single hair on his head was out of place. His breathing was normal. He seemed like he hadn't been exerting himself at all. "You are even more fierce than I recall, Hunter," the fallen angel said amicably, never looking up from what he was inscribing. "But you still think only in straight lines. As sharp as your sword is, you are only a blunt instrument."

Orion screamed in rage and hammered his magical blade against the circle's invisible barrier to no avail. It might as well have been made of adamantium for all the progress his blows made.

Finishing whatever he was writing in the dirt, Zagan stood and stared out at the three of us with smug satisfaction. "Thank you for this lovely circle, by the way," he said. "It will come in most handy." He threw his head back, dark eyes staring into the night sky, and began to chant in words that I could not stand to listen to. They burned my ears as I heard them. The language that he spoke was of the Eternal Night, the Endless Dark, and the Infinite Hunger. I didn't even know what that meant, but somehow I knew that was right.

Zagan began to rise in the air, floating on nothing. The ground inside the circle turned red and began to glow, like the earth was heating until it became lava. Orion continued swinging his magic sword like a sledgehammer, but even the Hunter's wrath could not penetrate the circle held by Zagan's will.

"What do we do? *Stop filming*," I snapped at Alex as I turned to my friend, who still had his phone pointed at the rising darkness of Zagan.

"Sorry, my internal journalist would die if I didn't capture all of this," Alex said, hesitating before lowering his phone.

"I'm pretty sure your external journalist is gonna die too if we don't figure something out!"

"This is so above our pay grade, dude," Alex despaired. He pointed at Orion. "If he's stumped, what can we do?"

Frustration burned in my chest, but I struggled to disagree with Alex. Standing before two beings like Zagan and Orion, I felt my mortality like a ball and chain around my ankles, a dead weight keeping me in my place. What hope did Alex or I have against a fallen angel?

The red ground beneath Zagan's floating feet continued to heat up. A giant bubble burbled in the center, before the whole ground popped and vanished, leaving nothing behind. A wave of heat came out of the abyss that I could feel even on the other side of the ring.

A clawed hand reached up out of the pit, its hands scrabbling for purchase on the edge of the circle. I stared in horror as a monstrosity pulled itself from the depths. It had long bony arms that its dried, leathery flesh stuck to. Its skull was triangular—all sharp corners and edges. The horns curling out of its skull ended in cruel-looking points. But the weirdest thing was a glowing red bulb that dangled off their forehead like a lantern—it reminded me of an angler fish, hunting in the deep.

"Oh great, now he has Trianglers," I groaned.

Alex sighed in frustration. "You are banned from naming things from now on."

The monster finished pulling itself out of the pit and stood on the edge. It was freaking tall. I was getting so tired of supernatural creatures that could look down on me. When could I fight a bunch of little goblins or something that only came up to my knees? I'm not *short*. I'm literally six feet tall. What more does the world want from me?

That rule I mentioned about demons not being able to summon more demons has some gray areas to it. That ban doesn't seem to extend to monsters and creatures from the Pit, like Lilith's hellhounds, which still give me nightmares.

"At least he only summoned one minion," I yelled to Alex. "It was way worse when we had to fight an entire pack."

Zagan kept chanting his spicy words. A second clawed hand reached up from the emptiness at his feet and grasped the edge.

My friend groaned. "You had to say something."

"Whoops."

A second monster climbed out of the pit to join its sibling and master. I sighed and rolled my shoulders a little. If we were playing pickup basketball, this wasn't exactly the three-versus-three lineup I would have chosen, but I had faith in my friends. We had survived worse odds… probably.

Three more hands reached up and grasped the edge of the circle, popping up like demonic weeds. Okay, this was just getting ridiculous.

Circles are tricky things. As I mentioned earlier, they are focuses, magnifying glasses of will that allow different worlds to meet and be contained. When we summoned Lilith way back when, she was able to break out of the rudimentary ring we had prepared for her. But that mostly had to do with me and my lack of belief in what the ring was made of. Construction material matters, but not as much as the will that is battery powering it.

I didn't have to be told that Zagan's will was hard enough to make diamonds look like a down pillow. Also, according to Orion, it was easier to break *out* of a circle than in. It has something to do with the surface area of the worlds that are colliding. Zagan only needed to have enough will to enforce the domain of Hell on the interior of the ring, which let him be very specific with his focus. The best way to break a circle is to damage the ring that contains it. Which technically made the hula hoop an incredible choice as a medium since we couldn't just scuff it like a line of salt.

To put that in less geometry terms and more in English, if Orion's sword couldn't cut through the will of the demonic CFO, then nothing Alex or I had was going to even leave a scratch on it.

Desperate, I cast around the dark crossroads, looking for a way out of this mess. We had to stop him from summoning more, or we were going to be overrun by a triangled horde.

Inspiration glinted in the light of Orion's burning blade. Zagan's Desert Eagle lay in the dust where he had tossed it. The next wave of pointy creatures were up to their elbows, so time was running out. With half a plan, I did what I do best and decided to make it up as I went.

I sprinted to the gun and dropped to a slide, scooping it up as I careened past it. Yes, it was super sick. But I didn't let the awesomeness of my move distract me from my goal. I raised the miniature cannon and squinted down the sight. At this range, I couldn't miss if I wanted to—and I definitely did not want to miss.

I filled the little notches with Zagan's chest and squeezed the trigger, like Orion had drilled into me a thousand times. The gun kicked like a mule, knocking me off my knees and onto my butt. I may have looked like an idiot, but my aim was true, and the slug smashed into

Zagan with the force of a stampeding bull elephant.

Father Time might give Immortals a pass, but Uncle Physics isn't as forgiving. A force in motion stays in motion, jerk. Zagan was a fallen angel, and therefore an Immortal, but the fifty-caliber round still sent him flying. He shot through the invisible barrier of his own will and crashed down to the ground in a burst of dust.

The abyssal circle closed instantly, reverting to the mortal realm's dominion faster than I could blink. The monsters that were in the process of crawling through the dimensional hole were swallowed alive like infernal weeds. Multiple skeletal arms wiggled in fury, like lizard tails cut off from their body, unable to break free into our world. One creature was buried up to its chest, mouth snapping at me in frustration as Mother Earth held it tight in her crushing embrace. It was a killer move, if I do say so myself. There was only one downside—the Trianglers that had already crawled out of the Pit to answer their master's summons had just been set free.

Orion leapt forward, channeling his frustration into destructive rage. I almost felt bad for the poor infernals. Imagine being ripped into a new world only to have the Hunter with his fiery blade waiting for you on the other side.

The first Triangler only got to have thirty seconds of breathing our sulfur-free oxygen before Orion split its skeletal form in half with a horizontal slash. My mentor spun into the stroke, sliding in between the other two creatures, who turned to face the Constellation-level threat in front of them.

Alex's pistol barked, and cold steel rounds ripped through the one on the right, punching through the back of its skull with the ease of a baseball smashing through wet newspaper. The weird red light that dangled in front of its face shone back at us through the new holes in its head. The Triangler staggered but stayed on its feet.

"Of course head shots don't kill them!" Alex snarled, reloading his pistol with a new magazine and continuing to blast away at the pair of demons Orion was dueling. The triangle creatures didn't look super impressive. Unlike the four-armed behemoth we had faced in the pizza parlor, these guys wouldn't be my first pick for my defensive line in a supernatural football team.

But they were vicious and fast.

They hemmed in Orion from either side, and the Hunter had to move quickly to dance around their razor-sharp claws as they slashed at him with reckless abandon. Orion deflected one attack by slicing its clawed hand off at the wrist. It didn't even blink, continuing its attack, trying to beat him with the black-blooded stump like a sledgehammer.

"Hey, Alex," I started to ask, a bad feeling beginning to creep up my spine. The next part of the sentence was "where's Zagan?" But before I could finish my question, the world was spinning as something sent me flying.

Found him.

Faithful as ever, Alex leapt between me and the fallen angel, his pistol blazing away at Zagan. Unfortunately, these rounds didn't send the demon flying. This time his feet were firmly planted on the ground, and the 9mm rounds in his pistol didn't pack the same punch as the Desert Eagle. A snarl settled on his face as the bullets peppered him like a swarm of bee stings.

Behind him, Orion slashed his way out of the Trianglers, black eyes wide as he tried to get to us. He was going to be too late. Alex threw aside his empty pistol and stepped toward Zagan, drawing a knife from his belt.

Groaning, I struggled to my feet, shock slowing my brain's ability to process down to a crawl. I had been knocked a dozen feet from where I'd been standing. My ankle was bleeding, but I couldn't feel it.

With a shout, Alex stepped toward the CFO, blade slashing. Zagan blurred forward, his empty hand lashing out at Alex like a cobra strike.

He lifted my friend off the ground by his neck, dangling him a few inches off the ground. Alex's knife flashed as he tried to slice Zagan's arm, but his blade didn't burn with a magic fire, and he might as well have been stabbing the demon with a peeled cucumber.

With a bored sneer, Zagan raised his fell blade and slashed the edge across Alex's chest. Bright red blood spurted from his body like paint splatter. The knife slipped from my friend's fingers and crashed down to earth. Someone screamed. It must have been me, but I couldn't be sure. My own body felt muted, like my mind was wrapped in a layer of cotton.

Zagan tossed Alex's limp body to the side like an old newspaper. Free of Trianglers, Orion sprinted toward us, his blazing sword casting his enraged face in a harsh light. Zagan glanced at the building on the side of the crossroads. It looked like some sort of industrial chute that was used to fill construction trucks with sand or gravel.

The fallen angel raised his empty hand in the direction of the chute and made a fist as if he was gathering up invisible threads, and *yanked*. As he pulled, something began to glow above his head. It was a dark smudge against the blackness of the night sky. It was like looking at the sun through an oil spill. Whatever it was, I couldn't look directly at it, but I got the sense it was misshapen, broken.

The structure groaned with the terrified squeal of tortured steel; slowly it fell like a tree, smashing into the crossroads, leaking gravel out in a flood. The earth shook with the impact of its landing, and it fell between Orion and us, cutting off the Hunter's charge like a dam. I buried my face in my arm, coughing as a cloud of dust and dirt swept over me.

As the air began to clear, it revealed Zagan, standing across from me like a Wild West gunslinger. The fallen angel glared at me, his two black eyes boiling with a deep rage. Alex's body lay in the dust behind him, partially covered in gravel.

"I begin to understand why Lilith hated you so," he snarled through gritted teeth. "Maybe the Pit is too good for you. Perhaps I shall ask my master to *unmake* you instead."

If I wasn't already sweating, that was more than enough of a threat to get me started. I don't know exactly what being unmade meant, but if Zagan thought it was worse than having my own personal circle of Hell specially constructed like an attached garage apartment to the Devil's house, I was going to pass, thanks.

"Well, Matthew Stephen Carver? No more glib remarks? No more sarcastic quips?" Zagan sneered.

For once in my life, I managed to keep very, very quiet. Even my instincts knew that I was in dangerous territory. Here there be monsters.

Suddenly Zagan was in front of me, having closed the distance between us in an instant, without taking a single step. His corrupted glow burned so brightly it blinded me. He backhanded me with his right hand and sent me rolling across the gravel road like an armadillo hit by a car. I could tell he was holding back a little, because my jaw was still attached to my face. The world was spinning. What year was it? My right leg hurt as I tried to put weight on it, ruining my attempt to stand up.

Despair settled around my shoulders like a wet towel, clinging to me and dragging me down. What chance did I have alone against a fallen angel? I didn't even have a weapon that could hurt an Immortal. I was about as dangerous as a baby bird in the clutches of a hungry cat.

Gasping for oxygen, trying not to cough on the dust in the air, I lay on my stomach, gaining new sympathy for a fish out of water. Zagan's boot dug into my spine as he loomed over me like a game hunter standing on his prize kill. He stomped down with crushing force. I felt like at any second my rib cage would shatter, and I would become just a Matt-flavored puddle of ooze on the ground.

"It's time you learn your place, maggot," the fallen angel panted.

This seemed like it was it. All things considered, I'd like to congratulate myself on exceeding expectations. I killed an Immortal and survived a year on Lucifer's Most Wanted list. If Vegas had been running odds on me, I could have made a fortune betting on myself. Granted, given that this was looking like my untimely demise, I wouldn't have gotten to spend it, but I could have died with a smug sense of superiority, which would have been nice.

Zagan increased the pressure. It felt like I was being crushed by a hydraulic press. I couldn't breathe. The edges of my vision were going fuzzy and black. In the back of my mind, I knew the final notes of my song were being played.

A burst of color filled my vision, pushing back against the darkness. A cluster of dandelions thrust their way through the gravel street that I was pinned to. They glowed with their own light, and the sweet scent of a summer field filled my nostrils. It seemed that my meeting with the Faerie queen was a more pressing—ha-ha—engagement than Zagan's boot crunching through my spine.

I didn't have enough air left in my lungs to ask questions *and* blow out a dandelion candle, so I ignored the demon and reached out with my right hand and snatched a dandelion from the bunch.

The weak little blow I managed had almost no effect. The dandelion seeds in the ball-like head waved for a moment, as if my life's last breeze was merely music for them to dance to. Then a single seed popped off, and for a moment it pranced a slow choreographed routine in front of my eyes, like a prima ballerina. A few heartbeats later, the white head of the dandelion exploded, and seeds shot everywhere, thrown around like nature's shrapnel.

Impossibly, I felt something reach up and hook into my chest through the ground, and suddenly I was pulled *down* through the gravel as if it were water.

"No!" I heard Zagan roar somewhere behind me. Something that sounded like his foot smashed into the ground after my body was pulled through, like a dull thud heard under water.

I was free. I could breathe again. Gasping, I struggled to fill my lungs with precious oxygen. The hook in my chest pulled like a fisherman reeling in its catch, hurtling me at speeds I couldn't even begin to process, the world flashing gold and yellow around me, splotches of colors dancing like we were in a kaleidoscope. Before I could get my bearings, something spit me out the other end. I burst through a wall that undulated like it was made of Jell-O and rejoined the physical world. My right leg flared in pain as I landed, and I fell to one knee, taking the weight off my ankle.

I was in a hallway that had to be part of a palace. White marble walls were accented with gold, and the stone floor was polished so brightly that I could see my own reflection. The trail of blood my ankle was leaking was very striking against this color palette.

None of that held my attention. I was staring at my hands, frozen in shock.

They were on fire. A ball of flame that danced with hints of red and blue consumed each of my hands like a pair of boxing gloves. Even though they were in the fire, my hands were not burning; they felt pleasantly warm.

"*Finally!*" a voice said brightly in my head. "*I can breathe again.*"

AHH!" I SCREAMED, flailing my candlelike hands as if I could put them out with a little breeze. "You can talk?"

"I can talk! I can also get headaches. Please STOP."

"Ahh! Sorry," I yelped, freezing my hands in place like they were suddenly as brittle as eggshells. I stared at them, trying to catch up. It had been so long since my hands had last become enflamed that part of me had secretly begun to think that it hadn't really happened. That it was all some sort of metaphor or something. But as I felt the strange warmth again, I knew that it hadn't been a dream. The talking part was new, though. That hadn't happened last time.

"Sorry I wasn't able to introduce myself before," the voice said cheerfully

into my head. It was a light and peppy voice, like a morning person comfortably hopped up on caffeine. *"I was almost all used up the last time we saw each other."*

Apparently burning down a building was even more exhausting for the anthropomorphic fire than it had been for me, because I had passed out after setting the blaze.

"Who are you?" I breathed, unwilling to believe my life had somehow gotten weirder.

"You can call me Willow, because that's my name!"

"Okay, Willow, do you think we could stop being quite so burny right now? It's kind of freaking me out a little."

"You're no fun," Willow said in a pouty tone, but my hands returned to their normal, non-immolated state. I tried to be subtle because I didn't want to be rude to my guest, but I did a quick spot-check on my hands to make sure there wasn't any burnt, crispy flesh left behind. They were a little banged up from being thrown across the road, but otherwise seemed unburnt.

"Sorry," I said. "I'm a little busy trying to figure out where I am."

"Why didn't you say so? We're in Goldhall, the palace of the Queen of All Fae. That's why I can breathe again!"

"You don't even have lungs!" I hissed at my now-flameless hands.

"Don't they teach you mortals anything? Fire needs oxygen. Magic fire needs magic oxygen."

I hated how much sense that kind of made.

I looked up from my hands to try to get a better handle on my situation. I hadn't known what to expect when I blew out the "Queen's Candle" as Robin had called it, but this was insanity on a new level, even for me. Only minutes ago, a fallen angel had been trying to make me one with the earth, and now I was bleeding on the floor of what was apparently a queen's palace while my fiery hands talked to me. I couldn't tell if my whiplash was metaphorical or a symptom of

Zagan trying to crush my spine.

I couldn't help but be a little in awe of the place I had been taken to. The white marble walls and vaulted ceilings spoke of a wealth beyond anything I had ever seen. I would go bankrupt trying to buy a single one of the chandeliers sparkling like miniature constellations in the hallway that I knelt in.

Before I could process the majesty of the place I was in, the door across the grand hallway burst open. I recognized the figure who strode to meet me.

It was Robin Goodfellow, my Faerie lawyer. His arms were spread wide in greeting, and a beaming smile lit up his face. His movement was fluid, like his whole life was choreographed. But the thing that stood out the most, other than his ridiculous tuxedo, were his brilliant golden eyes, bright as day compared to the abyss of Orion's.

"Finally!" Robin said with an enthusiastic clap. "I must admit I was beginning to get worried that you were never going to show up. Between you and me, the Queen was getting quite irked with your dilly-dallying and— ARE YOU BLEEDING ON THE QUEEN'S FLOOR?" His voice rose to a thundering shout as he pulled up short, a look of horror passing across his face.

"Oh, yeah, sorry about that," I said. "I was kind of in the middle of getting murdered by a demon."

Robin let out a faint choking sound.

"Not to be a presumptuous guest, but do you think I could get a bandage or something? Maybe some crutches too?"

"Matthew, I like you," Robin said with a strained tone, his face a little gray, "so I will betray almost everything that makes me Fae to give you this one piece of advice for free: *Do. Not. Leave. Your. Blood. There.*"

A chill settled in my stomach as I looked down at the pool of blood that had leaked around my right leg. If Orion had been present, he would have smacked me upside the head for forgetting one of his most important lessons. In a world filled with magic and monsters, there were no good outcomes to anyone getting a hold of my blood. I had plenty of enemies who would love to have easy access to me. Blood is magically linked to the body it came from. It's got DNA in it. Giving someone my blood was basically like giving someone the magical equivalent of a key to my house; with it, they could let themselves in at any time.

"Oh, right," I said, trying to figure out how I was going to clean it up. I started to grab some of the fabric of my sleeve to try to rip my shirt into a lame paper towel.

"I can help!" Willow's bright voice shouted in my head.

"Uh, okay, but maybe set the heat to low?" I replied hesitantly. "I can't afford to replace anything in this room."

"You got it, boss."

My hands burst back into flame, a smaller, cooler flame, and I knelt, sizzling my blood until it was consumed. Which smelled awful, by the way. Do not recommend.

"You have a Willow." Robin's voice was flat as he regarded me from across the room. His brilliant smile was gone. He stared at me with narrowed eyes, the golden orbs looking like a pair of rising suns.

"There's more than one?" I asked, surprised. "I thought that was more of a name than a species."

"It's both!" Willow replied in my head.

"It's both," Robin replied with a shrug.

I guess I shouldn't have been surprised. The Fae treat questions and information as being worth their weight in gold. I was going to need to get back into that mindset if I was going to survive here.

"So, about that bandage…" I said, trying to not make it sound like I was offering a deal. "I can't imagine it's proper manners for me to bleed my way through the palace, especially when I was invited."

Robin gave me a frank look. "Healing is one of the greatest gifts that can ever be given." Robin hesitated for a moment, eyeing my ankle with a practical air. "Still, when you are about to swim with sharks, it is best to not add blood to the water."

Gulp.

"*I can help with that, if you want me to,*" Willow's voice echoed hesitantly in my mind. I felt a burst of intuition of what the spirit was suggesting. It was like the idea of a picture communicated without visuals. I felt the phantom pain of a branding iron and grimaced. Cauterizing my own leg did not sound fun, but it was better than owing any Fae a big favor.

"Do it," I commanded Willow. I was a little shocked at how confident my voice sounded.

My right hand's flame increased in brightness, and for the first time, I felt waves of heat rolling off my own fire. Refusing to let myself think, I dropped into a crouch and pulled up my pant leg with my left hand, exposing a long scratch about the size of my palm. It wasn't terribly deep, but thick red blood still oozed out its length.

"Yeehaw," I said, which I assumed was what the cowboys always said before they branded their cows. Gritting my teeth, I used my red-hot fingers to close the wound and melt the two sides together.

"Gah!" I did my best to choke down a scream of pain. It hurt. It burned so bad it felt like ice. But it wouldn't do to scream in front of the Faerie, even if he was my lawyer. I counted to five. Not full seconds, I'm not that tough, but after holding it as long as I could, I pulled my fingers off and inspected the wound. It was ugly and tender, but it wasn't bleeding anymore.

Gingerly, I rose to my feet and tested putting my full weight on the ankle. It smarted a bit, but I could stand. All things considered, that could have gone a lot worse.

"Now, we must get you situated," he said, spreading his hands in a welcoming gesture beyond him, as if I hadn't just cooked my ankle like a steak right in front of him. "Right this way, Matthew."

"But my friends," I said, gesturing pathetically behind me. "We were kind of in the middle of a little argument with a demon. I can't leave them behind." Guilt stabbed a knife into my kidneys. I was no longer being flattened by a fallen angel, and my leg was sealed. I could go back and fight.

Robin's face twisted with something that might have been a flash of sympathy. He placed his hand on my shoulder like an out-of-touch older brother trying to comfort a sibling.

"The invitation was only for you, I am afraid," he said. "But I wouldn't worry too much about the Hunter. They don't give constellations to just anyone, you know." He gave me a cheery wink and patted my shoulder like the matter was resolved.

"Zagan didn't seem too impressed," I muttered.

"Zagan is in the mortal realm?" Robin hissed, his hand spasming closed in surprise. He was silent for a moment before he let go of my shoulder. "My bet is still on the Hunter. Orion has earned his reputation a thousand times over, my mortal friend. Let him fight his battle. You have your own to face now."

Robin spun on his heel and waved at me to follow him, trotting toward the door he had burst through. I followed him at a brisk trot, marveling at how much better my leg felt after getting off the grill. The lack of pain made plenty of room for a new twinge—guilt. I hoped Alex and Orion were okay. I knew in my head that I hadn't tried to abandon them. I had literally been cornered, in the process of being killed by a demon. But my friends were still fighting for their lives against a demon who was hunting me, and I wasn't there to help.

The doorway that I followed Robin through took me to whatever the Fae equivalent of the TSA is. A long hallway was dotted with doors identical to the one we exited—arrival gates, if I had to guess. At the end of the room, two liveried guards in white and gold stood on either side of what looked like a freestanding doorframe grown out of twisted oak branches.

"Ah," said Robin as we approached. "These fine gentlefae do need to run you through a quick security check before we go any further."

"Of course," I sighed. At least the line was shorter than LAX.

I stepped up to the structure and resisted the impulse to reach out and touch the branches that had been shaped to form it. One of the guards waved me through, a bored look on his face. Tense, I walked through the scanner. I knew a metal detector when I saw one. I didn't know what they were scanning for, but I was still carrying my gun, so I had a feeling I wasn't getting through on my first pass.

As I expected, the scanner let out an alarming gong, and red flowers sprouted out of the wood in an explosion of panic. There it was. I sighed as the guards closed in on me, suddenly alert.

"Sir, do you have any magical weapons, forbidden powers, or cold iron on your person?" the first one asked me, hand hovering over his hilt.

You know, in hindsight, I should have guessed the cold iron would have been the part they actually cared about. The gun wasn't the problem for them, but the bullets would be.

"Oh!" I said, as if I had casually forgotten about my supernatural killing weapon. "You know, I think I accidentally loaded the wrong bullets today." Slowly, I pulled out my pistol and held it up for the guard to see, being careful to hold it in a nonthreatening way.

"The bullets are cold iron?" the guard asked, eyeing my weapon with narrowed eyes.

"I think so," I said.

"Can you remove them, please?"

I ejected the clip and placed it on a side table. Hand still on the hilt of his sword, the guard waved me through the scanner again. This time there was no gong, no emergency flowers.

"We must keep the clip," he said with a shrug. "You can collect it when you are ready to depart. You're good to go. Welcome to Goldhall."

Tucking my now worthless pistol away, I followed Robin out of the security checkpoint. That might have been the most normal thing that had happened to me today, and it was still super weird.

We entered another long hallway made of marble and filled with wonders that I could never afford. We walked past a low table that had several Fabergé-type eggs casually piled together like someone might display a bowl of fruit. I saw a chandelier that seemed like it was made of emeralds and diamonds instead of colored glass. Every door handle looked like it was made of solid gold. The longer Robin led me through hall after hall, the more I suspected that if all the richest mortals in the world pooled their wealth together, they might be able to rent this palace for a few weeks.

The palace seemed to stretch for eternity. After a few minutes, I was hopelessly lost. Orion would have scolded me, but I think even he would have been distracted by the opulence that I was being pulled through.

Despite the wealth on display, I couldn't help but notice it was empty. A barren desert of gold instead of sand. We didn't pass another soul as our footsteps echoed through the sterile paradise.

"It is far too late an hour for the Queen to receive you tonight, I am afraid," Robin said, taking a left at a fork in the eternal hallways. "But have no fear! Our guest accommodations put your mortal hotels to shame. Or is it motels? I can never remember the difference between the two. Let us say both—our accommodations put them both to shame."

Thoroughly confused, I gave him a thumbs-up and kept following. My adrenaline from almost being squashed by a fallen angel was beginning to fade, so the crash that always comes after was on its way. I could sense its imminent arrival in the leadenness of my legs with each step on this indoor march.

"Is it much farther?" I asked after a few more minutes. "I don't suppose you guys have some of those golf carts that they use to drive people around at the airport? I'd be happy with a donkey or something."

"Just a few more turns," Robin promised, not even sparing me a pitying glance. Never before had I been happier that the Fae could not lie. I was beginning to feel like a man wandering in the wilderness, hopelessly lost with no idea how to get home.

True to his word, my lawyer led me up to what I can only describe as a Faerie hotel-motel. Seeing it, I understood why Robin had such a hard time keeping the distinction clear in his head. To the best of my understanding, the technical difference between a hotel and a motel is that a motel has doors on the outside of the building. Instead of going through a lobby, up an elevator, and down a hallway to get to your room, you just walk right up to the outside and let yourself in. There might be more to it, but I'm not an architect, so I don't know any of the more advanced rules. Like, for example, is it still a hotel or a motel if the doors are on the outside of the building, but the entire structure is still inside another, larger building?

The structure had three floors of wooden doors, all connected by an exterior flight of stairs and walkways built right into the wall. A larger set of double doors were set in the center of the first floor, and a wooden sign hung over the entrance, depicting three gold bars painted with pristine brushwork.

Don't get me wrong, just by being made out of marble and accented with gold, it was by far the fanciest hotel I had ever seen—but it might have technically been a motel. I suppose there was a chance it was a hostel, but that was mostly because I wasn't really sure what a hostel was. Structural decisions like that are above my pay grade.

"Ah, here we are!" Robin spouted cheerfully. "Behold, the Gold Bar and Inn. Guests of the Queen have been staying here in comfort for centuries."

Of course. It was an inn. I forgot about inns. I have absolutely no idea what makes an inn different from a hotel or motel or hostel, and frankly, I didn't care anymore. I was too tired and had way bigger problems.

"Come, let's get you a room." Robin led me toward the double doors on the first floor. As we stepped up to the door, he reached out and grabbed the handle before pausing and turning back to me with an odd look on his face. "It might be prudent," he said after a moment's thought, "to not mention your status as a squire of the Hunt to anyone tonight. At least not until you meet with the Queen."

"Why not?" I asked in surprise. "Usually that earns me a decent amount of street cred with the locals."

"It would certainly earn you a certain amount of credit here," Robin agreed somberly. "But the Hunt has many enemies among the Fae, and we Immortals are good at many things, but above all, we excel at holding grudges." His golden eyes flashed with a dark light. "We live too long and forget too little to be any other way, young Matthew."

A chill crept along the back of my neck at my lawyer's warning. I knew that once upon a time, Orion and the Fae had *not* gotten along. The thing about not getting along with Orion is that people in disagreements with him usually measure their blood loss by the gallon.

But I wasn't Orion, and he wasn't here to watch over me like a glowering statue. I could see how taking some credit from his account might get me wrapped up in some debts I wasn't interested in. I already had enough of my own. It's a good thing that I operate well under stress.

"Got it," I said, giving him a reassuring nod. "If anyone asks, I am just mortal Matt, here to see the Queen."

Robin gave me a reassuring nod and pulled the door to the Gold Bar and Inn open, revealing a small common room that looked like it wasn't sure if it was supposed to be medieval or the lobby of a five-star hotel. To my left, bright marble counters worked with golden accents ran through the room. Long, low tables made of smartly polished wood with equally well-made benches were farther in the back, next to a roaring fireplace. A dozen or so people dotted the room, drinking from mugs.

"Well, well, what have you brought me at this dark hour, Master Robin?" a man's voice called from the right. A Faerie man sat behind a thick marble desk with the word CHECK-IN carved in the front. He wore a suit jacket worked with gold thread, and a pair of half-moon spectacles rested over his golden eyes.

"My apologies, Seamus, for bringing you another guest so late, but this mortal has only freshly arrived to Goldhall this very hour. He is to have an audience with the Queen in the morning but is in need of a room for the rest of tonight."

"A mortal here to see the Queen?" Seamus asked, sounding a little shocked. "You always have something interesting going on, Robin."

"I try." My lawyer gave the innkeeper a tight-lipped smile.

"Well, we can certainly see to it that your mortal has room and board," Seamus said, turning to fuss with some papers on his desk. He stood, holding a golden clipboard in his hands. "I'll just need to see his papers and we can get him settled."

"My papers?" I asked with a lurch in my stomach. What kind of papers did you need to visit the Faerie Lands? "Uh, the guys who sent me through the cold metal detectors didn't stamp my passport or anything."

Seamus gave Robin a flat look. "They wouldn't," he said dryly. "But mortals need to have a signed Guest Visa to be allowed to stay as a guest in Goldhall."

I got the feeling when he was saying the word "guest," he meant it in the old-timey manner. According to Alex, being a guest in an immortal's home had more implications than being a guest in a mortal one. It went deeper than them needing to give me an extra towel and toothbrush. There was stuff like protection and trust wrapped up in guesthood that the host had to assume liability for. Which would definitely be a deterrent for anyone looking to settle a grudge with me on behalf of the Hunt. It seemed like Robin was trying to sneak me across the border, so to speak.

"Whoops," Robin said in a tone of voice that didn't sound like he really meant "whoops" at all. "It seems we missed that step." My lawyer stared back at the innkeeper, his golden eyes flat and daring. "Well, since we're already here, might as well get him checked in now."

"Absolutely," Seamus agreed firmly. "The moment he has his Guest Visa, I will hand him his key." He held up a golden key with a wooden tag on it and gave it a little rattle. I resisted the urge to wipe my sweaty palms on my jeans. I'd had enough trouble with mortal cops to be not that excited about an interview with immortal ones.

"Come now, Seamus," Robin murmured. "You're going to make a mortal visiting at the invitation of the Queen herself walk all the way to the nearest guard station over a formality?"

"If you need a guard, you don't have to go anywhere," a woman's voice cut off Seamus's response crisply, like a pair of cold scissors. A tall woman approached from the common area. She had pale skin that served to make her long black hair in an ornamental braid even more striking. Her ears were pointed like any Fae, but instead of golden eyes, hers were a slate gray with a mortal-looking pupil in the center.

"My lady," Seamus said with a nervous laugh. "It is nothing to trouble yourself with. Master Goodfellow has brought a mortal to get a room, but they have not obtained a Guest Visa for him yet. I was just telling him he would need to be granted one before I could—"

"Or I could interview him myself," the icy woman said, holding up one pale hand to stop the innkeeper's prattling.

My heart sank as I met her gray stare. Maybe we should have

gone back to the guard station. I didn't know who she was, but it was obvious that she was high up on the food chain that Robin had been trying to undercut.

"I apologize," Robin said smoothly. "This mortal is here at the invitation of the Queen. I was not trying to cause more trouble for you, Yo—"

"We're here now, Robin," she said with a stoic sigh. She held a hand out toward Seamus, who passed her the golden clipboard and a pen. "Very well, mortal, who are you?"

Mouth dry, I stared into the iron eyes of a very dangerous woman and did my best to tell only the truth that wouldn't get me killed. "My name is Matthew Carver, and I was sent a dandelion to bring me here."

"Well, that answers the next question," she muttered to herself, marking something down on the clipboard. "What is your profession?"

I opened my mouth and was about to blurt out something very stupid when out of the corner of my eye, I saw Robin shake his head ever so slightly, bringing me back to my senses. Not the Hunt. I was not a part of the Hunt.

"I'm currently funemployed," I said with a shrug.

"You're what?" the woman asked, looking up sharply from her notes.

"It means that he is in between jobs but is happy about that. It also usually implies a level of soul-searching about one's career and future," Robin confided to her conspiratorially. I guess when you do mortal lawyering you pick up some of the lingo. The guardswoman made a noncommittal grunt but went back to scribbling on the clipboard.

"Robin, are you willing to vouch for him as a sponsor and guarantee his good behavior as a guest?" she asked.

"With pleasure," my lawyer said with a broad smile. He tossed me a small wink. My spirits rose at his relaxed posture. This was going way better than I had been bracing myself for.

"Your Guest Visa is approved," she said, signing the bottom of the page with a flourish and handing it back to Seamus. "Be welcome at Goldhall," she said formally, dazzling me with a bright smile, shedding her professional composure like a glove. I felt a great weight slough off my shoulders as the innkeeper began collecting the papers on his desk. Finally, something had gone right.

"Out of curiosity, what does my mother want with a mortal with no job? Are you an artist or a trained chef, perhaps?"

I felt my brain shatter into a thousand pieces as I realized who I had just lied to. Being a daughter of the Queen would make her a princess, according to my simple knowledge of how royal families worked. Robin had just convinced me to pull a fast one on a princess of the Fae.

"Ah, no, uh, Your Highness," I managed to squeak. "I had a run-in with a demon who sort of stole my soul, and while dealing with that, I met Robin and freed him from a prison cell."

"So you are the one responsible for returning our illustrious Robin to us?" the princess asked, giving me a look of surprise. "Fascinating."

"Begging your pardon for the interruption, Your Highness, but this is the key to the room." Seamus handed me the golden key with a wooden tag attached to it bearing the number thirty-three worked in gold.

"I hope you get some rest, Matthew Carver," the princess said, giving me another smile that made her gray eyes lighten like parting rain clouds. "I look forward to hearing more of your story tomorrow."

DESPITE THE SURPRISING luxuriousness of the bed in my room, I spent my first night in the Faerie Lands a sleepless wreck. Guilt tormented my conscience for leaving Alex and Orion alone to deal with an angry Zagan. The fact that my two options had been die or leave didn't make me feel any less like a coward.

It wasn't like my escape had taken me out of danger. I wasn't at home, hiding under the covers drinking some nice hot chocolate while my friends battled for their lives. I was pretty sure I wasn't even on earth, per se. I got the distinct feeling that the Faerie Lands were somewhere *else*.

Wherever I was, I was now on a collision course with the Queen of All Fae, and if there was one thing that had been made abundantly clear to me during my time in the supernatural world, it was *do not make deals with the Fae*. This was an uncontested fact of life, like *don't go swimming with sharks while bleeding* or *don't talk to random demons in movie theaters*. I had a sinking suspicion that I was about to go shark diving without my trusty cage of Alex and Orion.

Plus, there was no white noise in my room. I'm one of those people who has to have a fan or something running to be able to sleep. The empty silence of night is oppressively loud to my ADHD-addled brain. It leaves far too much open space for all the thoughts I don't want to have to come out and play.

Zagan's sword slicing into Alex's chest played in my head on a loop.

He was tough, I told myself with the repetition of a panicked prayer. Orion would take care of him. He was going to be okay. He had to be. Still, I tossed and turned, battling with demons both inner and outer, and waited for dawn.

A sharp knock on my door announced Robin's arrival and woke me from a light doze. The night felt like it had lasted both an eternity and a single second. Bleary eyed, I shoved my legs back into my torn jeans and shambled across the room to open the door.

My Fae lawyer stood on the other side, dressed once more in a white-and-gold suit. In his outstretched hand he held a steaming mug of coffee. Desperate to jumpstart my brain, I reached for the drink, but then a dark warning instinct flashed through my brain. I paused, wrenching my foggy eyes away from the heavenly smelling coffee, and fixed Robin with a questioning stare. It is always wise to be wary of a Fae bearing gifts, especially if it is food or drink.

"Matthew, you are a guest," Robin said in a chiding tone that sounded almost offended.

That was good enough for me. "Bless you," I grunted, reaching out with both hands to take the steaming mug of brain gasoline from him. Blowing gently on the surface, I risked a quick sip. If I was going to survive today, I was going to need my brain awake as soon as possible. I'd risk scalding the roof of my mouth over having my mind be in a fog for a second longer. It was hot but delicious. I had to hand it to the Fae chefs, they could brew a mean cup of joe.

"Now that we've got you almost presentable," Robin said after giving me a few blissfully silent moments to sip my coffee, "we should get a move on. The Queen waits for no man."

Robin led me out of the Gold Bar and Inn back into the mazelike hallways. As we walked, I kept sucking on that blessed caffeine like my life depended on it. It felt like I was walking to a test that I had been cramming for, and I was sifting through all the little tidbits of knowledge over and over in my mind, like a desperate juggling act. Hopefully I wouldn't drop all the balls as soon as I got there. All I had to do was focus, listen for tricky half-truths. I could do this. I had to do this.

Just as I was getting close to the end of my coffee, Robin drew up a few paces down a hallway that dead-ended in a giant pair of curved mahogany doors. It was gilded in fancy designs and whorls with bright gold, and a pair of giant rubies were set in the handles.

"One last piece of advice, Matt," he said. "We'll call it attorney–client privilege, okay?" He held out his hand and took my coffee mug from me, casually placing it on a small table next to the doors. I guess it would probably be pretty tacky to waltz in to meet the Queen with a drink in hand.

"I'd appreciate it," I replied, surprised at how dry and thick my tongue felt. I had no idea what I was walking into, except that it was dangerous and I was in over my head. But what else was new?

"Number one: bow." Robin ticked off one of his fingers like he was counting a list. "Number two: don't speak until you are addressed. Number three: be polite. And number four, and I do truly mean this: *be careful.*"

I met his golden orbs and remembered that he couldn't lie. Fear gripped my spine in its icy grasp. For once, I had nothing flippant to say. I gave him a small nod. He gave me a small smile, different than his usual larger-than-life used-car-salesman grins. It struck me that I might be seeing his real smile for the first time as he turned and pushed on the pair of doors, throwing them open, pulling me into the Dandelion Court.

"It's showtime," he whispered.

Robin swept me into the throne room at a brisk pace. The room could easily host a royal ball and have plenty of space left over for buffet tables. But instead of a lovely tasting menu, the room was jammed with what I assumed was the upper echelons of the Fae nobility. It came as no surprise that they were stunning specimens—that was just par for the course. Fae of all genders were dressed in elegant suits and dresses that covered the entire color spectrum, pointed ears angled to the ceiling like a sea of grass.

A red carpet ran from me to the throne. At the head of it all, Queen Gloriana towered over them all, the topper on a fancy cake. She perched on a golden throne that sat upon a raised platform, looking down on her subjects.

She was divinely beautiful.

The Queen of All Fae's raven-black hair fell in waves to frame her round face, brilliant golden eyes dancing with their own light as she looked between Robin and me. Her bright red lips ticked upward in a slight smile at our approach, which made my stomach gurgle in a different but even more terrifying way. A simple golden crown was nestled in her hair, a brilliant emerald shining in the center. She wore a bone-white dress, with a train that swept down from her to the stairs approaching her platform. As my eyes followed the current of her dress, I belatedly noticed four more women sitting in smaller thrones a couple steps down from her. Each of them sported a different color, and they shone like moons reflecting the glory of their monarch.

I recognized the fourth, sitting all the way on the right. It was the dark-haired princess who had signed my Guest Visa last night. She gave me a shy grin as our gazes met. I hoped that my return smile looked friendly and not at all terrified.

"My queen," Robin bellowed, pausing to sweep into a dramatic bow, one arm extended behind him like the tail of a peacock. I wasn't nearly fancy enough to attempt his move, so I clamped my arms to my sides and bent at the waist, staring firmly at the floor. My heart was racing. I could feel a hundred immortal eyeballs resting on me with burning curiosity. But one pair felt heavier than all the rest combined.

"Allow me to present to you and to the Dandelion Court, Matthew Carver, Squire of the Hunt."

Unbidden, my hands burst into flame again.

"And bearer of Willow, who needs no introduction here," Robin added as an afterthought.

"*Do you mind?*" I hissed mentally at Willow.

"*It's rude not to bow to a queen!*"

There was a pause. I could feel sweat beginning to sprout on my scalp like dew among the weeds, but I kept my eyes planted on the red carpet below me like my life depended on it. The pause stretched into a moment and was on the verge of becoming a deadly silence when a warm voice broke the stillness.

"You may be a squire of the Hunt, but I can tell someone other than the Hunter taught you manners, and bless the stars for that! Rise, Matthew."

I rose from my bow, letting out a breath I hadn't realized that I had been holding. As I looked up, I stared right into the eyes of one of the other women seated before the throne. She was tan, with brilliant red hair that seemed streaked with gold, like flames. But her eyes were like mine—human. A pair of green emeralds gazed into me, and my heart skipped a beat. I was frozen. I could not have looked away to save my soul. She gave me the tiniest twitch of a smile and blinked slowly, kindly releasing me from the hold of her gaze and freeing my eyes to continue their trek to the Queen of All Fae.

I couldn't help but risk a glance at the icy princess sitting next to her at the end of the row. Her warm smile was gone, replaced with a rigid mask. Those two gray eyes stared at me like bullets. It seemed that Robin had been telling me the truth about the Hunt's popularity here at the Dandelion Court.

"We are very pleased that you finally found time in your schedule to see us," the Queen said, a half smile still playing at her lips.

Do not speak unless spoken to, Robin's warning echoed in my mind. That was a knife that cut both ways. I had been spoken to, now I was supposed to speak—and I had no idea what to say.

"Uh, sorry about that," I said, my voice starting out too quiet and then growing in volume. This was a room of predators. I could not appear nervous. "The arrangement did not specify a reply-by date, so I did not realize there was any urgency." Was that polite? I hoped it was polite. I needed to be humble but firm. I was not afraid. I was a squire of the Hunt.

There were murmurs from the gathered nobles on either side of me. Was it my imagination or did the redhead shoot me another grin? It was distracting having her right in my eyeline, sitting below the Queen.

"You bargain like a full-blooded member of my court!" she crowed, spreading her arm to the room. The lords and ladies in the peanut gallery chuckled along like good sycophants.

"I hope that does not imply any lack of gratitude on my part for the services of—"

The Queen waved a gemstone-encrusted hand to cut me off. "You gave no offense, boy, I merely thought that someone in your... devilish circumstances would be more interested when someone who could help them is knocking on their door."

My jaw dropped open, and any plans I had stored away in my head for this conversation made a jailbreak. Why had it never occurred to me that she might want to help? Robin gave me the clues when he helped me. He was the one who told me about the potential for war to break out over the stealing of my soul. He had basically told me that his queen wanted the peace to remain intact. If Gloriana didn't want a war, maybe she would be willing to appeal on my behalf.

"At last, he begins to see." The smile on her face grew even more. "Robin, dismiss the court—we have much to discuss with our guest."

The lords and ladies filed out without so much as a complaint and in an orderly fashion that would make any sports stadium manager weep for joy. It was almost like it was choreographed. The four women seated below the Queen, however, did not stir.

After a few moments, Robin returned, but strode to the dais and stood at attention behind the Queen's chair, hovering behind her right hand—the model of a perfect servant. Six pairs of eyes stared down at me as I struggled to think. Now, more than ever, I was grateful for that coffee.

"Matthew," Gloriana purred into the now-empty throne room. "I would deal with you. I would deal with you in the way the kingdom of the Fae and the kingdom of mankind has not dealt in centuries."

I gulped. Very quietly and only to myself. "What, uh, what did you have in mind?" I asked, clasping my still-burning hands in front of me.

Gloriana, Queen of All Fae, rose from her throne. Her white gown somehow cleverly separated from its train, and she strode down toward me. With a gasp, Robin lowered his head, and the seated women did the same, although more slowly. I went for broke and dropped to a knee, my heart hammering a beat in my eardrums.

I heard her soft footfalls and the gentle swishing of her gown as she approached. I kept my gaze down, my burning hands balled into fists, knuckles resting on the floor.

"If only half the Dandelion Court were so humble as you, Squire," she said dryly. "Do get up."

Hesitantly, I rose and stood before her. She was a tall woman, although not as tall as Orion. Her pointed ears were much more prominent this close, framed by the white wings of her gown's collar, which curved around her face.

"Oh, shush," she said softly, looking at my flaming hands.

Willow vanished like a blown-out candle on a birthday cake. The Queen reached out and took my left arm, intertwining it with her right. I managed not to squeak. She was warm like a summer morning and smelled like the beach—not like salt and brine but fresh.

"My offer is simple, young Matthew Soul-stolen. I offer you sanctuary in my nation, citizenship in my court, and a place in my household."

Robin let out a little cough of surprise, which I was pretty sure was the Fae equivalent of a spit take. Gloriana turned to arch an eyebrow at her servant with a wry smile but didn't comment.

"I apologize, Your Majesty," I said, wishing that Alex and Orion were here. Or maybe that I had never left them. Getting turned into road cheese by Zagan felt less dangerous than this moment. "I don't know all the rules. How would that help me with my soul, uh, situation?"

"You would become a citizen of my nation. As such, you would have the rights that any Faerie has. Our lawyers would begin working on your case immediately," she replied at once. "I understand you do not have an actual copy of your contract? A disgrace. We would demand it from Hell immediately. Furthermore, you would be under my protection while we built your case for a full reinstatement of your soul, plus damages."

"But if I, uh, *die* during this process. Or if my time runs out. Do you guys have a more fun place for my soul to go than where it is currently signed up for?"

"I can only offer this help to you, young man. There are no guarantees—but there is a chance." Gloriana looked at me with her golden eyes, and a small frown crossed her lips. "What Hell has done to you is unconscionable. The Dandelion Court has produced some of the greatest lawyers who have ever lived. I have every belief that they could wrench your soul free from the Pit itself if they had to."

A fighting chance. She was offering me a fighting chance to get my soul back. But there had to be a catch. She was Fae. The name might share a couple of letters with the word *free*, but they were about as different as could be.

"That sounds incredible," I managed, still getting used to the closeness of the Queen as she told me promises I wanted to hear. "What would you want from me in exchange for this help?"

"You are wasted in the Hunt," Gloriana said warmly, giving me a friendly pat on the arm. "You are a man. Although you have bonded with the Willow, so you must have some Fae blood in you. In order to join my court, you must become betrothed to one of my daughters." She gestured at the four women sitting across from me. It took every ounce of self-control that Orion had beaten into me in the last year to keep from twitching in surprise. I felt like a fish that had jumped out of its fishbowl and was now flopping around on some kitchen counter. This was not where I'd been expecting to end up.

Her four daughters were about as different as could be. While I knew one of them was a princess, I had assumed the rest were handmaidens or something—I would never have guessed they were related. But as I looked across them a second time, I saw traces of their mother in each of them. Not just her features or her beauty, but her aura. Each of them was a striking shadow of the Queen.

The first woman, all the way on my left, wore a bright green dress and had dark skin and even darker hair to match. Her eyes were a deep brown, and she stared at me like I was a slug she had found underneath her napkin.

Her sister to my right wore a yellow gown accented with the same white as her mother's gown. Her blue eyes twinkled as she tilted her head at me, her blonde hair spilling to her shoulders in golden waves.

The third sister was the one whose green eyes I was not sure I could handle meeting again. Her sun-kissed skin offset her red gown and redder hair. She dazzled me with a brilliant smile that made my heart race for all sorts of different reasons.

The sister I had already met sat all the way on the right, wearing a gown of ice blue slashed with black. Her black hair was in another highly architected braid, worked with silver. Whatever warmth our first meeting had inspired had been replaced by frost. Her gray eyes were flat and hard as she stared at me.

"Tania, Lady of Spring. Dawn, Lady of Summer. Ash, Lady of Fall. And Mav, Lady of Winter," the Queen said, gesturing from left to right down her row of daughters. All of them looked at me like fishwives at the market, sizing me up as the fresh catch.

I suddenly understood how salmon at a sushi bar must feel—raw and thinly sliced.

"I'm sorry, Your Majesty," I managed weakly, "I don't really follow. Why would you want this?"

The Queen of All Fae was silent for a time. Silent as only an Immortal can be silent. The room was a second sort of silent in obedient echo. It was the silence of a dog waiting for its master, or the forest before the sun rises. My breathing felt like an intrusion into that stillness. No one else disturbed the Queen's quietude, but that wasn't fair. I wasn't even sure any of them needed to breathe.

"Because, young squire, I *do not want a war.*" Gloriana turned to look at me, her hand firmly wrapped around my bicep, locking me in place. "The nation of the Fae is old and mighty. But we are not one of the great hosts. Do you know what happens when a World War breaks out? If you've read your own histories, you would. The smaller nations get invaded first, and the great battles of the wars are fought in their homes. I will do *anything* to protect my nation."

I nodded, my respect for her growing.

"You are a squire of the Hunt. But you are also a child. You do not remember the last time the Hunt was formed, but we do. The Hunt and the Fae were once enemies. I have no desire to see my people become sport for Orion Allslayer once again."

"I don't think he would do tha—"

"He is Nephilim. He is a Constellation. He is the Hunt. He must hunt. I would have him hunt other things, more worthy things this time. I would hope that you would speak for our people. I would hope that you would speak for *your* people."

I nodded again. That seemed like a reasonable request. I didn't want to make promises for Orion, but he had re-formed the Hunt to help me and Alex. I didn't think he was looking to fulfill some ancient vendetta against the Queen and her people. I was pretty sure we had our hands full of enemies already anyway.

"Finally, Matthew, I will tell you a hard truth. It is not a secret, only a truth. The Fae bloodlines are old and stale. Immortality and inbreeding have led to the dimming of our sun. The Dandelion Court has lost too many branches of our tree to time and ruin. My dream is to rebuild our bloodline—to bring strength back into it. At least a drop of Fae blood must run in your veins, or the Willow would have burnt you from the inside out. Your mortality can be fixed."

A shiver ran through my body as I wondered if that's how Lucifer had phrased it to Lilith when she had been a mortal.

"Yet even as a mortal, you are an Immortal slayer. Once, the Fae warriors were sung of, like Achilles and Prometheus, but we have been forgotten, our fire has begun to burn out. With blood like yours in our people once again, maybe during the next Great War, the Fae will be doing the invading instead of being invaded."

I blinked at the fierceness with which she spat the last sentence. Her hand gripped my arm even tighter, like a bear trap closing on its prey. I wasn't sure I understood everything she was talking about, but I thought I got the gist of it. If Hell started a giant supernatural war, she feared the Fae would get squeezed in the middle, like Poland or France in World War II. But if she helped me get my soul back, there might not be a war.

Plus, she would make an ally of the Hunt and bring new blood into the family, so to speak. I let out a low whistle in appreciation. The Queen truly was a master bargainer. This was efficient.

I didn't really know what to think about her claiming I was part Fae. I assumed that it was such a small part that it was basically worthless. It still felt nice to maybe belong to a similar club as Alex and Orion—even if it was a different branch.

I wished my friends were here to tell me if I was being played for a fool. Everyone knows making a deal with a Faerie is dangerous, but this one sounded pretty good. Realistically speaking, when was I ever going to get another offer like this? Never. Even if this was a bad deal, I didn't think I could afford to not take it.

"What do you say," Gloriana asked with a brilliant smile. "Do we have a deal, young squire?"

"Can I think about it?"

"Is that not what you are doing right now?" she replied, arching an eyebrow. I took that as a polite "no." Of course this was a limited time offer, why wouldn't it be? I didn't get to ask my friends or the internet what I should do. This was a decision I had to make on my own. Closing my eyes, I took a deep breath, trying to focus my thoughts. I knew what I had to do, but it was terrifying.

"This is real?" I asked, opening my eyes. I wanted to believe.

"I swear on the Dandelion Throne," Gloriana replied somberly.

"I accept," I said, my heart pounding like I had just thrown myself off the edge of a cliff. Here goes everything.

"Excellent!" Gloriana crowed as she slowly released her grip on my arm.

"You must meet each of my four daughters and get to know them all. We have a courtship on our hands!"

My new best friend Mav shot to her feet with the speed of a cobra. "I will not," she hissed, gray eyes dancing with a cold rage. "I will not be chained to some fiery brute from the Hunt!" Without waiting for a response from the Queen, she stormed out the side of the room, blue dress swirling in her wake.

I've had a lot of girls not want to date me. My hormones were not kind to me during my teenage metamorphosis process from boy to man. But referring to dating me as "being chained" was a new one, even for me. I saw the blonde daughter, Dawn, I think, roll her eyes at the back of her retreating sister.

A tiny sigh escaped from the Queen as she looked back to me. "On second thought, you're better off starting with my three responsible daughters," she said. Turning to my lawyer, she clapped her hands. "Robin also tells me that your birthday is fast approaching. Send word to the lords and ladies of the court. We shall have a feast!"

THE QUEEN'S STAFF took Gloriana's clapping very seriously. At her pronouncement, servants poured into the room and clustered around the royal family. The Queen swept into the middle of them, issuing commands with a firm tone, her pleasant smile never wavering. Her three remaining daughters rose to attend to her. My lawyer appeared at my elbow with that spooky abruptness that all immortals seem to share.

"Let's get you out of here before it gets truly chaotic," he murmured to me, gesturing to the side of the room. I followed his lead. I had nothing better to do. With the nobles of the court absent, crossing the yawning throne room felt like I was Christopher Columbus, sailing off into unknown waters, hoping to find land on the other side. More and more servants and attendants appeared out of hidden doorways as Robin and I made our way to safety.

We managed to exit through an equally ornate but much smaller door on the side of the room. I couldn't help but laugh as we emerged in yet another opulent marble hallway. You had to hand it to the Fae: their branding was consistent.

"We're going to have to find a place to stash you before everything gets out of control," Robin said as he took a turn down a different hall.

"It gets more intense than that?" I asked.

Robin's laugh was sharp and a little cruel, which I took as a yes. He didn't have to be so rude about it.

"So, a birthday feast?" I shifted topics. "That sounds fun. I've never been to a feast before."

"They never seem to go quite how you expect," he replied absentmindedly.

"I hope the catering's good at least."

Robin stopped dead in his tracks so abruptly that I almost ran into his tall back. He turned to face me, his face drawn tight.

"Matthew. You do realize that you just agreed to marry one of the daughters of the Queen of All Fae, don't you?"

That was certainly a sentence that sounded different than how I had been thinking about it in my head. The Queen had distinctly said "betrothed," and my mostly completed English degree had told me with a decent amount of confidence that that only meant "engaged," not "married." In fact, I had thought it was more like medieval dating. But Robin's golden eyes spun with an intensity that I couldn't discount. I had done it again, hadn't I?

"What, uh, what would it mean for me if I married a daughter of the Queen?" I managed to ask, doing my best to not sound as worried or stupid as I suddenly felt.

"It depends on *which* daughter," Robin said stiffly, resuming our walk.

"Hey, wait," I said, trotting to keep up with him like a little lost puppy. "What am I supposed to do for the next few weeks until my birthday?"

"Try to survive, mostly," he replied, giving me a side glance. "That's all anyone can do when they are in Goldhall."

Goose bumps ran up and down my spine like a football team of spiders hitting hill sprints. The Queen's offer had been a good one, I told myself; I needed allies like her. But just because she wanted to be an ally didn't mean I could trust her—or this place. There was a reason mortals chased the Fae away. They did not play nice.

"Can I bring my friends?" I asked him again.

"This is hardly a sleepover," Robin said, rolling his eyes at me. Well, I was sort of reading between the lines that he was rolling his eyes. When your eyes are one solid color, it's sort of hard to tell. But it was there in the tone, trust me. "You can't just invite all of your friends over for one of your mortal pizzas and watch a play. Maybe you already forgot, but your friends are not the most popular here. You'd need a really good reason for me to sell that."

"Hang on a second," I said, stopping, planting both of my feet firmly on the ground. "You're telling me that I, after being invited here by the Queen of All Fae, was invited to join her family and court one of her daughters, but I'm to do so without any of my attendants?"

"Attendants now, is it?" Robin asked, crossing his elbows as he turned to look at me. "You start dating royalty and suddenly you have an entourage?" His tone was severe, but he gave me a slow wink with one of his golden eyes that told me I was onto something.

"Obviously I would need my, uh, butler—"

"Manservant," murmured Robin to no one in particular.

"My manservant, Alex Johnson, to help me prepare for such an undertaking."

"That seems reasonable. A future noble cannot be expected to care for himself, after all," Robin allowed, his lips pursed in thought.

"But also seeing as this is a foreign land, I could not begin to travel without my bodyg—"

"Escort," Robin murmured again.

"There's got to be a better word than that. How about guardian?"

"Fine, guardian."

We stared at each other across the hallway for a long moment. Robin had his arms crossed and a frown on his face, but his golden eyes were dancing. I thought I was beginning to see the game we were playing. Every TV show I've ever seen taught me that a guest of royalty could expect a certain level of hospitality. I couldn't have my friends join me, but there was always a loophole. Robin is a confusing fellow, but he's a great lawyer to have.

"Let me guess," he said dryly, "your guardian just happens to be a certain Hunter."

"Oh, you've heard of him?" I managed to ask innocently. "He's the best. I simply *cannot* survive without him."

"*Don't forget about me!*" Willow's voice popped into my head.

"Also, my fire hands," I said, waving them at Robin.

He laughed. "I would be dragged out of the castle and fed to the Devouring Dark if I even tried to separate you from your Willow." He rubbed his chin in thought for a moment. "It would be unbearably rude to hold a feast in your honor but not allow you to prepare adequately," Robin mused. "If you must have your attendants, then so be it. The Queen would never allow for her prospective son-in-law to be embarrassed."

He spun on his heel and began leading me back the way we had come. "Come with me. We must see to this at once, before you are inconvenienced any further."

Robin led me through the a-maze-ing corridors of Goldhall at a brisk pace. Eventually I began to recognize landmarks. I had seen those Fabergé eggs before. The emerald chandelier was unforgettable. I realized that we were heading back to where I had popped out after blowing on the dandelion and getting sucked through reality itself. This time, I wasn't too disoriented to take in the radiant dandelion etched in the floor in gold of the arrival station of the weirdest subway in all of existence.

Robin led me to the wall next to the square I had arrived in, past what I was now calling the DSA, or Dandelion Security Agency. There was an old rotary phone that looked like it was from the late 1800s hanging on the wall. It was made of rich dark wood and gold, which fit the theme of the place. From beneath the phone, he pulled out a giant leather book as thick as any phone book I'd ever seen. He opened the book and started flipping through the pages.

My lawyer reached into his pocket and pulled out a gold coin, which he slid into the top like a payphone and began turning the rotary numbers one at a time. The sound of the spinning dial echoed like falling crystals. He dialed a 0, then let the crank reset before dialing 3-1-0 in rapid succession, which kind of freaked me out because that was the mortal code for a part of LA.

"Are you telling me the magic phone system uses area codes?" I asked in disbelief.

Robin kept dialing but flashed me a quick grin. "What can I say? Alexander Graham Bell was a mortal genius." He dialed a few more numbers and then listened before holding the phone out to me.

"Tell them to blow the candles. I cannot force them here. They have to choose to come."

I took the gaudy phone receiver and cradled it to my ear. Even the spiraling cord connecting it to the base was made of gold. The line was full of static, popping and hissing in my ears. It felt like I was listening to the voice of a great emptiness. It made my skin crawl. My heart was pounding, and my lips were suddenly dry.

Please be okay, I thought to myself.

"Uh, hello?" I asked. Thundering silence echoed back at me. My spirits sank. Maybe they were—

"It's one way," Robin corrected me. "They can hear you, but you will not be able to hear them. Think of it like being on the radio."

"Breaker, breaker, this is, uh, Big Cheese, over." I made static noises with my mouth that were probably unnecessary. I heard Robin sigh behind me. "Listen, Control, I'm gonna need you guys to find the nearest dandelion and blow on them. You won't believe what happens…"

I trailed off as Orion and Alex were spat out of the wall like empty pistachio shells, although both of the Nephilim landed much more gracefully than I had when I arrived. My heart leapt with relief in my chest to see both of my friends alive and in one piece. Stress rolled away from me like the waves retreating at low tide.

Orion looked like he was in as good of a condition as I'd left him. Maybe I should stop worrying about him. His blazing, Immortal-killing blade was clenched in his fist, and his dark eyes were narrowed to match the snarl on his face. He looked primed and ready for another fight. Whatever battle Zagan and his monsters had put him through had clearly left him in a bad mood.

Alex, by contrast, looked like he had gone a round in the ring with a blender. His right hand was in a sling, and his left had a firm grip on a loaded pistol. His face was drawn in pain, and he was paler than usual. But he was alive! I counted a win for the home team.

They both glanced around the white marble of Goldhall, taking in their surroundings. Then, in spooky sync, they turned and looked at me. I watched their concerned expressions go from my face to my burning hands.

"What did you do?" they asked in unison.

LET ME GET this straight," Alex said.

He was sprawled on an ornate golden couch in one of the living rooms of the ornate guest suite I had been upgraded to. I guess potential royal suitors didn't have to stay in the inn.

"You agreed to marry one of the Queen of the Fae's daughters, but you haven't spoken to most of them yet, except for the one that now hates you, *and* more importantly, you told them I was your manservant?"

"Why do I feel you're more upset about the second part than the first one?" I asked dryly.

"I am so not folding your tighty-whities," he muttered.

"It could be worse. Orion has to be my babysitter."

After helping me pull my friends into the Faerie Lands via the

Dandelion Express, Robin escorted us to a set of rooms that could have been the Presidential Suite in any five-star hotel around the world. Well, if it had some of the mortal basics like TV and electricity anyway. The ornate marble living area had three different bedrooms that branched off in each direction. It felt like I was living in a museum. Every piece of furniture was gilded. But the cushions were comfy and I'm a simple man, so I sat in my overstuffed chair and listened to my friends complain.

"You truly have a gift, Matthew," Orion grumbled from where he paced behind the couch like a caged shark. "I expected that Zagan would be the most dangerous opponent we faced this week."

"Speaking of that lovely individual," I said, ignoring the doom in his tone for a moment, like I ignore most of my emotional baggage. "I have a few questions."

"Here we go," Alex muttered.

"Oh, like you don't," I sneered. Just because Alex was over two hundred years old, didn't mean he knew everything that was going on, just more than I did.

"Let's get your questions over with." Orion sighed, pinching the bridge of his aquiline nose, which seemed needlessly dramatic to me. I wasn't even sure I believed he could *get* headaches. If they gave me a constellation in the night sky and I could still get migraines, I would ask for a refund.

"Okay, first of all, what happened after I blew the dandelion? How did you get away?"

"He didn't really stick around after you snuck out of your own party," Alex replied. "He muttered some vaguely threatening things about seeing us soon and stepped into a shadow and vanished."

I tried not to let that make me more afraid than I already was of the fallen angel.

"He just left?" I asked, stunned. And here I had been worried.

"Orion was quite *wroth*, I would say," Alex said dryly. "I think he figured facing down a furious Hunter wasn't worth the risk when you weren't even there for him to snatch up. He certainly wasn't worried about me." He gestured at his arm in a sling with a disgusted look on his face.

"Speaking of that," I continued, pointing a finger in the air, "am I crazy or did we almost beat him? I guess I thought a fallen angel would be like an order of magnitude more dangerous than that."

"You call what we just did 'almost beating' a fallen angel?" Alex lifted his wounded arm with an indignant stare. "Were you watching the same thing I was?"

"Okay, well, the end didn't go great," I agreed, "but we started out pretty strong."

"So, you're asking why we didn't get beaten harder?"

"Uh… essentially, yeah."

"Because he isn't allowed to beat us harder," Orion said, dropping into a chair across from me with a heavy sigh. "The limits of Zagan's powers are beyond anything you have seen. But if he unleashed his full potential, it would not go unnoticed."

"By whom?" I asked.

"Everyone," the Hunter replied. "If a fallen angel came to the mortal realm and unleashed his full power, that would draw the ire of every supernatural nation. Some of them might take it as a declaration of war."

"You're saying that's against the rules?" I asked in surprise. "Aren't fallen angels supposed to be, like, the original bad boys? Why should he care about some dumb rules?"

"I don't think that's Zagan's aim," Alex mused.

"What do you mean?"

"We already assumed he was here about your contract, right?" Alex rubbed his chin, as if massaging it was helping mold his thoughts.

"If his goal in getting you to sign an amendment for the contract is to legitimize it and torpedo your ability to claim that they stole your soul, then his job is basically to sweep this under the rug."

"So going thermonuclear on the problem they're trying to make go away would be stupid," I said, following along with Alex's thought. "That would only draw more attention to it. He's trying to lock me in place quietly."

"There are rules about how to go after a mortal's soul," Orion said. "Zagan is trying to keep his mission off the other supernatural nations' radars."

"Okay, so you're saying he was using the supernatural equivalent of a silencer to keep this quiet," I said.

"Sure." Orion shrugged. "That's better than most of your metaphors."

"Was Lilith holding back too?" I asked, thinking back on the fights we had with the former infernal VP. "I guess I never really got the impression that she was using all her tricks."

"Lilith wasn't a real demon, per se," Alex replied, wiggling his fingers.

"Yeah, you never explained what that meant the last time you brought it up."

"The original demons, the ancestors of the race, are fallen angels," Orion explained, a dark tone in his voice. I wondered if he was thinking of his own sinister ancestry. "In the generations since then, they have expanded their race with other bloodlines, human and otherwise. We call them demons, but they are different."

"So, Lilith was Nephilim or something, like you?"

"She was nothing like us," Orion growled, his voice so low and threatening that the hairs on my arms began to stand on end.

I held up both of my hands in placating surrender. "Sorry! Friendly reminder that I don't know what I'm asking."

"According to legend, Lilith was a human once," Alex offered, ever my wingman. "Some say that the Darkstar fell in love with her and stole her from her husband. Others say she seduced him. However it happened, we know that he made her a demon in his own image somehow."

"The Prince of Lies murdered an angel and fed her his still-beating heart," Orion said flatly.

Oh. Well then. Now that he mentioned it, I vaguely remembered her gloating about having eaten angels or something. I guess that was a big clue.

"So, this is basically a champagne thing," I said, trying to bring the conversation in for a landing. I thought I understood the difference between Lilith and Zagan but wanted to make sure.

Alex laughed. "Yes. The Devil and his fallen angels are the true demons. Everything else under the banner of Hell is really just sparkling evil."

"So, Lilith wasn't quite a nuclear warhead and was more like a cruise missile in terms of power, and that meant she was less... regulated?"

"I think that is a reasonable way to look at it," Alex replied, glancing thoughtfully at Orion, who shrugged dismissively. My mortal attempts to frame and categorize his side of the fence tended to make him itchy.

"That is a fire we can jump into later," Alex said after the silence became oppressive. "We've got a pan to leap out of first."

Orion and I both let out a humorless chuckle.

"Speaking of fire," I said, holding my flaming hands up before me. "Can someone explain what exactly Willow is to me?"

"*Why not ask me?*" Willow's light voice sounded in my head. Orion and Alex both cocked their heads in a way that told me they could hear the fiery spirit too.

"Okay, then, what are you?" I asked the dancing orange flames that I held in front of my hands.

"I am Willow. I am the Flame."

"That sounds awesome but doesn't actually tell me anything," I complained.

"I've heard of the Willow before," Alex offered. "They are a creature that is supposed to only live in the Faerie Lands and consort with the Fae."

"The Queen said that my connection with a Willow meant that I had some Faerie ancestry," I mused.

"You, too, are the fire. We are the Flame. We are alike, you and I."

"Willow, you said something about needing to come back here to be able to breathe?" I asked.

"You are in the Faerie Lands, of course! I can breathe again."

That reminded me of a discomforting thought I had last night. "Are the Faerie Lands north or south of LA?" I asked the room.

Alex shrugged. "Sort of in between?"

"Great," I sighed, turning my attention back to the fire spirit. "So, you can travel to the mortal world with me, but you only have so much power you can use before you need to come back here and recharge?"

"Now you're getting it!" Willow mentally shouted, their cheerful enthusiasm echoing in all three of our heads.

"Can I ask you something, Willow?"

"Anything! We're bonded now, so I guess we should start being friends."

"When I touched the minotaur that you were with, why did you come to me instead of burning me?"

"You called me! We are the same. We are both the flame! Besides..." The flames shifted from a bright orange to a cold blue and seemed to shiver for a second. *"Apis was very boring and smelled bad."*

I glanced at my two friends, who both shrugged. My fiery companion seemed eager to be helpful but wasn't the best at explaining. But who was I to judge? I'd never met any fire or flames who had a better command of the English language. I certainly couldn't speak a lick of Burnish, which is what I assumed a fire language would be called.

"None of this solves the most urgent matter." Orion waved our laborious conversation with Willow to the side with one of his long-fingered hands like it was no more than an old cobweb. "We have to survive the Fae gauntlet first. What exactly did you agree to?"

I caught them up on the Queen's offer: the courtship, the protection, her hope to build trust between them and the Hunt, and even the bit about strengthening the weakening Fae bloodline by adding me to it.

Alex almost fell out of his ornate chair, howling with laughter. Even stony Orion cracked a brilliant smile at that part.

"I killed an Immortal!" I protested over Alex's cackling. "You are the worst manservant." That shut him up.

"I need you to remember her words exactly," Orion said, leaning forward, fixing me with his obsidian gaze. "Was she vague? Did she leave any room for her to reinterpret her words later?"

My nervousness grew in my stomach as I tried to remember every detail. The palms of my hand began to get sweaty, which was surprising since my hands were on fire. You'd think any moisture would evaporate. I had been trying to listen to everything she was saying when she made the offer, but I was terrified I had missed something. I was only gambling with my life, after all.

"She said she did not want a war," I said slowly. "She said it clearly and plainly. I don't think she could be lying about that. She also said I would be a part of her house, and that she did not want the Hunt to come after her people again. She also said the Fae bloodline was fading, and she would do anything to bring power back to her people."

Orion and Alex looked at each other and shrugged.

"I mean, that sounds about as straightforward an answer as you ever get out of a Fae, let alone a queen," Alex mused.

"The Fae are only ever that honest when they are desperate," Orion said grimly. "And when they are, it's even more dangerous. This is a very bad idea."

I tried not to let that intimidate me too much. The thought of the powerful figure of Gloriana being desperate and cornered made me nervous. If she was feeling the pressure, what chance did I have? I felt a little like a banana right before the blender turns it into a smoothie. I was surrounded by better ingredients but about to get liquified all the same.

"You really love raining on parades, don't you?" Alex sighed, settling back in his gilded couch. "So all we have to do is find Matt the Faerie love of his life, not die, help prevent a war, continue not dying, and get his soul back?"

"That's it?" I asked.

"Yeah, you know, I'm not sure what we're going to do after breakfast. Our schedule is going to be wide open."

I **DON'T WANT TO** sound like I'm complaining. Living in luxury in a castle would be a dream come true for a lot of people, but in my humble opinion, the Faerie Lands were super boring. My friends and I spent the next few days lounging in our rooms, recovering. I had a bruise the shape of a size-twelve boot in my chest courtesy of Zagan. Rest and recovery when there's no TV or Wi-Fi meant we laid around on gilded couches and stared at the marble walls until our sanity was dangerously close to cracking. The Fae are very opulent, but in more of a medieval castle than billionaire's playground kind of way.

It had been a while since I had sat around and done nothing. I've never been good at it; I get bored too easily. After the high-octane year that I had survived, I was even worse at it. It turns out that laziness is a skill that you need to practice, and I was clearly rusty.

On the third morning of our imprisonment, a knock sounded on the door to our suite. I started to get up, but Orion held up a hand, stopping me.

"I have a feeling that it is time to play our parts," the Hunter said softly. "Alex, you answer it."

Alex let out a dramatic sigh but nodded before marching to the door with military precision. My alleged manservant swept the door open with his one free arm and stepped face-to-face with a woman dressed in the livery of the castle.

"Carver residence," he drawled in a perfectly bored tone.

"I come bearing an invitation from the Lady of Spring for your master," she said. "She is about to take her afternoon tea and wishes him to join her."

My heart skipped a beat. The Lady of Spring had been stunning, as all the daughters of Gloriana were, but I vividly remembered the look on her face when her mother presented me to her and her sisters. Her expression was identical to the one Chelsea Rivers gave me when I asked her to the sixth-grade dance—absolute disgust. Which hurt a little, but I've seen my face in the mirror. I get it.

The only sister who had been more disgusted by me was Mav, the Lady of Winter. Given that, I couldn't imagine a tea date with Tania would be very pleasant. I'd much rather meet Dawn, the Lady of Summer, or Ash, the Lady of Fall. They had seemed much more open to the whole courting situation.

But a deal is a deal. I had made it, so I should at least meet all the daughters. Eternity was a long time, and spending it married to the wrong woman seemed like trading one hell for another.

"Let me inquire with the man of the house," Alex replied in his dry manservant tone. "One moment, please." He closed the door firmly and turned back to me with a smug smile on his face. "This manservant thing is kinda fun. Well? Wanna go?"

"I should." I sighed, glancing at Orion. He nodded.

That's how I found myself sitting alone in a small parlor fifteen minutes later. The room had a plush red carpet and kept the Goldhall tradition of white marble walls and gold ornamenting. I was seated alone at an overloaded tea table weighed down with cakes and snacks. I was starving, but even my limited manners training told me it was rude to eat before my potential betrothed-to-be arrived.

I was wearing a pair of black slacks that had been in my closet, with a gray button-down. They both fit perfectly, which made me itch. I didn't like that the Fae apparently knew my exact size and had clothes for me just lying around. That felt like some Fairy Godmother type nonsense right out of Cinderella.

On my way out the door, I heeded my mother's training, and paused by the mirror to make sure that my brown hair was neatly combed, my blue eyes sparkling.

When meeting a princess, one must look their best. Assuming I ever got to meet the princess, and this wasn't some sort of elaborate way to stand me up. Bored, I tried to ignore the mountain of food in front of me and play it cool. Just because no one else was in the room didn't mean I wasn't being watched and evaluated.

Either princesses are always late, or she was deliberately waiting to see if I would throw a temper tantrum. Whatever the reason was, ten minutes went by before Tania, the Lady of Spring, strode into the room with a handful of attendants in tow, and tea abruptly began like a starting gun had been fired.

I am only a mere mortal, and an American one at that, so tea is already unfamiliar territory for me. But when I sat down, I thought I at least understood the basic concept: you boil the water, throw in some leaves, drink the dirty leftovers, and call it culture.

I was wholly unprepared for the production that is a royal tea party. One liveried servant rolled a golden cart next to me and began brewing a custom tea for me. With a start, I realized she was human. Her ears weren't pointy, and her eyes weren't solid gold, but a soft brown. I tried to imagine why a fellow mortal might be serving tea in the gilded halls of the Fae court, and a somber thought occurred to me. I remembered my undead sister's cooking, which tasted like sawdust and ashes. Alex and Orion had told me that producing art required a soul. I guess tea counted as art now. Who knew?

"Squire Carver," the Lady of Spring said, bowing her head ever so slightly to me from across the table. "Thank you for accepting my invitation." She wore a simple green dress, this time worked with golden thread, and a demure tiara sparkled in the nest of her dark hair. Her outfit felt like the royal equivalent of business casual.

"I was honored to receive it," I said, trying my best to be formally polite. She was a princess, after all. "I know that our reason for meeting is unusual—"

She cut me off with a snort. "You clearly have never been a princess. You get used to being put up for auction to any male who wanders by with something shiny your mother might want."

An attendant handed her a bright white teacup with a matching saucer. She held them in her hands, blowing on the liquid to cool it. Her tone had been light, but her brown eyes bored into me as she looked over her cup.

I swallowed a little and tried to give her a winning smile.

"It is true. I've never been a princess," I said with a forced chuckle. "Although I was almost prom king my senior year of high school."

"You are no king," she said with a laugh, sipping her tea. Her scorn cut a little deep, but I did my best not to show it.

"That's what the cheerleading team said too, now that I think about it." The attendant handed me my own teacup, and I copied the princess by bringing the warm liquid close to my face and blowing on it. The floral steam danced away from me as I made eye contact with the princess again. She gave me a small smile, her teeth dazzling white. I took a sip of my tea and did my best not to make a disgusted face. It was almost worse than an IPA. It tasted like someone had strained water through a bouquet of flowers and then let it rot for a few days. I was clearly too poor to understand why anyone would drink tea over good old-fashioned water, or a Coca-Cola.

"Very well, *King Matt*, let's discuss terms," she said, setting her cup down with a clink.

"Uh, terms?" I asked, copying her and setting down my own foul cup of liquid.

"Of course." She gave me a broad smile full of teeth that reminded me of the toothy grin of a predator. "What did you think? That I would just gaze into your blue eyes and fall in love? We would run off into the sunset together, driven wild by our passions, and live happily ever after?"

I hated how stupid that sounded when she said it.

"No, no," I said, coughing into my hand. "Although I did think courting might have a bit of a romantic or personal element to it."

"Oh, you poor lost mortal. You might have some smattering of Fae blood, but you are not one of us, are you? My sisters are going to eat you alive." A wicked smile flashed across her face for a moment before it was gone. "Or burn you," she murmured.

"I will have you know I graduated with honors from the University of California," I said, drawing myself up to my full height in the chair. "I am an educated man who can take care of himself. If your siblings wish to devour me, they can get in line. There are bigger fish waiting for their turn."

Then Tania did something that surprised me. She cocked her head and stared at me, like a bird eyeing a worm. I'm not sure what she saw, but she threw her head back and laughed. A true laugh, made of pure joy. The Lady of Spring had a rich laugh that was entirely on brand. It was like the first hint of life and warmth in a new year.

Despite her harsh demeanor toward me, I felt a smile grow on my face in response. I challenge anyone to have resisted her in that moment. Even a snowman's frozen heart would literally melt, such was her power.

"I must admit you have a certain charm, Matthew Carver," she said, her mirth fading. "My mother's choices usually possess far less personality."

Mentally, I added "Can Make Fae Princess Laugh" to my internal resume, next to "Matthew Carver, Squire of the Hunt."

"I offer you these three things." She held up three fingers to me across the tea table. "Freedom." She lowered a finger. "Our marriage will be one of business partners only. Take whatever lovers you wish; I will do the same." She gave me an appraising look. "You're not exactly my type, manling. Secondly, I offer you two children." She lowered another finger. "My mother expects our union to join your bloodline to the Fae, and we will satisfy her greed."

My nervous swallow was so loud the human attendant looked at me in concern. I waved her off. I did not need the Heimlich; I just have commitment issues.

"Finally"—the last finger went down, her hand closing into a fist—"I offer you protection. From my mother's plans, from my sisters' designs. If you agree to my terms, they will leave you alone. You can be the pig in the pen, free to wallow in whatever you want. No one will bother you for the remainder of your life."

A chill ran up and down my spine. I didn't know what to expect when I accepted this meeting, but this was not the direction I had thought it would go at all. Given Tania's disdain for me, I hadn't expected a marriage proposal on our first date. Were her sisters also going to propose deals on our first date? Did I have to have tea next time?

I would be lying if I said I didn't see a little value in Tania's offer. It didn't sound so bad, being a pig left to his own devices. My life had been too interesting lately. Interesting gets you killed. It might be nice to go play in the backyard while the adults handled everything. But I was also tired of the Immortals talking to me like I was a child. I had killed one of them. I was not some lost sheep. I was a man who understood. I had come face-to-face with the Devil. Well, at least his girlfriend, and survived. I was a squire of the Hunt.

"Oh boy," I said, stretching out my right hand to examine my fingernails. "I get to play in the mud as much as I want?" I glanced up to make eye contact with the Lady of Spring. "You truly are far too kind."

Tania had the grace to look slightly abashed.

"I assume you want something in exchange?" I said dryly. "So far it sounds like you're only offering, not asking."

The Lady of Spring shrugged. "All I ask is you leave me be. I told you that a princess's lot is to be sold away to the highest bidder. You let me run the House of Spring and rule our lands as I see fit. If you stay out of my way, I will stay out of yours."

Our lands. I couldn't help but blink at the thought of having a household, let alone lands. But I hadn't been thinking about all the implications of this arrangement. She was a princess. If we were married, that would make me some sort of noble, probably? We'd have to be in charge of something. Royalty usually likes having their ruling image reinforced by their children. I think that's literally where the term nepotism comes from.

Her angle actually made sense to me. She was going to be forced to marry someone for political reasons, like the old days. If she and I could make a deal, it was a safer bet than getting married to some fat old lord with sausage fingers. I guess in this case, I was the demon she knew rather than the one she didn't.

"You want me to be a puppet?" I asked, arching an eyebrow.

"I want you to be an absentee husband," she replied bluntly. "The gossips in the Dandelion Court will whisper and ask me how I cope with my husband always being away. I will quiver my lower lip and say that I make do. Everyone will nod. You and I both get what we want. My mother gets enough to be satisfied. Everyone wins." She spread her hands, encompassing the table. "Also, we will be very rich. I'm sure you will find some way to entertain yourself with a life of luxury. I certainly intend to."

As unromantic and transactional as this was, her offer was sounding more and more reasonable. Almost too reasonable. I needed help getting my soul back. If joining the Fae court meant that I would get a legal team that might be able to stand up to the Devil, then I should be willing to do *anything* to join. If this deal was essentially a supernatural green-card marriage that would make me rich and free to do whatever I wanted, what exactly was the downside? I would expect a Fae princess to take more advantage of a desperate mortal.

"And the whole part about my soul being stolen and helping me get it back?"

"That falls under my mother's purview as queen," she said airily. "But I have no reason to get in the way of it. By all means, get your little soul back. Put it in our vault. I don't care what you do with it."

"I must admit," I said after a moment of thinking, "that this is not the offer I expected from you."

"Oh?" Tania scooped up some pastry from the pyramid of sweets and took a gentle bite. You can always tell if someone grew up rich because they take small bites of desserts. They always eat as if someone is watching.

"When your mother introduced me to you and your sisters, you seemed even more unenthusiastic than the Lady of Winter," I said.

"Mav has the luxury of being Mother's favorite," she said, somehow sounding like her mouth wasn't even a little full. "But our temperaments are different. She gets her flair for drama from her father, I think, whereas my heritage likes to make the best of an opportunity."

"You and your sister have different fathers?" I asked, so caught off guard I didn't even realize it might be rude to ask. Although given the ethnic differences between the sisters, that should have been obvious to anyone with a brain, i.e. not me.

"All of my sisters and I have different fathers," Tania said with a wicked smile. "Mother takes the idea of strengthening the Fae bloodline *very* seriously. Plus, as far as she is concerned, eternity is entirely too long for monogamy."

I don't know why that felt so creepy, but a chill ran down my spine at her words. Maybe it was the reminder that the woman sitting across from me was not human. Her family was not human. Maybe it was from realizing that I was once again swimming with sharks, and I barely knew how to swim.

To cover my awkwardness, I took a tiny cupcake. I couldn't figure out how to eat it like Tania with multiple tiny bites, so I just popped the whole thing in my mouth in one go. At least I didn't get any frosting on my face. That would have been embarrassing.

Holy crap. It was the best cupcake I had ever had. It was moist and sweet without being overpowering. A guy could do a lot worse than being fed perfect cupcakes for the rest of his life. Tania smiled knowingly at me as she watched my expression.

"I understand what is expected of me," the Lady of Spring continued. "I am a princess of the Faerie Lands. My mother is Queen of All Fae. Elements of my life will be used to serve the court and the crown. But if I can control parts of those elements to make the most of my life, I will."

For a brief moment, I felt a pang of sympathy. My soul had been stolen from me. That was a decision I didn't get to make, but it still dictated my life. I know that's old news, but it gave me some perspective on what she was trying to tell me. She had been born a princess. She didn't get a choice on her life either. I was doing everything I could to wrest as much control back before time ran out. We weren't the same, but we weren't as different as a Fae princess and a mortal should be.

"It's a pretty good offer," I said after a moment of silence.

"It's a pretty *great* offer," she corrected. "I'm sure it's better than any my sisters have given you."

I was silent a moment, trying not to show that none of her sisters had even bothered to speak to me yet. A small smile on her face told me I shouldn't have bothered. The Lady of Spring seemed well aware of that fact.

"Do we have a deal?" The princess leaned forward, her brown eyes staring into mine with a hunger that she hadn't shown during all of teatime. It was kind of terrifying. Panicking, I tried to figure out a way to stall for time. No way I was going to sign the first dotted line a Faerie princess shoved in front of me.

"I promised your mother to court all of her daughters. Well, at least three of you," I amended, remembering the Queen's response to Mav demanding to be excused from dating me. "It would be a violation of my deal if I agreed to you without even speaking to your sisters. But I would be lying if I didn't say you've made an excellent opening offer."

The princess leaned back in her chair and crossed her arms. She scowled at me, but there was a dancing light in her eyes that hadn't been there before. A note of respect, perhaps? Or was it amusement at watching a mortal flail around at political games the Fae had invented?

"Maybe my mother wasn't completely wrong about you," she said with a begrudging tone.

As I left the meeting, my spirits were buoyed by my performance. I had gone toe-to-toe with a Faerie princess, an immortal being trained in politics and manipulation since the day she was born, and I hadn't been eaten alive. If anything, I had held my own quite well.

I'd like to say that I put off giving Tania an answer to her deal because I was a smart negotiator who had learned his lesson. I'd also love to say that I wasn't interested in speaking with the other sisters because I was hoping to find something more like a romantic connection than a cold business deal. I'd also *really* love to say that I was definitely not thinking about red hair and green eyes.

But I can't, so I won't.

AFTER BEING IN Goldhall for close to a week, I went from being bored to feeling like I had caught a case of palace fever, which is very similar to cabin fever, where you cannot possibly bear being cooped up inside any longer—only richer.

Goldhall felt like an ornate prison. Maybe this was what being a house cat was like. I hadn't seen the outside in days. I couldn't even find a window. The hallways always burned with the same unchanging light. My internal clock had given up and just blinked 12:00 over and over inside my head. My phone's battery had been dead for what felt like forever. There were no outlets to be found in the Dandelion Court. Time felt like it had no meaning in the Faerie Lands. I was ready to go to sleep or eat dinner at all times.

If I didn't know better—and if we're being honest, I *didn't* know better—this could all be some elite sensory-deprivation-style interrogation tactic to make me more receptive to bad ideas, like marrying a Faerie princess.

My birthday was a little over three weeks away. That was almost no time to make the life-altering decision of which princess I was going to marry. But it also was an eternity to not see the sun again. So, one Wednesday, when I woke up, I decided it was time I did something about the second thing, since the first thing wasn't going so well.

My entourage was nowhere to be found when I entered the living room. Alex was probably still asleep. I felt a slight pang of jealousy. When there's no TV or internet, sleeping is the best entertainment money can buy. I thought about waking up my "manservant" out of spite, but then I remembered that I didn't pay him. The dude barely needs to sleep under normal circumstances. But he was in the process of recovering from a gnarly sword cut, so if he was actually resting, it was probably better to let sleeping Nephilim lie.

Orion's door was open, his bed perfectly made. I'm sure if I took a ruler to his sheets, they would be folded with military precision. I took his absence as permission to slip off by myself. A symptom of both palace fever and cabin fever is being sick to death of your roommates, so the prospect of some alone time sounded exactly like what the Matt had ordered.

I wandered out of my apartment into the never-ending halls and took a right. I had been in Goldhall long enough to have learned my way to a few places—the eternal buffet was a personal favorite of mine—but I had almost given up on trying to memorize the entire thing. All I had to do was wander until I ran into some liveried staff, and they always got me back to my room.

Now that I thought about it, Goldhall almost felt more like one of those all-inclusive resorts rather than what I expected a palace to be. Food and drink were always available, the staff wore matching uniforms, and everything was free.

Determined to satisfy my wanderlust, I took turns at random. For the most part, I saw more of the same. It was like being trapped in a house of mirrors, but instead of my own reflection, all I saw were marble hallways, thick carpets, and priceless pieces of art. I know that might sound unappreciative, but a man in the ocean soon grows tired of water.

In the end, walking was an excuse to think. I'm not sure if it's a symptom of ADHD or something else, but I always think better when my body has something to do. I've got one of those legs that starts bouncing if I think too hard. Bleeding off some of my excess energy seems to let my brain finally focus on a single thing, and boy did we have some things to focus on, mostly about me being single.

It had been three days since my meeting with Tania. I still hadn't encountered any of her sisters to see what they had to say, but her offer dominated my thoughts. Heavy is the head offered to marry the crown, I guess. In a weird way, Tania's offer felt like a perfect copy of her mother's. I wasn't excited about it, but it made sense. I've heard that no one is supposed to be happy in a compromise, but I also grew up on fairy tales and rom-coms. I wanted to have cake and ice cream, to fall madly in love, *and* to get my soul back, thank you very much.

The problem I was struggling with was I couldn't find a good reason *not* to take her offer—other than the fact that I didn't want to. But was that a legitimate reason, or was I channeling my inner Icarus—daring to fly too close to the sun, just because I wanted more?

It was entirely reasonable, I assured myself, for me to wait and hear the other daughters out. Even though I couldn't find a blasted clock anywhere in this marble palace, I knew that didn't mean time had stopped ticking away. I did need to decide, but not yet. I still had time.

I took a few more turns. By now I was completely lost, both on the inside and on the outside. I'd seen a couple servants as I wandered, but for the most part it was always echoingly empty. After being in close proximity with my friends for so long, I found myself enjoying the silence. I'm not exactly an introvert. I think I'm too loud. But it was nice to get some alone time to recharge occasionally.

"Whatcha doing out here?" a playful voice interrupted my silent healing. My whole body jumped in shock, and too much of Orion's battle boot camp took over. I leapt to the side and dropped into a crouch, fists raised.

"Oh no," Robin said, slowly raising both of his hands. "I surrender."

I sighed, lowering my hands. "Well, that's embarrassing."

"No, no." He laughed. "Quite intimidating." He held up his hands and shadow-boxed a few punches. A brilliant smile lit up his face as he dropped his fists. My lawyer wore a white-and-gold outfit that marked him as a servant to the Queen, although his was much fancier than everyone else's.

"Were you following me?" I asked him, narrowing my eyes.

"Matthew, you know I cannot lie," he said, drawing himself up tall and stiff. "So, I will not deign to answer that question."

"Fair enough." I rolled my eyes. "I wasn't up to anything sneaky, just looking around. Are there any rooms with a window or something? I'm going stir crazy locked up in these marble halls. I haven't seen the sun in like a week. I'm craving some vitamin D bad."

Robin was silent for a moment, his golden eyes thoughtful. "Come with me," he said abruptly. He began power-walking back the way I had come. I had to trot to catch up with his pace but managed to fall in step with him.

He led me through three turns before we entered a hallway that ended abruptly. It felt short, like a nail that had been clipped too close to the cuticle, or an amputated limb. I hadn't thought about it before, but I realized that almost every hallway I had seen had been identical, the same length, except for this one.

At the end, instead of an ornate wooden door, was a pair of black iron doors. I raised my eyebrow at Robin. Given how dangerous iron was to the Fae, that was like me having a door made from enriched uranium.

"What's behind that door?" I asked, suddenly feeling a little nervous. All I had asked to do was see the sun. This seemed a little more dramatic than what I signed up for.

Robin ignored my question and approached the door. He raised his right fist, which had a golden signet ring, and inserted the ring into a little golden receptacle on the wall. There was a faint hum, and a chime sounded in the room.

"I know I'm supposed to be the one to open doors for a guest," Robin said, gesturing at them. "But I don't have my gloves with me, so if you wouldn't mind."

I gave him a skeptical look.

He laughed. "It's nothing that will hurt you, Matthew. You have my word."

Mollified, I reached out and grabbed the bar on the door. I felt the usual tingle from cold iron, like I had jammed my hand into arctic waters, but I gritted my teeth and gave the door a pull.

It swung open smoothly. I didn't want to know how they managed to oil the hinges without dying. That was probably another use for the human servants on their staff. They could handle the cold iron their masters could not.

My concerns about hypothetical iron-door maintenance fell out of my head as I stared at what was behind the door. I expected the outside of the palace to be something from traditional fairy tales, or at least a mediocre fantasy novel. I thought I would see something like a sprawling city with classic fantastical buildings: a tavern, a blacksmith, and a wizard's tower. If not that, then maybe an endless forest filled with bright colors and chirping birds or something. But I've come to learn that behind every good fairy tale or myth is a marketing machine that would make Mr. Disney himself impressed.

The iron doors ushered us into a long rectangular room that ran perpendicular to the truncated hall we exited. This must be where all the glass was kept, because I finally found the windows I was looking for. The entire wall across from me was one giant window that ran from floor to ceiling, the length of the room.

Beyond the walls of the palace was nothing. Instead of sunshine and forest, the only thing that waited outside the cold marble walls of Goldhall was an even colder abyss.

For a second I thought I had been sucked into some weird sci-fi movie. I felt like I was on the bridge of a battlecruiser prowling through the stars. No, I realized, looking out into the emptiness on the other side of the glass. There were no stars out there. There was only nothing.

I stared out of the glass for a long time. For once, I was truly speechless. Robin stood next to me, hands stuffed down his pockets, shoulders slumped. His angular face wore a pensive frown as he gazed out the window with me.

"You could have just told me there was nothing to see," I grumbled after what felt like five minutes.

Robin arched an eyebrow. "Would you have known what I meant?"

"No," I sighed.

"Now you do." My lawyer didn't sound smug, only tired.

"Now that you have seen Nothing, you can begin to understand," a new voice cut through our quiet pondering of the abyss. Robin and I both spun to find Queen Gloriana standing in the open iron doorway.

Willow immediately burst into being on my hands, immolating them in its gentle fire.

"*Show-off*," I thought at the weird Fae spirit. Willow was silent, but somehow I got the impression they had stuck their tongue out at me.

Robin bowed his head low, and I, completely out of my depth, copied him. I wasn't sure if I was supposed to kneel again. For all I knew, Robin had a higher VIP status than me, and I was being super rude. But the Queen had said she wanted me to join her family because of my strength, so I decided to bank on that.

Gloriana wore what I assumed was as close as a queen gets to wearing casual attire. Instead of a gown and crown, she wore a simple white pantsuit, worked with golden thread that matched her golden eyes. Her head tilted as she regarded the two of us, like an amused aunt catching her nephews with their hands in the cookie jar.

I felt a little uneasy. Was I breaking any rules? I felt guilty about being here but didn't even know if I was in trouble or not.

"Robin, would you give us a moment?" she asked softly.

"Of course, Your Majesty," Robin said, dipping his head again. As he passed by the Queen, she placed a hand on his shoulder and murmured "thank you" so quietly, I wasn't sure I had heard it. My lawyer nodded once and stepped through the iron doors, closing them behind him. I wondered if he had found his gloves or if he burned himself to follow his queen's commands.

I was more worried about me—all alone with the Queen of All Fae.

I was nervous. I couldn't tell if I was in trouble, being seduced, or about to be eaten. This is what I got for wandering off without my babysitters, I guess. No one ever mentions the fourth little pig who was too stupid to stay in the house and got eaten by the Big Bad Wolf out on a walk—no huffing or puffing required.

Gloriana walked up to join me at the edge of the Nothing. I turned to stare back out into the emptiness with her. There was something about it that made it hard to look away. A haunting tug of command that demanded my attention, like an intrusive thought. Part of me wanted to leap through the glass to touch the void, to taste its nothingness.

"Matthew!" the Queen barked, snapping a finger sharply.

I flinched in surprise, tearing my gaze from the mesmerizing abyss and looking at her.

"Don't stare into it for too long," she said, a soft expression on her face. "Your mind is far too open to handle it."

"What is it?" I asked, swallowing a blob of fear in my throat. Of course it could kill me. Was there anything in the supernatural world that couldn't devour my mind, body, or soul?

"You have proven to be a bright young star," she said, holding my eyes with her golden gaze. "What do *you* think it is?"

"I know it's nothing," I said.

"No, it is Nothing." She emphasized the capitalization in her tone.

"What's the difference?" I asked.

"Other nothings are but a shadow of this Nothing," she said, turning to gaze out the window once more. I decided to follow her advice and kept my eyes trained on her face, which was equally mesmerizing in a different way. "A black hole could never be as Nothing as this is. For this, young Matthew, is where reality ends."

Without a conscious thought, my head turned back to staring at the blackness beyond. A dreadful chill passed down my spine, and I found myself wondering if the glass was thick enough to hold back the abyss. I managed to not take a giant step backward, but only because I was more worried about looking weak in front of the Queen than I was about being devoured by the darkness.

"What does that mean, exactly?" I asked.

"This is what it is all about."

Weird. I always thought that was the Hokey Pokey. Regardless of my confusion, I kept my deep philosophical thoughts to myself for once. Gloriana didn't seem the type to turn herself about, but more likely to turn me inside out, and that didn't seem worth the risk.

"Did you know that once, Goldhall was surrounded by trees as far as the eye could see? You could travel for days to the different palaces of the Fae. You would have thought this palace was a hovel compared to the splendor of Tír na nÓg or the halls of Annwn."

"What happened?" I asked. My eyes felt as round as saucers as I stared out at the blackness that had eaten all those strange-sounding places.

"We ran out of souls." The Queen snorted at my slack-jawed expression. "Did you think that we collect souls because they are pretty little things, Matthew? I have many pretty little things in my home. None of them are as valuable as souls. The greatest art ever made is worth its weight in gold, but souls are worth their weight in reality."

"Let's say hypothetically, I was trying to explain this to my friend, and he just wasn't getting this at all," I said. "What would you tell him?"

The Queen's mouth quirked in a small smile as she turned to look at me again. "I would say your friend is in good company. Even we don't really understand how souls work."

"Hang on," I interrupted. "You're telling me that Immortals use souls to carve out their own little bits of reality, but they don't know how they work?"

"Surely a *mortal* is not criticizing his elders for using something they don't fully understand," Gloriana said, eyebrows furrowing.

I had to admit she had a point. I use the microwave all the time, and I have no idea how it works. Radiation, I heard someone say once. Still, it was a little depressing to find out that even the Queen of All Fae still had mysteries she couldn't explain.

"Okay," I managed. "Let's try this again. This void exists because you couldn't afford to pay your mortgage, which is paid in… souls." The part I found hardest to believe about all of this was that the Queen of All Fae and I had something in common—neither of us could afford property in this economy.

"A tacky explanation, but it will work for now." She sighed. "Reality is the domain of mortals. It exists for you, or because of you, or for some other reason. But our reality is not the only thing that exists. Our universe is a bubble of light surrounded by the hungry dark."

"Okay, but what is the bubble?" I asked. "Did someone make it? Was there a Big Bang? Did someone say, 'Let there be light' or maybe 'Shazam'?" My head was spinning. Trying to sort this new worldview felt like trying to shuffle a deck of cards while wearing thick gloves. I kept dropping all my ideas on the floor.

"Matthew, I am ever so old, but even I have a beginning," the Queen said, her voice rich with indignant amusement.

I took that to mean that she didn't know that either. I guess that would be too easy. I don't know if it made me feel better or worse that an Immortal didn't know the answer to the basic question that plagued the mortal existence: Who are we and how did we get here?

"What happens if you run out of the rest of your souls?" I asked.

"We are in no danger of that," the Queen said, sounding far too calm for someone whose kingdom had been mostly devoured by Nothing. "When our harvests began to fail centuries ago, we liquidated our lands and budgeted fiercely." A small, proud smile graced her regal lips. "We sacrificed everything but Goldhall and have been investing our profits ever since."

I let out a low whistle. Capitalism really had gotten its finger into all of the pies. Goldhall wasn't really a palace. It was a gilded Doomsday bunker for the One Percent.

"Do you know why I allowed you to see this, Matthew?" Gloriana asked.

"To terrify me?" I offered.

"So that you *understand*. You know that I am Fae. I cannot lie. But now you know that when I told you the sun of the Fae is setting, I was not exaggerating, I was not dancing around a hidden truth. It is already being devoured by the dark. Our blood is weak, our people scared. This is what the Dandelion Court has been reduced to. Cowering in a bunker on the edge of the eternal night."

I turned to gaze back into the abyss with new eyes. I was willing to admit that this was all very convincing. I realized this wasn't the first time that I had seen Nothing before. I've seen reflections of it in the eyes of an ex-girlfriend. Where once there was light and laughter, now there is only a resounding stillness. It's not just an emptiness, but an absence where there should be something more. The Nothing was that little glimmer times infinity.

But as convincing as the whole presentation was, a cynical thought forced its way to the surface in my mind. If the Fae were truly this desperate, was it smart to put the safety of my soul in their hands? I was a nobody. Why would the Queen be so invested in recruiting me if her nation was teetering on the brink of oblivion?

She had admitted that my access to Orion and the Hunt was a part of the equation. That explanation made sense to me. As far as I could tell, Orion would be a starting player for any team that could recruit him. Furthermore, he was probably one of the most dangerous free agents floating around the supernatural league. If the Queen locking me down got her access to Orion, I could see how she would think that was worth it.

"Matthew, I have a favor to ask of you," the Queen said, interrupting me working through my supernatural politics flowchart. "I know that we are not formally family yet." A small smile brushed across her elegant face. "But I would be in your debt if you were to assist me with an urgent matter."

My ears perked up and my heart started beating a little faster when she said "debt." I was already in deep with the Dandelion Court, adding another marker to the bill did not seem like a good idea—the house always wins eventually.

"What troubles you, Your Majesty?" I asked, choosing my words carefully.

"There is a cancer growing in my court," she said after a moment of reflecting. "We have the same enemies now. Lucifer and his ilk will not simply roll over and let us take what he sees as his."

"What do you think they will do?" My mouth went dry as I processed what she was saying. It made sense, of course. Zagan had already made sure I knew that the interest in me from downstairs was personal. I hadn't been assuming that having the Queen of All Fae on my side guaranteed that I would get my soul back, but I had been hoping that someone else would be doing the heavy lifting.

This will sound stupid, but I think the hardest part about having my soul stolen and trying to get it back wasn't fear of failing. The whole eternal damnation in the fiery pits thing sounds terrible, but it's also very abstract. I've never seen a single fiery pit before. I have no frame of reference other than "it's bad." No, the hardest part was simply that it was *hard*. I was one mere mortal treading water in the deep sea—and I was getting tired. I didn't want to stand up to demons and debate with Fae. I wanted some cookies and a nap.

"I do not know," she confessed, raising one of her hands to study her golden nails. It felt like she was trying to decide if she should say more. I was silent, letting her have her internal debate in peace. "I am worried, Matthew," she said after a long moment.

It took all my self-control to keep my eyebrows from leaping off my forehead in complete shock. One thing that I have learned during my brief tenure in the supernatural world is that predators, the ones on top of their respective food chains, *never* worry. They don't show weakness or fear; they have to be above it. For the Queen to admit this to me, especially when our alliance was still so tentative, was not normal.

"There are elements of my court that are not happy," she admitted. "My people chafe in this restricted corner of our world. The Fae were made to be wild and free, but now we are confined to this cage of marble and gold. There are those amongst my people who blame me for our troubles, as if my wisdom has not kept us alive." Her golden eyes flashed with anger.

"How is that connected to the demon problem?" I asked.

"I have already said that I do not know!" she snapped. "But there are demons here." My gut clenched. "And they need to be watched."

"You want me to spy on the demons that are in Goldhall and figure out who they are talking to?" I repeated, panicking a little. This was way beyond a small favor. This had to be at least a medium one, getting dangerously close to a big favor. "No offense, but are you sure you want to trust me with this? Shouldn't *you* handle it?"

"Have you learned nothing from your time with the Hunter? Having power to do something doesn't always mean you have the freedom to do so. There is a reason the Darkstar does not come after you himself but sends his minions. If I respond to the demons' creeping, it becomes an incident. If you do it, it is barely a footnote. Besides, who is more motivated than you?" she asked with a shrug, as if she hadn't just asked me to spy on demons. "It is in both of our best interests to know what the infernals are plotting."

There were some absolutely magnificent mental gymnastics being performed. I resisted the urge to groan. How in the world was I supposed to spy on demons? They probably invented lies and spies. This was like asking me to race a fish in swimming. I wasn't built for this. I was in serious danger of drowning.

"Since we're putting our cards on the table," I said, following a nagging thought, "may I ask you something?"

Gloriana sniffed. "Asking to ask a question is rude and inefficient."

She was right, but I took that as permission. "You told me you were helping me because you did not want a supernatural world war," I began. "Seeing what you've shown me, I understand why."

I felt my eyes narrow as a hint of suspicion crept into my tone. "But it seems like by allying with me, you're antagonizing Hell on purpose. Why is that?"

Gloriana, Queen of All Fae, stared at me for a long, long moment. Her exquisite face was as smooth as the marble prison she had built for her people. Had I been too blunt? They say to never look a gift horse in the mouth. I have no idea what that means, but maybe I had just done it on accident.

"Lucifer has ever thought himself my better. It's about time I reminded him that he is not," Gloriana said with a glint of something in her golden eyes.

I blinked in surprise. I hadn't considered that this vendetta was personal in multiple directions. What had the Devil done to get under the Queen's skin enough that she would risk her struggling nation to cross him? Maybe I didn't want to know.

"Okay, great," I said with a sigh. "I'll just slip a little subterfuge into my schedule between courting three of your daughters so I can spy on some demons. What could go wrong?"

"This is an opportunity for you to prove yourself, manling," the Queen said sharply. "I chose to give you a chance to join my family because of your potential, not your sense of humor."

I didn't have the heart to tell her that all my potential was a joke anyway. Besides, I could read between the lines. The Queen was being polite by saying that this was a favor. The truth was, if I wanted her help getting my soul back, I was going to have to prove her right—I had to be useful.

As far as a Fae asking for a favor went, it didn't seem that bad. The demons were a common enemy. I could only benefit from getting a chance to observe and learn about what they were planning. If it helped me show my value and secure a legal team to help me get my soul back, I counted that as a two-for-one special.

"I'll keep my eyes open," I promised. "Where are the demons hanging out here?"

"At least one has been spending time in the palace, visiting my daughters," the Queen practically spat. "Skulking about as if I did not know what they were up to. They think I am blind, but soon we will show them how well we see, won't we, Matthew?"

That sent a shiver down my spine. I'm not sure if it was fear or excitement. I liked the sound of that. Hell had gotten the upper hand on me too many times lately. I'd love to even the score a little.

"I'll see what I can find out," I promised, doing my best to keep the deliverables of my promise vague. The Queen had given me no reason not to trust her, but she was still a Faerie. I had learned my lesson about making deals. Even if I hadn't actually made one, I had learned the lesson.

"Well?" Gloriana said after a moment of silence. "What are you waiting for, Matthew? Immortal I may be, but time waits for no one."

I'm not the sharpest knife in the cutlery drawer, but I have the good grace to know when I'm not wanted anymore. I turned to leave, giving the Queen a slight bow from my neck. It seemed respectful. I made it halfway to the iron doors before I paused, one last question floating in my mind.

"You mentioned that in order for me to bond with a Willow, I had to have Fae in my bloodline," I said, turning back to the Queen.

Gloriana turned to meet my eyes, her golden orbs unreadable.

"How does that work? Do you know where I got it from?"

"Your mortal scientists would tell you it is genetic," she said with a slight shrug. "But there's more to it than that. Of all the immortal races, ours integrates with mortals the easiest. Many families have a hint of Fae blood and never even know. A changeling can appear human in every way, and without proper guidance would never become anything more than mortal. One of your parents must have passed their heritage on to you."

"Thank you for explaining." I filed that info away for later. With everything on my plate, that seemed like a mystery for another day.

A **FTER BEING SHOWN** the devouring abyss and getting a secret mission from the Queen, I decided that I needed to become more proactive in this courtship process. While my stupid brain, which had seen too many rom-coms, was holding on to a faint hope that one of the sisters would sweep me off my feet, the calculating part had been nudged awake by Tania's offer. The point of this deal was to get my soul back, to stop a war and save my life. I was not the star of a dating reality show. I was a man trying to not get sent to the Bad Place when the soul collectors came for him in nine years.

Suitably motivated by those fears, I pulled Robin aside the next time I saw him and asked where I might come across either of the other two sisters that weren't Mav. She had already made her opinion pretty clear, so I figured I'd save her as more of a Hail Mary date option.

Besides, the other two sisters had seemed to be a lot more open to the whole situation. Spring was just the thaw of Winter, so it made a weird sort of sense that Summer and Fall might be friendlier seasons, right?

Maybe I was overthinking this seasonal theme thing.

I was nervous about talking to other sisters. I've never been good at this whole dating thing. I never know what I'm supposed to say. There's an art form to being forward but not too forward, and whatever it is, surely evades me. I only have two modes: quiet little church mouse and bull in a china shop.

My plan was to do what I always did with something that made me nervous: put it off as long as possible and hide it by doing things that were easier so no one could tell I was a coward.

Unfortunately, I didn't have any easy wins like "put away socks" on my to-do list. Instead, I had to woo royals, recover my soul, and ferret out demon spies. Light work for a Thursday. If today even was Thursday. I had lost track.

It turned out that the dating task was actually the easiest item on my to-do list, which was how I found myself marching off to ask a princess out. How had my life gotten here? If only I hadn't gone to see *Citizen Kane* on my birthday, I'd still be a souled young man. This series of events further proves my theory that black-and-white movies are bad.

Alex, Orion, and I followed Robin's directions to the Lady of Summer's home. Well, Orion followed his directions. Alex and I followed Orion. My sense of direction is terrible. Thanks to the magic of GPS and smartphones, I've never had to learn the basics of navigation. I know the sun rises in the east and sets in the west, but other than that, I'm hopeless. Also, for a nation that exists entirely inside a marble mega-palace, would it kill them to put some street signs? Well, hall signs, I guess. Everything looked the same. It was enough to drive a man mad.

When we found the Lady of Summer's place, I realized that I still had no concept of how rich the Fae were. I had begun to feel a little fancy in the three-bedroom luxury apartment that the Queen had stashed me in. After seeing where her daughter lived, I realized that I might have been living in a spare janitor's closet.

Dawn's residence was a separate mansion stuffed inside of a palace. That's a ridiculous sentence, but I can think of no other way to explain it. It was like seeing a cake inside a pie, baked by some mad pastry chef. The marble halls of Goldhall opened into a self-contained glade inside of a giant square room, like a terrarium for rich people. The ceiling was painted the vibrant blue of the sky on a perfect summer day. Painted puffy white clouds somehow drifted lazily across it. A brilliant golden sun gave off light and heat like it was real. Perfectly manicured grass led to a sweeping estate at the top of a small hill. As I watched, a startled pair of deer fled into the woods flanking the three-story mansion. The entire estate was an idyllic Van Gogh painting come to life.

"Oh okay, sure," I said, staring in awe at the recreated forest before me. "And I thought the Fae weren't able to do art."

Orion grunted. "Makes you wonder who they had make it for them." He started walking up the gravel drive that led to the front door, leaving me staring at the scenery with a new perspective.

We crunched our way to the front door, and with each step I felt my tension increase. I didn't have a good plan. I didn't really know how to ask a normal girl out, let alone an immortal Faerie princess. Goldhall could give Rodeo Drive in Beverly Hills a run for its money any day, but I didn't think it had a movie theater or coffee shop. What were we supposed to do on our date?

"I have no idea what I am doing," I muttered.

"You could pick her some flowers." Alex gestured at a patch of immaculately curated flowers growing along the path.

I snorted. "Hey, I stole these from your garden, wanna get married? Great, thanks for the advice, stud."

"Maybe ask her to go for a picnic or something," Alex replied.

"Aren't you like two hundred years old? Shouldn't you be better at this?"

"I've been in LA too long." Alex gave me a big grin. "Dating is impossible there." He certainly had that part right.

I sighed, glancing at Orion. "What about you, Mr. Star? Do you have any advice for me in courting an Immortal?"

"I usually tell them a joke to break the ice," Orion said evenly. "Humor is an excellent weapon when it comes to romance."

Which just says everything there is to say about the Hunter. I rubbed my face as hard as I could, trying to scrub away the headache I could feel brewing behind my eyes. I don't know what I expected. Being in the Hunt sometimes felt like I was in a supernatural fraternity.

"Jokes. Got it," I muttered darkly. "Tell her a joke or *be* the joke?"

That's as far as my planning got before we arrived at the beautiful gilded oaken doors of the marble mansion inside the marble palace of the Fae. Screw it, I decided. I would just wing it, as usual. It's not like things could get worse.

Ha-ha.

I gestured to Alex to knock on the door. He was my manservant, after all, and still had one working arm. It wouldn't do for me to knock myself. I was practically nobility now.

Alex's fist beat out a staccato rhythm on the door that matched my heart. The door swung open to reveal a sallow, long-faced Fae waiting on the other side. He wore a tuxedo and a disdainful expression that were a matched set. His severe frown deepened enough to rival the Mariana Trench as his gaze flicked from Alex, to Orion, and landed on me.

"Yes?" he sneered in a rich tone oozing with enough oil that some countries would probably be tempted to invade him.

"Squire Carver to see the Lady of Summer." Alex drew himself up stiffly in response to the servant's tone. He might have been wearing a T-shirt and jeans, but he matched the pure contempt perfectly.

"Do you have an appointment? No, you do not."

People who answer their own rhetorical questions should be shot.

"No appointment, except the one of the Queen to court her daughters," Alex replied smoothly.

The servant's expression grew even more dour. He stared at me again like I was a dog turd that someone had tracked into the mansion on the bottom of their shoe. I gave him a smug smile and waited.

He sighed after a long staredown. "I shall see if my lady is available." The door slammed shut in our faces like a bolded period on his displeasure.

"You could learn a thing or two about being a manservant from him," I whispered to Alex.

"He's a butler. It's an entirely different thing."

"Maybe you should try buttling too."

"That's not a word."

"Actually, it is," Orion rumbled from behind us.

The door opened as the butler returned, his face a judgmental mask. "Lady Dawn has granted you an audience," he said with an uppity sniff.

He led us through the opulent mansion at a brisk pace. The interior of the Summer home broke from the style of the rest of Goldhall. It was all dark wood and plush carpets. We passed sitting rooms and drawing rooms, which are apparently different things, but don't ask me how.

The grand hallway spat us out into a central courtyard, where several Fae lounged about. A bubbling natural pool took up the center.

As I watched, one of the bathers dove into it with perfect form, slicing through the water like a shark.

Several more Fae lay on lawn chairs, tanning themselves in bathing suits. It was such an odd collision of a trust fund kid's backyard and forest copse that I thought I might get whiplash. Laughter and conversation echoed lightly around the pool as a servant offered a platter of drinks. I guess wealth lives the same on either side of the mortality line.

Dawn, the Lady of Summer, was seated in one of the chairs, wearing a white bathing suit that was the Faerie equivalent of either a bikini or dental floss. I suddenly felt very overdressed. Given some of the fairy tales I have read, I suppose we were lucky they were wearing clothes at all. Glancing at the Fae around the yard, I couldn't blame them for their clothing choices. Immortality appeared to also preserve your metabolism, because there wasn't a spare pound in sight.

"If it isn't the infamous Squire Carver. And he brought a Constellation and a *runt*," the princess said, leaning forward with interest. I felt Alex stiffen slightly next to me, but his face remained impassive. I did my best to follow my friend's lead. Dawn's blonde hair fell in waves to her shoulders, and white teeth flashed in her smile. "He is the talk of the court, and yet here he is, visiting my humble home."

Some muted chuckles echoed from her entourage.

"I'm sorry to barge in," I said, giving her a slight bow and slapping a smile on my face. "I was in the neighborhood and heard we might be getting betrothed, so I thought I would stop by."

"Yes, Mother did dangle that out there, didn't she?" Dawn mused, perfect smile not faltering. Her blue eyes stared at me without blinking, pinning me in place. "I suppose that might be an excuse for you to call on royalty *uninvited*. What do you think, Dawson? Is it presumptuous of our little manling to interrupt my day?"

Dawson was evidently the name of my least-favorite butler, who now hovered at Dawn's shoulder. I wondered if she had hired him because their names were similar. That seemed ridiculous, but also something I would not put past someone who might be richer than the United States government.

"Extremely rude," the butler huffed.

The courtyard was silent. Every Fae's attention was focused on us with an intensity I could feel. I was half surprised to not see a dozen golden dots like a sniper's red laser dancing on my chest. It occurred to me that I didn't know why Dawn's eyes were a normal blue, when all the other Fae's were solid gold. Probably wasn't the time to ask.

"Please forgive me," I said through gritted teeth. "I meant no disrespect. I am a mortal and clearly do not know all the intricacies of Faerie etiquette. We mortals visit each other all the time."

"Yet even mortal children know which lunch table to eat at," Dawn said, her smile still as big as it had been. Now that I was up close and personal, I realized that it didn't reach her eyes. I had thought Mav was scary, but the Lady of Summer was in a league of her own. Crocodiles have big smiles, but it is just to hold all their teeth. Her cronies all around us chuckled in chorus like a well-trained pack of hyenas.

"I never did well in school," I said with a shrug. I could feel my cheeks beginning to flush as the fires of anger spread through me. I have pretty thick skin, but I don't like bullies. This Summer chick was getting under my skin. It felt like middle school all over again.

Tania's offer was getting more appealing by the second.

I glanced over Dawn's shoulder at a woman sprawled on a lounge chair by the pool. Unlike the rest of the trained pack of Fae, she hadn't leaned forward. She seemed to be the least interested person in the courtyard. That's what made her catch my eye. Her black bathing suit and black hair shone in bright contrast to her pale skin.

She glanced my way, revealing her secret—she had the black eyes of a demon. The demon noticed me notice her, and so did the Lady of Summer. Her fake smile grew tight. Her blue eyes flashed with something other than anger. Was that fear I saw?

"Here's a free lesson for a silly squire," she said. "Don't speak unless you are spoken to. Don't enter where you are not invited. And don't"—her unwavering smile widened—"let the door hit you on your way out." Her coterie let out another burst of wild laughter.

Well then.

I didn't.

IF THERE'S ONE thing the Hunt is good at, it's stalking. Wait, that sounds weird. Not that kind of stalking. Well, yes, that kind of stalking, if we're talking about following our prey in a wolf kind of way, not in a creepy one. The point is, once we have a target, we're pretty good at tracking them. Orion's sense of smell could make a bloodhound jealous.

It didn't take much convincing to get Alex and Orion to agree to help me spy on the demon I had seen at Dawn's. None of us like demons. I know most people don't like demons, but for us it's pretty personal. Plus, we were all super bored. A week in a marble cage will leave you desperate for anything to break the monotony. Give me some paint, let me watch it dry.

While I've boasted about our prowess, keeping tabs on the demon wasn't hard. Goldhall sprawls for miles upon marble miles, but the demoness was firmly ensconced in Dawn's party palace. Orion, Alex, and I took shifts watching from the fake woods surrounding Dawn's mansion to see if we could catch her on the move. Fae came and went at all hours. It seemed like her house was the official headquarters of the party that never ends, it just went on and on, my friends. But our demonic quarry never left. Orion's eagle eyes occasionally spotted her through the front windows, but whatever she was up to, it was happening behind doors that were closed to us.

I knew the Queen wouldn't accept a closed door as an excuse to ignore the demon. What kind of spy lets that stop him from exposing a conspiracy? I needed to be in the room where it happened, so I needed to secure myself an invite. I was pretty sure I knew how— I just needed to cheat a little. All I had to do was tag along with someone who couldn't get kicked out. Fortunately, in Goldhall, there were plenty of royals in the sea, and at least one of them wanted something from me.

I sent Alex to Tania, bearing a little notecard that asked her for a meeting. I hoped she could read it. I can't remember the last time I wrote something by hand; my cursive looked like a drunken kindergartener's. I couldn't believe that was how I had to contact her; it was such an inefficient way to communicate. If the Fae had dandelions that could follow me around and pull me between worlds, I didn't see why they couldn't also have a magical form of texting.

Alex came back with an acceptance from Tania, which was how I found myself standing outside another princess's house. Tania's style was markedly different from her sister's. Whereas Dawn's palace stood out like a sore thumb, Tania's could have been confused for a closet. Her quarters were in the halls, behind a door that looked like all the other doors of the palace.

Worried I had the wrong place, I knocked several times and took a step back. After a moment, the door opened, and a female Fae answered with a smile. She wore a green sundress and had dark hair that flowed past her bare shoulders in waves. Her golden eyes beamed with a warmth that was reflected in her smile.

"You must be Squire Carver," she said. "Please come in. She is expecting you."

I stepped into the apartment and blinked in surprise. There were windows! The far wall was made up of floor-to-ceiling glass panels that revealed a breathtaking view of the New York City skyline. I had somehow been transported to a penthouse apartment in the mortal world.

My mind reeled. How could this be? The Queen had shown me what lurked outside of Goldhall. It was *not* New York. As a born-and-raised member of the West Coast Best Coast committee. I'm more than happy to call NYC and all its boroughs a bottomless abyss of despair that is only good for bagels and pizza. Yet given the choice between the Nothing I had seen and living in New York, I'd take the Big Apple... probably.

"How is this possible?" I breathed. As I asked my question, I noticed something was off. The Twin Towers stood proud and tall on the skyline. This wasn't real, I realized. But the plants on the balcony were waving in the wind. I could see a flag flapping in the distance. It *felt* real.

"Do you like it?" Tania asked, entering from a side room. "I understand that it is from one of your cities." She strode over to the woman who had let me in and placed a hand on her shoulder. "Thank you, Grace," she said, dismissing her. The woman beamed at her and then at me and excused herself, slipping out of the room.

"Is it a projector?" I asked, still awed by what I was seeing.

"I don't know what it is, really." The princess shrugged. "Some sort of magical trinket. I found it in one of Mother's storage closets a decade ago, a forgotten gift from a forgotten mortal. She gave it to me, and I've lived with it ever since. My father lived somewhere out there once. Seeing it reminds me of him."

It sure beat living in a windowless box floating in the void. I stared out of the fake windows, drinking in the sights of my world. If I ever got out of here, I was going to go see New York for myself, I decided. Just to see what all the fuss was about.

"But you didn't come to see the mortal world," Tania said, clapping her hands together. "You came to see me."

"I did." I tore my eyes away from the fake windows to focus on the princess. Unlike the Faerie who answered the door, she was all dressed up, wearing a brown pantsuit with a matching jacket and a white shirt underneath. I tried not to feel insecure in my jeans and T-shirt. I really did not have the wardrobe for courting royalty.

"Made up your mind already? I know I'm a catch, but this is faster than I expected." A small smile played at the corner of her lips.

Explaining my plan was going to be more awkward than I thought. I was here to ask the one sister who had been open to marrying me to set me up with her sister. In most families, once you pick a sister, you're done, no matter if you got the date or not. You might as well be radioactive to the rest of the siblings. I hope it didn't work the same way in royal courtships too.

"No, no, no decisions yet," I said, holding up both my hands in mock surrender. "I was hoping you could help me in my decision-making process."

"That sounds very close to asking for a favor," Tania remarked dryly, brown eyes narrowing.

"I wouldn't call it a favor, more like an opportunity to demonstrate what an excellent partner you might be."

The princess barked a short laugh. I gave her a smile that was all teeth.

"What sort of opportunity did you have in mind?" she asked, arching one royal eyebrow.

"I need someone to get me in to Dawn's never-ending pool party," I said, wincing in anticipation of her reaction. I was pretty sure my reasoning on why she should help me would hold up to Fae logic, but if it didn't, I might damage my only relationship with a reasonable Faerie royal. The more I met the daughters of Gloriana, the more I felt like reasonability was in short supply.

"To prove my potential as a partner, you want me to help you court my sister," she said in a flat voice. "I know I proposed an open marriage, Squire Carver, but this is a bit bold if you ask me."

"It's not like that." I waved a hand as if I could shoo her accusations away like they were a fly. "I promised your mother I would court three of her daughters—"

"Yes, yes, we've been over this," Tania interrupted. "You made that quite clear during tea. I fail to see how you needing to sample the merchandise is something I should help you with."

"Well, the problem is, I tried to have a nice little meeting with Dawn yesterday, and she sort of kicked me out."

"Oh, trust me, Matthew, *everyone* has heard about that."

My ears burned with embarrassed heat. I bet they could have given Rudolph's nose a run for its money. I don't care how immortal you are, I have become convinced that none of us ever truly escape high school. Dante wrote about the wrong place when he tried to capture eternal suffering. The seven circles of Hell? Chump change compared to the seven tables of the lunchroom.

"Well, that's awesome," I said with a sigh. "The problem is, our meeting was so brief that my conscience doesn't feel like I've fulfilled the heart of the agreement if I write her off."

"You'd like to give Dawn a second chance? After she filleted you in front of her whole court and made you look like an idiot?" Tania asked in shock.

"Okay, well, agree to disagree on the looking-like-an-idiot part," I replied. "But that's the problem. I don't see it as a *second* chance at all. More like she only got a half a chance to begin with."

"And because she didn't get a whole chance, you're worried that will prevent you from fulfilling your agreement with my mother?"

"That's about the half of it," I said with a rueful grin. "I'm just trying to be a mortal of my word."

Tania sighed but nodded. "Fine. I will help you. But when Dawn tears you to shreds, remember that you wanted to be there."

TRUE TO HER word, Tania took me to the VIP pool party. Orion kept watch over the palace during the night, making sure our demonic target didn't sneak off in the dark. Alex requisitioned me a bathing suit from somewhere in the depths of Goldhall.

"How did I live without a manservant before this?" I demanded as he handed me a pair of blue-and-white-striped trunks. "If I had any money, I would totally give you a raise."

"Don't worry, once you're a member of the Fae royalty, I will be sending you a bill for back pay and health insurance," Alex replied with a disgruntled nod at his arm, which was still resting in its sling.

I met Tania at her quarters. She greeted me wearing a gauzy green coverup and a big hat. Belatedly, I realized, as I stood before her with my towel thrown over my shoulder, that the pool parties I had gone to as a poor kid growing up in LA were probably different than the pool parties of the Fae elite. You can take the kid out of Northridge, but you can't take the Northridge out of the kid, I guess.

"This should be fun. I cannot *wait* to see what Dawn thinks of your outfit," Tania snorted, giving me a once-over. Her remark cut as deep as any cheerleader captain's. It was good for me, though. If my self-esteem was too healthy, I would be too powerful. I needed to have at least one weakness to give everyone else a chance.

Underdressed or no, Dawson was forced to let me in without more than a small sneer. Today I wasn't a mortal squire of the Hunt, I was arm candy to a royal, which put me in an untouchable social tier.

"The Lady of Spring and Squire Carver," Dawson announced dolorously to the courtyard.

I followed a half step behind Tania as we stepped back into the pool party. It was much as I left it a few days ago, but most of the cast had at least had a wardrobe change. I guess that's a downside of immortality: you better not get bored easily, because you've got an eternity of sitting next to a pool ahead of you.

Sounds rough.

The courtyard was littered with Fae sunbathing or swimming. I scanned the area, looking for my true prey. I spotted the demon lurking in a chair off to the side, away from the nucleus of the party.

Her black eyes met mine as she looked up. I gave her a small smile, all teeth and threats. She didn't react, staring back at me with a bored expression. *Don't go anywhere*, I thought in the demon's direction. The second I was done making appearances, she was my target.

Dawn sat up on her lounge chair throne at our approach. She was wearing a big hat too; apparently it was Big Hat Day, and no one told me. Her iconic broad smile split her face, but her blue eyes danced with a dangerous glint.

"Sister, darling," she purred. "I see you have emerged from your cave! Does this mean that we will have six more weeks of winter?"

Tania snorted and rolled her eyes. "You tell me, Dawn," she replied. "Do you want to have to listen to Mav for an extra six weeks?"

"It could be worse." Dawn smirked. "It could be six more weeks of fall."

Tania let out a snide laugh and sat down on a chair next to her sister. This was the first time I had been up close with two of Gloriana's daughters at once. Despite their different fathers, there was no missing that the genetics of the Queen ran through their blood. Tania was dark while her sister was pale, but they had the same jawline, the same regal brows, the same sharply pointed ears. It was like a master jeweler had cut a ruby and a diamond into the same shape.

"Squire Carver, how lovely to see you again—and so soon! Did you miss me already?" Dawn fluttered her eyelids at me in a flirtatious gesture.

"You know," I said, with a flash of insight, "the last time I was here felt so short. We mortals say that time flies when you are having fun, so by definition, that must have been a blast. How could I ever stay away?" Dawn let out an amused little laugh that came out as a short burst.

"Thank you for not dressing up," she remarked, eyeing my casual bathing attire. "I hate it when my guests make me feel out of place in my own home."

I did my best to ignore her very distracting outfit, which made excellent use of negative space to draw attention to itself. If Dawn could be made to feel out of place by others being dressed better, there was no hope for the rest of us. Clothes are the accents that complete us, the frame on the painting. The finest tuxedo in the world can't fix my face, but hers didn't need any help.

"I thought it might be fun to dress in the traditional mortal way," I said, matching her vicious smile with my own. "I am from a place called Los Angeles, the City of Angels. It's where the mortal stars live."

"This is mortal fashion, then? Tania, dear, I think Mother *was* right. The mortals' culture really is falling apart."

Whoops, it hadn't been five minutes, and I'd already managed to embarrass my entire species. I apologize to humans. I did my best, but I was sparring far outside of my weight class.

"I don't know," I said with a shrug, "it grows on you."

"Like a fungus, I'm sure," Dawn mused.

"Dawn, must you play with your food?" Tania sighed from the chair next to her sister. "You're worse than a cat with a mouse."

Ouch. I knew I was losing, but I didn't think I had been doing *that* poorly. I glanced down at my chest to make sure I wasn't bleeding from her razor-sharp barbs on my white shirt.

That would have been embarrassing.

"Speaking of fungi," Dawn said with a dramatic sigh, "you seemed to have grown back on my lawn, even though I'm pretty sure I plucked you just a couple days ago."

"You said it yourself." I shrugged. "I am a fun guy. I always come back."

Dawn stared at me with a flat expression, refusing to acknowledge my pun. That felt like my first point. It was a cheap win, but beggars can't be choosers.

"Lady Tania invited me," I said after Dawn didn't crack. "It would have been quite rude of me to turn her down after the deal I made with your mother."

"Ah, yes, you're working your way through the family at a record pace, aren't you? Nothing makes a girl feel more appreciated than being measured against her sisters like a cut of beef at the butcher's."

Tania arched an eyebrow in silent agreement.

"I didn't make the rules," I said softly. "I'm stuck in the game just as much as you."

"Then I recommend you play better," Dawn said with a sniff. "At least you left the runt at home this time. Very well, you're here, then. Let's get your pitch over with."

"My pitch?" I repeated in surprise. "What pitch?"

"Why should I become your betrothed? What do you have to offer me?" She clapped her hands twice, cutting through the general conversation like a pair of gunshots. "House of Summer, gather round, friends," she crowed. "Matthew is going to propose."

My gaze slowly turned to meet Tania's brown eyes. She gave me a small smirk and an arch of dark eyebrow that seemed to say *I told you so*. I guess she had. Following their princess's orders, the supernatural day drinkers gathered around like a pack of scavengers.

"Whenever you're ready," Dawn drawled, leaning back in her chair to grab a champagne flute from the table. "I'm on the edge of my seat."

When I was planning how this party invasion was going to play out, I hadn't considered that Dawn would play along with the whole courtship bit. I didn't have my own elevator pitch ready like I was an indie movie producer desperate for funding, I was going to have to make it up as I went.

How the heck was I supposed to make myself appealing as a romantic interest to a Faerie royal? I didn't have a lot going for me. What was I supposed to say? "Hi, I'm Matt. I have no soul, no money, no properties, but I think you're pretty?" Something told me that wouldn't make me stand out—at least, not in a good way.

Tania saw an opportunity for freedom in me. But my astute judgment of character told me that Dawn wasn't motivated by the same things as her sister. No, the Lady of Summer was her own woman. What was she looking for? I decided to see if I could find out.

"Your Highness, esteemed guests." I gave a small bow at the hips, the towel over my shoulder swinging forward like a loose toga. For a moment I felt like a Roman senator, standing before the emperor. "Thank you for taking the time to listen to my proposal. Today I will show you that I am a worthy suitor for Dawn, Lady of Summer."

Dawn scoffed quietly in front of me. Muted chuckles ran through the group of immortals, but I ignored them. The time for jokes would come later.

I was so glad Alex and Orion weren't here to see this. I'd never live it down.

"My name is Matthew Carver." I gave the audience a big smile. "The rumors are true. I like to be up-front and honest. I don't have a soul. It was stolen from me, and I'm trying to get it back. But that's not who I am, just a tiny little red flag. I am a squire of the Hunt. I am a friend of the Fae. I rescued Willow from the horns of a minotaur." I held up both my hands, and they burst into flames right on cue.

"*Thanks!*" I thought at the weird little fire spirit. I still didn't really understand what Willow was, but the audience seemed impressed. That was good enough for now.

"*Tell them who you are!*" the quiet little voice cheered from inside my head.

"I walk with Constellations and defy dragons," I continued. "I've fought ghouls, hellhounds, and demons. I slew the Immortal Lilith with a flaming sword of judgment." I held my right hand up so the princesses could see the scar the hilt had branded into the palm of my hand. I didn't know if it meant anything, but I thought it looked cool. "All of that, my friends, was accomplished in my first year of leaving the safety of the mortal world. Imagine what I will accomplish in my second."

The courtyard was totally silent. I allowed myself a smug little smile. When I compared my accomplishments to my friends, it was easy for me to doubt myself. But I had to admit, my resume was not too shabby. I could tell by the echoing silence that Dawn and her cronies had been caught off guard—

Dawn's peal of laughter interrupted my internal victory lap. The Lady of Summer threw her head back and let out a scornful sound that was more like a falcon's shriek than a laugh.

"That's it?" She casually placed her champagne flute back on the table and sat forward to spear me with her blue eyes. "Little manling, changeling, whatever you are, my father is a *god*. My mother is the matriarch of an entire race. Do you think that your achievements are impressive? Your friends and teachers are the discarded offspring of power you can't even comprehend, tainted by humanity."

Holy crap. My brain didn't know how to respond to *that* piece of information. Fortunately, my mouth has never been fond of checking in with mission control for permission to spout off. "Give me a few years," I drawled. "I'll see what I can do."

"Very well," Dawn sneered. "I'm sure we're all eager to see what *magnificent* thing you accomplish next. Do keep me in the loop." She clapped her hands twice again. "As you were!" she ordered her retinue.

The Fae scattered back to their lounges and the pool like dandelion seeds dancing on the wind.

"By the way," she said, not done slicing me with her razor-sharp words. "I'd keep that little burn scar on your hand to yourself. You are like a toddler that tried to hold a burning log and are proud of their scars. We already know you like to play with things you don't understand. You don't have to prove it."

I gave her a tight smile and a shrug, but that barb got to me a little. I don't really know much about Orion's sword, but I know that it's a big deal, and I am, at best, a small deal, if even a deal at all. Although he's never told me so, I suspect the burn on my palm was because I wasn't worthy to wield his blade like that. I could see how my betters would see it as embarrassing rather than beneficial.

"Matthew, I have been very nice and listened to your pitch," Dawn said, turning back to me. "Now that it's out of the way, shoo. Leave me and my sister alone from your incessant advances and let us breathe a little air untainted by mortality."

Dawn was trying to put me in my place by sending me packing, but that was what I wanted anyway. The demoness was off on her own. The princesses were busy. Not bad, Matt. Not bad at all. I did my best to hide a pleased smile as I bowed to the two ladies.

"Of course, Your Highnesses. Thank you for taking the time to speak with me, Lady Dawn."

Dawn made a rude noise and waved me away with her hand. I was happy to follow her orders. I could practically feel the princesses' eyes stabbing me in the back as I skedaddled. Whether or not either of them wanted to marry me didn't mean they weren't keeping an eye on me.

This next step required a subtle transition—my specialty. If it was too obvious that I came here to speak with the demon, I might offend one or both of my hostesses. Plus, Gloriana's mission felt like it required a measure of subterfuge. If she only needed the demon interrogated, she had people for that. There was a bigger picture here, and I needed to help her paint it.

The first part of my plan was to be so boring that everyone forgot I was here. All I had to do was keep my big mouth shut and not cause a scene. How hard could that be?

Okay, given that it is me, probably harder than it should be, but still, doable.

I've found that I'm much better about keeping my mouth shut when it's stuffed with food, so I headed straight to the buffet, because of course Dawn's pool party was catered. The three human servants were making tacos to order, grilling chicken and beef right in front of me.

I'm picky about my tacos. I grew up in LA. Our street tacos are better than anything you can find in most cities in the U.S. I was completely unprepared for the transformative experience that was these Faerie tacos. I don't know who these humans were or where they had been hired from, but their cooking was nothing short of divine. My first bite made me gasp so hard I choked on a piece of onion.

Needing to clear my throat, I snatched a champagne flute from the end table and gulped down something that tasted of watermelon and bubbles. Aware that everyone was staring again, I gave an ashamed duck of my head and made my way to sit down at an empty chair. I can't even eat without being an embarrassment.

The nearest free seat just happened to be next to the sunbathing demon. What are the odds? I guess I *had* to sit there to eat. I was only trying to get out of everyone else's way, like a good little mortal. I perched on the edge of the chair and started scarfing down my tacos. I was hungry and they were delicious. No one said I had to suffer while I was spying on the demons.

Out of the corner of my eye, I studied the demoness. Her skin was so pale that I wondered what kind of supernatural SPF she was using. Was it even possible for an Immortal to tan? I had no idea if Dawn's fake sun generated UV rays. Hopefully it didn't. I burn easily, and the last thing I needed while trying to convince princesses that I was a good marriage prospect was to have a bright red peeling nose to make me more resemble a clown.

The demon was leaning back in her lounge chair, eyes closed. Her shoulder-length black hair was a sharp contrast to her skin. She appeared not to have noticed me stuffing my face next to her. That was fine by me, as I didn't want to seem too eager to talk to her, and I still had two more tacos. The demon could wait to answer a few questions until after I finished my lunch. I didn't know how many chances I was going to get to eat like royalty, so I darn well was going to take full advantage of it.

"I don't work in that department," she said without opening her eyes. I paused mid-bite of my final taco. With a small sigh, I placed it down on my plate and turned to face her.

"What department?" I asked.

"The Soul Sales Department," she replied, rolling her shoulders to get more comfortable. "You were sneaking your way over here to bother me about getting your soul back, right?"

"Who, me?" I placed a hand against my chest. "No, no, I was just eating some tacos. Have you tried them? You must, they're heavenly—sorry—they're really good. This seat was just the first open one I saw," I protested. She opened her eyes, the twin black orbs staring at me with an expression of flat disbelief.

"Now that you mention it, you are a demon, aren't you? I hadn't even noticed."

She closed her eyes and leaned back against her chair with a caustic laugh, almost like the caw of a crow.

"Yes, now that you mention it, I suppose I am," she said dryly. "What impressive observational skills you have, Matthew Carver."

"You appear to have me at a disadvantage," I protested. You know my name, but I don't know yours." Those black eyes opened again, and she stared at me for a long moment.

"You may call me Sam," she said at last.

"Very well, Sam. What department of Hell do you work in, if it isn't the sales one?"

"I prefer to think of myself as an ambassador of sorts." Sam's eyes were closed, and her body language could not have been more bored. But that felt like a distraction. My experience with demons was that they loved to talk. Even Dan loved to talk, though he wasn't very good at it. I had never been given the infernal cold shoulder before. Armed with Gloriana's suspicions, I wasn't buying it.

"Interesting," I said, leaning forward slightly. "I didn't know Hell had much of an ambassador program." Gloriana had promised that the Fae would intercede on my behalf to Hell. There had to be some sort of channel they could use to do that.

"I bet there's a lot of things about Hell you don't know about." A small smile played across her mouth, which made me feel uncomfortable. Was this demon playing with me?

Stupid question—duh.

I made a noncommittal grunt. I simultaneously felt like I knew too much and too little about Hell and its denizens. "I'm guessing it's a pretty cushy gig," I said, trying to figure out how to keep her engaged. Small talk can be brutal.

She snorted. "No demon wants to spend their career trotting around and mingling. It's a glorified desk position."

"Sorry, it's just, you're sunning yourself in a bathing suit next to a pool in a faerie glade, so I assumed that was a pretty big step up from your ambiance back home."

Sam cracked open one black eye and stared at me through her long lashes. A wicked smile crooked at the corner of her mouth as she shifted back into a comfortable position. She closed her eye and murmured, "Maybe you're a little smarter than I gave you credit for."

People tell me that way too often, I've decided. Do I look that stupid? I'm at least smart enough to know I don't want to know the answer to that. Maybe I should start wearing a fake pair of glasses so people think I'm intelligent.

"I guess you'll find out about the ambiance in due time, won't you?" the demon said in a calm tone.

I glanced back to see both of her eyes were open and staring at me. "I thought you said you didn't work in that department?"

"I don't." She shrugged. "But it's not like I haven't heard about you. You killed *Lilith*. I haven't seen Him that mad in centuries."

I didn't need to ask which "Him" we were talking about; her tone made it crystal clear that she meant her boss's boss. The big cheese himself, el Diablo.

"He's that upset, huh?" I asked. This wasn't news to me. Zagan had made it clear that Hell's desire to execute the contract and procure my soul was personal.

"You killed the only girlfriend he has actually *liked*," she said with emphasis. "Maybe if you had knocked off some of his other girlfriends, he wouldn't have been as wrathful, but Lilith was special to him."

I wondered what girlfriends the Devil might have in his past and decided I didn't want to know. I couldn't believe more than one person had been willing to date him. Talk about ignoring some red flags.

"I've heard the whole doom-and-gloom pitch from Zagan, thanks," I said with a flippant wave of my hand. "I'm more curious about you. You're the first demon I've met who hasn't been trying to eat me or steal my soul."

"Like I said, not my department. Not my circle, not my imps." It sounded like she had a surprisingly healthy work– life balance. Even though she was a demon, I was a little impressed. I kinda figured Hell had invented hustle culture. Or maybe they did, but it didn't seem like it had its hooks in Sam.

"What does fall under your department's job description, then?" I asked. I was supposed to be spying on her for Gloriana, but I also had no idea what I was looking for. So far, Sam seemed to be kind of lazy. A salaried employee taking advantage of her hotel's amenities and enjoying the fact that her bosses weren't around to keep her on the clock. It might have been the most I've ever related to a demon on a personal level.

"Oh, you know, the usual," she said airily. "Butter up royals, apologize for doing things that we're going to do again and aren't actually sorry about, and make sure to slander other organizations we don't like."

If only our own politicians were as honest.

"Speaking of royals." She sat up, looking over at Dawn and Tania. "You did me a favor. I've been trying to get a chance to speak to Tania for a week now, and she's been impossible to catch. It's been lovely to meet you. I'll be sure to pop by and say hello sometime during your eternity of torment. But if you'll excuse me, I have to go do my job."

Sam popped out of her chair and trotted to the sisters before I had the chance to stop her. Tania rose to meet her, and the two shook hands warmly. After a moment of chatting, they strolled off, arm in arm. Dawn watched them go with an odd expression on her face.

My gut told me that might be important, so I filed it away under "Miscellaneous" in my brain's system. Maybe Gloriana would know what it meant. But demons were definitely talking to her daughters. As different as Sam was from the other demons I had met, she was still an employee of Hell.

Dawn's gaze slowly turned from the retreating backs of her sister and the demon ambassador and back to me. Her blue eyes stared at me sharply, like two icy daggers. There was no fake smile on her face now, only a coldly cunning expression. It was the gaze of a predator deciding how hungry she was. A shiver ran down my spine despite the warm weather.

Dawson, the obnoxious butler, appeared at my elbow as if summoned by his mistress's glare.

"Time to go?" I guessed, matching Dawn's stare with my own as best I could.

"Immediately. You have quite overstayed your welcome," Dawson said.

"I didn't even get to go swimming yet," I grumbled, rising to my feet. I wasn't too bummed that I was being kicked out. My plan had already run its course. I had gotten inside Dawn's party, so I could check her off my list, and I had information for the Queen. By Matt Plan standards, today was a resounding success—as a bonus, nobody lost their soul or died. But my gut told me this was only the beginning. If there's one thing I've learned about demons, it's that they're always up to something. So what did an ambassador of Hell want with Dawn or Tania? I didn't have a single clue, but it was my job to find out.

"Right this way, Squire Carver," Dawson urged, gesturing me toward the exit.

"Don't worry. I know my way out," I said, leaving him in my wake.

AFTER THAT SOCIAL nightmare, I was left
with one princess to woo. I assembled the brain
trust for a long board meeting. I don't know why
I thought that the courting bit would be easier than this. I never get
to do anything the easy way.

Alex suggested, and Orion agreed, that if a princess didn't invite
me to have a meeting with her, finding an organic way to cross paths
with her was better than just waltzing up to her residence unannounced.
I wish he had pointed that out before I insulted 33.3 percent of my
marriage options, but it is what it is.

Robin was only too happy to be of help. He told me Ash spent
a lot of her time in Goldhall's training facilities, pursuing just about

every combat practice known to man or beast. Armed with this information, I decided to pull the middle-school boy special—hang out at a place obsessively until I happened to "casually" run into my crush. Although in this case, my "crush" was a Faerie royal who I needed to convince to enter an arranged marriage with me on favorable terms and not Whitney from algebra class.

Tomayto, tomahto.

My version of the plan had been to lounge around an armory trying to look cool and bored. Instead, I was dodging a sword. The moment Orion heard a single whisper of a place to train being available in Goldhall, he insisted we resume our workout regimen. According to our fearless leader, being stuck in the Faerie Lands and courting Fae princesses was not a good enough excuse for a squire of the Hunt to slack off. Especially not after our narrow escape from Zagan. So for the past week, Orion had marched Alex and me into the ring to try to pour more of his martial prowess into us, which felt like a fire hydrant trying to fill two shot glasses with knowledge.

Alex's practice blade slashed past me as I danced out of the way and struck back with mine. The lesser Nephilim twisted, faster than he should have been able to, and caught my attack on the edge of his dulled sword. His sling was already off, thanks to the unnatural healing of his Nephilim blood. From the tight look in his eyes, I suspected he felt some pain while swinging his blade, but he fought like a man on a mission.

"Well done," Orion called from the sidelines, clapping his hands once in confirmation of his praise.

A small smile flashed across Alex's face and was gone as fast as one of his lightning-quick slashes that took all of my speed and focus to avoid.

"Well done," I mimicked back at Alex, my voice a higher-pitched cadence of the Constellation's. Alex's eyebrow twitched. I think my constant irreverent treatment of Orion bothered him more than he let on. It was like we were being taught to shoot hoops by Michael Jordan himself, but I kept making fun of him under my breath. It was wildly disrespectful, which is one of my most endearing qualities.

Either way, it was a bit of a distraction. Alex was not nearly as Nephilimed as Orion, but he was still stronger and faster than me. He also had a century or two of training to back it up. So obviously, I cheated whenever I could.

"What are you going to do when you find yourself fighting some ancient being that doesn't speak English?" Alex asked, feinting a low thrust at my gut. I stepped aside, keeping my blade hovering between us. Our blades flashed several times in quick exchange as Alex continued to press his attack. There was an urgency to his training that hadn't been there before. Getting sliced up by a demon will do that to you.

"I know a joke in Latin," I said, taking that instant to execute a series of thrusts that my friend turned easily as we began circling each other. Our eyes were locked, and I could feel a grin on my face that mirrored his. Sword fighting is an art. It is a conversation—or maybe more accurately an argument. You and your opponent both make your points with the point of your blade. I had much to learn before I could be considered any good at it, but I was finally able to speak fluently.

"Oh, this should be good," he said with a groan.

"*Semper ubi, sub ubi!*" I cried, launching an attack. I slashed down across his chest, anticipating him catching my blade. When he did, I slid my sword down his and stepped across him to my left, hoping to slide underneath his weapon and be inside his guard.

With a curse, Alex dropped his wrist, letting his blade go limp as he leapt back. Feeling confident, I stepped into the space he had created, crashing a flurry of blows down on his defense. Alex was fast and strong, but I had been learning from the Hunter too.

Alex retreated from my onslaught, both of us getting sloppy in the heat of the moment.

"Footwork!" Orion bellowed from the sidelines of the practice ring.

With a jerk, I tightened up my form, and I saw Alex twitch with a similar response. We looked like a pair of chastised students caught slumping in their desks by the teacher.

The end came quickly, as all violence tends to. I landed a blow on Alex's left arm and, feeling confident, pushed for the finish. He retreated a few steps before lashing out with one of his long legs, sweeping my front foot as I stepped. I staggered, catching my balance, but not before the Nephilim lunged, his dull blade resting at my throat.

"Always where under where?" he asked, referring to my Latin joke. "Oh, holy crap," he swore. "Now I hear it! Did you really make a pun in two different languages?"

"You're one to complain," I groaned. "Since when do you do kicking moves?"

"Since I don't want to die to an insane fallen angel," he replied with a shrug.

"That is a really good point. Show me that kick thing again?"

Before Alex could demonstrate his leg sweep, a commotion burst out at the entrance to the square room. Ash, Lady of Fall, swept into the room with an entourage that would make any celebrity jealous. Ash was dressed for combat, in a pair of bright yellow training leathers, her fiery red hair pulled back into an athletic ponytail.

The training facility was a large square room with vaulted ceilings. This was still Goldhall, so the walls were peerless marble, with gold scrollwork accenting everything. The center of the room held the large sandy arena Alex and I had been sparring in. One wall was entirely covered with weapons: clubs, spears, swords, and everything in between. The other was covered in mirrors three times as tall as me, to practice your forms in front of. It was a beautiful room, a work of art worthy of Leonidas or some other legendary warrior. It was the literal definition of martial art. It deserved to be a museum and film set all at the same time. But all of those details faded into the background.

I only had eyes for her.

Ash's green eyes sparkled with an inner fire as she met mine across the room. An impish smile spread across her face as quick as a flaring match. I could feel my own leap to answer hers.

"You there, mortal, get off the sand," a sneering male voice cut in on my moment. "Your betters are here now."

With more effort than I would like to admit, I managed to tear my gaze away from the beautiful green pools that I had been relaxing in to face the speaker. The newcomer was one of the Fae who had come in her retinue. He was tall and lean, with light blond hair and angular features. He wore a pair of green training leathers that were cut at the shoulders so his—admittedly impressive—muscles were on display.

"My betters?" I asked, sweeping my arms out and looking around the room in an exaggerated gesture. Seeing no one I immediately deemed better, I turned back to him and shrugged.

"Oh boy, here we go," I heard Alex mutter to himself. I ignored him. This was my moment; I wasn't going to let him rain on my parade. This was where I could prove myself in front of one of the Queen's daughters. Tania had offered me a deal, but it had nothing to do with me or what I brought to the table. She just saw me as an opportunity to rubberstamp her own escape. Dawn had laughed me out of her presence. I could be more than either of those things.

I've said it before, and I will say it again: Supernatural beings are all about chutzpah. Swagger is a core to their being. They're all predators, every single one. They speak in predatory tones and only understand the language of predation. This Faerie frat boy thought he was someone and that I was no one. I was going to disabuse him of that notion.

"Yes, your betters," he growled, taking a step onto the sand.

"Squire Carver, have you met Rogan, Lord of Earth?" Ash's strong voice cut between us like a police tape cordon, preventing this from turning into a murder scene.

"A squire, is it? Not even a proper knight? Who let you into this room?" Rogan pressed on, ignoring the Lady of Fall's graceful attempt to defuse the situation.

"A squire of the Hunt," I replied with a steely smile.

The room went silent. You could have heard a pin drop on the sandy floor, which is even harder to hear than a pin dropping on a regular floor.

Ash was standing behind the obnoxious lord, and I had a perfect view to see her face light up with a wicked smile of her own. Maybe she wasn't a huge fan of Rogan either. I couldn't blame her; he looked like a Rogan. I don't know what that means, but it's true.

Rogan's gaze slowly turned to take in Orion and Alex with me. He looked confused, like a toddler who has just learned that Santa Claus isn't real.

"A mortal? A member of the Hunt?" He turned to look at Orion. "Surely you jest, Hunter."

Orion shrugged.

"Tough times," Alex said from next to me.

Rogan's eyes narrowed as he took in Alex. "You're practically mortal yourself."

"Mortal or not, we still killed Lilith pretty dead," I said, speaking up for my friend. Technically it had been me who had been stupid enough to swing the final blow, but I consider it a team effort. It made me feel better to spread the blame—I mean credit.

"*You* slew the Dark Mother? You're the one?"

I held up my right hand, which still bore the scar from the hilt of Orion's sword, seared into my palm like a brand. I know Dawn had told me it was embarrassing, but I wasn't so sure I wanted to live my life according to her rules.

Rogan did not disappoint. He pulled back with a slight shudder, like someone who has just felt a spider crawling along their shoulder. A wicked smile that was all my own crept across my face. Have I mentioned I have no patience for bullies?

"Whoever you are, you still must surrender the training field," the Faerie lord said, regaining his composure. "Her Highness, the Fall Lady, requires it."

I turned to look at Ash, arching an eyebrow. I was just about to give her a sweeping bow and offer the princess my place, but she beat me to the punch.

"Oh, Rogan, I'm in no hurry." She gestured lazily to a wiry old Fae standing next to one of the weapons racks. "Sir Raynar wanted to have me test the new hilt on my blade today before I used it anyway. If you're in such a rush, why don't you warm up with the mortal squire?"

The smile on her face was absolutely predatory now. Her deep green eyes found mine, and her left eye twitched in the shadow of a wink. My heart rate doubled, its beat setting a pace that any rock band would be hard-pressed to keep up with. The room had been silent when I claimed to be a member of the Hunt.

Now it was frozen. Everyone in the room might as well have been carved from the same marble that made up the bones of Goldhall.

I flashed my most winning smile and met Rogan's full golden eyes. "I suppose I could squeeze one more in," I heard myself say above the rushing blood in my ears.

I won't lie, I wanted to fight Rogan. But I wasn't sure I stood a chance. I'd learned a lot from Orion, but I still struggled against Alex. And he wasn't even a full-blooded immortal. Rogan was apparently some Lord of Earth, whatever that meant. He was almost certainly packing power in a way that put him a weight class beyond what

I was ready for. But as some poet once said, "Nothing ventured, nothing gained." Which basically means you miss every shot you don't take, just in fancier, older English.

This was my chance to prove myself worthy of the reputation of the Hunt, mortal or not. I wasn't going to throw it away.

I could almost see the calculations running behind Rogan's yellow eyes. He knew one of us had been offered up as a tribute, but he wasn't sure which one. I guess I couldn't really be sure either. This was a win for Ash no matter what happened. If her companion beat me, it would call into question if I had the strength her mother wanted to bring to the bloodline. If I beat him, she earned points with me by being supportive. It was a clever move. I was also proud of myself for reading that so well. Maybe I had learned a little from surviving Lilith's manipulations.

"Very well," Rogan said as the room eased back into motion. "I suppose I could do with a light warmup." He held out a hand and snapped his fingers. An attendant tossed him a practice sword from the wall, which he caught without looking. He brought the blade up into a salute with a flourish as he stepped into the ring.

A creeping fear tingled up my spine as I saw the casual confidence that he had with his blade. His style was stupid and flashy, but it was obvious that he had spent many hours practicing to be that way.

Alex rapped his fist on my shoulder as he walked past me toward Orion. "Take him down a peg or two for me, will you?"

"Only two?" I shot back.

Alex grinned as he stepped up next to our fearless leader, who was as still as stone. Orion gave me one slow nod and crossed his arms in front of him. Tension built in my shoulders as the weight I was carrying settled on them. As Fae gathered around the ring to watch our match, they left a noticeable bubble of space around the imposing Hunter, like a void hanging around a star.

"First to three touches?" I asked Rogan as he set himself across from me.

"Whatever you prefer, mortal. It will be a short bout however you want to score it," he replied arrogantly.

I gave him a confident grin that didn't necessarily match how I felt on the inside and raised my own blade in salute to match his.

He took that as the start signal and launched at me like a supernatural torpedo. Holy Toledo, he was fast! I was used to sparring against Alex and other minor Nephilim, and they were quick. But Rogan was something more. He blurred toward me, blunt sword extended to stab into my chest. Already, I knew he was one of the fastest people I had ever faced in a dueling ring.

But he was not the fastest.

He was not the avatar of the Hunter.

I have never beaten Orion in a sparring match, but that doesn't mean that I haven't learned a few tricks to survive against his onslaught. I sidestepped the Lord of Earth's lunge, letting my blade kiss the side of his and shove it lightly to my left. I used the resistance of pushing off his blade to fuel a backward spin of my own, so that I turned and slashed at his heels as he flew by. I felt my blade hit his leg as I came around.

Rogan let out a surprised grunt and skidded to a stop, his feet digging furrows in the sand. He turned back to face me, a startled expression on his face.

"Golly, you're fast. But I think that's one for me," I said with an innocent smile, setting myself into a guard position with my blade angled forward. Behind me, I heard a woman's laugh, and I felt my smile grow even larger. He had underestimated me. He knew I was in the Hunt but had still assumed that because I was a mortal, I could not be a match for him. Only fools ever doubt Orion. I could see by the flush of red that was creeping up the Fae lord's neck that he realized how stupid he looked.

Embarrassment is sharper and deadlier than any blade; it cuts from the inside out. Rogan might have all the pedigree in the world on me, but he was proud and hotheaded. I could work with that.

Eager to even the score, Rogan advanced on me at a more measured pace. He closed in with a slash that I caught on my blade, and our swords slid apart and into the rhythm of a dance. Seeking and turning, we exchanged half a dozen blows in a matter of seconds. His gold eyes narrowed in concentration, and he began to speed up his pace, relying on his supernatural genetics to batter his way through my defenses.

I will give credit where credit is due: Rogan's form was incredible. He was well trained and comfortable flowing through his attack stances. His strokes were fluid; he never fell into a pattern that I could exploit. His ego was not completely unfounded. He knew what he was doing.

I did my best to turn his attacks, but bit by bit he began to grind through my defenses. I was falling behind on the pace of the exchanges, and eventually I was going to miss one.

Like that! A heavy blow that I was not quick enough to catch landed on my left shoulder, and I rolled with it, using the force of the blunted blow to spin me away and out of his reach for a moment to reset. Just because the practice blades didn't have edges didn't mean they didn't still *hurt*. I moved my arm experimentally. I would probably bruise, but nothing felt broken.

Rogan's golden eyes bored into mine. He wasn't smiling or show-boating anymore. His face was a mask of focused anger, smooth as the marble walls around us.

Whoopsies, I might have upset him a little too much.

He didn't gloat on his point, and instead he continued his attack. This time I didn't stay back and take it. He was faster and stronger than me—the only way I was going to beat him was to force him to make a mistake. Given enough time, he would eventually break through my defenses, so I had to deny him that time.

I lunged toward him, getting inside his guard, where I was too close for him to comfortably slash at me. Our blades met, I raised them up high and body-checked him with all of my weight.

The noble staggered back a few steps. I disengaged my blade from his as he reeled back, and brought it down in a diagonal slash across his chest, bouncing off the strong training leathers with my blunted edge. Another point for me. Fighting like a brawling ice hockey player is absolutely not how you're supposed to fight in a courtly dueling ring. I was counting on that catching him off guard.

My blow landed before he could recover his balance, and he staggered back another step before falling onto his rump. This time I heard more Fae than just Ash laugh.

"You cheating bastard," Rogan roared, leaping to his feet, his face fully flushed. Seeing the crazed look on his face, I realized something. Rogan wasn't a soldier. He wasn't a warrior. He was a rich boy who had been taught how to hold a sword, with none of the other training that is necessary to make you deadly. Any idiot can be taught how to hold a sword or shoot a gun. That's a basic skill, just like brushing your teeth or using a fork and knife. Having one singular skill does not make you dangerous. The real training is the part that makes you able to think while you are fighting—the wisdom to guide your skills.

Maybe that was what the Queen had meant when she said her people had gone soft.

"I'll show you your place, mortal," the blushing noble growled, and he raised his left hand in a claw. Goose bumps ran up my arms as all the hairs on them stood on end. The ground beneath my feet began to wiggle. Horrified, I looked down to see a widening crack opening in the sand, right between my two feet.

I had a guess what the title "Lord of Earth" might refer to now. Instinctively, I leapt to the left, landing on one side of the mini fault that was opening up beneath me. As an LA native, this was one of my worst nightmares—an enemy who could control earthquakes. The line in the earth cracked and splintered, more tendrils reaching toward me like the dark arms of the kraken. Dorothy, I don't think we're having a sword fight anymore.

I dodged backward again from the branching faults that were hunting me, my mind scrambling. Could I make my way over the faults without falling in, then hit him one more time? Would he even stop if I did? Was this why the stupid practice ring was filled with sand?

Slowly, one thought forced its way to the front: When in Rome, fight fire with fire. Actually, I'm pretty sure that isn't quite how the saying goes, but it was close enough. I lifted my left hand off the hilt of my sword and sent a silent thought to my companion, Willow.

Burn.

Instantly, both of my hands were swallowed by the friendly fire that was Willow. Distantly, I heard a murmur of shock run through the room. I guess word of a mortal having a Willow hadn't spread to the entire court yet.

"Hey, boss, just so you know, I don't do ground stuff," Willow's light, breezy voice said directly into my head.

"I got a different plan," I shouted at my burning hands. I extended my sword like a tip of a spear and pointed it right at Rogan, whose golden eyes went wide. Willow picked up on my train of thought, and a portion of our flames flowed off my hand, swirling down the practice blade before shooting out like a flaming lance.

The Fae lord swept his left hand up, and the sand rose, forming a shield that caught my blast before collapsing back to the earth in a miniature dust storm. But while he did that, the cracks stopped growing. A predatory smile grew on my face as I met his wide golden eyes.

"How do you have a Willow?" he demanded in awe. "It's impossible! Ever since the Lord of Fire—"

As interesting as whatever fact about the Willow he was about to share probably was, I had no interest in letting him regain his cool. I was here to win a duel and impress a princess. Gossip could come later.

I know, who *am* I?

Mentally, I ordered Willow to send another flaming lance shooting at the lord, interrupting his speech. Another sandy wall came up to block the fire, but his defense had a downside: it also blocked his line of sight. The second his view of me was eclipsed, I sprinted toward him, throwing another fireball with my left hand as I ran, pumping my legs as hard as I could.

His shield popped up, absorbed my fire blast, and dropped to the ground. I still had fifteen feet to go. I threw another fireball. He shielded again. Ten feet now. Another fireball. Another shield. Five feet.

This time when the shield dropped, I could see Rogan's eyes up close as he realized I wasn't going to stop. The cracks at my feet began to widen, but it was too late.

Once more, I threw another fireball. Rogan was forced to throw up his sand shield to deflect it. I could see something that looked like despair on his face as he did. He knew that he was stuck. The sand blocked the fireball, but it wasn't solid enough to stop my lunge.

I burst through the sand barrier in a fencer's lunge, sword extended, both knees pointed forward with all the velocity of a runaway train. Rogan tried to turn my blade, but every single ounce of force my six-foot body could muster was behind the thrust. The tip of my blade speared into his shoulder, and he staggered from the force behind my strike and fell once more into the sand.

"Three," I said softly, looking down at him.

Behind me, a solitary pair of hands began applauding. I looked up to see Ash, the Lady of Fall, standing at the head of the arena. Her clapping hands were wreathed in a fire identical to my own.

"Hey, look, it's me!" Willow said.

ROGAN STORMED OFF after our duel ended, but I stuck around to watch Ash work with her trainers. As she progressed through her sword forms, I soon realized that she was in an entirely different class of swordsmanship than the Lord of Earth had been. Every movement and stroke she made was calculated and precise. At one point she fought two of the sword masters at the same time and held them both at bay. Rogan had been a boy playing with swords. She was one with the blade.

Even Orion grunted appreciatively once or twice, his obsidian eyes watching the lady train with sharp interest. His approval is as rare as a lightning strike, and worth its weight in gold.

When she was done, she approached me with a bright smile on

her face. Her red hair was bound tightly in a single braid, making her look like a superheroine stepping off a movie set. Despite her rigorous training, I don't think she had even broken a sweat.

"That was well done," she said warmly as she drew close. "Rogan has always been an ass. I'm glad someone finally bit back a little."

"I suspect you would have no trouble doing that yourself," I said, gesturing at the practice field behind her. She laughed, a delightful sound that was so genuine I couldn't help but smile in response to her joy.

"You might be right," she conceded, "but it has quite a different tone when a member of the royal family does it to a vassal, instead of a mortal slapping around a Faerie noble as if he were a child."

Well, that certainly sounded like a familiar excuse. It seemed all the people in power wanted to talk about were the things they couldn't do. I didn't think it had been that easy, but I smiled and inclined my head, accepting the compliment.

"You honor your teacher," she continued with praise, turning and bowing slightly to Orion. Alex and I glanced at each other, eyes widening slightly. I am not fully educated on courtly etiquette, but I know that royals don't bow to *anyone*, not even the literal stars. That's not how it works.

Orion returned her bow with a mild one of his own, something like a small smile playing at his lips, like a shadow at high noon. "As are you to your masters, Princess," the Hunter said softly. "Do you know that your sword master Raynar once gave me a scar?" He pointed at his left hip. Behind him, Alex's eyes were now as round as saucers. "Few have ever lived who were his equal with the blade."

I glanced at Ash. Her excited expression mirrored Alex's. I tried to imagine a swordsman who could meet Orion's raw strength and skill in combat. Even Zagan had struggled to keep up with the Hunter. I glanced at the wiry, gray-haired Fae with a pair of thin swords strapped to his waist, who had been instructing the princess during her training. Never had I seen a Fae who showed their age. How old did he have to be for Father Time to finally show a little wear and tear on the face of an Immortal? I didn't think I wanted to know.

"I don't suppose you would be willing to give us a demonstration?" Ash breathed softly, a fanatical excitement tinting her voice. She sounded like a hardcore sports fan thrilled to see two legendary players finally face off.

"Some things are better left undemonstrated," he said gently, turning to look at the Fae swordsman for the first time. Both of the sword masters were as stiff as boards. It must be awkward to spend time in a room with someone you had tried to kill before. I think I would rather spend time with an ex-girlfriend. Granted, my last girlfriend was in middle school, but I'm still confident in that choice.

"Of course," the Fall Lady said, bowing again. "Forgive me, Master Hunter, I forget my manners."

Orion brushed her apology away with a wave. "None needed, Your Highness. You are not wrong—it would certainly be a sight to see."

This time I was certain a vicious little smile tugged at the corner of his mouth. A small whisper of excitement ran down the back of my neck. The call of the Hunt was a part of who he was, a carnal need that he could not ignore.

"Would you walk with me, Squire Carver?" Ash asked, turning to me. "I would love a chance to show you some of my home if you could find a way to squeeze me into your busy schedule."

I felt my mouth go dry as her green eyes met mine. Who the heck put all those butterflies in my stomach?

"I am not really the keeper of my own calendar these days," I said, turning to look at my "manservant." "How's the old schedule looking, Alex? Think we can carve out some time for Her Highness?"

Alex stared flatly at me for a second, his face dead and unamused.

Ash let out a most undignified giggle as she watched our exchange. It was cute.

"Well, let's see," Alex said, holding his hands up in front of him like a make-believe book. "You have a nap at two p.m." He leaned conspiratorially close to Ash and stage-whispered, "He really shouldn't miss it, Your Highness, he gets very cranky—"

"Sounds like I have the time," I said, stepping past Alex, cutting him off before he could really get going. I didn't want all my credibility going out the door after I went to all the trouble to beat up a Faerie lord to earn it.

"I'm delighted you could make it work," she said, stepping close to me and taking my arm. A thrill went through me, like a static shock but much more pleasant, as I felt her arm nestle against mine. Despite having just finished an intense workout, her arm wasn't warm or damp, which is some real magic. "Come with me and let me show you the wonders that Goldhall has to offer."

Not long into the Fall Lady's tour, I realized that I had been too harsh in my judgment of Goldhall. You can only look at so many gilded marble hallways until it becomes garish and boring. The human mind can get used to anything. Somehow even too much ice cream can get tiresome.

But the real treasures of Goldhall were not its walls but the literal treasures hanging on them. The Fae were obsessed with art, and their home was packed with a more robust collection than the British Museum. Ash led me through hallways that had missing paintings from Renaissance masters. One room had a piano that was enchanted to eternally play every lost piece composed by Chopin on a loop. It was kind of cool, I guess. Since immortal Fae could not create their own art, only steal it, they had been busy.

I suppose a true artist would probably declare immortality not worth it, that they could not live without their art, their passion. But all I have is a fake English Literature degree, and I think I'd rather have the immortality. I guess the grass is always greener on the other side or something.

Despite all the glory and glamour of Goldhall, Ash only had one thing on her mind.

"What's the mortal world like?" she asked as we walked past what I thought was a missing Picasso hanging unguarded on the wall like an ordinary painting.

"What do you mean?" I asked, surprised. "Have you never been?"

"I've never left Goldhall," she said with a somber tone.

"Wait, really?"

"Mother says it's too dangerous. We have too many enemies. Only Mav has ever been outside these walls."

I was quiet for a moment, digesting this news as we strolled, still arm in arm. The Queen had told me that she wanted to rebuild the strength of her nation. I didn't know that times were so bad that she didn't let her daughters go outside. I was *not* trying to end up in some weird Rapunzel situation. Plus, if she was worried that she couldn't protect her daughters, how could she protect me from my enemies?

"Is it true that your king also lives in a marble house?" Ash asked.

"Well, it is a white house," I said, slowly connecting the dots. "I don't know if it is really made of marble. It's a lot smaller than your home. Also, we call him a president, not a king. We're very particular about that. There was a war and everything."

"What's the difference?"

I paused for a moment, trying to think how to explain how a crumbling democracy operated to an inhuman Fae who had never even left the two hundred walls of her marble castle.

"It's probably about the same," I said with a shrug. "We just feel better pretending that it's different." I suddenly remembered I was talking to a daughter of a queen. "No offense," I added hastily.

Ash only smiled.

"I've always wanted to see the mortal world. Everything I've read makes it sound so exciting." She gestured at another priceless piece of art resting on a wall. "Any place that can produce such wonders must truly be magical."

I couldn't help but laugh at the irony of a Fae princess wishing to visit the "magical" mortal lands. Ash's face fell, and her arm went slack.

"You're laughing at me," she said in a slightly bitter tone.

"No!" I protested, patting her hand before she could pull completely away. "Well, yes, but not at you. We mortals would say *this* is the magical place. That the endless halls of a queen's castle are something right out of a storybook, and most people would give anything to see it just once."

It occurred to me at that moment that even though I was horrifically unlucky—my soul had been stolen, after all—I was also quite lucky to see these wonders. A small moment of gratitude amid the storm of my life.

"The truth is, the mortal world is not that different, my lady," I said, picking the thread of conversation back up. "We have the same colors, breathe the same oxygen. We just have email."

"What is email?" she asked, no longer sounding offended.

Somewhere behind me, I heard Alex chuckle. How in the world do you explain email to an Immortal who has never seen a computer?

"It's like the dandelion thing, but even more obnoxious."

She laughed brightly, any earlier tension forgotten as she clutched my arm a little tighter. I couldn't get over how different this was from my meeting with Tania. That had been all business and negotiation. This was... fun? I was having fun?

"I have a question," I said after a few moments of companionable walking. "I noticed that you also have a Willow."

She held up her right hand, and it burst into a cheery flame.

I copied her movement, holding up my free left hand, and gave Willow a mental nudge. A second fire lit the room, dancing on my own hand. I couldn't help but notice that her flames were a little brighter, a little bigger. They burned a brilliant orange, whereas mine had streaks of blue dancing in the flames.

"It's very impressive that you did that, by the way," she said, eyes staring deep into her own flames. "It's quite rare that Willow bonds with anyone anymore."

"They bonded with you too," I replied.

"Fire is under the purview of the House of Autumn." She shrugged. "There wasn't much choice in the matter."

"I've got to admit," I said, following her into yet another gallery of exquisite missing art. "I don't really understand the titles that everyone has here. In the mortal world, we'd just call you a princess. But you and your sisters are all tied to seasons, and then there are lords of... elements?"

"It's quite simple, really." Ash paused in front of a glass box that held an old document. My eyes glanced over it before doubling back in shock. As a survivor of the American public education experience, this was the first document that I recognized on my own. My eyes rushed to the bottom where it spotted a series of familiar names. Washington. Jefferson. Adams. Hancock. Unless I was a complete idiot, I was pretty sure it was the freaking Declaration of Independence. Someone had stolen it. I decided not to ask. I didn't want to know.

"My mother is Queen of All Fae," Ash recited, holding up a finger. "Each of her daughters is the head of a specific season's house. We are expected to help her rule during our term. Since it is spring, my sister Tania serves as her right hand. That is why the rest of us had to wait until she had spoken to you."

"She got first dibs?" I thought about her pressuring me into making a deal at our first meeting. Tania had implied that because none of her sisters had spoken to me, they were uninterested, but it seemed like that was not entirely the truth. Clearly she was not as open-handed and kind as I thought. A good reminder for this mortal stuck in the land of the Fae. Some members of the royal family had been nice to me, but that did not mean they were kind. It did not mean they had my best interests at heart. No, they were playing their own games.

"Then there are lords and ladies of elements. Your new friend Rogan is a Lord of Earth. They are individuals who have bonded with one of the elemental spirits."

"Is that like Willow?"

"Got it right on the first try." She smiled at me, and for a second, I lost myself basking in the shine of her pleasure. "Although his spirit's name is Gome, not Willow."

"So there are many Lords of Earth?"

"Rogan is *a* Lord of Earth, not *the* Lord of Earth, if that is what you are asking. Although it is a noble title, it can be held by anyone who has bonded with the spirit of an element. Some spirits of other paths are more eager to bond with us than others."

"I think I got confused because I've heard several people reference *the* Lord of Fire," I said, copying her emphasis.

"I told you that bonding Willow was very impressive. There are no other members of the path of fire," she said with a bit of a shrug. "Before you got here, I was the only member of the court with a Willow."

I let that sink in for a moment. Robin's shocked expression when he saw me summon Willow made more sense now. So did the Queen's delight at meeting me. I didn't know what other elements there might be spirits for, but it seemed obvious that fire was useful when it came to combat. Lazarus's lab knew that only too well.

"What happened to the last Lord of Fire?" I asked.

"He had a falling out with my mother and left." Ash shrugged again, turning away from me. Her shoulders slumped a little. "It was before I was born."

"So, fire falls under the season of fall, you said?"

"I really prefer autumn," she said with a deep-seated weariness that seemed to come from her bones.

I turned, surprised by the change in her tone. This was not the strong, enchanting Ash I had met before.

I risked a glance over my shoulder at Alex, who had been following a few steps behind with Orion and some of her entourage. He made a confused face and shrugged. Thanks for nothing, manservant. You get what you pay for, I guess.

"My sisters have convinced everyone that fall is a more fitting title for me," she explained softly.

To fall. To fail. An entire season's court with no lords or ladies. I thought I was beginning to see the whole picture. Ash's house was weaker than her sisters'. They were her family, but also her rivals. If they each took turns ruling, it stood to reason there wasn't a formal heir. They were all jockeying for their chance to maybe one day be queen. Once their Immortal mother died, I guess.

I felt a sympathetic twinge of pain in my own chest. I might be a squire of the Hunt, but I still felt like I was on the outside of this world. Most supernatural beings reviled me before they even knew me, because they thought I had sold my soul to the Devil on purpose or because they didn't like mortals. Maybe it was because I had a touch of Faerie in me, but this was the second Faerie princess that I felt like I could relate to.

"What would it mean for your house to have another Lord of Fire?" I heard my voice ask without consulting my brain first. I hate it when it does that. It always gets me into trouble.

Ash's head came up, her green eyes now tinted with red. A solitary tear trickled down her cheek, which damn near broke my heart. To see someone so bright and shining in such a vulnerable moment felt like a sin. Like seeing a Christmas present in your parents' closet before it was wrapped.

"It would mean that no one could say I have ruined my house," she whispered fiercely. "That I am unfit to rule. They would not dare call me the Lady of Fall ever again. I would be Lady of Autumn once more."

I blinked in surprise at the ferocity of her response. The princess clearly felt the sting of disrespect keenly. I've noted before how much of the supernatural world is about reputation and perception. Power was held by those everyone assumed to have power. If everyone thought she was a fallen failure, then in some ways, she was. Belief mattered. Not just in gods, but in men and the things in between that go bump in the night.

"What would it mean if the first Lord of Fire in a long time joined a different house than yours?" went my stupid mouth, asking another question without waiting for a permission slip from my mind before it started running.

Ash was silent for so long I wondered if she had heard me.

"Then I would fall for real," she said eventually, whispering the words with reverent tones.

This is how I always get myself into trouble.

MATT, WHATEVER YOU do, do not choose
Ash," Orion's soft voice echoed through our luxury
apartment in Goldhall. It wasn't the first time he
had told me that in the several days since we had our run-in with the
Lady of Autumn at the training hall.

The three of us were huddled up in the living room, trying to make
sense of the players and information we had. Despite all my respect
and appreciation for my friend, my spine stiffened at his imperative
tone. I don't mind feedback, but I have a hard time being told what
to do. It probably reminds me too much of my childhood.

"She is very pretty," Alex offered from the couch that he was once
again sprawled on, feet dangling over the edge like a lazy fisherman
in a rowboat.

"Pretty dangerous," Orion countered, his stone face serious.

"Are any of the daughters of the Queen not dangerous?" I shot back.

"A wounded predator is even more dangerous than a hungry one," the Hunter replied. All his analogies are aggressive like that. I think it's part of the job description.

"I don't know," I said with a sigh. "Tania might not seem as desperate on the surface, but she was manipulating me from the start. She tried to pressure me into accepting her offer before talking to any of her sisters and made a big deal out of the fact she was the first one to bother reaching out. I get the point you're making. I truly do. But I think the Lady of Spring would have me neatly wrapped with a bow before I even knew what happened."

Orion grunted in the way he does when he doesn't agree but grants that you have a point. He's a bit stubborn, even for a Nephilim.

I knew that I was at least partially being swayed by pretty green eyes and a charming personality, but that didn't mean I was completely wrong. Plus, there was a good chance that Rogan was a part of Tania's court, seeing as how he was a Lord of Earth. I figured earth wasn't aligned with winter or summer. Don't ask me why, but that just made no thematic sense in my head.

Bumping into Rogan at the courtly barbeques would be a little awkward. Or whatever it was that the Fae did for fun—pool parties, apparently. Whatever other social activities there were, I stood by my point: I didn't think Rogan and I would be chums anytime soon.

"Willow," I said out loud, struck by a sudden burst of inspiration. I looked down at my hands as they blazed with the fire spirit's familiar warmth and light. "What made you decide to bond with me when you haven't bonded with anyone in such a long time?"

"*You're a Fireheart,*" Willow's voice echoed into everyone's minds.

"I don't understand," I said, glancing at my friends. They both shrugged.

"He asked me to wait for more Firehearts," the spirit replied.

Frustrated, I gave up on questioning them. Explaining things was not one of Willow's gifts. Maybe it's harder to get a firm grasp on concepts when you're only as solid as fire. With a sigh, I relaxed my nudge on Willow, and the flames on my hand went out like two birthday candles.

"So, what, I'm a fireheart?" I asked. "Is that like being pure of heart or something?"

Alex snickered. "Well, we know that one isn't true."

"It could be another attribute," Orion mused slowly. "Perhaps brave or heedless of danger."

"It could mean hungry," Alex offered. "Flames love to devour things."

"Maybe he's extremely warm in bed, like a heater."

I hated when the Supernatural Bros started riffing. Partially because it was like being picked on by two Navy SEALs, but also because as a self-proclaimed smart-mouth, I hated their jokes. Orion was really bad at them. Their comedic routine hurt my feelings emotionally *and* professionally.

"Calm down, Abbott and Costello," I grumbled. "It clearly means *something*. I'm just trying to salvage my entire life's future here, no big deal."

Alex rolled his eyes and grinned at me, but mercifully, he and Orion stopped their comedic assault. We were silent for a few moments as we each puzzled what being a "fireheart" could mean. For the life of me, I couldn't come up with anything that didn't sound super lame, like a bad YA fantasy novel. I just hoped there weren't any prophecies about me. That would be super embarrassing.

"Maybe you're prone to heartburn?" Orion offered into the silence.

I wondered how long he had been sitting on that one. I sighed dramatically as Alex cackled. I don't want to sound too harsh, but that might have been the best joke Orion ever told.

"Can I ask a question?" Alex said, finally getting serious. "What about the other sisters? All this Tania versus Ash drama doesn't really encompass the full equation, does it? There's still the Lady of Winter. We only have part of the picture anyway, so this whole trying-to-make-a-decision meeting is sort of a waste of time."

"Oh, no, I think we're set," I said with a mild shiver. Mav didn't scare me, per se, but I didn't have any interest in spending alone time with her. "Mav basically told the Queen that Hell would have to freeze over first."

"I'm just saying that it seems silly to not even try." Alex sat up to press his point. "We should still try to get the full lay of the land before we go too far down this road. Maybe you can use some of your charm and convince the fourth sister that you're nice and funny."

"Is that a polite way to say someone isn't very smart?" Orion asked.

"Listen here, I've about had it with Open Season on Matt Day," I growled. I had a whole rant ready to go—when someone knocked on the front door.

The three of us leapt to our feet, exchanging stressed looks. We weren't very good at the whole noble household act that had been my excuse for getting my friends here in the first place. That's the problem with having a manservant and guardian who are your friends instead of paid employees.

I pointed at the door to Alex, who shrugged and looked at Orion. Orion shrugged back, an equally blank look on his face. I pointed at Alex and then the door more fiercely. He gestured at his pointy ears as if to say *sorry, can't hear you*, and looked back at Orion.

"Will you—" I hissed, before being cut off by a second knock, this one sharper.

"Say please," Alex said, crossing his arms.

I stared at him.

There was a third knock.

"Fine, fine, I'll do it." Alex turned and made his way to the door. Orion shuffled to the side of the room like a diligent… bodyguard. Alex grabbed the front door and pulled it open in a swift gesture, catching the Fae on the other side with their fist raised, about to knock yet again.

"Carver residence," he said in a bored tone, like a proper noble attendant. Clearly he had taken some notes from Dawson.

Robin wandered in with an amused nod at Alex. "You're getting better at that," he remarked dryly.

Alex rolled his eyes and shoved the door shut behind him.

"Well, you've certainly been busy." The Faerie's golden eyes danced as he looked over toward the seating area. I flopped back down in my chair. That might be rude in front of fancy company, but I wasn't worried about formality. I don't think you need to be a stickler for manners with someone you've saved from an evil scientist's lab. But maybe that's because I grew up barely middle class. Robin must have agreed with my sentiment, because he threw himself onto the couch with casual grace.

"What now?" I groaned.

"Let's see." He began counting things on his long fingers. "The Lady of Spring is telling everyone what a lovely tea you had. She's apparently *quite* smitten with you." He winked at me, which made me feel like he knew the truth of the game that princess was playing.

"You got thrown out of the Lady of Summer's pool party—twice, no less—days before revealing that you are apparently the first Lord of Fire in almost four hundred years. A fact that you demonstrated by publicly drubbing a lord from a rather powerful family."

I rolled my eyes at the word "apparently." Robin was the first person to identify my relationship with Willow for what it was when I arrived in the Faerie Lands. He could have given me a heads-up on the stir it was going to cause. But he was a Faerie and there are rules.

Of course Rogan was from a powerful family—of course he was.

"And you were seen leaving the training halls for a long walk with the Lady of Autumn. We may not have actual paparazzi here in the Faerie Lands, but you certainly are the talk of all the gossips at court."

"How am I doing?" I asked.

"I honestly couldn't say." He waved a hand down his gold-and-white livery marking him as a servant of the Queen. "I literally cannot," he amended.

Stupid Fae and their rules they can't break.

"But that's not why I am here." He clapped his hands and sat up on the couch like an excited conspirator. "I have been commissioned with throwing your birthday party feast."

I let out a groan. I hate my birthday. It's never gone well for me. I didn't need any more birthday surprises.

"I'm sorry, my friend, but this whole shindig is being thrown in your honor," Robin said with a small smile. "You might as well try to enjoy a little of it."

"I like ice cream cake," Orion offered from his chair across from me. I gave him a surprised look. He shrugged. "It's ice cream and cake, what's not to love?"

"Don't you remember, like, the wheel being invented?" I asked.

"Mortals didn't peak until ice cream cake." The Hunter crossed his arms. I think he was being serious.

"I'm fine with ice cream cake," I said with a shrug to Robin.

"It is traditional to ask your parents or patron for a gift," he remarked, golden eyes dancing.

I snorted. "There's no way my father's getting me anything."

"The Queen considers herself something of a patron of yours at the moment," Robin said idly, leaning back in his chair and watching me with keen eyes.

I tried to not let my shock show on my face. The Queen of All

Fae wanted to know what I wanted for my birthday? How in the H-E-double hockey sticks was I supposed to know what to ask for? A billion dollars? A house? My own TV show?

My panic must have shown on my face because Robin let out a booming laugh. "She's already planning on giving you one of her daughters. Don't be afraid to be bold."

I found that description a tad old school for my modern sensibilities, but I got the implication. *She's already giving you the moon, so shoot for the stars.*

Still nervous, I drummed my fingers on my thigh while I tried desperately to be clever. No, not clever. I am often clever. Being clever does not keep you out of trouble or make you friends. I needed to be wise. It only takes a little cleverness to come up with sarcastic one-liners. It takes wisdom to not say them to powerful Immortals' faces.

Alex raised his hand from across the room. I pointed at him. "Yes, you in the back, you have a suggestion?"

"Laser gun," he said, lowering his hand. Robin, Orion, and I all sighed at the same time.

Stupid as it was, I had to admit Alex was on the right track.

Shoot for the stars.

My eyes fell on Orion's sword, which was leaning against the table. It was an Immortal-killing blade. I was collecting powerful enemies at an alarming rate. Having a way of defending myself couldn't hurt.

"What about a magical sword?" I asked.

"It's generally bad form to ask an Immortal for a weapon that could be used against them," Robin said with an apologetic smile. "I said shoot for the stars, not the sun."

"Technically—" Alex began, but I interrupted him. I had a new idea.

"How about a way to go home?" I offered. "I have things I need to do back in the mortal world, and no way to come or go of my own volition."

Robin was silent for a moment as he pondered my suggestion. His answer was interrupted by another knock at the door. Apparently, I was very popular today. I looked at Alex, who immediately pointed a finger at Robin. Robin kicked his feet up on the coffee table.

"Holy crap, you lot are lazy," Alex grumbled, stomping off to answer the door again. This time he had no smooth greeting. He jerked the door open and stuck his head out. "What?" he barked at the servant on the other side.

The individual waiting on the other side was human. Where did the Fae find all these human employees? Like Robin, he was dressed in the gold-and-white livery of the staff of Goldhall. In his hands he bore a silver tray covered by a cloche, making it look like a delicious little entrée plate.

"Your master's presence is required," the man said, bowing and offering the silver tray like a waiter.

Alex turned to look at us, an expression of *What the heck do I do now?* on his face. I motioned for him to remove the dome. He grimaced but turned back to the waiting servant.

With a delicate hand, he lifted the silver cover to reveal a fancy envelope with a large yellow wax seal. He reached out and swiped it off the tray before returning the lid.

"Got it," he said with an awkward nod to the servant before slamming our door shut.

"This came for you," he said, tossing it to me in a sideways arc that fluttered wildly before crash-landing at my feet like a failed paper airplane.

I dropped to a crouch and grabbed it from the floor. It said SQUIRE CARVER on the front in scrawling cursive letters. On the back was a blob of golden wax that had been stamped with someone's ring, leaving the imprint of a giant sun in the middle. I shrugged and broke the seal, opening it.

"Her Majesty the Queen of All Fae requires your attendance at once," I read out loud.

A more urgent knock sounded at the door. I felt my stomach slowly curdle in dread. Had the Queen heard about me beating up a noble on the training ground? Why did this feel suspiciously like being called to the principal's office?

With a sigh, Alex opened it to reveal the same man holding the tray, patiently waiting.

"I was told to bring him immediately," he intoned flatly.

Wordlessly, Robin gestured for me to hand him the envelope. He turned it over once in his hands, a small frown on his face. He stared at the seal for a long moment before shrugging and handing it back to me.

"Best hurry, then," he said with a tight smile. His golden eyes weren't laughing anymore.

I'**VE NEVER HAD** a great relationship with authority. *Shocking*,
I know. I've never really been comfortable with anyone telling
me what to do. I don't like it. It makes me mad in my bones. As
the human servant led Alex, Orion, and me through the golden halls,
I tried to figure out how to process what I was feeling.

On the one hand, I was nervous. Had I made a mistake in showing up Rogan? Was he some favorite pet of the Queen's? Had I upset
one of her daughters? I had been playing fast and loose with the rules.
My mind raced, trying to figure out what Gloriana might want to see
me about. It was entirely possible that she wanted an update on her
demon problem. Would she be satisfied with my progress?

"What do you think you did?" Alex, my physical conscience, whispered from my shoulder as we walked.

"As you know, *we've* been behaving ourselves," I managed through gritted teeth. I can never tell if he's being the worst on purpose or not. Maybe that journalist's brain of his can't help but be curious, even when it is beyond obnoxious.

"This way, sir," the servant cut in, pausing to open a small wooden door on the wall. It opened to a much smaller, less ornate hallway than any I had seen so far. It was so narrow we were forced to follow our guide in single file down the narrow passage.

I realized that we must be using the staffing tunnels when we burst through a pair of swinging doors and into a giant industrial kitchen. After spending so much time in the prim and proper world of the Fae, the hustle and commotion of the kitchen felt like suddenly being in the middle of Times Square in rush hour. Men and women shoved past us, carrying platters of ingredients to and from cooking stations. People yelled at each other, calling for ingredients and cooking implements. It was a very human space, I realized, looking around. A corner of mortality hidden away in our elder's house.

Apart from a few Fae managers, as far as I could tell, all of the chefs toiling away, and their line cooks, were mortals. I paused for a moment to take in the chaotic scene, remembering my realization from teatime. They had human chefs for the same reason they wouldn't want my sister cooking for them.

"Cooking is art," I murmured, watching my fellow mortals toiling away.

"Bingo," Alex said, standing at my left shoulder. I glanced at him and was surprised to see a touch of anger on his usually amused face.

The Fae were obsessed with art, that was clear to anyone who had spent five minutes in Goldhall. I doubted they would be satisfied eating terrible food. I wondered how much better an egg scrambled by a mortal versus a Fae was. Did the ingredients matter? Could a Fae with perfect ingredients create something better than a mortal with the cheapest quality? Or was the rule something more foundational? I couldn't imagine not being able to make decent food. Scrambled eggs aren't hard. With enough butter and milk, even I can make them taste amazing.

But why suffer through your own miserable cooking when you could hire humans to do it instead? Looking around the kitchen, I was sure this was a collection of elite Michelin-starred chefs working in a different style of restaurant. Heck, I wouldn't have been shocked if you told me the Michelin Star program was a front for Fae kitchen recruitment.

"I wonder where they recruit and hire all these mortals to work in the Faerie Lands?" I mused to my friends, watching the kitchen move in an intricate dance like a delicious ballet. Both of my friends turned to look at me, their faces scrunched with concern.

"What?" I asked, looking between them.

"These mortals aren't *hired*," Alex said slowly.

"They are fools who made bad deals with Fae," Orion said in his harsh way.

A chill settled in my spine as I looked around the kitchen with new, clear-seeing eyes. I wasn't looking at hustling entrepreneurs bringing elegant cuisine to a new world. These weren't willing servants.

They were slaves.

Sympathy rolled through me like a tidal wave of grief. I hadn't made the deal that had taken my soul from me. Orion would call me less of a fool than the individuals in this room. But when Dan had approached me with his offer a year ago, I had been scraping along rock bottom. I knew better than to take a deal from a demon, but even at my lowest, I was better off than many. I wondered how many people in this room had fallen through greed and hubris, and how many had been pushed.

"Sir? It's this way." The servant who had been leading us gestured to another set of swinging doors across the kitchen. Wordlessly, my companions and I followed him. The tidal pools of the kitchen surged around us, but the workers ignored us, hustling to prepare for whatever Fae nobles awaited their meals. With a guilty twitch, I realized that often included me.

We followed the servant through the other doors and into another series of staff hallways, meandering our way through the secret passages of Goldhall like it was a giant anthill. I was thoroughly lost and beginning to wonder why we were being kept off the beaten path. The best reason I could come up with was the Queen did not want us to know where she was, or she did not want anyone to see us meeting with her. I wasn't sure either of those options sounded great for my current standing with the Dandelion Court.

Finally, we exited the staff corridors and reentered the main passages of Goldhall. It felt like we had made our way to a distant corner of the palace, one that wasn't as populated. There wasn't an obvious reason that it felt that way. The halls were just as clean and regal as the rest of the palace. But there was a deeper silence, an echoing emptiness that the other halls did not have. Somehow, I could feel in my bones that there was less life here.

Our guide led us to a large pair of closed doors and swung them open. He paused at the doorstep and motioned for us to enter. I followed Alex into what must have been an ancient ballroom, a large rectangular room with a smooth, polished floor. But whatever it had been, it was a storage locker now. Dozens of pieces of furniture crowded the room, covered in white sheets, like ghosts of when they had been among the living. I guess even the Fae had to deal with dust bunnies.

The center of the room was clear, like a miniature eye of a furniture storm, and we threaded our way toward it. Distantly, I heard the doors close behind us, sealing us into the mausoleum.

Slowly, I turned around the center of the room, taking in our surroundings. The ever-present light of Goldhall was dimmer here, as if they were conserving whatever magical power fueled it—souls, maybe. Our footsteps echoed on the floor as we walked. We were completely alone.

"What do you think she wants?" Alex asked, idly eyeing the furniture around us.

"This is weird, right?" I asked, ignoring Alex's question. "Like, why are we out in the boonies of Goldhall?"

"Can you blame her for not wanting to be seen in public with you?"

"She literally had a giant reception with me in front of the entire court."

"Matt's right," Orion intoned from somewhere off to my left. "Whatever is going on here, we were deliberately taken away from witnesses."

I let out an irritated sigh and began wandering out from the harbor in the center of the room, among the sea of stored furniture. Was this another demonstration of the waning sun of the Fae? I didn't need any more. I believed Gloriana.

"Frankly, I'm surprised we're in a room like this," Alex commented after a few minutes of idle inspection. "The Fae are so obsessed with appearances and forms that this feels a bit like seeing Goldhall naked."

"It is unusual," Orion mused. I could practically hear him rubbing his chin in thought.

I never got a chance to hear what his theory was. As I started to turn, my eyes caught a hint of motion under one of the sheets covering a table of some sort. My vision locked on to a pair of golden eyes in the gloom underneath the hem of the sheet.

They immediately snapped shut, vanishing. For a second, I stared at the pool of shadows under the furniture, trying to convince myself I had imagined those glowing orbs.

"Hey, guys?" I called out, still staring at the spot under the table. "I don't think we're alon—"

There was a jarring crash from somewhere behind me. My head whipped around to see a figure rising from beneath a sheet, the book-case they had been hiding next to toppling as they emerged. Tall and lean like a Faerie, they were encased entirely in black leather. They wore a golden masquerade mask that covered their whole face, like the ones mummers wear in plays. Not an inch of their skin was exposed.

In their hand, they held a rapier, which gleamed in the dim light.

I **GLANCED BACK AT** the table to see another, similarly dressed figure rising from beneath the cloth. They adjusted their mask as they stood.

"Sloppy," I commented dryly. All around the room, assassins popped out from where they had been hiding beneath dust covers like evil prairie dogs. My adrenaline surged, and I could feel my heart pick up the set of drumsticks necessary for battle tempo.

I looked over my shoulder toward the center of the room where I had last seen Orion and Alex. The first assailant took that as a cue. They leapt at me, rapier extended like a lance. A year ago, I would have died to that first strike. A year ago, I was a terrified boy playing with things he didn't understand. Now, I was a terrified man playing with things he understood even less. But fear was far more familiar now. It wasn't a friend, exactly, more like a coworker. Being afraid came with the territory. I was afraid when I spoke to evil scientists and made deals with queens. I had learned to channel my fear into action.

I dodged backward, making sure to keep my legs spread and stay on the balls of my feet. I cursed myself for not insisting on being allowed to carry a sword. My assailants didn't hesitate. They rushed me, rapiers whistling. I continued my dancing retreat, trying not to get sliced and diced like an onion.

A brilliant light cut through the dusky room. It was different than the warmth that came from Willow's light. Awful and terrifying, it was the light that devours, that consumes. Somewhere, Orion had drawn his blade. Fire calls to fire. I sent Willow the mental nudge to wake up, and my own hands burst into flames. Both assassins paused in the light, as if surprised.

Somewhere behind me, a voice screamed in pain. I felt no sympathy. We are not the hunted. We are the Hunt. Pride surged in me at the hesitation of my attackers. I delighted in their realization that I was not some poor mortal, easily killed. I was a Lord of Fire.

My left hand slashed diagonally across my body, sending a line of fire out of my hands like a whip, cracking at both of my enemies. They danced around my attack like graceful acrobats, lithe bodies twisting through complex choreography to keep them unburnt.

Okay, so they weren't easy pickings either.

I retreated another step back toward the middle and my friends, sending a pulse of flames at my attackers. They each leapt to a different side, splitting my vision. My flames slammed into a boxy piece of furniture, whose dust cloth immediately burst into cheery flames.

Tracking both of the assassins, I aimed a hand in each of their directions and sent lances of flame shooting at them. Effortlessly, they dodged and continued to circle me, like a pair of lions herding their prey.

I have already covered my opinion on being prey.

Since they were separated, I decided to take the initiative. I leapt to my right, over some sort of dresser or chest, and rushed toward one of my attackers. The leather-clothed figure surged to meet me, their performer's mask as still as death.

I had no sword to block with, so I had to strike before they got in stabbing range. I raised my left hand and had Willow send a burst of flame at their chest. They dodged with the same fluid grace, angling their body sideways and turning on one foot to let the blast go past.

That move made it very hard for them to dodge the second whip of flames that leapt from my right hand, which I swept diagonally across my body. The living flame bit into my attacker, its fire spreading quickly across their chest like a swarm of ants over a picnic. I heard a horrified scream as they dropped to the floor, beating at the flames with their gloved hands. Conscious of the assassin behind me, I continued my sprint toward my downed enemy and leapt over their burning body, trying to keep the distance I had created between us. As I passed over the burning Faerie, I sent another ball of fire at their downed form. The Hunt does not show mercy.

I dodged around a shrouded armoire and spun on my heel, fiery hands raised to catch my assailant in hot pursuit. For several eternal seconds, I waited, my breath coming in ragged gasps. I could hear fighting happening closer to the center of the room. At least one of my friends was still up and swinging. I could only hope they both were.

As I continued to wait, I got the bad feeling that my second attacker wasn't going to fall into my trap. Slowly, I lowered my hands and started to lean back around the armoire. As soon as my head came around the side, a throwing knife slammed into the dresser, inches from my head. I twitched back behind my cover with a curse. I wasn't due for a haircut for another week or two.

"Screw this," I said. I summoned Willow's flames and set the armoire I was hiding behind on fire. With a flicker of thought, I tossed fireballs at other pieces of furniture nearby. If the Queen wanted me dead, I might as well take some of her furniture with me, or if this was all a misunderstanding, I could apologize later.

"You want to play games?" I snarled as the inferno began to grow around us. I could feel the heat from the fires, but to me they felt warm and pleasant. I suspected that was not the case for people who weren't protected by the spirit of fire.

"Come out, you coward, and face a mortal Lord of Fire," I called, my voice mocking. Ash really shouldn't have told me about the fancy title. It had gone straight to my head.

Maybe my goading got under their skin, or maybe the fires burned too bright. The assassin stepped out from behind the piles of burning furniture, rapier extended, moving lightly. I gave them my best predator's smile, all teeth. The faceless mask stared back at me, implacable.

"Are we gonna waggle our eyebrows at each other all day, or do you want to dance?" At some point during this battle, I had gotten separated from my fear, and all that remained now was fiery anger. They wanted to kill me and my friends? Let them reap what they had sowed.

My assailant obliged me by blurring forward, blade extended to strike. They were fast, faster than any human could be.

But they were not the fastest. They weren't even faster than Rogan. Compared to Orion, they might as well have been running through a field of molasses.

I copied the move that the last masked attacker had used and slid to the side, twisting my body to dodge the thrust that shot toward me like a bullet. Unlike the burnt husk that had tried to murder me, I kept both of my feet on the ground. I did not forget my footwork. I could hear Orion's voice in my head yelling at me as I stepped through motions I had practiced a thousand times.

The blade shot past me as I dodged, whistling as its razor-sharp edge sliced the very atoms of the air. My would-be killer stepped into grappling range, golden eyes wide behind their mask. I reached out and placed my right hand on their chest.

"*Burn*," I ordered Willow, and the fire on my hands went from bright to incandescent. The last time I had called on my fire spirit with that kind of power, we had burned down a building. The Faerie assassin I was holding crisped like a potato in an air fryer.

With a snort of disgust, I pulled my flaming hand away and turned toward the center of the room and my friends, leaving my attacker crumbling behind me. The Hunt does not hesitate.

I raced toward the sound of battle, parkouring around a few pieces of ancient furniture that were not on fire and burst into the open center of the room.

I pulled up short, in awe of the scene unfolding before my eyes. Black-clad figures lay strewn around the room, broken, like they had tried to box a bear. At least five more were still in the ring, doing their best to survive against the terror that was Orion the Hunter.

I have seen Orion face down fallen angels. I have seen him duel Lilith, VP of Hell, without even drawing his blade. I have seen him battle ghouls and other creatures of the night. But I had apparently never seen him hold nothing back.

His fiery sword blazed in his right hand as he danced among the five rapier-wielding assassins, like a farmer harvesting his wheat. Orion swung the flaming blade up, slicing cleanly through one of the skinny rapiers as though it were made of wet newspaper. As the blade came down, he spun backward, lashing out with his left foot in a roundhouse kick that clobbered another attacker closing in behind him.

Not slowing, the Hunter sprinted at the reeling Fae he had kicked, shoulder-checking them as they tried to regain their balance. The lithe assassin went flying and slid on the polished floor like a hockey puck. The Hunter was already engaging his next target, blade flashing as he reduced another blade into a little nub with his magic sword.

This was the Constellation of the Hunter, and today he was hunting Fae once again. This was exactly what Gloriana had been afraid of.

I threw a fireball at the still-reeling hockey puck, who was safely out of the tornado that was Orion's battle dance. I was afraid to take a shot at anyone closer to him. He was so fast, I'd probably miss and end up with a singed Constellation.

"I hate to interrupt, but this isn't actually a spectator sport." Alex slid out of the dark furniture jungle to stand next to me. Concerned, I gave him a quick once-over. He looked fine, but his shirt was a little sliced up. We really didn't have the budget to keep replacing those. He carried a pair of rapiers that had more blood on them than his shirt did. He shot me a grim smile, an air of satisfaction radiating from him as he gave one of his blades a little swing.

"You sure about that?" I asked as we watched the Hunter do what he did best. The five attackers were down to three, and I saw more subtraction imminent in their future. More black-clad assassins trotted out of the darkness to join the circle, waiting for their turn at him.

"You had to ask," he said with a bitter laugh. He held out the rapier in his left hand to me.

"Yup, that's on me," I replied, taking the blade from him. We clinked our swords together in a grim sort of "cheers" and turned to the new wave of attackers.

"Come and face me, little Fae!" Alex roared, leaping toward them, blade raised. "There's enough of this runt to go around!"

I hate rapiers. They're my least-favorite type of sword. They're long and lean and don't do any of the things I think a sword should do. Rapiers are all about lightning-quick movement, perfect footwork, and patience. Attributes that would not be found on my character sheet in a tabletop game. They are precise scalpels for sophisticated duelists. I'm more of a back-alley brawler type.

A rapier won't cut someone's arm off. They are more like the sword equivalent of slicing someone with a piece of paper. You give your opponent a thousand little cuts until they bleed out of energy and let you stab them right through the heart, just to finally get it over with.

Alex and I joined Orion in the center, turning our backs to each other to form the final two wedges of the triangle of death. That's not what it's really called. I just thought that sounded cooler than calling it a "triangle."

Orion set our pace, stepping slowly to the left. I knew without looking that his steps were perfect and precise. I did my best to keep his tempo, as I had been trained. The result was our formation slowly spinning to keep its eye on the circle of enemies around us, like a prickly little cactus on a lazy Susan.

Step. Parry. Riposte. Step. Dodge. Slash. Step. Fireball. Slowly we turned, surrounded on all sides. Our discipline held against their assault like the cliffs against the waves. One by one they attacked and died, yet still the tide of attackers came on. There were at least a dozen enemies I could see. Who knew how many more lurked in the dim room, waiting for their turn at the Hunt? My arms were tired; they felt like lead. Every block, every slice took all my will to drive it. Even Willow's flames began to dim.

An inevitable feeling of dread began to creep into my heart. There were too many. None of them were more skilled than Orion, but they were more than human, and there were a lot of them. They would drown us eventually. Alex still raged at the Fae, but I could feel him slowing down next to me, both of our rhythms falling out of sync with Orion's indefatigable movements. All of us, even the Hunter, were bleeding from a number of small cuts, leaking precious energy out of holes in our bodies.

The crushing weight of the sea of enemies pushed down on us, threatening to tear our prickly little formation apart. This was it. I was going to the Bad Place, where You Know Who was waiting for me, rubbing his hands together in anticipation. Fear, my old coworker, came back from his lunch break. I didn't want to go there. This was not how my story should end, with me and my friends dying in some forgotten, lost place.

Orion threw back his head and let out a primal scream, more chilling than any wild animal. "I am the Hunter," he cried. "Come and greet the Reapers tonight. They walk in these halls!"

Needles ran down my spine as the hair on my arm began to rise. Orion's blazing sword dispatched two more assassins in a series of sizzling slices. A second wave of adrenaline coursed through my veins, and I tried to make the best out of it, slashing with renewed vigor. What was I talking about? We were *the Hunt*. We were the predators, not the prey. My rapier found its way under an assailant's guard and bit deeply into their chest. What does the lion care for the circling of the hyena? I could feel the pressure of our attackers begin to crumble under our renewed assault as they realized that it was they who were trapped in here with us.

A dozen more swings and there were only three assassins left standing—one for each of us. Although statistically speaking it was more like two for Orion and one for Alex and me. The three of them lined up across from us, and we stepped out of our triangle to meet them.

I felt cold. Was it from the blood loss or the fear? Had I gone into shock as Death's clammy hands wrapped me in a final embrace? I hate the cold. If eternal death was cold, I was going to be pissed. Although given the resort where my soul currently had its eternal reservation booked, maybe I should enjoy the cold while I could.

But it wasn't my body shutting down. I could see my breath in the air as I panted. I could see everyone's breath, I realized, looking around. This wasn't shock. This was something else.

A horrific cracking sound cut through the din of combat. A wave of frost swept across the floor as the temperature plummeted from cold to penguin paradise temperatures. I spread my legs, trying to keep my balance on the slippery floor. My shoes were not rated for winter, and I could feel them struggling for purchase.

"*Undi!*" Willow gasped in recognition.

One of our attackers was caught midstep and slipped. Another kept his balance but could not stop sliding. They skidded away from us on two feet like a first-time skier until they bounced off a piece of burning furniture. I couldn't help it, I laughed. Alex joined in, our cruel laughter mocking the clumsy fool who had tried to murder us. The third assassin turned and tried to run, but instead they flailed like a cartoon character on an oil slick. Another wave of ice swept over our feet, going from liquid to solid, locking us in place like the safety restraints of a roller coaster.

Mav, Lady of Winter, stalked into the circle, and she had golden eyes dancing with rage.

We stopped laughing.

My heart froze in my chest. If she was here to kill me, I didn't know how much fire I had left in me. She wore a formfitting suit of armor with ice-blue and black leather that was both stylish and practical. Her raven-black hair was tied tightly into a single braid that flowed over one of her shoulders. In her right hand, she held a naked sword made of a dark material that might have been obsidian. Instead of a straight edge, wicked teeth dotted the edge like barbs, hungry to rip and tear.

Mav looked around the room, a furious snarl on her face. I gathered what strength I had left, while trying to not fall on my face. If I was going to die, I was going to face it on my feet—hopefully.

"You dare strike against my mother?" she hissed, looking at our black-clad attackers.

No one responded. I barely managed to not choke in surprise. Mav hadn't ordered this attack herself? A few of the assassins shuffled to their feet nervously. I didn't move a muscle in case T-Rexes and Fae princesses both had vision that was attracted to movement. Maybe she hadn't noticed it was me they were trying to kill. Once she did, I was afraid she might change her mind and join them.

"Speak!" she cried. The room shook with the power of her command. Goldhall itself recognized the authority of the Lady of Winter. But the assassins were silent. No one dared answer her.

"Very well," she said after a frigid moment. "The penalty for treason is death." She rotated her obsidian blade through a twirl before settling into a traditional guard stance. "And judgment is upon you."

Where was the spoiled daughter who had demanded Mommy not make her date the bad man? That had given me a different impression of the Lady of Winter than the terrifying warrior who stood before me now.

Mav struck at the nearest assassin, her blade cutting deeply into him with a hunger that made me uncomfortable. The blade seemed to bite on its own, like a shark turned into a sword. The Fae let out a horrific scream and dropped to the floor, leaking everywhere.

No thank you. Absolutely not.

Mav moved on the next assassin with brutal efficiency, flashing across the ice like it was solid ground, blade slashing in vicious arcs. It was almost enough to make you feel bad for them.

Almost, but not quite.

I had no time for sympathy for my would-be killers. I was worried I might be next on the menu, and I was currently frozen to the floor. But I had a sneaking suspicion I might be able to do something about that.

"Willow?" I shouted in my head. *"You won't burn me, right?"*

"I would never!" their bright voice responded immediately. *"Well, unless you told me to do it, or it was a different me—"*

"Great, thanks!" I yelled, cutting the spirit off. I pointed my free hand at my feet and sent a stream of fire shooting straight down.

"Please don't burn. Please don't burn." I gasped.

The flames passed harmlessly over my feet and melted the thin layer of ice. Suddenly my shoes had friction again.

"I'm a geniu— Gaah!" I yelled, looking up just in time to dodge being skewered by the last assailant, gliding toward me like a curling rock with a sword. Their blade missed me, but my attacker couldn't stop on the frictionless floor and slid right into me, knocking me over. The force of their body slam threw me out of my patch of friction, and we both fell to the ground, sliding through the battlefield like an out-of-control Zamboni.

My golden-masked attacker and I wrestled on the icy ground as we slid. Our rapiers had gone flying in the collision, so we fought in the ancient way, with hands, legs, and teeth. I grabbed a fistful of something and sent a pulse of fire through my connection with Willow. My opponent screamed and tried to pull free. I didn't let go, sending more flames while I held them tight until they went limp.

Our slide ended as we bumped into some dumb dresser or something. Whatever it had been, it was a bonfire now. I pulled myself to my feet, scooping a discarded rapier up off the floor as I did.

In the center of the room, the last assassin fell under the obsidian blade of Mav. Then there was only absolute and terrible silence. The kind of silence that only follows a parent's furious outburst or a lover's quarrel. It was the silence of empty and broken things. Looking around the burning storage room, I saw at least a dozen bodies and knew there were almost as many more hidden behind pieces of furniture.

My eyes were pulled to the Lady of Winter, who stood in the middle of the room like an executioner. One by one, all three of the members of the Hunt turned to stare at her. Her authority pulled our attention like the sun's gravity holds the earth in its grasp.

But unlike the earth, the Hunt was not helpless against the thing that held its attention. I'm not sure who started it, but I found myself gliding over the ice with Alex, coming to hover behind Orion's shoulder as he stared at the Fae princess.

The big Nephilim was wound up tighter than usual, as if diamond could have a human form. His sword was still naked in his right hand, its fiery aura casting an even brighter light than the furniture pyres burning all around us.

His left hand was clenched in a fist.

"Well?" he roared, stalking toward the princess like an unchained tiger. "What are you waiting for, icy one?"

Mav eyed the three of us coolly for a moment, her eyes returning to a human gray. With glacial slowness, she returned her sword to its sheath on her belt, her eyes never leaving Orion's. Slowly, ever so slowly, she raised her two empty hands and presented them to us. Although she gestured in surrender, a slight sneer tugged at the corner of her mouth.

"The treaty hangs but by a thread," Orion whispered into the terrible silence.

I had a sudden bad thought. A familiar itch played up and down my spine. This felt too similar to the tune Lilith had us dancing to a year ago. Events were interconnected in ways I did not understand and were spiraling out of control.

The Queen had made one of my conditions of her helping me get my soul back the preservation of the treaty between the Fae and the Hunt. I looked around the room of broken Fae and realized with horror that their true target might already be dead.

Mav, icy executioner that she was, didn't blanch at his threat. "After centuries?" she whispered softly. Her cold, gray gaze turned to lock on me with a sudden intensity. I knew that look. I've seen it on parents and friends my whole life. It says *do something*, but so loudly that you feel your bones rattle.

"Hey, uh, Orion," I stage-whispered from his right side. "I think there might be a teeny tiny bit more going on here—"

"The Queen led us like lambs to the slaughter," Orion snarled, ignoring my input. His blood must have been boiling in his veins. I could feel rage pouring off him like an oppressive heat, melting some of the icy floor around us. Okay, maybe some of that was the fiery sword, who knows. "Gloriana, of all beings, should know better. The Stars do not so easily fall."

Which, if you think about it, is so badass.

"My mother upholds the treaty," Mav replied, a little too quickly.

"Then why did she send her seal to summon us to this forgotten room?" Orion took a half step forward and ripped one of the faceless golden masquerade masks off an assassin's body. "With Gilded Dancers waiting for us?"

I had not realized that these were famous assassins.

Mav had no answer for him.

"Where is your mother?" Orion growled, each word bitten off as they forced their way through clenched teeth.

"She is in session with her advisors. She cannot be seen."

"Are you denying me, Lady of Winter?" Orion's voice was as hard as granite, as cold as a blizzard's heart.

The Faerie princess was silent for a long moment. My heartbeat accelerated in anticipation of her answer. Her gray eyes measured each of us. I could only guess the political math she was running in her head. Whatever sum it worked out to, she didn't love. I didn't blame her. Adding Orion to any situation was like trying to divide by zero: it broke everything.

With a sigh, she stepped aside and gestured at the doors we had entered through. "See for yourself," she offered coldly.

TWENTY-ONE

MAV LED US at an aggressive trot through the back halls of Goldhall. The human slave who had brought us to the slaughterhouse was nowhere to be seen. That was probably the smartest thing he could have done. I doubted he had been in on the ambush itself, but I didn't know how rational Orion was right now. When he was in judgment mode, there were few powers on earth or in the Faerie Lands that could stop him from administering it.

As we stormed through the palace, I did a double-time march to catch up with Mav at the front. The icy princess gave me a sidelong glance as we swept along, her black cloak billowing behind her.

"Do you have a plan, Squire?" she asked out of the side of her mouth. I don't know why she bothered whispering. Orion's hearing could make a bat seem like it needed hearing aids.

"I'm working on it," I whispered back. Not for any pretense of secrecy, but it felt like it matched the mood. "But I'm missing a few pieces of the puzzle here."

I took her silence as an invitation to continue.

"How did you know to come rescue us?" I asked, turning to stare at her as she walked. She really was beautiful, despite her harsh demeanor. She reminded me of an Alaskan glacier, all sharp edges. Her mother's exquisite bone structure was visible around her eyes and cheeks. But I am a professional. I didn't let that observation distract me, not even a little.

"I am captain of my mother's personal guard," she replied coolly. "If someone dies in this palace, the wards report it to the guards immediately. If a lot of someones die in short succession, it comes to me directly." She glanced at me, as if remembering she was talking to an idiot. "A ward is a magical—"

"Yes, thank you, I've read a book before," I said with a sigh. "So we set off an alarm because we killed so many of the assassins that were trying to kill us?" I was a little impressed at the intensity of their security system. It must be very hard to be a professional assassin in a palace that literally set off an alarm when someone died.

"So many Reapers were detected in the palace, I was worried we were being invaded."

"Then why didn't you bring an army with you?"

"I did." She gave me a smug smile, full of teeth.

I thought about her savage grace and devouring obsidian blade and resisted the urge to shudder. She had a point. "New question," I said, trying to breeze past acknowledging how impressive I thought she was. "The Gilded Dancers, what are they?"

"Fae assassins," she replied with a shrug. "Very expensive."

"Well, I guess that's sort of a compliment if you think about it." I sighed. "I wouldn't want anyone to think they could kill us with cheap assassins. Why would your mother want us dead?" I asked, switching topics.

"She does not," Mav said with an emphatic snarl, some of her original anger toward me creeping across her face like frost on a windowpane.

"Wait a second," I said, my eyes narrowing. "I thought you weren't supposed to be able to lie?"

"We cannot lie, mortal." There was an exhausted tone to her voice, as if my questions were wearing her down.

"Then how could we receive a summons from the Queen if it wasn't from the Queen? Because she summoned me, and there were assassins waiting for us. That seems pretty cut and dry from where I'm sitting."

Mav turned and stared at me for a moment as though I was the biggest idiot she had ever met. To be fair, if she had spent most of her life hunkered down in Goldhall, that wouldn't be a difficult title to claim. That's a very small sample size.

"Did you actually hear one of *my* kind tell you that the Queen summoned you?" she asked.

A whole bunch of things clicked into place for me rapid fire. The human slaves weren't only kept because they could cook real food. They could do something far more valuable than sous vide a steak to perfection. They could *lie*. A human had brought us a piece of paper—that had been the trap. No Fae had actually spoken those words out loud to us.

"Can you order a mortal to lie for you?" I asked with narrow eyes.

"Not directly." She shrugged, turning back to focus on the hallway she was leading us through. "I cannot tell you that three plus three equals seven. I could not write it down either. But I could commission a servant to write it on a random piece of paper for me as a piece of *art*."

"So, anyone could have gotten their hands on the royal seal and told a mortal servant what to write on a note accompanying it?" Another layer of the Faerie game clicked for me. I wondered how many of the mortals amongst the chefs and artists had experience as forgers. "That's a pretty significant loophole."

Something like a pleased predator's smile flashed across her face for a moment. It was the same kind of smile that a boxer gets after an opponent tells them they have a killer right hook. A tight, self-satisfied grin that said *I know.*

"It tends to be wise to be skeptical of information sent via writing in the Faerie Lands," Mav said.

I remembered Robin's frown as he looked at our summons, and a slow chill settled over me. I trusted Robin. Well, I thought I did. He had helped me out of more than one bind, but he had also *owed* me. Debts were more serious to the Fae than taxes were to the IRS. He didn't owe me any longer, and he had looked at the summons and said nothing.

"So we don't even know for certain that was your mother's seal," I said, thinking out loud. "I imagine a seal could also be some sort of interpretive art made by some talented mortal?"

"Easily enough." Mav nodded. "Although forging the Queen's seal would be treason, and even the boldest of nobles would hesitate before crossing that line. My mother has never been hesitant to prune her garden."

Somehow, I didn't doubt that at all.

Well, crap. Someone was not as excited about my possibly joining the royal family as I would like. Had I embarrassed Rogan enough that he had hired these Gilded Dancers? A different dark thought whispered in my mind: Was it one of the Queen's own daughters? Maybe Mav wasn't the only princess who wanted nothing to do with me.

My gut told me it wasn't pragmatic Tania or fallen Ash. Tania wanted me alive as a get-out-of-jail-free spouse, and Ash wanted to rebuild her house. Neither of them gave me the feeling they hated me.

Dawn, on the other hand, I wasn't so sure about, plus I knew next to nothing of the politics of the larger court. I eyed Mav slightly out of the corner of my eye.

"There's always the chance," said the Lady of Winter, flashing me another toothy grin, like she knew exactly what mental math I had just completed, "that something else entirely is going on."

"I don't like the sound of that," Alex grumbled from behind me.

"It's Faerie politics. Nothing is ever actually about what it's about," the princess offered.

I glanced behind me at the storm cloud in human form that was Orion. The Constellation brooded behind us like the sweeping of a cold front, although the temperature drop felt more like the cold of an empty grave that swirled in his wake. He looked grim enough that I felt like we were lucky that he wasn't carrying his flaming sword in his hand. The Immortal-killing blade's hilt peeked over his right shoulder as he swept behind me, its ruby eye glistening in the bright lights of Goldhall with its own hunger.

Orion was a wrecking ball, able to smash through anything that stood in his way. But I have firsthand experience of that going wrong. The Queen's command for me to speak on behalf of the Fae echoed in my mind. I gave Mav a nod and dropped back a few steps to fall in line with my fearsome leader.

"Hey, big guy," I said in a low voice. "How are you feeling?"

Orion was silent for a moment, only the deliberate tread of his booted feet making any sound. Instinct told me to wait, so I did, trotting along as his unfairly long legs devoured the hallway floor with every step.

"The treaty is broken," he rumbled after a few moments.

"Is it?" I hissed back at him. "We don't know who ordered the attack on us. You storming the castle gates and shredding the treaty past any point of repair could be exactly what they want!"

"We have been wronged. We deserve vengeance," Orion said through gritted teeth. "We are *guests.*"

"I'm not suggesting that we just lie here and take it," I said. "But going off half-cocked is how we ended up with a dead Immortal last time. I know you're the Hunter, but sometimes it's okay to lie in wait for your prey a little, isn't it?"

Orion was silent for another long moment. I could practically hear him grinding his teeth in frustration. For as much as he is superhuman, he is also less than human. Being a Nephilim gives him great power, but also makes him inflexible about certain things. Having that much demon blood pumping through his veins meant his free will was hanging on by a thread. He could not be different any more than the stars could not come out at night. It was burned into his bones in a way that I could never understand.

"What do you propose?" he managed after some prolonged internal struggle.

"Be yourself." I shrugged. "Be angry. Demand judgment. But don't burn *everything* to the ground yet. If they offer to investigate, then make sure they're very motivated to find out who did it."

"You think this wasn't Gloriana?"

"She straight up told me that she didn't want you Hunting the Fae again. Faerie queens can't lie either, right?"

Orion grunted in assent.

"I also gave her my word that I would do my best to keep the peace."

The Hunter was silent for a time, chewing on my point.

"Very well," Orion said through a long exhale, like a volcano venting a blast of ash and steam before an eruption. "We will do this your way."

"Okay, good." I rubbed my hands together. "You scare the crap out of them, and then I'll talk them into fixing it."

"If you're good cop, and he's bad cop, which cop am I?" Alex asked from the other side.

"Uh, you can be handsome cop," I offered.

"Does handsome cop get any lines?"

"Yeah, you come up with a good zinger to open everything up."

"Are you making me come up with the opening line because I'm a writer?" Alex asked with a dramatic sigh.

"I always forget about your credentials," I said. "I just assumed you'll forget any lines I give you by the time we got there."

Alex's indignant reply was cut off as we turned a sharp corner and did something that almost never happened in Goldhall—we passed another group of travelers.

My new friend Rogan was leading a pack of laughing Fae. At the sight of us, he stopped dead, his face going pale. The rest of his entourage screeched to a halt around him, their momentum carrying them a few steps like a heavy train hitting the brakes. I saw the Lord of Earth's hands ball into fists at his side.

"Still alive, then?" He sneered at us while the audience watched.

There were probably a lot of things he could have said in that moment that would have shown his clique that he wasn't scared of the fiery mortal and his Nephilim friends. Unfortunately for Rogan, that was the one thing that he should *not* have said.

There was a blur of movement, and a black-and-blue streak slammed the lordling against the wall like a linebacker. Given what I have been shown of the Nothing, I don't know if there's a foundation under Goldhall, or if it's just floating in the void, but part of me fancied I felt the entire structure shake from the force of the blow. Horrified gasps emerged from Rogan's cronies as they realized what had happened.

Mav held Rogan against the wall, one hand clamped around his throat. The other slid down to wrap around the hilt of her obsidian blade, like a boa constricting around its prey.

"Did you have something to do with this?" she demanded, her voice ringing with fury.

Rogan let out a squeak that was reminiscent of a field mouse.

"Answer me!" the Lady of Winter demanded, drawing her terrifying blade.

"With what?" the pinned Faerie managed to gasp out through her viselike grip.

"Did you try to kill these guests of the Queen?" Mav asked, her voice a frozen wasteland. I could see how she was a terribly effective captain of the guard.

The room went still. If the temperature had been reduced to absolute zero, it could not have been more frozen. Every member of Rogan's retinue was staring at the exchange with their mouths hanging open. Even Rogan's eyes looked like they might pop out of his head, but that might have to do with how hard Mav was squeezing.

Rogan tried to speak, his mouth moving a few times, but no sound came out. I felt Orion's attention sharpen, zeroing in on the Lord of Earth's hesitation.

"Are you accusing me?" he managed to croak out after a few tries.

It was Mav's turn to twitch. Sensing her discomfort, the lord pressed his advantage, which only sounded slightly ridiculous wheezing through his constricted esophagus.

"Have I been called before the Iron Table? Am I compelled to bare my soul to you, Lady of Winter?"

Mav stared at him for a long moment, every muscle in her body tense. She was rigid like a hunting dog waiting for the order to kill. With a small sigh, she released her death grip on his neck. He slid down the wall like a slug, his golden eyes wide, as if he couldn't believe that had just happened.

"Not yet," the Lady of Winter replied, turning on her heel and storming away from him in a style that would make Orion proud. "But perhaps soon," she called over her shoulder as she led us down the hall.

I gave Rogan and his friends a little wave as we passed. The Lord of Earth glared at me from the carpet where he sat. After not dying, that was my second favorite thing that had happened today.

More than a little confused, I waited until we turned the corner before I dropped in step next to Alex. "What just happened?" I whispered.

"Mav accused Rogan of being behind the assassins," he replied.

"Yes, thanks, I got the part that was in normal English," I snapped back. "I mean the rest of it. The table thingy and the fact that he didn't answer her question?"

"The Iron Table is where Fae are brought to be judged," Orion answered calmly from a few paces ahead. His batlike hearing let him butt in.

"Is it a big iron table that burns any Faerie they put on it?" I asked, wincing in sympathy.

"Pretty much," the Hunter replied.

"So he basically told her to take him to court? But like way worse than our court? I feel like I'm still missing something."

"Forcing a being that can't lie to answer questions is... complex," Alex said. "There's a lot of vulnerability there that doesn't exist for the non-fibbing-impaired like us."

"You mean like white lies and stuff?"

"Exactly. They can't tell their Aunt Mildred her meatloaf is delicious and not too dry at all even when it's horrible, so they don't demand answers from each other. No Faerie can be compelled to answer a question unless they are on trial."

I blinked a couple times, processing the weird idea that Alex was explaining. I thought it made sense. If your species could only *not* answer a question or confess, I could see how they would take their Miranda Rights even more seriously than we did.

Mav had tried to demand a back-alley confession, and Rogan had told her to make it official and do it in front of a judge. That didn't mean that he was or wasn't guilty; it just meant we couldn't shake him until he told us the truth.

My education on the Fae justice system was interrupted by a pair of gorgeous double doors waiting ahead of us. Three Fae guards stood outside, dressed in full suits of armor, decorated with the white and gold of the Queen of All Fae. The center guard stepped up to intercept us as we drew near.

"Apologies, Your Highness," he said, bowing his head at Mav. "Your mother is in session with her high council and is not to be disturbed."

The Lady of Winter turned to us with a little shrug, her icy gray eyes daring.

Orion let out a growl that would make a Doberman proud and took a step forward. The guard took an instinctive step back, his hand falling to the hilt of his sword. His two companions moved forward to join him, which I thought was brave. Stupid, but brave. Each of their faces bore the haunted look of men resigned to die.

Orion drew his sword with a smooth flourish, and its bright flames danced on the walls of the hallway, casting long shadows for all of us.

"I think you'd better let the Hunter in," Mav murmured in a low voice that sent a thrill running down my spine.

Slowly, the guards parted, stark relief showing in their eyes that they did not have to stand between the wrathful Nephilim and their Queen.

"Showtime," Alex said.

In a burst of motion, Orion strode forward and wrenched the door open. I followed the princess and the Constellation into the room, trying to emotionally prepare myself to face down a queen.

The throne room was much emptier than it had been about a week ago when I had been paraded in like a circus animal. Gloriana was sitting on a tall wooden chair in front of the stairs that led up to her proper throne. On her right stood Tania, and on her left was good old Robin. His usual cheerful expression crashed to horror as his eyes flicked from Mav, to me, to Orion with his naked flaming sword.

A smattering of Fae lords and ladies stood behind her, or so I guessed from the fancy clothes and pointy ears. They all regarded us with varying degrees of shock as we burst into their closed council meeting.

But they were not alone.

TWENTY-TWO

A **SINGLE MAN FACED** the assembled Fae council, seated in a fancy wooden chair with his back to us. He turned, and I felt a punch in my gut as I realized I knew him. Zagan's black eyes took in our furious little troupe, and his obnoxious smirk spread across his face like a forest fire. My brain locked up in complete shock. "The Queen of All Fae having a secret meeting with the CFO of Hell" was not on my bingo card. Doubly so for having it while someone tried to kill me. Suspicion flared in me as I took in the room. Maybe I was completely wrong and the treaty *was* broken. Had the Queen agreed to assassinate me for Zagan?

For a moment, both sides of the room studied each other. There was an oppressive heaviness to the room that comes from jamming too many powerful people into too small of a space. It's like trying to shove a billion jellybeans into a mason jar. Maybe that's why the kings of England made their ballrooms so big. It was to spread out the tension, and definitely not to compensate for anything.

Alex decided that moment was primed for his zinger. "What the hell is going on here?" he demanded. I did my best not to sigh.

My friend's voice cut through the stillness of the room with all the grace of a boulder landing in a lake. Queen Gloriana rose to her feet, chin raised. Her features were no longer beautiful but terrible as wrath gathered on her face. Her baleful yellow eyes were fixed on me, searing me like two burning suns.

I definitely was not intimidated. Nope. Not in the slightest.

"You dare intrude?" she hissed. Behind her, the Fae nobles shouted their displeasure, like a medieval rapper's entourage. Robin, however, lowered a hand to the back of his liege's chair and bent over slightly. I didn't hear what he said to her; my ears aren't pointy enough to hear a butterfly's flutter or whatever the expression is. But his eyes were fixed on Orion's bared blade. I could guess what he drew Gloriana's attention to.

The Queen's eyes snapped to the Hunter, and the room fell into a second silence. Like most sequels, it was harder to bear.

"Delicious," murmured Zagan from his chair.

I decided to ignore him for the moment. I had bigger fish to fry. Well, actually, I wasn't sure which of them qualified as the biggest fish. I had a different fish to fry.

"What is the meaning of this?" Tania demanded. "Have you come to break the treaty at last, Hunter?"

"It is not I who has broken it!" Orion fumed. His anger was so palpable that I worried he had forgotten the plan. Acting was not one of the big guy's strong suits.

"Your Majesty, if I might—" Robin interjected.

"You may not." Gloriana's tone was absolute, as hard as the marble her throne was made of.

"Your Majesty," I said, "my friends and I received a note asking us to attend you. It bore your seal. But the servant led us to an abandoned room, where we were attacked by a swarm of golden assassins."

There was a metallic clatter as Alex tossed a bloody mask to the floor between us and the throne. I guess those writer instincts were good for something, because that was cold. The Queen froze in the Immortal way.

"If not for the intervention of the Lady of Winter, my companions and I would be dead in your own home." Only the Queen's eyes moved, snapping to look at her daughter, who stood to my left. Mav nodded slowly, her face impassive.

"Well, I think that's my cue," Zagan said. He slapped his hands on his knees and popped to his feet. "It sounds like you have a lot going on, Gloriana darling. It was lovely to see you. I think this audit will be quite fun. We can circle back and finalize details whenever you aren't so… busy." Zagan gave me a smug smile as he turned.

I had a half second to wonder if Zagan was allowed to address the Queen of All Fae so casually. Gloriana promptly sat down, deflating like an immortal whoopee cushion. Her golden eyes flickered between me and the demon.

"Yes, very well. Thank you, Zagan," she said stiffly.

"See you tomorrow," he said to me with a wink.

The CFO of Hell strolled out of Goldhall's throne room like he didn't have a care in the world, whistling a little tune to himself as he took his time. He knew we were watching him.

"What was *he* doing here?" Alex managed after we all collected ourselves.

"I gave my word to Squire Carver that I would lobby on behalf of his soul, did I not?" Gloriana drew herself out of her slump on her chair, the marble flowing firmly back in her spine. "How exactly did you think I would accomplish that?"

I definitely hadn't thought that hard about it.

"Where did this attack take place?" Tania demanded. "How do we know you are not lying?"

"It took place in the Fireheart Ballroom," Mav spoke, her voice brittle. "I saw it myself. I struck down our own kinsmen in the act."

Tania looked like she was about to protest her sister's testimony, but her mother raised a hand, silencing her. Gloriana was quiet for what felt like an eternity, her gaze flicking between the members of the Hunt, the shadow of some dark thought lurking in her eyes.

"Are you going to strike me down, Hunter?" the Queen asked, staring down the deadly Nephilim with his Immortal-killing blade. "Or will you listen to reason and pursue the peace that has existed between us for centuries?"

"Matthew believes you are not responsible," Orion growled, his voice rough with unrealized violence. He lowered his sword to his side, pointing it at the floor.

"You have my thanks for your faith, Squire Carver." The Queen turned to regard me with a surprised expression. Surprised that I had stood up to Orion? I found that a little insulting. Yes, he's a big scary warrior of myth and legend, but I'm not that much of a wimp. I was born missing the part of the brain that tells me when I should shut up and keep my mouth closed.

"I gave my word," I said. "I believed you when you told me that you wished to maintain the treaty between the Hunt and the Fae. I still believe that now."

"The treaty demands justice," Orion interrupted me, iron in his voice.

"And you shall have it." Gloriana rose and glared at Mav for a long moment, her gaze unreadable. She turned back to address us. "Before my throne, I acknowledge insult has been given by my people to the Hunt. I decree that those responsible be found and punished for their crimes against the peace.

"I swear by the marble of my home that those responsible have endangered their people and as such are named traitors. I vow by the gold of my crown that we shall not rest until justice is welcomed amongst us. I name the Lady of Summer my executor in this matter. Know that when she speaks, she speaks with my voice. Obey her as such or find yourself on the Iron Table next to those who have betrayed their people."

I wasn't sure what to make of Gloriana choosing Dawn over one of her other daughters. The Lady of Summer didn't strike me as the crack investigator type. I would have been happier if Ash or Tania or, hell, even Mav had been chosen. Mav might not want to date me, but she had been honest and fair and saved my life. That earns you a decent number of points in my book.

"Mother, I would be more than willing to—" Mav began.

"You have failed me enough today," the Queen cut her off with the voice of final judgment. "Your sister will clean up this mess."

I glanced at Tania, standing behind her mother's throne, her face as hard as the walls surrounding us. Mav looked as if she was barely holding back tears. Gloriana ignored both of her daughters' reactions, her golden eyes locked with Orion's black ones.

"I give you my oath, the word of Gloriana, Queen of All Fae, that we shall balance the scales between us, Hunter. So let it be ordered. So let it be done."

Orion held the silence for a long moment, like a headsman waiting to drop the axe. But as the tension and collective blood pressure of the room soared way past stroke levels, he simply nodded once and sheathed his sword in one fluid motion.

"I accept your oath and give you one of my own. Not even my

stars falling from the sky will spare you from the Hunt if you fail to right this wrong. I will tear down your throne and your halls and leave them a ruin. I am Orion. I swear this by my Constellation."

Sheesh. Even Zagan could learn a thing or two about threats from Orion. Somehow, Robin's face got even paler. I eyed the servant with a new sense of distrust; he certainly had the access to set up this trap.

Gloriana accepted Orion's pronouncement with a small nod, as if she expected nothing less. She raised her hands and clapped them once, golden rings flashing. "Go. Carry my will and orders to my daughter. Bring to justice those who would bring the terror of the Hunt back to our doors for their own greed."

A flurry of motion erupted behind her, as nobles dispersed in every direction like a startled flock of pigeons. I saw several servants flat-out sprinting to carry out their Queen's commands. In a matter of seconds, the room emptied out until only Tania and Robin remained with the Queen.

"Robin, you wished to say something earlier," the Queen said softly. "It was rude of me to not allow you to. Please forgive me."

I felt my eyebrows leap to the top of my forehead like a rocket breaking into the stratosphere. I didn't think queens were supposed to apologize to their servants, no matter how trusted they might be.

"It is forgotten, thank you, Your Majesty," Robin replied smoothly, bowing slightly as he did. His face showed no hint of being upset at being interrupted. "I only wished to say that I was present at Squire Carver's apartment when the summons for him arrived."

"You knew that the Queen was meeting with Zagan?" I asked. "Why didn't you warn us that the summons was fake?" I tried to keep my voice neutral, but I could hear the accusation creeping into my tone like mold.

"I knew that the Queen was occupied, yes," Robin said. "But that didn't mean she hadn't sent you that summons. For all I knew, she was moving you farther away from the audience for your own safety. Zagan hates you with the fury of his master, Matthew, and trust only goes so far with someone like him."

"The Fallen can be unpredictable," the Queen agreed with a small sigh.

"If I had even an inkling of a threat from our people toward you, I would never have let you go," Robin continued. "I swear upon my life and my fealty to Gloriana, Queen of All Fae."

Orion let out a quiet grunt that sounded satisfied. I squinted against a mild tension headache forming behind my eyes. I felt like a grandmother trying to put together a thousand-piece puzzle without the picture on the box. I didn't know where my corners were, and all I had were a few floating pieces that went somewhere in the middle.

An awkward silence began to grow between the two sides. If we had been friends visiting for dinner, I would have said we had long overstayed our welcome. The conversation topics were exhausted and so was our host's patience.

But we weren't friends. I don't care what Caesar said about the enemy of my enemy. That wasn't enough. Not after today, not by a long shot. I still had questions, and I wasn't leaving until they were answered.

"What did Zagan say about my contract?" I asked, looking at Gloriana.

"He claims that your deal with me is not final, so you are not yet my subject. Therefore, I have no right to petition on your behalf," she said with a small shrug. "He stalls for time, but he is not completely incorrect. However, he has agreed to allow an audit of your contract."

It was probably very American of me, but I couldn't help but prickle at the term "subject." George Washington must be spinning in his grave to see one of his metaphorical constituents willingly choosing to join a monarchy. I'm sure it wouldn't help his historic judgment that as far as I could tell, the Fae were kind of British in their origin. But even with all of my freedom, I had no good options. At this point, I'd drink as much tea as I needed to in order to get my soul back.

"So, when do we start?" I asked.

"Immediately." Gloriana stood, joining the rest of us in the room. "The audit tomorrow is but the first step. Once you are betrothed to one of my daughters, Zagan and his master will have no choice but to respect my claims on you and cooperate." Gloriana's voice was as hard as the iron she could not bear.

It all sounded so easy. All I had to do was pick a Faerie princess to marry. Tania gave me a knowing stare from behind her mother's shoulder. I knew what she wanted.

"The ball is a week away," the Queen said lightly, like the slow step of an assassin sneaking up on their target. "Have you chosen one of my daughters yet?"

Tania froze behind her mother. Her face was impassive, but I had gotten used to reading the Fae enough to recognize it as a mask. I was surprised to feel Mav stiffen next to me. I wasn't sure what she was worried about. She wasn't in the running. She had made it clear she would not participate in this supernatural dating show, and her mother had excused her.

This was a trap. It wasn't the biggest trap I had ever faced. Heck, it might not even be the biggest trap I had faced today. It hadn't even been an hour since assassins had tried to kill me! But it was still a probe, trying to get something from me when I was off-balance.

"Your daughters are without equal," I said, choosing my words with the precision of a neurosurgeon. "You ask me to choose between the sun, the moon, and the stars. How could any man make such a choice? I could spend an eternity and not be any closer to making a decision."

"Your wisdom does you credit, Squire Carver." Gloriana's lips widened into a surprised smile. "Yet even Sisyphus eventually completed his eternal task."

"I shall roll the boulder up the hill one final time," I said, surprised that my literature knowledge didn't fail me like I failed that ancient literature class. "But I beg your patience as I use every moment of my time."

Both Tania and Mav relaxed like pufferfish deflating after the shark swims away.

"You must forgive me," Gloriana replied smoothly. "Even a queen is still a mother. An agreement was made. You shall have the time you were promised. I would sooner press cold iron into my own heart than break my word."

"That's so metal," Alex said under his breath.

TWENTY-THREE

DESPITE THE QUEEN'S ironclad oaths to serve justice up like an appetizer for us, the cynical part of me hadn't missed that there was no deadline to the promise. When you live forever, you have plenty of time to make good on an open-ended promise without technically "breaking" it. I fully expected that there would be some paper shuffling, a few people pretending to work on it, and that would be the end of that.

I did not expect a personal visit from my least-favorite Faerie princess.

Dawn herself knocked on my door first thing the next morning. Alex was asleep, so I let her in. I didn't *need* a manservant to do things for me, I just thought it was funny. Dawn wore an outfit that seemed to fit Mav's aesthetic far more than her own. Black combat boots covered by black cargo pants with an equally dark top to match. Her blonde hair was pulled back into a ponytail, and she wore no makeup. I, on the other hand, was still in my bathrobe and hadn't had my coffee yet—and I needed my coffee.

"Good, you're up." Dawn let herself into my apartment, casually cruising past me without a second glance. "We've got a lot to talk about before things get wild today." She plopped into one of the chairs at my little table and waved for me to join her.

I groaned and tried to rub sleep's sand out of my eyes as I took my seat. Dawn was an even worse person than I had suspected. She was a morning person, my true mortal enemy. I'm convinced people who wake up early and bounce out of bed with their brains firing at full speed must have sold their soul to the Devil. It's the only explanation I am willing to accept.

"What are you doing here?" I grumbled.

"Saving the world, or something like that," Dawn replied in a crisp, businesslike tone. "An attempted assassination of a soon-to-be member of the royal family is a serious offense."

I realized I was staring at a stranger. Where was the obnoxious, mean Dawn? Gone were the fake smiles, the popular girl routine. Whoever this was sitting at my dining table was all business. Clearly there was more to Dawn than I had thought.

"You're looking into that?" I asked in surprise.

"No," Dawn corrected me, her blue eyes hard, "I am going to *handle* it."

I couldn't tell if this was another one of Dawn's games. Was she toying with me? "Why did your mother put you in charge of finding out who was behind this instead of Mav?"

"Mav is her blade." She said it slowly, as if she was trying to make sure I understood what it meant. "She excels at chopping her enemies into little bits. She's a lot like your Hunter. But I am much more suited to hunting those lurking in the shadows."

I blinked once or twice in surprise. I hadn't expected such a straightforward answer. Even if what Dawn was saying was true—and it had to be—she didn't like me.

"But why do you care? You're not exactly president of the Matthew Carver Fan Club."

"I care about the strength of my kingdom," she snapped. "I will not let it rot from the inside."

Ah. That made more sense to me. It wasn't for my benefit at all. I could work with that.

"Great. What do you need me to do?" I wasn't sure if I found her confidence reassuring or off-putting. It might have been a little attractive too—if it had been anyone other than Dawn. This was the woman who had thrown me out of two pool parties in a row. I didn't find her attractive. That would be stupid, very, *very* stupid, and I am only a little stupid—most of the time.

"I've reviewed the scene of the attack," Dawn said, pulling out a notebook and a nibbed pen. "And it is quite a mess. Your bond with Willow must be very strong if you were able to channel it so effectively."

"Uh, thank you?" Was that a compliment? It felt like a compliment, but I wasn't sure. Dawn would never compliment me. I was beginning to think I had never met the real Dawn before. Maybe the party girl was an act, camouflage as effective as any hunter's.

Dawn ignored my comment. "Did any of the Fae that attacked you demonstrate any prowess that would mark them as a lord or lady?"

"You mean, like, having a Willow, or whatever the earth equivalent's name was?" I asked.

"Yes, I mean a Faerie bonded to Gome or one of the other spirits, Sylph and Undi."

"No," I said, thinking back to the hectic battle. "The only other element I saw being used was when your sister froze the entire room."

"Tell me about Mav." Dawn leaned forward in her chair, like a panther preparing to strike. I felt one of my eyebrows twitch in surprise. Did she suspect the Lady of Winter was involved? Or did she hope she could catch her sister in something? Dawn said she was worried about rot inside the Fae kingdom, but she hadn't specified what that rot was.

"Mav was incredible. She swept in on this tidal wave of ice and wiped out the last of our attackers," I said, realizing that was true. "She also took initiative in questioning Rogan when he implied that he had been involved in the assassination attempt."

"This would be Rogan, the Lord of Earth who skulks around my younger sister?"

"That sounds like him," I confirmed.

"How did he imply this?"

"He said he was surprised that I was still alive, and when Mav questioned him, he refused to answer if he had been involved in the assassination attempt. He asked her if she was accusing him before the Iron Table, and she dropped it."

Dawn's face twitched in an irritated expression for a moment.

"I assume one of your friends explained what that meant?"

"My understanding is that you're not allowed to shake down a fellow Faerie for a confession on any old thing."

"You are correct. To call someone before the Iron Table is a most dire accusation. For someone to do it, they must put their own life on the line."

"I'm sorry, what?" I asked. This had not been in the briefing Alex had given me.

"Among our kind, lying mortal, if someone is forced to answer every question, they are fully exposed, more naked than the day they were born. If someone would see another Faerie laid bare before their peers, they must put their own safety on the line. If their accusations prove false or unfounded, they may find themselves on the Iron Table instead."

"So Mav backed down because Rogan was basically asking her to bet her life on it?" I asked. Dawn was way better at explaining the intricacies of the Faerie justice system than Alex had been.

"Exactly," Dawn agreed, with a curt nod. "But let's focus on the fight a little more. Did she say how she knew to come to your rescue?"

"She said that she was the captain of your mother's guard, and she had access to some sort of magical security system that detects if someone dies inside of Goldhall."

"Well, she certainly gave away a lot of information, didn't she?" Dawn said dryly, making a few notes in her book. "Did you see any beings other than Fae? Demons, Nephilim, or angels?"

"I don't think so." I shrugged. "They were all wearing masks, so I couldn't be sure."

"Tell me more about the summons you were sent."

I told her the full story, how a mortal man had come with a note and led us a long way through the halls. She asked me to describe the servant, and I did my best, although I was embarrassed to realize I couldn't remember him very well. I'd only been in Goldhall a few weeks, and already I wasn't paying attention to the staff like I should. The trappings of nobility apparently rub off on you quickly.

"You mentioned that Robin was present when you received the note?" There was a dangerous calm to her tone, like a placid lake teeming with alligators lurking just below the surface.

"Yes, but he gave his word in front of your mother that he did not know there was any threat behind the note."

Dawn grunted in what might have been mild annoyance. It must be very nice to conduct investigations amongst a species that could not lie. The eyewitness account of a Fae would count for a lot more than Joe Mortal on the streets of America.

"It's interesting that the ambush was set in the Fireheart Ballroom. Do you have any idea why you were taken there?"

"I don't even know what that means," I said. "What is a fireheart? What do you think it means?" I remembered Mav and Willow mentioning the term, but I hadn't attached any real importance to it.

"The Firehearts were an old Fae family, but they're long gone now. The last Lord of Fire was a Fireheart before he vanished."

"*Do you know anything about this?*" I asked Willow inside my head.

"*The return!*" the spirit cheered. Which wasn't a particularly helpful answer, but I guess it meant that Willow was a fan. I made a mental note to look into that situation when I had time. As the first Lord of Fire in over four hundred years, I should probably figure out what happened to my predecessor. Wouldn't want the same thing to happen to me. I just got here.

"Well, then I guess it's a start." Dawn sighed, starting to rise from the table.

"If I may," I said, interrupting her exit. "I have a question for you."

"This should be good," she said, a hint of the old Dawn's scorn creeping into her tone. But she sat back down and fixed her blue eyes on me in a flat gaze. "Well, out with it."

"Why you?" I asked.

Dawn looked at me for a long moment. She knew what I was asking. I didn't need to spell my question out for her.

"Someone has to care for this kingdom. The Dandelion Court is a shadow of what it once was. If nothing changes, I may well rule over a marble broom closet by the time I am queen. So why not me?" she fired back, tilting her head slightly to peer at me through her lashes.

I refused to be distracted, even if that showed off her good side. Who was I kidding? She was the daughter of a god and the Queen of All Fae. All her sides were good sides. I didn't know which god, but

I figure once you get the "g" in your title, you can make your cheek-bones as defined as you want them to be; otherwise, what's the point?

"I think," I said slowly, pulling on the thread of a plot that I was only just beginning to see, "I think that if one of your sisters is in charge of the guard, another sister might be in charge of information." The difference in Dawn's personality was beginning to make sense to me now. She was undercover. No one would ever suspect pool-party-throwing, reckless, cruel *Dawn* of being her mother's spook.

Come to think of it, Gloriana hadn't told me that either. She had ordered me to spy on her daughters to see why they were hanging out with demons but left out some key details. Did Dawn know what I was up to? Somehow, I doubted it. I got the sense the Queen was playing her cards very close to the chest on this one.

Dawn's right eyebrow quirked up in surprise. She raised her hands and gave me a quiet round of applause. Somehow, she managed to make it sound both authentic and sarcastic at the same time. "Well done," she mused. "Better than half of my sisters, no less."

"Your sisters don't know?" I asked in surprise. "How is that possible?"

"Oh, this will be very fun." Dawn laughed. "Who do you think is the eldest of the daughters of the Queen of All Fae?"

"Uhm," I said stupidly, suddenly afraid to answer. My mother taught me many things. I don't want to ever give the impression that she skimped on my education. But high up on the list is an entry that reads "never ask a lady her age." It sits right in between "give up your seat on the bus for pregnant ladies," and "always put the toilet seat down." I don't know why, but those rules are seared into my brain like a brand on cowhide.

"Come on, Matthew, don't be *boring*," Dawn teased. Her eyes danced with the first genuine light of amusement I had seen her direct at me. "Just when you were starting to be a little fun."

I did something rare for me. I took a moment to think. Immortality is a tricky thing when it comes to age. I realized now that I had assumed all the sisters were contemporaries. But as I thought about it, it was entirely possible that the sisters were born decades, or centuries, apart. They were siblings, but that did not mean that they overlapped in age.

If Mav was in charge of the Royal Guard, and Dawn was in charge of the spies, or whatever her title was, that made me think they were the two eldest. She had said two of her sisters did not know her secret. It would be odd for the person in charge of security to not know. It seemed to me that those two roles should be working together. Dawn had known Mav's role, so if Mav knew hers, that left two sisters in the dark. My guess was they were the younger two. That made sense, right?

"There's no way to tell," I said after a moment. "But if you are forcing me to guess, I would choose the Lady of Winter."

Dawn's smirk grew into an impressed smile, a quick beaming grin. "Well done, Squire." She nodded her head. "And what about me?"

"Second eldest," I guessed. "Your sisters don't know that you are your mother's spy master because you've been doing so since before they were born."

Dawn let out a surprised laugh, clapping her hands together once. She had a nice laugh—her real one. It was bold and rich, like a trumpet of joy. It could not have been more different than the scornful screech I had heard before.

"Very clever." She grinned. "How did you guess that Mav was the eldest?"

"Honestly, it was just a feeling." I shook my head, trying to figure out how I had known. "I think it was when your mother introduced us, and she stormed out of the room. That screamed 'firstborn' to me."

"My elder sister was here a long time before the rest of us came along. She's never quite adjusted to having to share Mother's love."

Dawn laughed again. Every time she did, I found I liked it a little more and hated her a little less. It was a shame the real Dawn hid behind a mask of cruelty and laziness. It had to be a lonely life. It reminded me of the mask I had to wear whenever I spent time with Connor and Violet. They knew a different Matt, a dead one.

"Why don't the Ladies of Spring and Autumn know?" I asked.

"Mother has terrible taste in males," Dawn said with a shrug. "Tania is the daughter of some mortal that she fell in love with, who only watches out for herself. As for the youngest... the Lady of *Fall* can't even care for her failing court. Neither of them has the pedigree to rule the Fae. Only I am truly worthy to reign after our mother."

I felt a flash of irritation at Dawn's use of the cruel nickname for Ash's court. Maybe it was because I'm the youngest and seeing the older siblings gang up on the youngest felt too familiar. Dawn gave me a smug smile, complete with a slight tweak of her eyebrow that made me wonder which Dawn was the mask.

That reminded me of another question that needed to be asked.

"What about the demon who has been hanging out at your pool?" I asked. As nice as Dawn was being to me, only an idiot would take a Fae at face value.

Dawn was silent for another moment. She tilted her head to the side and bit her lip as if trying to decide what to tell me. "I was trying to contain the demon," she said finally.

"What do you mean contain her?" I asked.

"I mean that someone dragging my impressionable younger sister to my home rather ruined that plan." There was a hint of the familiar glare in her blue eyes.

Oops. I winced slightly, remembering Tania walking off arm in arm with Sam the demon. Her name was Sam, for crying out loud. How much damage could a demon named Sam do? Demons with human names like Dan or Sam seemed to be the junior, less-competent ones. In my experience, the ones with the weird names like Lilith and Zagan were the ones to watch out for.

"Speaking of my sisters," Dawn said after a pause. "A word of free advice, mortal. Call it reparations for almost being murdered while bearing a Guest Visa."

I sat up straight at that.

"The idea of a twin flame is very romantic, I know. But remember that little boys who play with fire often end up burning themselves."

I didn't know what to say to that. Stunned, I stared at her for a moment with my mouth hanging open. It was obviously a warning against choosing Ash and the House of Autumn, but why? Dawn's blue eyes stared into mine with an amused glint before she pushed back in her chair and rose to her feet.

"I think that's enough court gossip for one day. I do have a traitor to hunt down, after all." She turned to go, then paused, glancing over her shoulder at me. "I almost hope you pick me," she said. "Tormenting you might be more fun than I thought." Something close to a genuine smile played across her lips.

Stunned into silence, I raised my hand in farewell, and the Lady of Summer left.

AFTER DAWN LEFT at the crack of, well, dawn, I had a few hours until I needed to be ready for the audit. I didn't know what to expect. My favorite part of *Law & Order* had always been the Law parts. I tended to tune out during the Order scenes.

I spent most of the time in the shower, practicing yelling things like "I object" and "order in the court." I didn't think either of those were my lines, but it couldn't hurt to be prepared. As a bonus, it kept me distracted from thinking too much.

I refused, absolutely *refused* to get my hopes up. How many times had hope been snatched away at the last moment by some trick pulled by a demon? At least several. I was committed to not getting ahead of myself today. My hopes and dreams would cross the street at the crosswalk when the light said "walk" and not a moment sooner.

It was a good thought, but I totally failed. By the time I got out of the shower I was so excited for the audit, it might as well have been Christmas. How could I not be? After all the flailing around, trying to find my way in the supernatural world, it felt like I had finally landed on my feet. The employees of Hell had been cleaning my clock, but today we had them in our sights. It was time for some retribution. My hopes were at an all-time high.

Sigh.

The worst part of making stupid decisions is being smart enough to know they are bad decisions, and then doing them anyway.

Robin collected the three of us and led us to a room that could have been a corporate conference room at any company. Not that I've been in any, but I've seen movies.

The brightly lit room had gold murals etched into its marble walls, with a thick yellow carpet covering the whole floor. A full-service buffet, piled high with fancy breads, cheeses, and fruits, that I now knew were all prepared by indentured human labor, ran along the far wall.

In the middle of it all sat a long wooden table. On one side sat my legal team, Robin in the center, with me at his left and the Queen on his right. My lawyer wore a business suit, tailored in the Queen's gold and white. Tania stood behind her mother's chair, while Orion hovered behind mine.

Glancing around at the august company I found myself in, I felt a little underdressed in my combat boots, dark jeans, and T-shirt. Nobody told me the audit dress code, okay?

Alex sat next to me, plopping a little book and pen on the table.

"Taking notes?" I asked, eyeing him.

"You never know," he replied with a shrug. "Something interesting might happen, even during an audit. Oh, hey, they have watermelon.

I'll be right back." Alex scampered toward the buffet tables.

Across from us sat the Hell legal team. Zagan loomed in the middle, wearing his preferred dark suit and arrogant smirk. Two demons sat on either side of him, dressed to match, minus the cocky swagger. With a start, I realized I recognized one of them. Sam the pool party demon sat at his right. She gave me an impish smile and a little wave as she saw recognition bloom in my eyes.

That was something to deal with later, I told myself. Today was the first real step in getting my soul back. I couldn't afford to trip because I was distracted.

"Let me do the talking," Robin murmured to me as everyone settled in. "Remember, anything said here will be on the record in front of witnesses."

"What does that mean?" I asked.

"It means if you say something stupid that gives the implication that you signed the contract or wanted to sign the contract, they will have proof of you saying it." His golden eyes searched mine to make sure I got the message.

Well, that was terrifying.

"I was definitely under the impression *they* were under the microscope today," I complained in a whisper.

"They are," Robin said with a smile, "but that doesn't mean they stop being demons."

"That checks out," I muttered darkly, glaring at Zagan and his legal team. The CFO gave me a cold smile in return, black eyes shining like a beetle.

"Don't worry, my friend," Robin said with a bright smile, a hint of his usual cheerfulness lurking under his professional exterior. "This is my arena, my dueling ring. Today is a day that we get you some answers."

"Enough stalling," Zagan growled from his side of the table. "Let's get this formality over with and stop wasting everyone's—"

Clank! Alex's plate rattled as it crashed down on the conference table, loaded with watermelon pieces. "Sorry, sorry," he said, grabbing a giant piece and popping it into his mouth.

"—time," Zagan finished with an irritated sigh.

"Very well," Robin replied. "In the presence of Her Majesty Gloriana Tanaquill, the Golden Flame, the Marble Hearted, Queen of All Fae, let this dandelion audit be called to order. I am Robin Goodfellow, counselor to the Queen, representing Matthew Carver, soon-to-be member of the royal family of Goldhall. Henceforth, let everything here spoken be on the record and witnessed by Immortals."

"On behalf of Hell Incorporated, I am Zagan, CFO, authorized representative of Lucifer, the Darkstar."

"The first item on our agenda is to assess the alleged signing of an infernal contract by Matthew Carver—" began Robin.

"Point of order," Zagan interjected dryly, "we have not agreed to discuss anything regarding the *signing* of the contract at this time. This is purely a courtesy to allow Matthew's new masters to review his contract before entering into any form of agreement with him. Think of it more like a buyer beware."

A nervous itch creeped up my neck at the demon's words. I hadn't thought of it from that angle. I had no idea what the contract actually said. What if we found some clause in there that made the Queen cancel her offer to have me join her court?

Robin was silent for a moment before smiling as if that was what he wanted to hear the whole time. "Excellent, let us then review the contract *in depth.* The Queen appreciates Hell's full candor in this situation and takes it as a gesture of good faith between our two nations."

Zagan's eyebrow twitched ever so slightly in annoyance. I glanced between him and Robin, trying to read their expressions. Had my lawyer already scored a point? By forcing Hell to define exactly what they would cover, maybe now he couldn't hide as much? I remembered Zagan sneering that most lawyers ended up in Hell's clutches. I think I saw why now—even the good ones were sneaky. To Zagan's right, I thought Sam rolled her eyes.

Zagan snapped a finger at the demon to his left, who picked up a briefcase from the floor and plopped it on their lap. The two clicks of the locks being opened sounded like gunshots throughout the room, the opening fire between these two supernatural nations.

The demon pulled out a black scroll that was worked with red lines pulsing like a heartbeat. In a flash of intuition, I held my fingers to my neck and checked my pulse. The tempo of its flashing matched *my* heartbeat. I suppressed a shudder. I guess that was one way to verify a signature. Zagan accepted the scroll and placed it on the table before passing it to Robin with a bored expression.

"This is the contract we have with your client," he said. "You may review it during this meeting."

"Will you provide us with a copy for our records?" Robin asked.

"Absolutely not," Zagan scoffed. "There are no copies of an infernal contract, only the original. You are free to measure his heartbeat to verify its legitimacy."

Robin nodded to one of the other Fae waiting behind us, a woman with dark hair and a permanent business scowl etched on her face. She produced a stethoscope that split halfway down the rubbery rope and ended with two heads instead of one. She inserted the ridiculous-looking device into her ears and placed one flat head on the contract. The other she placed on my chest.

The room waited with bated breath. I didn't know what would happen if my heartbeat didn't match the one on the scroll, but I imagined it wouldn't look great being on the record for the brimstone team. For a moment, I forgot to breathe, until the Faerie scolded me with a dark look. "Please breathe normally."

"Sorry," I muttered, feeling like an idiot. A few moments passed, measured in my deliberate breaths. Apparently satisfied, she stepped back, pulling the stethoscope out of her ears and nodding sharply.

"We agree that the heartbeat is a match," Robin said with a slight frown. I decided to not let that get to me. The contract not matching would have been too easy.

"Well." Zagan gestured lazily at the scroll on the table. "Have at it, then."

Robin scooped up the scroll and opened it. His golden eyes began blurring from side to side as he began to read at an impossible rate. It reminded me of the first time I met him, trapped in a cell in Lazarus's evil science lab, where he was speed-reading ancient mythologies to pass the time.

Curious, I tried to glance over his shoulder. Each word was hand-written—or maybe claw-written—in calligraphy and what looked like very archaic English. I saw a lot of "thees" and "thous" as the scroll blurred by at top speed. Just trying to process the words as they flew by made me feel dizzy, so I gave up.

Suddenly, Robin froze. His eyes, which had been blurring back and forth, paused, and he stopped scrolling his way through the contract. The room was silent in bloodthirsty anticipation. I leaned forward in my chair, not daring to breathe as Robin's eyes flicked up from the page to stare at Zagan. The CFO of Hell didn't react. He didn't even blink.

The scroll's magic lights pounded in time with my own racing heart. What had he found? How bad was it? Maybe I had been better off never looking for answers.

After a tense moment of staring between the two lead counsels, Robin resumed scanning through the rest of the scroll, which seemed longer than those eternal drugstore receipts. When he finished, he rolled it back up and placed it on the table in front of him.

My lawyer was silent for a moment, his usual smile gone, replaced by a stoic seriousness that I had never seen on his face before. Had he found something in the contract that was going to make the Fae toss me out like a used paper plate?

My nervousness did not go unnoticed. Zagan gave me a knowing look, glancing from the flickering scroll to me, his black eyes glimmering under an arched eyebrow. That was extra annoying. I didn't love having a visual representation of my nervousness on display for all the super predators in the room.

"If there's nothing else…?" Zagan said, starting to reach for the scroll. "I have some paint to watch dry."

I called it. I *knew* they did that in Hell.

Robin didn't respond to the CFO's question right away. Instead he paused, his head tilted to the side as if he was trying to process the metric ton of letters and words that he had just poured into his skull like a torrent of water gushing out of a fire hydrant.

"Well?" Zagan demanded after the silence began to grow heavy.

With a twitch, Robin snapped out of his thousand-yard stare and looked at the fallen angel with a look of mild surprise on his face. He held up a single finger to the delegation from Hell, and unrolled the scroll, reading it from the beginning with the same lightning speed.

Zagan flopped back into his chair with a dramatic sigh. "I didn't mean to rush you. Is it too complex for you, Faerie? I'm sure we can get someone to explain it to you."

Robin ignored him, his eyes still blurring as they moved across the page.

I tried not to let Zagan's snide remarks get under my skin. I had no reason to doubt Robin's ability as a lawyer. He had gotten me out of my issues with the mortal law just fine. Granted, that had relied more on some sort of hypnosis than actual legal work, but the Queen trusted him, and she had given me no reason to doubt her judgment.

Robin reached the end of the scroll again and absently set it down, a strange look passing across his face for a moment before it vanished behind a mask of neutrality. My panic grew as I saw his expression. What had he seen?

The edge of Robin's lip quirked in what might have been a challenging smile.

Without a word, my lawyer slid the glowing scroll across the table, returning it to Hell's custody. I could see my heart's furious beat in the blinking lights as Zagan slowly closed his fist around it. For once, the fallen angel didn't have an acerbic comment ready. A shadow of a frown grew at the corner of his mouth as he looked from my lawyer's face to the scroll and back again.

"Do you think you're clever, little Faerie?" Zagan asked in a low, dangerous voice.

What was he worried that Robin had seen?

"Thank you for your time," Robin said in a too-calm voice. "The Dandelion Court is most appreciative of Hell's cooperation—"

"Spare me," Zagan snapped, handing the scroll back to his demon aide who had the suitcase. His black eyes danced with fury as he stared at Robin. The shadows in the corners of the room seemed to warp, expanding like tendrils. The smudgy light I had seen above his head the day he tried to smash me into a Mattcake appeared like blinding sunlight on a cloudy day.

"Zagan! Control yourself." Gloriana's voice cracked like a whip, causing the demon to flinch. The crawling shadows abruptly retracted, and his greasy light vanished. "You are not a child," she hissed, rising to her feet. "You will control yourself in my kingdom or face the *consequences.*"

"My apologies, Your Majesty." Zagan bowed his head to the queen and held it down for several seconds. He seemed genuine in his apology, which surprised me. Maybe even fallen angels had to respect the Queen of All Fae in her home.

"Now, if there is nothing else," Gloriana said, her voice still tinged with a sharp edge as she looked at Robin, who shook his head. "Then we will adjourn this meeting between our two nations. Tell your master that I appreciate his candor."

"Rest assured, Your Majesty," Zagan said, his black eyes turning to lock on me, "I will tell him everything."

HEART RACING, I followed Robin out of the meeting room. I kept thinking about what else might be lurking in the contract.

I know you're supposed to read contracts before you sign them, but *I didn't sign it.* All I knew was the basic pitch: ten years of a good life in exchange for my soul. Some of the perks of the "good life" had been pretty obvious so far. I was a miraculous college graduate and my sister had come back from the dead. Even without seeing the fine print, I'm willing to give Hell the credit on those two.

"The Queen wants to meet with you," Robin told me, causing my stomach to plummet even further. "Alone." He glanced at Orion and Alex.

Orion frowned but said nothing. Fallen angels and the Hunter both have to respect a queen in her castle, I guess. I gave Alex a fist bump and let Robin whisk me away down a couple hallways to some cozy sitting room I had never seen before.

In the doorway, my friend paused, his golden eyes sparkling with a poorly contained fire. "Now the game really begins," he whispered to me, and then we were through the door before I could ask him any questions.

Gloriana was waiting, seated on a giant overstuffed white couch with gold trim. Tania, her ever-present shadow, stood at her side. Robin and I bowed, and the queen waved impatiently for us to sit in a pair of chairs that matched the couch.

"Well?" she demanded without preamble. "What did you find?"

"I have only seen one infernal contract before," Robin said slowly, "but I am convinced whoever wrote this one didn't know what they were doing. I suspect that the bumbling demon who forged Matthew's signature also made his own edits."

"He did say that he was giving me the deluxe edition because he felt bad," I remembered. "He might have gone off script."

"It's all over the place," Robin agreed. "I will need to think on it further, to make sure there are no traps that I missed, but it's far from ironclad."

"So you found good news?" I asked, not daring to hope.

A wicked smile spread across Robin's face as he looked at me. "I found a way to get your soul back, my friend," he gloated.

I stared at him, unable to comprehend the words coming out of his mouth.

"What do you mean you found a way to get it back?" I demanded.

"I don't suppose you've suddenly come into any large lump sums of cash in the last year?" Robin asked, his grin somehow still growing.

"I found twenty bucks in a pocket of my jeans that went through the wash."

"Then it sounds like you're still missing four million, nine hundred thousand, nine hundred and eighty dollars." My lawyer chuckled.

I blinked, trying to understand the impossible number I had just heard. "Did I win the lottery or something?"

"There's a stipulation in the contract that you are to be paid a yearly salary of five million dollars. If you do not receive it, then they would be in breach of the contract and required to release you."

"Oh, well done," Gloriana crowed, clapping her hands in delight.

I didn't know what to say. I stared at Robin for a moment, my mouth hanging open. Could it really be that simple?

"So just to make sure I understand," I said, when I could finally form a coherent sentence. "If they don't give me five million dollars by the time Dan signed the contract on my birthday, the contract is voided?"

"There would be a few steps after that." Robin grinned. "But yes, that is the basic explanation."

"So all I gotta do is hide for the next six days," I said, a giant grin of my own breaking out on my face, "and this is all over." This didn't feel real. It couldn't be that easy, could it? I never get to do things the easy way. One legal loophole and I would have my soul back.

"I'm not certain that Zagan even knows." Robin laughed, clapping me on the shoulder. "Dan the Demon may have made promises Hell does not know they need to keep."

"Then it is time for you to make your decision," Tania said curtly. "We have been true to our side of the bargain and helped you regain your soul. You must make your choice." Her brown eyes glowed with fury as she stared at me.

Dawn's words of warning about Tania echoed in my head.

"I am very appreciative of the help that has been given to me," I said slowly. I needed to be careful here. Oh, so very careful. "But the deal was I had until my birthday."

"You're stalling," Tania snarled. "Tell Mother you choose me now or—"

"Enough!" Gloriana cut her daughter off with an indignant glare. "A deal has been made, and it will be honored."

"Mother, don't let him take advantage of us—"

Gloriana raised a hand and snapped her finger once. It cracked like a gunshot, cutting her daughter off as effectively as an executioner's axe.

"Leave," the Queen said in a very low voice, like a junkyard dog's growl. It didn't need to be loud to be menacing. A thrill ran across my arms, making the little hairs stand on end.

Tania glared at her mother for a moment, and then at me. I did my best to meet her enraged stare with an emotionless one of my own. I could tell from the fury that washed across her face that I failed. The Lady of Spring stormed out of her mother's sitting room. The pressure in the room abated so quickly that my ears almost popped when she was gone.

Gloriana stared after her daughter for a long moment, her ageless, perfect face unreadable, eyes as hard as diamonds. That stony gaze swept from the door to me, pinning me in place.

"Rash and rude as my daughter is, she has a point," Gloriana said in a flat tone. "I have acted in good faith with you, Squire Carver. Have you been about my business? Tell me what you have found out."

I did my best not to gulp as the Queen stared down at me. I didn't know where exactly Gloriana sat on the power scales. Was the Queen of All Fae as mighty as a fallen angel like Zagan? I don't know. He sure got respectful any time she snapped at him. Orion also treated her with wary respect, so that was really all I needed to know. Sitting in her judgmental stare, I thought I knew how a moth felt right before it was pinned into a shadowbox—tiny and terrified.

I hoped what I had discovered would be enough to satisfy her. I wasn't entirely sure what quality of work I needed to turn in to get an A; there wasn't a syllabus for this class. I certainly didn't have good news. Hopefully she didn't decide to shoot the messenger. Parents get prickly when you criticize their children. I bet they get extra prickly when you implicate some of them in treason.

"I have personally witnessed several of your daughters meeting with the demon ambassador," I said, suddenly glad that Tania wasn't in the room anymore.

"What do you mean 'demon ambassador'?" the Queen interjected. "Demons don't have ambassadors. What would the point be?"

I paused, caught off guard. Using all the processing capabilities of the hamster wheel that powers my brain, I recalled very carefully what Sam had said to me. "Well, actually, the demon said that she liked to *think* of herself as an ambassador. I suppose that doesn't have to mean she actually *is* an ambassador."

"Which of my daughters has this demon spoken with?" the Queen asked me in a serious tone.

I hesitated for a moment, wondering if I should lie. My conversation with Dawn had turned my perspective upside down. Yesterday I would have been more than happy to send the Lady of Summer up the river, but I wasn't confident that I understood the game I was playing anymore. The rules were made up, they changed by the day, and no matter what I did, I never seemed to have the right pieces. But the Queen had been faithful to our agreement. I decided I owed her the same in return.

"She has been a guest at Dawn's pool parties," I said, "but she seemed eager to meet with Tania as well. They left together and alone."

The Queen's silence was so absolute that I thought I could hear an echo of Tania's outburst still reverberating in the silence. Gloriana did not move for a dreadful moment. Her golden eyes seemed to be peering into my very soul—assuming it was still there. I'm a little unclear on where exactly it was being stored during this phase of the deal.

"Do you know this demon's name?" Robin asked.

"She told me it was Sam." I shrugged.

"I don't know of any demons named Sam," Gloriana snapped, a frustrated look creeping onto her face. It was eating at her, I realized. How devastating it must be to fear that your children have turned on you. For a moment, she reminded me of a majestic cliff by the sea, being slowly carved away by the ocean below.

"She was at the audit," I said, trying to be helpful. "Sitting right next to Zagan."

"You don't mean Samael…" Robin said, his voice full of horror.

"Pale skin, black hair, looked super bored the whole time?"

"SAMAEL?" the Queen shrieked. She leapt to her feet in a fury. Her hands were clenched into fists at her side. The chandeliers in the center of the room exploded in a shower of crystal and glass. Robin and I both leapt to our feet, backing out of range of the clear shrapnel that was raining down from above us.

"The Poisoned One has been wandering unchecked in my kingdom, consorting with my daughters?" she raged, her fury a physical force that pushed me back another step. "Why was I not told?" Her furious gaze leapt between Robin and me, eyes molten like lava from an erupting volcano.

"Dawn told me that she was trying to isolate Sam from the rest of her sisters," I continued, trying to be honest. "She hoped to prevent the demon from speaking with the rest of her sisters. But she was not able to." I decided not to mention that might have partially been my fault. I wasn't on trial here. Well, I wasn't on trial for consorting with demons, anyway.

"There is no containing the Seducer," the Queen hissed. "You might as well try to hold a shadow."

"Then her presence seems like something your daughters should have brought up," I said quietly.

That seemed to deflate Gloriana's rage. She collapsed back onto her couch with a sigh. It seemed that Dawn hadn't been completely honest with me. Now that I knew the cunning that lurked beneath the veneer of her party-girl nature, there was no way I would believe that she didn't know who Sam—Samael—was. Why had she kept the demon's presence a secret from her mother? The same went for Tania. I was very glad this was coming to light before I had decided to marry one of them. For some reason, I doubted that anyone who hung out with demons would be interested in helping me get my soul back. Not to make it all about me, but you know, a little about me.

"I have not seen the Lady of Autumn or the Lady of Winter speaking with Samael, but I cannot be everywhere at once," I said, trying to make sure I was honest as I pointed fingers.

"We must be very careful." The Queen steepled her long-fingered hands in front of her nose, deep in thought. "We are in the eye of the storm now. The waves will get taller from here on out. But there is a path if we are brave and skilled enough to sail it."

I didn't love the sound of that. The waves felt plenty tall to me already. I had no desire to see them get even bigger.

"Three things we must do," she said. "Hide you from the demons until their contract has been violated, rekindle the flame of the fire spirit, and tie our bloodlines together."

"What was that second one?" I asked. That sounded new to me.

"It is no matter." She brushed it aside with a wave. "You began that the moment you took your Willow from the minotaur."

I've been paying attention, so I had a guess. I was the first Lord of Fire in four hundred years. It didn't take a genius to figure out that "rekindling the flame" meant triggering new Lords of Fire to rise amongst the Fae. It seemed that I was some sort of catalyst that I didn't fully understand.

"*Do you know what I did?*" I asked Willow, thinking in its direction.

"You freed us," the spirit's soft voice said. *"We can spread again."* A vision of a wildfire consuming a forest danced in my head. I suppressed a shiver at the thought. Willow was my friend, or at least my friendly parasite. They gave me access to power that had saved my life many times, but it was also a living fire, and an unchecked fire is more dangerous than any wild beast.

The Queen stood, gathering Robin and me in her wake. "Matthew, you will be moved to new, safer quarters from now until your birthday. We must keep Zagan away from you."

I nodded emphatically. There would be no arguments from Team Matt. I wanted my soul back. I didn't care how long I might have to hide in a broom closet to get it. If Ash and her sisters could live their entire lives locked away in Goldhall, I could handle six days.

"Robin, it is time that the delegation from Hell leaves. The ending of Matthew's audit gives us a reason to send them home. Make sure he takes *all* his kin with him."

"He'll be furious." I snickered.

Gloriana shot me a vicious little smile. For a moment, it felt like we were bonding over hating the same sports team. I wondered what Hell had done to the Queen of All Fae that she was willing to spite them for little old me. Then I remembered that her kingdom had been reduced to a mansion floating in an empty abyss. That might be the answer to my question.

The Queen gave me a long, ponderous look. "You have done well, Matthew. I am pleased to have you become a member of my house. I will not forget your honesty to me on this day." A small, tired smile lit up her face for a moment before it was gone, like a match lit on a windy day. "It's nice to have a Lord of Fire among my court once again."

The Queen of All Fae swept out of the room, leaving the two of us in the wreckage of shattered glass.

"Well done," Robin agreed, turning to follow in the queen's footsteps.

"I have a question," I said, stopping him in his tracks. "If the contract is breached or whatever, and I get out of it, does it say what happens to my sister?"

Robin gave me a small, sad frown. "In this case, the contract would essentially be annulled, allowing both parties the right to reclaim their original assets."

"So, my asset would be my soul, and Hell's would be my sister?"

"I'm sorry," Robin said softly, "but she was already dead. There's not much that can be done about that."

I nodded, and the Faerie lawyer clapped me on the shoulder once before leaving me to my grief. It seemed that all I had to do to get my soul back was kill my sister all over again.

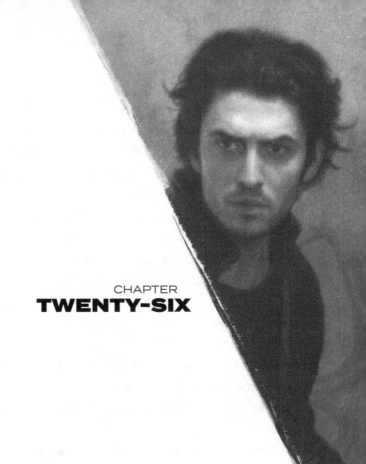

TRUE TO HER word, the Queen had me moved to a new apartment inside of Goldhall. For some reason, when she said I would be going to a safer location, I thought that meant we would be roughing it. In my mind, a safe house is a run-down shack hidden in a bad part of town, with boarded-up windows and ancient appliances. That might be how the CIA does things, but the Fae don't let a little thing like hiding from demons interfere with their luxury.

According to Robin, Zagan and his entourage had been success-fully hustled out of the Faerie Lands, but this close to the finish line, it was better to be safe than sorry. For the better part of a week, we had camped out in this cavernously empty Fae mansion like a trio of squatters sneaking into some billionaire's vacation home.

These new quarters were so much nicer than my original apartment that it kind of hurt my feelings a little. Instead of a three-bedroom apartment reminiscent of how the upper crust of Manhattan lived, our new residence looked like something from the heart of Beverly Hills. My bedroom alone had more square feet than our last place. The members of the Hunt were now living like kings. I was going to get my soul back while relaxing in first class.

Despite the luxury, a shadow of guilt hung over me as I counted the hours down until my sister's life would be reclaimed by my enemies downstairs.

"You know, when you first told us the plan to get your soul back, I was skeptical," Alex remarked as we lounged next to our indoor pool—that's right, we had a pool now. He took a crunchy bite from a giant red apple and plowed on with his sentence. "But I could get used to this."

Orion snorted in derision from where he perched on the edge of a reclining chair. Unlike us, he was fully dressed, from leather jacket down to combat boots. If Superman's ultimate weakness was kryptonite, I'd have to guess that Orion's is relaxonite. The rigid Nephilim avoided it like the plague. Even alone in our mansion, his black eyes never stopped scouring the room for hidden assailants. "A gilded cage is still a cage," he muttered. "Just ask the princesses."

I felt my mouth sour a little as I digested his point. The novelty of staying in a home that my entire family could not afford to rent for a single night would fade. If I had gotten used to being chased by demons and making deals with Fae, then I could absolutely get bored of this.

"It's only for two more days," I said, helping myself to a peach from the tray Alex had raided. "Tomorrow is my birthday, and we can get out of here."

My promise sounded weak to my own ears. It hadn't occurred to me that I might not be allowed to leave once I was a member of the Queen's family. Some of her daughters had literally never even left Goldhall's marble corridors. Why should I be any different? Would I get my soul back but be trapped in this marble prison for the rest of my days?

Suddenly the thick walls felt malicious, impenetrable. There would be no digging through them Shawshank style, with forks and spoons carving out a hole behind one of the giant paintings hanging in the living room.

Well, I thought as I took a bite of the peach, at least this prison wasn't on fire, that was a definite step up. If I had to be in a prison for the rest of my days, I would still choose this one over the downstairs option every time.

But even if I was not allowed to leave, I was sure the Queen wouldn't dare try to contain the Hunter against his will. No matter what, my friends would have to leave; we couldn't keep the sleepover going forever. The Hunt was the first place I had felt like I had belonged since my mother and sisters died. It was my job, my purpose, but also my home. I didn't want to lose that.

"Speaking of the princesses," Alex said, interrupting my introspection, "who do you think you're going to choose?"

"That's really the five-million-dollar question, isn't it?" I groaned, leaning back in my chair. Never mind that I was hiding from the Devil and his cronies while trying to sniff out a demonic conspiracy infiltrating the Dandelion Court, I was supposed to pick a relative stranger to marry. I'd never missed being a deadbeat loser more than right then. I used to be able to take naps.

"You should choose none of them. We should leave," Orion grumbled. I was well aware of my mentor's opinion on this plan. But it's easy enough to shoot holes in plans without proposing better ones.

"Look, in a few weeks, they've already made more progress in getting my soul back than we have in an entire year." I glowered at the big Nephilim. "We're on the clock here. If I don't take their help, who is left? It's not like there's a line of applicants waiting to take their place."

Orion simmered in frustrated silence for a moment. "You shouldn't trust them," he growled. "They are Fae. Lying by omission comes as naturally to them as swimming comes to a fish."

"Oh, they're keeping something from us," I agreed without any hesitation. "Mav is a no go. Tania has tried to bully me into marrying her the entire time. Her offer is that we get married and then leave each other alone. I would be free to do whatever I wanted, as long as I fulfill my obligation to her house."

"Honestly, not bad," Alex said through another mouthful of apple. Orion grunted in irritation.

"I don't know." I sighed. "There's something about her that makes me… itchy. She feels desperate and I don't like that."

"Someone get me a mirror!" Alex shouted down the hallway toward the rest of the house. There were no servants in our quarters. That would sort of defeat the purpose of a safe house. Which was fine. I didn't actually need a mirror to see his point. Tania wasn't the only desperate person in this equation.

"Then there's Dawn," I continued, refusing to rise to Alex's barb.

Alex made a rude noise.

"Yeah, yeah, I know. But there's more to her than meets the eye," I replied, thinking about our private meeting. When no one else was around, Dawn was a completely different person. Unless that was the fake Dawn, and the real one was who she was in public.

Somehow I doubted that.

What was it she said to me? Tormenting me for the rest of my life might be more fun than she thought? "Dawn is playing a different game. She wants to rule, and I think she sees me as a step to the throne."

Alex pretended to choke on his apple. I ignored him. I knew

it sounded ridiculous. It *was* ridiculous. But I was the first Lord of Fire in four hundred years. I had no idea why that was the case, but it meant something to the royals. For all I knew, marrying me really was a step to the throne.

"That leaves Ash," I said softly.

My companions were silent. Ash was a mystery to me. Well, no, that wasn't entirely accurate. She was pleasant and nice. Unlike her sisters, she didn't try to coerce me into a deal or treat me like a chess piece. It was her lack of manipulation that made her confusing.

She asked me about my life and my thoughts and treated me like a person, despite having the most to lose if I married another one of her sisters. The Autumn House was the traditional home of the Path of Fire. If the only Lord of Fire in a generation married into another house, hers might collapse. Plus, she had the prettiest eyes. But that didn't have any weight in my decision-making.

It didn't.

Seriously.

None.

Three bad choices, each one worse in their own way. There were no good options, but there was one that was inherently worse than the rest. One of the sisters had to be behind the assassination attempt on us. I had a one-in-four chance of marrying myself to the mastermind who tried to whack me and my friends. The same sister that was probably under the influence of the very demons whose thumb I was trying to get out from under. Marrying the wrong sister would be like a fish jumping out of the ocean directly into an open cooler on a fishing boat. I might as well shove a hook in my mouth and call it good.

Both Tania and Dawn had been talking to the demons. Dawn claimed that she had been trying to keep the demons from getting access to her sisters, but who knew what dark truths she might be holding back? From that angle, it meant Ash would be the safest bet.

But Ash ruled over the weakest court. Did she have enough power to stand up to Hell and help me get my soul back?

Dawn was cruel and cunning enough to go toe to toe with Zagan. She had power and wanted more. She could help me—unless she was the one trying to kill me. Or was Tania desperate enough for freedom to sell me to the demons?

I sighed. Who let this get this complicated?

"Life's tough when you have to pick your actual poison, huh?" Alex asked. "Oh no, which beautiful psychopath will I marry and live in miserable luxury with for the rest of my days?"

"I can't tell if you're trying to cheer me up or make me feel stupid."

"A little bit of both." He shrugged, leaning forward to sift through the remaining food in the charcuterie board that Robin had dropped off a few hours ago. In an effort to keep as few people as possible from knowing where we were hiding, the Faerie lawyer had been personally delivering our meals.

"Well, only one of them is working."

"In the end, it is your choice, Matthew," Orion said, rising to his feet. "None of us can stop you from making this decision. Nor can we make this choice for you. All we can do is stand with you when the chips fall."

With that, my two friends left me alone to think and try to make a choice.

I don't know what sound chips make as they are falling. For that matter, I wasn't exactly sure what the chips were made of or where they were falling from.

I didn't expect them to sound like unlocking doors and soft footsteps.

It was late. I was alone in one of the lavish sitting rooms—or was it a den? I don't know. To me it was a thinking room. I had been pacing across its plush carpet for an hour, wearing a circle in the threads of the carpet and in my own arguments. The old-school clock tick-tocked away, chipping at what little time I had left to make a decision with the patient swing of a miner cutting through stone.

Faintly, I heard a dull click sound from the hallway. I turned in surprise. Robin had already made his food delivery for the evening. He didn't usually return until the morning. Glad for any excuse to stop dwelling on my impossible decision, I walked out to greet him.

Instead of Robin, I found myself facing five strangers who froze at the sight of me. My first thought was to panic. Had the demons found me? Despair rolled through my body like a wave. I had been so close!

Belatedly, I realized the five figures were dressed in the same black formfitting outfits and golden masks that the assassins who had ambushed us before wore. Each of them carried a pair of wicked-looking knives.

"Oh, thank goodness," I breathed to the frozen group of invaders. "Sorry, for a second I thought you guys were here to give me five million dollars."

"Extinguish the Flame!" one of them cried and hurled a knife at me that howled as it sliced through the air like a deadly frisbee. I dropped into a crouch, letting the blade sail over my right shoulder. All of them leapt into action, rushing toward me.

"Orion!" I bellowed—or tried to. As I screamed, the air around me distorted and warped. I heard my own cry distantly, as if I were standing at the end of a distant tunnel as my ears popped, like when you abruptly change elevations. Mentally, I gave Willow the nudge to awaken. My hands whooshed with the familiar burst of fire, and I flung my power with my right hand in a contemptuous gesture at the leading Fae assassin.

Instead of fleeing, the assassin raised her hand, a wave of frigid cold sharpening in the room like the edge of a winter wind. Something dark and frozen sliced through my fireball. The flame evaporated in a burst of steam that gave off a muted sizzle.

A chill settled over my heart. I had bested a Lord of Earth in combat once, but if we were being fair, I had caught him off guard with my powers. I had never fought against a member of the Water nobility before. I had seen Mav wield her powers to devastating effect, but that didn't give me any ideas on how to fight someone whose powers so directly countered my own. Maybe I had found my own kryptonite. Plus, unless I missed my guess, a Lord of Air was stopping the sound from traveling, preventing my warning cries from reaching my friends. That was just obnoxiously useful for an assassin.

If I couldn't scream like a damsel in distress, I would have to go get my friends myself. There was no shame in a tactical retreat; if you are outgunned, outmanned, and unable to get reinforcements, prudence demands that a smart general live to fight another day.

I turned to sprint toward the bedrooms, but the marble floor flowed like water, a stone wave swamping my feet before turning solid and locking me in place. Holy crap, they brought the whole circus. Whoever wanted me dead was throwing the entire kitchen sink of Fae magic at me in one attack.

"*What do we do?*" I shouted mentally at Willow, hoping the Lord of Air couldn't block my brain waves as effectively as he was blocking the sound waves.

"*Don't let them put me out, don't let them put me out, don't let them put me out,*" Willow sent back, their voice brimming with panic. "*Burn them all. BURN THEM ALL.*"

The color of Willow's fire around my hands shifted from a bright orange to a merciless white hot. Even I recoiled a little from the heat powered by the spirit's fear. The assassins paused in their advance, the blinding light of my fiery hands dancing in the reflection of their gold masks.

"I hope you know how to extinguish yourselves," I snarled, hurling a ball of flame at the leading Fae. Again, the Lady of Water cracked her icy whip, and my fireball sizzled in complaint, but this time, the fire did not go out and screamed toward my enemies. The assassins did a passable impression of a set of bowling pins and scattered before the ball hit any of them, but I was willing to call it a strike.

Trusting the fire spirit that was riding along with me, I slashed my left hand down at my feet. The white-hot flames boiled the marble, allowing me to pull my feet free from the gum-like stone. Remnants of the sticky floor clung to my shoes like they had been covered in chewing gum. Someone owed me a new pair of sneakers.

The golden-masked attackers stared in stunned silence, and I showed them my teeth in a predatory smile. Just because I was not the Hunter did not mean that Matt Carver was easy pickings. Silently, they spread out, circling me like a pack of wolves stalking their prey. I held myself loose, like a gunslinger ready to draw at the slightest twitch.

"Now, then," I said, my voice still sounding distorted and strange in the bubble of the Lord of Air's power. "Which one of you is controlling the volume?"

No one answered. I figured they wouldn't be nice enough to point him out. Assassins tend to keep quiet as a general rule of thumb—conversation ruins the whole mystique. Whoever was controlling the wind was the only thing that was keeping me from waking up Orion. If I could get rid of them, then the rest of my attackers would be screwed.

If they weren't going to offer up their comrade on a golden platter, I'd have to do what I did best: make a blind guess with nothing to go on, and hope it worked. That was how I passed more tests in school than anyone would believe. Then again, considering how I actually ended up graduating, maybe they would believe.

I chose the guy to my right. I didn't like his look. He wasn't on fire enough. Fortunately, I had just the thing to help with that. Gritting my teeth, I swung my arm, sending a burst of white-hot flames roaring at the Faerie. I didn't wait to see if my attack landed; instead I leaned into the turn, spinning to face the assassin that had been behind me. I held out both hands, pouring all my fury and will into the flames that hurtled toward him.

The assassin leapt backward, but I pressed the attack, fire spewing from my hands like a flamethrower. I spun in a circle, still pouring on the heat, pushing back the little stabbers trying to sneak up behind me with a wall of flame. Once I created a gap for myself, I turned back to my original target.

I didn't choose him at random. I had no idea if he was the Lord of Air or not, but he was the one with his back to a wall, which meant he wouldn't have anywhere to run. I know that's a little cruel. It's not my fault that five assassins picked a fight against one dinky little squire of the Hunt. I had to play for keeps or I was going to die very quickly.

The assassin's back smacked against the impenetrable wall, and my heart had to be just as hard as the marble that it was made of. I took two steps forward, immersing him in the spew of fire. He didn't even have time to scream before the flames were on him. He went full stop, drop, and roll, but Willow's furious fire would not be denied. It spread across him like it was starving and he was the first food it had seen in a month.

Satisfied that he was the Flame's now, I let the hydrant of fire die out as I turned to face the other four. The air was still distorted. That left four options, a twenty-five percent chance to guess correctly. My back was against the wall now, but I preferred it that way—no room for anyone to sneak up behind me and steal one of my kidneys.

The two assassins on the left made my odds even better. The Lady of Water made a slashing motion at me, and a half dozen ice blades emerged from her arm, shooting at me like missiles. With a snarl, I swept my hand through them, letting the heat evaporate them into nothingness. While the steam cleared, the Lord of Earth raised his hand, triggering a miniature earthquake. The floor bucked beneath my feet, sending me stumbling back against the wall for support.

A third assassin leapt at me, blades extended, while I was regaining my balance. I gritted my teeth and sent a pulse of fire, forcing him back. That left one who hadn't moved toward me—an accidental reveal? Good enough for me. I raised my left hand and threw a blast of flames at the fourth assassin. Golden eyes widened behind the mask before a gust of air swept across the room, diverting my attack like a fencer's blade, sending the fireball corkscrewing wildly.

My ears popped as the air bubble collapsed from the force of the currents inside it. I could hear again.

There was a moment of crystal-clear silence as the assassins froze in reaction to sound returning to normal.

"Enemies at the gate!" I bellowed, shattering the silence like a dropped chandelier. Somewhere behind me, I heard a door bang against a wall as it burst open. "Heh, heh, heh," I cackled at my attackers. "If you start running now, I'll give you a head start."

"I will not." Orion's voice was colder than the frost of the Lady of Water. He looked furious, like a looming thunderhead. His fiery sword was already drawn, held in a low guard. He wore a pair of striped pajama pants and no shirt. I knew Orion was in good shape, but holy crap, it looked like his abs had abs.

The Hunter did not pause for negotiation. He waded into the thick of the assassins, blade singing. The Lord of Earth sent the floor to grab his feet, but Orion gracefully leapt over the stone waves. I hurled fireballs at the Lord of Air and Lady of Water, keeping them distracted as one of the deadliest swordsmen in the history of the universe closed with their little band. There are two things that are inevitable in life: death and taxes, and I was pretty sure it wasn't Faerie Tax Day.

The only living Fae who didn't seem to have a magic spirit leapt at Orion, daggers flashing. Orion didn't bother to dodge. He brought his sword up, catching the leading blade and searing through it like it was made of paper. His stroke continued into the chest of the assassin and smashed him into the ground like a volleyball spike. I ran parallel to Orion, throwing suppressing fire on the remaining lords and ladies.

The Lord of Earth met his end head on. He attacked Orion with chunks of the floor, ripping them out with some sort of earth telekinesis and sending them flying at the Hunter like deadly baseballs. Orion never slowed, twisting smoothly around the hurtling chunks of marble as though participating in a choreographed dance. Panicking, the Faerie tried to form a bubble of stone to protect himself from Orion's terrifying sword. The burning blade bit through the shield like it was air, and the assassin screamed in terror as he died.

I had my hands full with the remaining elemental Fae combo pack. The Lord of Air constantly deflected my fireballs, sending them spinning away from my target. I felt like I was a baseball pitcher in the middle of a tornado. The Lady of Water, on the other hand, had no such issues with crosswinds. Her deviously sharp frozen needles flew at me in a vicious barrage that I had to use all my focus to avoid. We were playing the world's deadliest game of dodgeball, and they were cheating.

That was fine by me. I was going to cheat too. If anything, their cheating would probably help me with the guilt. I gathered Willow in my left hand, winding up for another pitch. But instead of a fast ball, I gave it a half-hearted lob that would have barely made it a portion of the way to my enemies. The Lord of Air didn't even bother to bat it around with his winds. I could almost feel the contemptuous sneer behind his golden mask.

My furious little ball of fire, glowing like a dying star, fell to the ground short of my opponents. Right on the edge of the carpet they were standing on. "*Burn*," I commanded Willow, and the spirit took me literally.

The fire spread in a ring, faster than an out-of-control forest fire. The starving flames devoured the thick carpet, trapping the two Fae in a matter of heartbeats. Then it began to constrict, closing like a noose around my would-be assassins. The Lord of Air panicked, sending winds rushing at the flames, which only fed their fury. The Lady of Water jammed her hand on the ground and sent out a wave of ice to combat the circle. The two elements met in a hissing clash of steam as we strained against each other. But no matter how hard she pushed, the circle continued to constrict. Willow's fury would not be denied.

"Surrender!" I snarled, watching as the flames closed in on them. I wanted to take one alive, to find out who was trying to kill me and my friends. Then the Hunt and those people were going to have some words. We just wanted to talk—with our fists and maybe a magic sword.

"Surrender and I will spare you," I shouted again, the flames closing quickly. The heat had to be unbearable, Willow was still burning white hot. They had only a few moments of burn-free existence left. The two masked figures looked at each other, then slowly they turned to face me, ominous specters framed by the leaping flames.

"Extinguish the Flame!" the Lord of Air shouted.

"Hail the three Houses!" the Lady of Water cried.

In one fluid motion, without a shred of hesitation, they plunged their knives into their own chests. One after the other, they leapt into the flames and fell to their knees. Shocked, I ordered Willow to extinguish, but it was too late. The fire feasted on them, leaving only gruesome remains. Even Orion was stunned, frozen mid-stride, black eyes wide.

"Will you guys stop making all that noise?" Alex complained, shuffling in like he was still half asleep. "I know I don't technically need that much shut-eye, but it's still nice—" His voice cut off as he took in the carnage in our entryway. "There goes Alex, missing another fight. No one needs his help, as usual."

I protested weakly, trying to catch my breath. My brain could not believe what we had just seen. What secret were the assassins guarding that they would rather die than be captured? I glanced down at my hands. They were still burning, but the flames had faded from the brilliant white to its normal orange.

"Willow," I said slowly, trying to process all the thoughts in my head. "Does 'Extinguish the Flame' mean anything to you?"

"Must be free. Must spread. Cannot go out." If the spirit had lungs, I would have said that it was close to hyperventilating. Orion's and Alex's heads both twitched, which told me they could hear it as well.

"Why would you go out? How would you be extinguished?" I pressed. "I want to help you, but I don't understand what they were trying to do."

"If Willow's fires go out, Willow goes out."

"How would your fires go out?" I had a sinking feeling that I wasn't going to like the answer to my own question. "Am I one of your fires?"

"Yes."

"So, if all your hosts die, you die?" I said, beginning to understand. I felt like I had finally found the box for the puzzle I had been trying to solve the entire time I had been among the Fae. Unfortunately, the picture was terrifying, and not two kittens frolicking in a field like I had hoped. This had always been about power. "Willow, how many fires do you have?"

"There are only three still burning. The rest have gone out." Willow's voice was very quiet inside my head, spoken in hushed fear.

My mind reeled as I processed this information. Everyone had made a big deal out of my bonding with Willow, but I didn't realize the fire spirit was that endangered. "Let me guess," I said. "Me, Ash, and the missing Lord of Fire? The one who made you promise to not bond with anyone else?" I ticked off the names on my fingers as I counted.

I took Willow's silence as confirmation.

"Uh-oh," Alex muttered. "Here we go again."

"Why would you do that? Why would you agree to let yourself get so close to having your flame go out?"

Willow was silent for a long moment. I could almost feel the spirit borrowing my brain to formulate its thoughts. *"He said it was the only way."*

I didn't know much about this rockstar Lord of Fire, but he sounded bossy and domineering. I got the sense we wouldn't get along very well. For some reason, I don't respond well to megalomaniacs. Call it generational trauma.

"The only way to what?"

"Stop the Queen."

I blinked my eyes in surprise. That was not on my bingo card either.

"Willow, why would you want to stop the Queen? Stop her from what?"

"Burning the whole world."

Remember a few moments ago when I said I had finally found the puzzle box? Turns out I was wrong. That was a different, far-less-terrible puzzle. *Now* I had the right puzzle box, and it was a damned nightmare pressed onto cardboard and cut into jigsaw pieces.

"What happened to the rest of the Lords of Fire?" I asked. "Surely when the last Fireheart left, there were more than just two of you."

"When they realized no new Lords of Fire were being bound, they began to hunt my fires. They put them out, one by one."

"Who did? Who put them out?" I demanded.

"The Queen's enemies."

This was it, my gut told me. This was the thread that was going to answer all the questions. Who was trying to kill us, which sister to marry, and the rot inside the Queen's court all rolled up into one burrito. I had the pieces, I had the box. All I had to do was channel my king's horses and men and put it back together again.

"But now that you bonded with me, you're free of your promise, right? Isn't that what the whole return thing is about?"

"*It may be too late,*" the spirit said somberly. "*The Autumn House is a shadow of what it once was. There are but a few Fireheart souls left for me to bond with.*"

Ash's desperation about her court suddenly took on a new light. The youngest Fae princess, had to watch as her people were murdered from the shadows one by one. That was why she was a disappointment to her mother. She had let the power of her house fade, and there was nothing Gloriana valued more. No wonder she had been so eager to bring me into her family. I was the path to restoring one of the weapons in her arsenal.

I glanced at Orion, then at Alex, who finally seemed completely awake. "What do you think?" I asked.

"I think that I was right," Orion growled. "We should never have stayed here."

"Oh, congratulations." I sighed. "No one likes gloaters. I meant what do you think we should do *right now.*"

"If they're trying to extinguish all the fires of Willow," Alex said slowly, his blue eyes flicking between Orion and me, "does that mean Ash is in danger too?"

Of course she was. If she was one of the last flames of Willow, then she was in as much danger as me. Maybe more, given she was the leader of the house. If someone was trying to remove the House of Autumn completely, it made sense they would go straight for the head. Incidentally, if it was called regicide when you kill a king or queen, was it houseicide when you wiped out an entire house?

"Do you think they would send assassins after both of us at the same time?" I asked Orion.

His face was twisted in annoyance. I knew it was my fault he was here. He didn't want to get involved.

"The last time the assassins tried to kill us, it was just you. They didn't attack her," he offered with a dismissive shrug.

"That we know of," Alex pointed out. "If I were fighting a shadow war with members of the Fae court, I wouldn't broadcast surviving an assassination attempt."

I gave Alex a sharp look. It seemed he and I were working on similar theories.

"Maybe time is running out," I mused. "The ball for my birthday is tomorrow. Could that somehow be related?"

"What are you trying to do here?" Orion demanded. "Should we go rushing through the halls until we find Ash to make sure that she is safe from assassins?"

"Well," I said sheepishly, "you could put a shirt on first."

"This is a bad idea." Orion's voice was as hard as his abs. Which, take my word for it, might be firmer than diamonds. "Why do you need to be involved? What do you care if Ash lives or dies?"

"Well, I tend to take a fairly dim view on murder," I said with as little hypocrisy as I could, standing above the smoldering corpses of my enemies.

Orion rolled his abyss-filled eyes. "These are not your people. This is not your fight. As long as you stay alive, so does Willow. There is nothing to be gained by throwing yourself in the middle of a war that started long before you got here."

"Yeah, until I'm the last Lord of Fire standing, and they come for me too," I snarled. "I think I'd rather stand with an ally than die alone."

"Oh, good, I was worried we would be dying with you," Alex remarked.

I bit my lip in frustration. I understood their point. I did not have to do anything. I could choose Tania and have my business marriage, get my soul back, and keep my neck out of things it didn't belong in. But I knew now that there was no way that whoever was trying to extinguish Willow was going to let me go. They couldn't risk leaving me alive so the flames could spread again. Just like a fire, as long as a single coal still burned, there was a chance.

I shook my head. "Even if I do nothing right now, they will come for me again. What does it matter if I die last if I still die? The more of Willow's fires that still burn, the better chance we have to stand against whoever is hunting us. Ash might even be able to tell us who it is.

"Besides, weren't you super pissed when someone tried to kill us last time?" I accused the Hunter. "It was all I could do to stop you from stalking through the halls hunting every Fae under the sun. This time we're not holding back. Offense has been given, Orion. What was the oath you gave to the Queen again?"

A frustrated sigh escaped Orion's lips before he stormed toward his bedroom at a quick pace.

"Where are you going?" I called after him.

"To put on a shirt!"

BY THE TIME Orion finally put his shirt on, I was a nervous wreck, prancing by the door like a kid late for his own birthday party. Every moment we delayed felt like *the* moment, kind of like the Butterfly Effect. If we didn't leave by a certain time, no matter what we did, we would be too late, but if we had left ten seconds ago, we might have still been in time. A feeling of inevitable doom towered over me like a tombstone.

If anyone asked, I would have told them that my fear was caused by the fear of losing a potential ally. With only three flames left, even one more fire being extinguished would be a major loss. Especially when the only other remaining flame hadn't been seen in centuries. I didn't imagine the last Lord of Fire and I would be teaming up anytime soon.

And that answer would be true. But it might not be the only true answer I could give.

"We gotta go!" I yelled down the hallway, doing my little anxious shuffle. A more cynical man might think that Orion was stalling on purpose. If we were too late, then we weren't involved. But that kind of passive aggression was not his way. After what felt like an eternity, the two Nephilim came to meet me at a trot, Orion no longer shirtless. Sorry, ladies.

We emerged from our mansion like the world's lamest raiding party. We didn't even have a dog or a scarecrow. Now all we had to do was find a princess and save her from an assassination attempt.

Alex and I armed ourselves with a pair of daggers that our attackers had been kind enough to deliver to our apartment. Their weight in my hands was comforting. There's something about holding a weapon with a good heft to it that makes you feel stronger.

The knives were made of something that I was told was called "faerie steel" which was legally similar to, but distinct from, cold iron and its derivatives. Sounded to me like the Fae had figured out a way to synthesize a hard metal that wouldn't burn to the touch. Good job, Fae scientists, you did it.

The mansion we had been hiding in was somewhere in the abandoned Fireheart territory, far away from the portions of Goldhall's maze that I had become familiar with during my stay. But I didn't know where Ash lived. I had been to Tania's and Dawn's, but the Autumn House's location was a mystery to me. Even more frustrating, since we were in an empty wing of the palace, there wasn't any staff wandering around, which was sort of the point of a safe house, I know, but darned irritating when we needed directions.

"What's your plan?" Alex asked as we jogged down a long hall. "Run around yelling, 'Ash, Ash, darling, let me save you,' until we scare any assassins away?"

"No," I lied, mentally scratching that off my list. I was pretty sure that the main palace was in this direction. If we went far enough, eventually we would find some servants who could help us.

"Are you telling me your Nephilim powers don't include the ability to always know where north is or something?" I complained. "Seems like a feature that should come standard with sporty editions like you."

"North here is not like north in the mortal world," Orion said with a shrug. "It changes."

"How the hell does it change?" I demanded. "That's like scientifically improbable, I think. I don't really remember how the poles work, but I know it has something to do with magnets." I suddenly remembered that Goldhall wasn't on a floating ball of mass like good old Mother Earth. It didn't have any poles to be polarized or magnetized or whatever. Checkmate, Einstein.

"North always points to the seat of the Queen's power in the Faerie Lands," Alex shared in a conspiratorial stage whisper.

"Well, that just seems inefficient," I grumbled. "What happens if she moves it?"

"What indeed," Orion agreed.

I decided to ignore that tangent. I had enough stress at the moment.

"Wait, does that mean you can tell where the throne is at all times?" I asked, a plot beginning to form in my mind.

"That way," Alex said, pointing straight ahead of us.

"More correctly, it is that way," Orion said, pointing about forty-five degrees to the left.

Alex rolled his eyes, and I thought I heard him mutter something about "pointy ears" under his breath. Orion ignored his grumbling.

"Okay," I began, thinking slowly. "There's no way the assassins would strike while the Queen was near Ash, right? The Queen wouldn't be in on it. She's trying to strengthen the power of her people. She needs the Autumn House stronger, not dead."

"So, you think Ash isn't near the throne right now?" Alex asked.

"If Ash is somewhere public and close to the Queen, it's less likely that they would risk attacking. They need her to be alone, or at least not with the most powerful Faerie of them all."

"So, if the Queen's power is left, we go right," Orion said.

"That's all I got." I shrugged.

We began to cut right. Whenever we found a fork in the halls, we took the right one, angling ourselves away from the Queen. It was a stupid theory. For all I knew, the daughters' apartments were clustered around the Queen's throne like a pearl necklace. But somehow, I doubted it. All of the princesses struck me as an independent lot who wouldn't tolerate a helicopter mom—queen or no.

We walked for what felt like an hour but was maybe ten minutes according to Father Time. Each passing second, my stress compounded. We were going to be too late. We had taken too long. We were going the wrong way. Ash was going to die, and I wasn't going to be able to save her.

Finally, we made our way into the more populated main corridors of Goldhall. I accosted the first human servant who trotted past us, carrying a silver tray of food.

"Excuse me," I shouted, not caring who else heard. "Where does the Lady of Autumn live?"

She gave me a nervous smile but didn't say anything. I guess if I worked in the White House and three armed men demanded to know where the president's daughter was, I would be nervous too. But I didn't have time to convince her that I wasn't the danger. We were already late. So instead, I showed her that I was the danger she should be worried about. Willow burst into flames on my hands, and I growled in my best Orion impersonation, "I won't ask again."

"Keep going this way, take three rights, and look for the double doors with the phoenix on them," she blurted, silver tray rattling in fear.

"Thank you!" I called as I led my friends in a sprint past her. I was so stressed that I barely registered that I am a genius. I mean, I registered it—just *less* than usual. My theory had worked, we were going the right way.

There might still be a chance.

True to the servant's word, after three turns we found a pair of double doors with a golden phoenix emblazoned on it, a wing on each half. The image of the legendary bird that rises from its own ashes felt like a good omen to me. I only hoped that the Ash inside was in a better state than the one on her door.

The three of us huddled up outside the door, like a football team planning their play. "Should we knock?" Alex asked.

"And give the assassins warning?" I asked.

"But what if there are no assassins and she's in the shower or something? That would be super awkward," Alex said.

Orion nodded. "It could be seen as very rude not to knock."

"What the hell happened to the specter of judgment you used to be?" I complained, looking at the Constellation. "You literally were prepared to tear the Queen's doors off of its hinges."

"She hasn't broken her promise yet." Orion shrugged, as if *that* explained everything. Stupid supernatural beings and having to keep their word. Sometimes mankind's fluid relationship with the truth is so much more efficient. This rigid honesty was going to drive me up a wall.

"Fine, we will knock," I snapped as I pictured an assassin stabbing Ash over and over while we had this stupid argument. "But have your sword out, just in case." I stepped up to the phoenix door, and with my heart in my throat, I knocked on the door with my burning hands, three sharp times.

The door popped open as soon as I finished knocking. Ash herself stood in the doorway, wearing an orange cocktail dress. Her red hair was done up in an elegant braid, like she was expected at a fancy dinner party any second. Relief flooded through me like a pipe cleaner punching through my panic blockage and letting the fear drain out.

Ash's face fell when she saw me, her skin turning pale and her eyes going wide. "Squire Carver," she greeted me in a low voice, "what a surprise." Her green eyes tracked from my Willow's fire to Orion's blazing sword, and an eyebrow arched in surprise. "Now isn't a great time..." she started, but I cut her off.

"You're in danger," I hissed, also keeping my voice low.

"Since the moment I was born," she replied in an amused tone.

"We came to protect you."

"I appreciate the thought. But as I said, this is not a good time." She started to close the door.

Frustrated, I held a hand up to keep it from closing all the way. Why wouldn't she listen?

"They're trying to extinguish the Flame," I pleaded.

Ash froze. For a brief second, she was a statue instead of a living, breathing thing. Every inch of her was still, from her red tresses to the folds of her orange cocktail dress. She tilted her head, green eyes assessing me with a new glint.

"So," she said, the hint of a sad smile playing across her face, "you're beginning to understand the real game. Took you long enough."

I blinked. That was not the reaction I had been expecting. I guess none of this was news to her. It would have been nice if anyone had felt the need to clue me in earlier. I was just trying to help!

In hindsight, I suppose that it should have been more obvious to me. How many times have I repeated to myself that supernatural creatures are predators? How often have I lectured myself on the importance of not looking like prey? The first warning Robin gave me was to be careful in these waters, because it was where sharks swam. Ash had admitted that her house was hurt, in danger of bleeding out. Her sisters were just doing what sharks do. I had been told exactly what was going on, just in the Faerie style—which is the nice way of saying "backwards and upside down."

"What is taking you so long?" a familiar voice demanded.

My eyebrows twitched in surprise as Dawn stepped behind her sister in the doorway. A smug smile spread across her lips as her blue eyes settled on me.

Ash let out a tiny sigh, opening the door all the way. "It seems Squire Carver and his friends were in the neighborhood and decided to drop by for a nightcap," she said, giving me a glare.

"Ah, yes." I coughed, hiding my burning hands full of knives behind my back. I heard a slight rustle as Orion sheathed his sword. "I love nightcaps. I have them all the time." I had no idea what a nightcap was. I hoped it wasn't a mushroom. I hate them. For some reason, it wouldn't surprise me if Fae sat around eating mushrooms. That seemed very on brand for their lore.

"And here I thought I had taught you a valuable lesson about turning up at princesses' homes uninvited," Dawn said, her vicious smile growing. "But it seems you still have more to learn, Squire Carver. Oh, do let them in, sister. This should be most fun."

My heart fell. Despite knowing and kind of liking the other side of Dawn, I doubted that anything she found fun while playing this role was something I would enjoy.

"Please come in," Ash said, stepping aside and gesturing for us to enter. Her green eyes had a desperate gleam to them, as if she was trying to tell me something. I've heard couples can develop a level of instinctual telepathy over a long enough period. That one look from a wife to a husband is worth a thousand words. Unfortunately, I was untrained in the art of look-deciphering, but I was pretty sure she wanted me to come in and play it cool. There was also the chance that she might want me to turn her down and leave. It was definitely one of those two things—probably.

"We'd love to," I said, stepping into the doorway.

Ash rolled her eyes.

Oops.

Dawn's grin grew even larger, like a cat that had swallowed a whole flock of canaries. It struck me that she didn't seem upset I was here. Which meant that she wasn't upset that I wasn't bleeding out in my apartment right now. Did that lower her on the suspect list? Maybe a little. Or maybe she was just a good actress—maybe that should move her *up*. My head hurt. Just once, I'd love to have a straight-up good guy versus bad guy fight to settle this. All this cloak-and-dagger nonsense was going to give me an ulcer… or death. Or both. Can you die from an ulcer?

At Ash's invitation, I stepped into the Lady of Autumn's apartment. The apartment was wildly different from the other princesses' residences I had been in. While Tania's was modern and Dawn's was opulent, Ash's had the silent calm aura of a library. The bright colors of autumn decorated everything, every wall bearing a beautiful work of art or a shelf stuffed to the brim with books. It was the lair of an inquisitive mind that treasured knowledge like a dragon hoards its gold.

My feng shui psychoanalysis was interrupted by something far more pressing demanding my attention. In the sitting room off the entry hall was a table with four chairs. Two were empty, but the other two were filled. Mav and Tania gave us appraising glances as we entered the room. For the first time since I had been presented to the Queen, the four seasons of the Fae court were gathered in one room before me.

Cold sweat began to slide down my spine as I glanced between the four women. One of them had ordered the Hunt's death tonight. Now I was trapped in a room with them.

Out of the frying pan and into the shark tank.

Good thing I made Orion put on a shirt.

DAWN JOINED HER sisters around the table, while Ash produced three more chairs for me and the gang to sit in. As we took our seats, the four daughters of the Dandelion Court stared at us from across the dark oak. Each one was as unique as a snowflake, and yet the strength of their common DNA shone through in the weight behind four pairs of eyes that held me down with what felt like physical force.

I found myself overthinking their expressions, as if I could catch the Dandelion Traitor just by looking in their eyes. None of them seemed surprised to see me. Well, I guess a better way to put that was that none of them seemed *extra* surprised to see me, in a "hey, why isn't he dead?" kind of way. Of course not, that would have been too easy.

Alex and Orion sat at my shoulders like literal wingmen, although their service went far beyond the casual use of that term. I had a bad feeling that the conversation at this table would be more dangerous than any dogfight.

"I must say, it's so lovely of you to drop by so unexpectedly," Dawn said into her wineglass, taking a healthy sip. A flash of displeasure rang across Tania's face before vanishing behind a stoic mask. I could practically feel frustration boiling off her in rolling waves.

Dawn's implication was clear—I had chosen a favorite daughter and was sneaking to her place late at night. It was shocking to me how innocent that felt. I wished my only agenda was one of a blushing boy who was head over heels for a green-eyed, red-haired princess. Instead, I was trying to thwart assassinations and prevent the extinction of a multi-presence spirit.

"Here at the Hunt, we do our best to be lovely," I said, giving Dawn my most winning smile. Even if the real Dawn was much more pleasant than she let on, I couldn't afford to give her an inch right now. "That's actually the second-highest score we get on exit surveys."

"Spare us the games. What are you doing here?" Tania demanded, her voice cold and empty of any of Dawn's playfulness. The Lady of Spring's brows were furrowed in frustration, and I thought I saw a single vein pulsing a drum solo in her temple. I couldn't help but take a tiny bit of satisfaction at her stress. Tania wasn't the worst of the sisters, but she had tried to play me like a fiddle. It was cathartic to see her do a little jig of her own.

"Well," I said, then held up my hands to accept a glass of wine from Ash. "Ah, thank you! Well, we were in the neighborhood and thought it might be fun to have one of these nightcaps I've heard so much about."

"You were in the neighborhood," Dawn repeated flatly. "At just a few minutes shy of midnight?" She pointed at an old clock ticking away on the wall.

"Have you never heard of the nightcapping hour?" Alex offered, but the princesses ignored him. I thought I saw Ash's lip tweak in a half smile, but it was gone as quickly as a match's flame.

"Why aren't you in your safe house?" Mav asked, arching an imperious eyebrow. "Mother has gone to a lot of work to get your soul back. Surely you are not taking her gift for granted?" A low murmur ran through the four sisters as if they were suddenly a flock of distraught hens.

I hesitated for a moment. Mav's question was a fair one, and an important one. To the elder races like the Fae, things like favors and hosting were not given lightly. Being a rude guest here was even worse than if you were raised in the tradition of Southern hospitality. If I was being dismissive of the Queen of All Fae's kindness, that would be a level of insult that could not be ignored. Also, of course the desperate mama's girl brought that up.

The easy answer was that it turned out my safe house wasn't that safe. But if someone in this room had ordered my death this evening, I didn't want to give them any information. This called for a little Matthew Carver charm to grease my way out of a sticky situation.

"Robin said that all the demons have been *expunged*." I did my best Robin imitation, affecting a strong enunciation.

Ash snickered. Even Dawn arched an amused eyebrow.

"And Orion got a really bad case of mansion-fever, so we figured a late-night prowl wouldn't be much of an issue. What are the demons gonna do, invade?" I gave a sarcastic sniff.

"Idiot," Mav muttered to herself, but seemed willing to drop it. I tried not to feel too offended. I *am* an idiot, but for different reasons. The smartest way to get out of a situation is to make everyone think you're the dumbest person in the room. All you have to do is be willing to take a few blows to your pride. Fortunately, my pride is like one of those Crown Vics from the eighties—it can take a beating and keep trucking along.

"Oh, you never know," Dawn said with her vicious little smile, "they're nasty little devils, capable of things you wouldn't believe. Don't you agree, little Ash?"

The Lady of Autumn's green eyes flashed at her sister, but her face was poised as she took a sip of her wine. "The Darkstar and his ilk have no boundary they will not cross," she said, a faint touch of heat coloring her words.

One thing I liked about Ash: She appeared to be an astute judge of character. She hated demons and seemed to like me. That was a platform I could get behind. I gave her a firm nod to show that she had my full agreement. I came here expecting to fight for my life—but I thought the battle would look a little different.

"So, tomorrow is the big day," Dawn began, changing subjects. Inwardly I suppressed a groan. I could guess where this was going. "It's your last night as a free man. Are you nervous?"

I could *feel* without even looking that Tania's eyes sharpened as they tried to pin me in place. I met Dawn's stare with a smile on my face. She was enjoying this; I could see true delight sparkling in her blue eyes.

"I'm looking forward to it!" I said with extra enthusiasm. "It's the opportunity of a lifetime. Who wouldn't be excited? I really appreciate each of you having so much patience with me during this whole process. You've really shown me who you are, and I am so honored to have had the opportunity to get to know each of you."

"Oh, save the speech," Mav grumbled into her drink, rolling her eyes. I saw Tania's knuckles whiten as she gripped her wineglass like it was the only thing keeping her from falling into the Nothing. Ash favored me with one of her lightning-quick smiles, which almost made the whole thing worth it.

"I think what Matt means is that he—" Alex began.

"Don't worry, we know what he means," Dawn said, her smile even wider than it was before. She was so strange when she wore this face. I think she liked it when I fought back. Fine. If she wanted to play hardball, we could do hardball. No more easy questions.

"Say, Dawn," I drawled, trying to sound more relaxed than I felt. "Did you ever make any progress on the whole 'someone tried to murder the Hunt' thing?" I used air quotes to show how unbothered I was about the whole affair. I looked very calm and relaxed.

Orion's deep growl behind me was so primal it could have protected five different junkyards at the same time. It was a struggle to keep my smirk from growing as Dawn's face went smooth in the blink of an eye. A struggle, but I persevered. Mav leaned back in her chair, a hint of satisfaction lurking at the corner of her lips.

"Have no fear, Hunter," Dawn replied, no hint of playfulness in her words anymore. "The Dandelion Throne has made an oath, and it will be carried out. We grow closer to uncovering the truth every day. It is only a matter of time before the traitors bask in the wrath of the Queen of All Fae."

You know, the weird thing was, I believed her. I wondered if she knew that I had almost died again tonight.

"Well, we definitely appreciate your effort." Alex's reply was so laden with sarcasm I was surprised that it didn't make a puddle on the table.

Dawn's eyes danced with genuine anger. "Quiet, runt, your betters are speaking," she sneered before turning her gaze to me. "Do try to keep your servants in line, Matthew. It is unbecoming of a future royal."

"I think that's enough for me." Mav threw back the rest of her wine before standing from her chair. She scooped up her obsidian blade and belted it on over her dark pants. "I can only listen to you all squabble like children for so long before I get the urge to stab someone." Her gaze swept across the room, pausing on Orion for a long moment before it landed on me. "I could not be happier to be free of all this," she said.

That felt a little harsh. And here I was thinking we had started to become friends. The Lady of Winter left a cold breeze in the wake of her exit. And then there were three. Well, technically six, counting us, but three sisters—one of whom I desperately wanted to get alone.

Not like that. Well, maybe not *not* like that. I don't know, it was complicated. Right now, my interest was purely survival, I swear.

Sigh.

"Such a promising quality in the heir apparent," Dawn remarked to an empty room, "overcome by some wine and a few cocktail guests. If only Mommy dearest could see her now."

Tania snickered, and even Ash managed a flat-lined smile that was tight around her eyes. Regardless of my romantic feelings for the Lady of Autumn, I hated seeing her so diminished. It was like watching someone stomp through a flower bed on purpose.

"It's her Nordic blood," Tania replied, leaning back in her chair. "She's too Viking to be civilized. She'd rather be in a mead hall than suffer the courtly pursuits."

"I agree," Dawn drawled, looking down at her fingernails in a disaffected manner. "Blood always tells."

The Ladies of Spring and Autumn both stiffened at Dawn's words.

"You're awfully quiet, Hunter," she continued, ignoring her sisters. "Do you agree? You are an expert on such matters."

Orion's silence was as stony as the mountains. I could all but feel the glare of his black eyes over my shoulder. There *was* a literal biological difference between him and Alex. The amount of supernatural juice flowing through their veins directly impacted their physical capabilities. When I first met him, he had been dismissive of Alex for the same reason that Dawn was, but despite being an old, old dog, he had changed his perspective and learned a new trick.

"I think that people can—" I started.

"*We* are not people, my sweet little mortal." Dawn sliced through my sentence with the ease of a master sushi chef, blade sharpened to infinity. "You would do well not to forget that."

No, you're sharks, I barely managed to keep myself from replying, but the Lady of Summer's attention wasn't on me. Her blue eyes were fixed on Orion with a singular focus.

"You aren't the only one in Goldhall with the blood of Hunting in their veins, Orion. I, for one, am fascinated by how similar your temperaments are, aren't you?"

"What is she talking about?" I asked Alex softly. He shrugged with a sour look on his face. Even though he had been dealing with comments like hers his entire life, I didn't imagine they ever felt good.

"Her father, Ullr, is much the same," Orion agreed.

Dawn's wicked smile grew. I still had no idea what she was getting at. I felt like I had heard the name before, but I tend to stick to the A-listers when it comes to ancient pantheons. My poor little brain only has so much space to hold all these facts.

"Ullr is a Norse god of, like, winter and hunting and stuff," Alex whispered to me.

I wondered how it would feel to be the child of a hunting god and have to stand in front of the Constellation of Hunting. I thought it might be like being a painter and meeting Michelangelo or any of the other turtles.

I was still unclear exactly *how* one becomes a Constellation, but instinct told me that being one didn't make you popular with the rest of your peers. No one likes a sore loser, but everyone hates a winner. Maybe some of Mav's ire toward the hunt was jealousy for her father.

"Would you say that dear Mav's heritage influences her behavior?" Dawn pressed Orion, her fingers drumming on the crystal edge of her wineglass. Tania and Ash looked even more uncomfortable, like they were embarrassed to even be present during this conversation. I had a feeling that Alex and I looked very similar from their perspective.

"Sometimes, the blood tells," Orion admitted grudgingly after a moment.

Dawn sniffed but seemed pleased with her victory.

"Now, mortals, Squire Carver," she said, fixing me with a stare. "Mortals are something different entirely."

"I think you've made your point," Tania snapped, rising to her feet. Her face was flushed. I think it was the first time I had ever seen a Faerie blush. It was so out of place, I found myself staring. The princesses were usually in such control of their emotions, seeing Tania come close to losing it was like seeing a tutu on a pig—it didn't belong.

"Whatever do you mean?" Dawn asked, a false note of surprise ringing in her voice. "Oh, darling, certainly you know I don't mean you! You are only *half* mortal anyway."

Tania ignored her sister's appeasing words and fixed me with an angry stare. I wondered for a moment if she was upset at her sister or if she was angry that I was still alive. But that wouldn't make any sense! She needed me, right? Right?

"You better make the smart choice tomorrow," she hissed at me, turning on her heel to storm out. She slammed Ash's door so hard that the whole apartment rattled slightly.

Then there were only two daughters left.

Now all I had to do was outlast Dawn's fierce tongue and I would have a chance to talk to Ash and finally get some answers about who was trying to quench Willow's flame. Should be easy, right? One final boss to go.

"Was that entirely necessary?" Ash growled at Dawn.

"Maybe not entirely." Dawn shrugged. "But I enjoyed seeing that spoiled brat squirm for once."

Dawn's animosity had vanished in an instant, like a light switch had been flipped. Ash looked more relaxed, and so did Dawn. I gritted my teeth in irritation. This had all been another game.

It should come as no surprise that I am just about worthless when it comes to conversational chess. I was pretty sure that Dawn was in the middle of playing a master-level game, eliminating her sisters from the conversation one by one. Even as I realized it, the Lady of Summer made her next move for checkmate, bingo, or whatever.

"Well, it has really gotten to be quite late," Dawn said with a chuckle. "We have far overstayed our welcome, little Ash. I'm so sorry to keep you up so late."

"It's really no problem," Ash replied evenly, a smile plastered on her face that failed to seem completely real. "I hope you have a pleasant rest of your night. Don't worry about your wineglass. We'll clean up after."

Dawn paused in mock surprise. "Surely you aren't suggesting I leave you alone with this gentleman caller at such an hour? You have no servants or chaperone! What would Mother say?"

Now that she mentioned it, Ash's quarters were the only place I had been in all of Goldhall—other than my safe house—where I had not been accosted by some butler or servant about something. Ash had served the drinks and provided seats herself.

"I'm sure the presence of the Hunter and his other squire is more than sufficient, Dawn," Ash said through gritted teeth.

"It would be the height of impropriety! As your elder sister, it is my responsibility to look out for you. I must insist, if only for your sake. You three, up!"

None of the members of the Hunt so much as twitched. I could feel Alex's and Orion's gazes settle on me, waiting to see what I wanted to do. My heart was racing. This was the moment, I realized. We were about to lay all the cards on the table and see who was bluffing and who had won. I had run out of time. Tomorrow was judgment day. Well, engagement day, but what's the difference? I couldn't afford to wait to talk to Ash later. I could only hope that I had played my hand as well as I could. I had a soul to win and a fire spirit to save.

Stalling for time to think, I licked my lips and glanced at Alex and Orion on either side. The Hunter's face was stony, as it had been for most of this adventure. With an irritated shrug, he gestured for me to get on with it. I think he didn't care what happened as long as we got this over with. Alex looked stressed—welcome to the club, dude.

While I knew Dawn had her own motives, the fact that she was bound by the Queen's oath was the safest piece of driftwood I had to cling to. I was adrift in a sea of intrigue, and it was time to grab on to anything that could float.

"Assassins attacked the safe room tonight," I blurted out to the two princesses. "There were Lords of Air, Earth, and Water with them." I deliberately left out the part about "extinguishing the Flame." I wanted to see what Dawn had to say first. Just because it was the final hand didn't mean I had to play all my cards at once.

Dawn was totally still. Her only reaction to my news was a slight flaring of her pupils. My ears popped as a current of wind swirled around us, cocooning us in a silence that was a little too familiar. Dawn leaned forward in her chair, her face riveted with intensity.

"No one can hear us. Tell me everything," she demanded, pinning me with a fierce gaze.

"You first," I said, tilting my head.

"What did you say?" Dawn asked in surprise.

"You are *bound*, Faerie," I hissed. "The Dandelion Throne made the Hunt a promise and named you as the executor of it. From where we sit, the promise is nothing but empty wind, blowing dust in our faces."

"Nice," Alex said, "because she's probably a Lady of Air." Alex is the greatest hype man I could ask for. I held out a fist, and we rapped knuckles. I might be backed into a corner, but I wasn't going down on someone else's terms.

Dawn was silent for a moment, a contemplative look on her face. After a while, she leaned back in her chair and fixed me with a frank stare. "Why do you think the demons were here?" she asked.

"I assumed that they were here to keep me quiet, so I didn't start a supernatural world war," I replied.

"Oh, some of them were here for you." Dawn waved my concerns away. "But not all of them."

Now that she mentioned it, Samael had already been here when I showed up, but Gloriana had already been worried about the demon's presence before I got added to the equation. Zagan and his posse didn't show up until after I arrived. I had assumed that they were connected, but that felt kind of naïve now. I might be on Lucifer's personal hit list, but that didn't mean that *all* the fiery pits of Hell revolved around me. Wow, did I have an ego? No, I was pretty sure I was very humble. I call myself an idiot all the time.

"They know we are weak, and they want to keep it that way," Dawn told me with a sidelong glare at Ash. The Autumn Lady bowed her head in shame but was silent. "The Path of Flames was the backbone of the Dandelion Court's strength for thousands of years. With it in shambles, we are a shadow of what we once were."

Frowning, I glanced between the two sisters. Having now fought against at least one member of each of the other three paths, I could see how the other ones were useful—but they weren't fire. None of their power had exuded the *hunger* that Willow's flames did. All of the other paths had utility that wasn't centered around combat. Fire pretty much only cooked stuff or burned it.

"You're saying the demons wouldn't want the Path of Flames to return to its previous strength?" Alex asked.

"Precisely. The same way your own nations try to limit their rivals' access to more powerful weapons." Business-mode Dawn answered Alex without a trace of her usual disparaging tone toward him. Yet again, it felt like there were two Dawns—one was a daydream, the other a nightmare. Unlike Dr. Jekyll and Mr. Hyde, both versions were still drop-dead gorgeous.

Alex and I exchanged glances. That sounded a little too familiar. "Now that you mention it," I said, as if I had forgotten this tidbit, "one of the assassins yelled something about 'extinguishing the Flame' before they died."

Dawn's face hardened into a furious statue. Not the fake pleasant cruelty of a cheerleader, but something harder, like a mountain. "Those fools!" she screamed, slamming her palm down on the table with a loud crack. Everyone jumped in surprise except for Orion. "They get a little bit of power, and they sell the ship out from under themselves to keep it."

I thought I finally understood what was going on. When the last Lord of Fire had left and convinced Willow to stop bonding with more lords and ladies, he had effectively defanged the Fae court. Without the ability to recruit new soldiers, "the Flame" would die out. A fire needs more fuel to keep burning. The fall of the Path of Flames would have created a vacuum, and if there is one thing I know about Mother Nature, it's that she abhors those things. Someone else got the opportunity to fill the space and increase their power. I bet the other lords enjoyed the power shift and had been only too happy to profit off their nation's decline. It's what we mortals would do. So the question was: What house and path rose to new heights, to new power, that they would do anything to keep?

It wasn't Ash, obviously, as hers was the fallen house. I still didn't think it was Dawn either. She wouldn't put her house's success over the entire court. Her goal was to rule the whole dang thing. Tania didn't seem capable of this either. No, to do this to your own family, you had to be ice cold.

"Dawn," I asked, after a moment of reflection, "I don't suppose the last Lord of Fire used to also be the Queen's captain of the guard, did he?"

"Yes, Mav took up that mantle after he left," she replied.

"Would you say that the favor of the House of Winter has grown with the Queen since the Path of Flames began to wane?" I pressed.

Understanding dawned in her eyes as she did the same mental math I had. Ash shifted uncomfortably in her seat.

"Also," I continued, playing my final, damning card, "isn't there some sort of magical security in Goldhall that's supposed to alert her when people start dying? I just find it interesting that she was here, enjoying a lovely glass of wine, instead of coming to save me."

"But she saved you the last time," Dawn pointed out. Her brows were furrowed as she thought.

"We were fine," Orion grunted.

"In hindsight, it was more of a symbolic saving than anything else," Alex said. "If we're being cynical, one could argue she finished off the last of the assassins so they couldn't be questioned."

That was a good point. I hadn't even thought of that.

"Lords and Ladies of Fire have died off over the last four hundred years," Dawn breathed in horror, picking up my train of thought. She turned to her sister, her blue eyes wide. "After you took over your house, we blamed you for not protecting your subjects. But if the captain of the guard was opening the doors for Gilded Dancers to strike them down, there was nothing you could have done to protect them."

Ash stared at her sister for a long moment, her chest heaving as she struggled to keep her cool. Her green eyes danced with a fire that I didn't need to use Willow's senses to feel. Silently, she rose and strode across the room to a coat closet. With a vicious wrench, she jerked it open.

The bodies of three golden-masked assassins were crammed inside, like a toddler had shoved their toys into a box they didn't fit into. They were scorched and broken. I could tell from a glance: they had died quickly and poorly.

"Well, I feel a little stupid," I muttered to Alex. We had rushed to try to save Ash, but if anything, maybe it should have been the other way around. I couldn't help but be impressed—the Lady of Autumn had dispatched several assassins and then hosted a cocktail hour for her sisters without anyone noticing.

"It's good for you," my friend muttered back.

Orion let out one mirthless laugh that was somehow a compliment to Ash while mocking me. I don't know why I bring my peanut gallery with me anywhere. The only thing they're good at is making fun of me and fighting monsters. I'm not sure the tradeoff is worth it.

Dawn stood slowly, walking over to inspect the bodies, her mouth hanging open. The real Dawn isn't the worst, but I still took a small boost of delight in seeing her shock. "My sister," she said in a soft tone, taking Ash's hands in hers. "I owe you such an apology."

Ash tilted her head, staring at Dawn as if seeing behind her mask for the first time. I felt another pang of sympathy for how lonely it must be to walk the Path of Wind and Secrets.

"Thank you," she said in a gentle tone. The two sisters held hands and looked into each other's eyes for a long moment.

I felt like I was hosting one of those reality shows that reunited families. But mending sibling bonds with centuries of trauma wasn't what I was here for.

"Hang on," Alex said, holding up a hand like a student in class. "I just want to make sure that this is crystal clear. You're saying that Mav has been killing off the members of Ash's court so that she could be Mommy's favorite, and now that she's desperate, she's turned to the demons?"

"Like Matt said, when the Lord of Fire left and locked the Path of Flames, Mav became the person that my mother depended on to fulfill much of his duties," Dawn answered, tucking a strand of blonde hair behind her ears. "She became my mother's hatchetwoman, her tool for violence, and apparently she would do anything to stay Mother's favorite—even betray her, although I would never have guessed that she would turn to demons for allies."

"It seems to me that we all share a common goal," I said after a moment of thought. "The preservation of the Dandelion Court. I was tasked with rooting out the demons and those undermining the Dandelion Court by your mother." Both Ash's and Dawn's eyebrows rose in surprise. "Meanwhile, you, Dawn, are supposed to be hunting down the assassins who tried to kill us and the Lady of Autumn."

"How lovely for us that they're connecting," Dawn grumbled.

"I think the intention is clear," I continued, feeling my confidence rise. If this was what it was like to finally feel like I understood what in the world was going on, I could get used to this. "Mav and the demons would both profit from seeing the Fae remain weak. Whether Mav was working with them or on her own doesn't matter; they wanted similar things. The assassins don't need to kill me and my friends to be successful. All they need to do is kill the treaty between the Hunt and the Fae."

"That would put a damper on you joining the family," Dawn agreed, tapping a long finger against her chin.

"There is still a way that you can keep our oaths and preserve the treaty. But if we're going to do this, we need to do it in front of a crowd, so there is no way anyone can deny that she confessed, and she can't run," I continued. "Plus, it would be a really thoughtful birthday present."

"You want to make a scene," Dawn said coolly.

"Correct me if I'm wrong, but now that you know who tried to kill us, and we know that you know, there's not a lot of wiggle room left, is there?"

"There is not," Orion interjected, a hint of his former dark anger lurking in his tone, like a trail of smoke from the mouth of a volcano.

"He's right," Ash agreed, turning tô her sister. "To do nothing would be to break the oath."

"I'm aware." Dawn drummed her fingers on the table in irritation. "I just dislike being backed into a corner."

"It was not my intention to do so," I said, realizing she meant what I had just done. From her perspective, this might look a lot more planned out than it was. I had put the pieces together on the fly. Not bad for a rush job.

"I believe you," the Lady of Summer replied with a small smile. "But accident or no, it's not your body that will be burning on the Iron Table if we get this wrong."

Touché.

"You've uncovered a conspiracy to hobble the Dandelion Court and extinguish the Flame," I pressed. "My friends and I have identified the rotten portion that has made alliances with demons. Dawn, this is a win."

The Lady of Summer was silent for a long moment, an irritated look on her face. Ash reached across the table and laid a hand on her sister's arm.

"Please," the Lady of Autumn said to her older sister. "Avenge my people."

Whatever resistance that was left in Dawn's mind broke, and she let out a defeated sigh. "Very well, Matthew, you shall get your present. May I be the first to wish you a very happy birthday?"

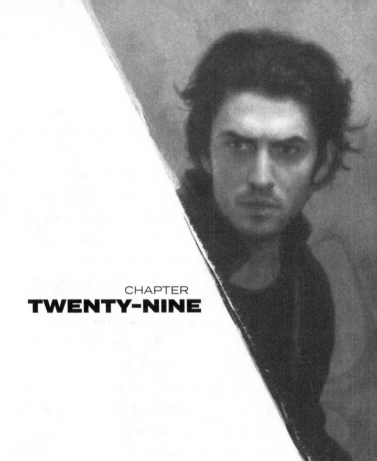

TWENTY-NINE

I **NEVER WENT TO** any of my high school proms, so the procedure of getting ready for a formal ball was far outside of my comfort zone. The California casual dress code is baked into my bones. I'm in my element in a pair of comfortable sweats and a band T-shirt, which was how I had spent most of my birthdays so far. I don't have many good memories associated with dressing up. The last time I wore a suit, most of my family was being put in the dirt.

So it might be understandable that as I stared in the mirror on my twenty-fifth birthday, I didn't recognize myself. I was wearing a *cummerbund* for crying out loud. I certainly couldn't spell that without a dictionary, let alone begin to tie it myself.

But tonight wasn't just my birthday party. Oh no, that would be too easy. Tonight's agenda included exposing a traitorous princess, securing my soul, and getting engaged to a different, less-traitorous princess. All while wearing a stupid tuxedo.

At least, that's what I thought I was doing. I was a little vague on the exact details of what "betrothing" is and isn't, and I didn't have access to the internet to look it up. I knew it was somewhere between strangers and pregnant but was struggling to narrow it down any further, and I had been too busy to ask anyone.

Alex executed his manservant responsibilities with only mild complaints. Together we wrestled with my tuxedo, bending it into some semblance of proper shape. It felt like trying to assemble a tent in the dark. I don't know if we got it exactly right, but I figured as long as everything was covered, it was probably close enough. Despite being stuck in a Faerie castle far away from the mortal lands, the black tuxedo felt like it wouldn't have looked out of place at a formal mortal event, which somehow made sense.

I found it more than a little ironic that somehow, even in the middle of this political maelstrom, I still couldn't avoid my birthday. I hate my birthday. It has only ever brought me trials, tribulations, and ugly socks. The worst day of my life absolutely was on my birthday; it was just hard to choose which birthday it was. Either the time most of my family died or when Dan the Demon stole my soul.

The one ray of sunshine was, if I managed to not Pass Go, and not collect five million dollars tonight, then I would be free of that soul deal once and for all. Given the fact that the Queen had thrown every single demon out of her private world just for my birthday, I felt pretty good about those odds. Of course, if I did get my soul back today, it would also become the new anniversary of my sister's death, which would be a whole other can of trauma.

I stared into my own blue eyes in the mirror and let out a big sigh. It didn't fix any of my problems, but it made me feel better for a few seconds. Tonight at the ball, I had to tell the Queen of All Fae which of her daughters I wanted to seal our political contract with. Which, on top of being a rather gross practice, would be a lot easier if I knew the answer I was going to give.

At least one of the ladies was easy to remove from the list. Mav, the Lady of Winter, had flat-out refused to be a contestant on this dumb dating show, *and* she had tried to assassinate me—twice. That was a hard no from me.

Tania, the Lady of Spring, was also lower on the list. She saw me as an object, a chess piece to help her get free of the Dandelion Court's games. After playing them for over a month, I couldn't blame her. But that didn't mean I wanted to join her team. People have a bad habit of sending their pawns to die when it is useful to them.

It was with the remaining two daughters, Dawn and Ash, that the scoring got murky. Their style as potential partners could not be more different. Dawn was smart and capable, and her game was to rule. If I was going to escape Hell's clutches, I needed backup that had Power with a capital P. Even if I did manage to get my soul back, the scales between me and good old Luci-You-Know-the-Rest wouldn't be balanced. An ally like Dawn could keep me alive.

Ash, on the other hand, hadn't made me any offers or tried to negotiate a contract. She hadn't tried to lock me into her big plan. I just wished I could have spent more time getting to know her. If I didn't know better, I'd say she was avoiding me.

Despite the short amount of time we spent together, I couldn't get her out of my head. She was smart, fun, and she had been nice to me. I know that sounds stupid, but it was something to consider.

She reminded me of Violet.

Not in any way that makes sense. You couldn't put the two of them in a lineup and be like "oh, I totally see it!" But I liked her for the same reasons that I had once loved my best friend's fiancée. Talking to her was like breathing. It was something I instinctively knew how to do. I didn't have to put on a mask and pretend to be someone else. She laughed at the real Matt's jokes, not the deliberately funny Matt's scripted ones. Besides, we were bound by the Flame. I would be lying if that didn't add a little spice to the situation.

I was torn between the logical choice of Dawn and the interesting one of Ash. The need for entertainment has always been one of my greatest weaknesses. The whispers of my id have never been angry or greedy. They have echoed with the vacuum of boredom, of a life lived without anything exciting to frame it. Those same whispers ate at the foundation of my logical choice like acid.

What is the worth of regaining my soul only to wither away in a different kind of hell, a different prison? Was it enough to survive the damage done to me or did I need to thrive? How would Dawn help me to Live, Laugh, Love?

A knock on my bedroom door pulled me out of my desperate emotional cramming session. I felt like I was about to take a test that would affect the rest of my life, but I was a dog trying to answer calculus equations—no matter how much I studied and went back over the coursework, I just wanted to do a few tricks and get a treat.

"Come in," I yelled, trying to kick my pity party to the curb.

My door slid open a crack, and Robin Goodfellow stuck his head in, his eyebrows arched even though his eyes were closed.

"Are you decent?" he cried.

"Depends on who you ask," I muttered.

My friend cracked one eye open with a dramatic flinch, as if worried he might see some eldritch horror instead of me without my shirt on.

"What do you want?" I asked, a hint of bitterness creeping into my voice. I was feeling pretty down about the system right now. Robin, despite being a friend, was also very much a cog in the machine that was forcing me to make big decisions.

"Testy, testy, my mortal friend," Robin clucked as he let himself into my room. "It's almost like you don't want the gift I have been sent to bring you."

"What gift?" I asked, narrowing my eyes. It might have been my birthday, but I was still suspicious of Fae bearing gifts. According to Shakespeare and Orion—and between the two of them, they have the subject rather covered—that was how they got you.

"It is your *birthday*." Robin put a hand to his chest as if he was insulted. "Even the Fae give gifts freely on a birthday."

"It's not free if you give them while expecting a gift on your birthday," I said, turning to face him. His white suit made it look like he was the one getting married. His shirt and buckles were all a shimmering gold that almost matched his eyes.

"For a mortal, you understand the Fae a little too well." He chuckled. "If I didn't know better, I would say we were losing our touch. You are quite right. Mine is in August, by the way." He stepped into the room, keeping his arms behind his back.

"I'll add it to my calendar," I promised, turning back to the mirror to fuss with my bow tie. Why was there a bow tie? "Fine. Before you explode, tell me about the present." Just because I was asking about a present on my birthday did not mean I was enjoying my birthday, for the record. But if I had to have one, I might as well cash in on the few perks—it was only practical.

"I was bidden to give you this in secret, for it is yours by right." He pulled his right hand from behind his back and held out a small black felt box. It was wrapped in golden lace tied into an immaculately perfect bow.

I reached out and took it from his hand. Slowly, I pulled on the ends of the bow and let the lace flutter to the floor. I pried open the lid like a velvet oyster, but instead of a pearl I found a ring. It was a simple golden band, proudly displaying the wealth of the Fae. In the center was a rectangular ruby that winked darkly in the bright lights of my room. The precious gem was surrounded by a circle of small diamonds, like a cluster of stars around a red sun.

Hand shaking, I reached out and picked up the ring. Willow immediately burst into flames as my finger touched the ring.

"*Ours!*" they cried in my head.

"It would not be fitting for a Lord of Fire to attend his own birthday ball without a mark of his station and favor," Robin pronounced with a note of triumph in his voice.

It took me a moment to process what he said. All I could do was stare at the ring. The light inside of the ruby seemed to glow, and I felt a kindred warmth bloom in my chest.

"Put it on," he urged.

"*Put it on*," Willow echoed.

I slid it onto my right ring finger. It fit perfectly, like it had been cut specifically for me. My suit had been the same way, even though I had never been to a tailor in my life or met anyone named Taylor. It was just how the Fae were.

"Not bad for the appetizer gift," Robin said, beaming.

"This wasn't my birthday present from the Queen?" I asked, surprised.

"No, your royal gift will be given to you at the party, for everyone to see," Robin chuckled. "This was something just for you." His golden eyes danced in the light as we stared at each other, his amusement growing the longer the silence stretched. I was beginning to get the feeling that I was being given a nudge.

"You can't tell me who this is from?" I asked.

"Sworn to secrecy," he replied with a shrug.

"And no one else sent anything?"

"I was only given the one present to deliver," he replied, his smile widening.

So that's how it was. I looked down at the ring on my finger. It felt heavier than it did a moment ago. The weight of an unspoken promise pulled on it with gravitational force that would make Newton proud.

I remembered the earnest look on Ash's face as she told me what it meant to her that I was a Lord of Fire and could help her rebuild her court. Now I wore the ring she had given me as a mark of station. Robin was wrong; the Fae might give birthday gifts, but they were not free. I had new levels of empathy for a fly wrapped in the strings of a spiderweb.

"You wouldn't be playing favorites, would you, Robin?"

"Come now, Matthew," he replied with a laugh. "You know better than that. I am Fae. I do not play."

THIRTY

THE MATTHEW CARVER Birthday Bash Ball
started an hour to midnight. Mortals would call that
eleven p.m., but that kind of newfangled time tracking
doesn't fly in the old-school circles.

The official invite was delivered on a scroll and said to arrive before
the witching hour, which was oh so unhelpful. Also, what kind of birthday party starts an hour before the birthday is over? Fortunately, Alex
was there to translate the invite into modernity for me, or I might have
missed my own birthday-slash-engagement-slash-villain takedown.

My two friends were dressed in tuxedos similar to mine. Robin
had given me a bright red pocket square, which felt a little on the nose,
but I went with it. Orion and Alex now rocked similar flares of red,

which I guess was our equivalent of a jersey for this social scrimmage. I was glad we got shirts instead of skins; I had no interest in showing up to my birthday in my birthday suit.

Robin led us to the Queen's grand ballroom, my nerves spiking as we drew closer. It felt like the butterflies in my stomach were hell-bent on trying to create a tornado inside my guts, collapsing me in on myself and creating an anxiety black hole that would devour all of Goldhall. I knew that Dawn and Ash were on board with the plan to take down Mav, but there was a lot of room for things to go wrong.

Alex slid next to me as we followed the Queen's servant through the halls. His blond hair was slicked back, and he wore the suit with a natural comfort that I was jealous of. I felt like a tub of putty shoved into a pair of fancy pants.

"How ya doing, boss?" he asked in a low voice.

"You know you're not actually my servant, right?" I shot back in the same hushed tone.

"You look nervous, so I figured I'd give your ego a nice little pat before you go swimming in the shark tank."

"I don't think it works if you tell me that you're lying to make me feel better," I grumbled.

"Have you made up your mind yet?"

"About what?"

"About which course you want for dinner. Come on, dummy, get your head in the game." My friend shot me a glare. "Matt, this is serious."

"I know, I know." I sighed. My palms were sweaty. I rubbed them on my sleeves as we walked. It didn't help. Whatever horrific cloth suits are made of, they are not absorbent. "I keep getting so distracted with the whole traitor plotline that I forget to focus on phase two."

Alex gave an amused snort.

"Who do you think I should choose?" I asked.

"They all terrify me." He shrugged and thought for a moment. "Definitely not Mav."

I chuckled. "Thanks for the killer analysis. Hadn't figured that one out on my own."

"Listen, man, all I'm saying is—are you sure you'd rather get *married* than go to Hell? How bad could it be there?"

I laughed. He laughed. We both looked at Orion, who stalked behind us like the fusion of James Bond and the Grim Reaper in a sports jacket. He did not laugh. His black eyes were dark and terrible.

"This is a trap," he said.

"Yeah, obviously," I hissed at him. "You were there when we planned it as a trap. If we're planning on bringing a trap, I'm sure everyone and their mother is bringing one too. It's BYOT. I'm open to better ideas. We're down to nine years. I know you're immortal, so time doesn't mean anything to you, but that's not a lot of time, and I'm the one going to the burny place."

"It's your *choice*," he said. "I cannot gainsay you your free will."

There it was. Gloriana had alluded to this when she showed me the Nothing. Power and immortality have some sort of inverse relationship with free will. The more you have of one, the less you have of the other. Life's a playground, and we're all sitting on the seesaw apparently. I was mortal. I had— Well, I was *supposed* to have a soul. Actually, I think I technically still owned my soul, but it was in some sort of escrow. The point is, I had free will in spades. Alex had a little less, and Orion a lot less. It's the same reason the Fae can't lie. They didn't have the free will to, even if they wanted to.

Orion could hate my choice all he wanted, but even though he was the big boss of the Hunt, he couldn't take it away from me. All he could do was be a big grumpy rain cloud.

"Seriously, guys." I stopped walking, and they both turned to stare at me. I could see the big double doors that led to the ballroom at the end of the hall. This was it, the final pit stop before showtime. "Speak now or forever hold your peace. If you have a better idea, I'm all ears, but I can't just do nothing until they come to collect me in nine years."

My two friends were silent. I glared at both of them, giving them their chance to derail this whole project. Part of me hoped they would come up with a better alternative. I wasn't thrilled about my chances walking this path, but as far as I could tell, it was the only one before me.

"It's not like I'm going into this with my eyes closed," I said after a pause. "I know the Fae are tricky and dangerous. But if I get dragged down into the Pit without trying every opportunity that comes my way, it will burn even hotter."

Orion eventually grunted, which was as much of an agreement as I could hope for, and we resumed our march toward my future. Alex started humming "Here Comes the Bride" under his breath, and I let him have it. It was a good joke.

A trio of servants waited for us at the door. A bright golden carpet had been rolled out of the entrance, and I watched some sort of fancy-dressed Fae be admitted ahead of us. Robin spoke to one who was apparently a chamberlain, a man wearing a white powdery wig and a scowl. In his hands he held an ornate wooden staff with a golden ball on the top and bottom.

"Squire Carver and the Hunt," Robin said by way of introduction.

The chamberlain pulled out a golden pocket watch on a chain and frowned at it for a moment, then closed it with an aggressive click.

"You're early," he complained.

"It is his birthday party," Robin pressed with a charming smile. "Announce them."

"You may be Her Majesty's favorite, but your father—" began the haughty chamberlain, but Robin interrupted. He stepped close, inside the range of the heavy-looking staff. He pulled a golden knife from one of his white sleeves so fast that I barely processed seeing it, but the chamberlain sure felt its cold edge pressed against him. His complaints cut off, and his furious golden eyes leveled on my lawyer with an icy promise.

"I *am* her favorite," Robin purred, knife firmly pressed against the chamberlain's kidney. Well, I assume. Do the Fae have kidneys? I have no idea. "That's why she trusts me to do her bidding and why you will do mine. Announce them."

The two immortals stared at each other for a long moment, arguing with their eyes or telepathy. The chamberlain didn't say anything, but Robin seemed to sense that he was capitulating. The knife vanished back up his sleeve with a flash of gold, and he stepped back, his smirk wider than before.

The chamberlain glowered at us but turned and nodded to the pair of servants manning the doors. They threw the doors open, and a wave of sound crashed down on us.

I had thought the great hall had been packed the first time I was brought to meet the Queen, but that was nothing. The room itself had *changed*. Instead of being a large reception hall, it now looked like it could hold a football field. The ceiling was open to the night sky, where brilliant stars shone down on us, unhindered by any light pollution. Idly, I wondered how many souls it cost to make the Nothing retreat enough to bring the stars back.

The floor was gone, replaced by thick green grass sprinkled with dandelions. Young trees had grown throughout the entire hall. Bright lights that had no form or substance to them hung in the leaves of the trees. Smaller lights zipped through the air like giant lightning bugs. As one shot right in front of us, I realized with a start that it was a pixie.

The glade, for a glade it was, was packed with Fae who laughed and drank and danced through the hall turned field. Music assaulted me from every direction as different bands played their own songs that had nothing to do with each other. But the partygoers only danced harder and faster, their movements oddly precise, reminding me of the halting mannerisms of praying mantises.

The chamberlain's staff crashed down on a chunk of the old marble floor preserved by the door. The golden cap on his staff rang like a bell. The music cut off harshly, as if the maestro had shot his first-chair violinist in the middle of a performance. The dancers stopped on a dime and turned to face the door. In the space of a heartbeat, the glade went from the ruckus of a frat party to the silence of a funeral. Hundreds of immortal eyes stared at us from around the forest.

"Presenting," the chamberlain's voice rang out cold and clear through the entire glade like a creek of snow melt, "Orion Allslayer, the Hunter; Alex Johnson, Squire of the Hunt; and Matthew Carver, Squire of the Hunt."

I gave the crowd a small smile. The hairs on the back of my neck all stood at attention like recruits at bootcamp. This was worse than being introduced to a new class after moving halfway through middle school.

Robin gave a pointed cough from my side into the silence. I glanced back at him, but he was glaring daggers at the chamberlain. My lawyer's hand snaked out and grabbed my right fist, holding it forward so the ruby on my finger glinted under the faerie lights.

"… and Lord of Fire," the chamberlain said through gritted teeth.

A rush of murmured surprise swept through the glade like a forest fire. I guess that cat was officially completely out of the bag.

Somewhere in the sea of the guests, one of the bands resumed their song exactly where they had left off, with the discordant whine of string instruments. Not to be outdone, a member of the band on the other side started playing a trumpet solo that was in a different key and tempo.

One by one, the guests stopped staring at me and my friends, sucked back into the rhythms of the party by something that seemed almost magnetic. Like a school of fish, they were unable to resist their nature. A dozen different dances spun through the same space but somehow never collided. Food and drink flowed, and laughter filled the gaps between every leaf and blade of grass.

As I took in the sea of inhumanity swirling around me, I realized there was a method to their madness, an order to their disorder. The Fae wore a riot of colors, but once I thought about what I was looking at, patterns leapt out. Members of the House of Winter always had the deep blue of the arctic accented in their clothing. Tania's followers wore green for Spring, and the House of Summer was decked in a bright yellow, the color of ripe wheat. Most of the attire was formfitting, silken clothing that would have been more appropriate for a rave than a formal ball. My tuxedo felt very stuffy, like I was a finance bro who showed up at his artist friend's birthday party.

Every once in a while, I saw someone wearing the bright orange of the flame of fall—of the House of Autumn. I had no idea how many hundreds were crammed into that glade, but orange was a rare find.

"No time to dawdle," Robin said as the party resumed its frantic pace. "The Queen will be waiting."

Adrenaline roared through me, sharpening my focus and my fears. Tonight, we were playing for keeps. If this went sideways, I might not ever get my soul back and then die. Happy birthday, me!

I followed in his wake as he led us deeper into the dark forest of the Fae. All around us, the partygoers swirled like barely contained waves of debauchery, caught in tide pools or dashing against the rocks. I felt a little flattered. I don't think anyone had ever had this much fun at my birthday before. Not even when I was thirteen and my parents rented out a laser tag place. Robin led us like a rave Moses, the Party Sea parting before us, and we walked on sober land.

I felt a sudden pressure on my arm as someone slipped theirs through mine. I turned, barely managing to stifle a surprised twitch to find Dawn, the Lady of Summer, walking beside me.

She wore a brilliant yellow bodysuit that clung to her with all the desperation of a man to an empty canteen in the desert. Something that I would describe as a half dress, like a cape but only around her hips, trailed down to her ankles. Her arms were bangled in gold and gems. On her forehead, she wore a black tiara set with a diamond the size of my thumbnail. She dazzled me with one of her brilliant smiles, but I knew her well enough now to know that I was about to experience another rousing conversation shootout with the Lady of Summer and not Dawn.

"A Lord of Fire?" She purred in a sultry tone. "No matter how much you dress up a donkey, it's still just a donkey, I'm afraid." Dawn beamed at some of the Fae dancing around us, like a good politician posing for photos.

"That might be the sneakiest way anyone has ever called me an ass," I said, echoing her smile to the nearby partiers who had clocked that I was walking arm in arm with one of their princesses. "Ass I may be, but if you're walking on my arm, I think that makes us a pair of cheeks."

"I know it's your birthday, but I can't wait to see what trap you fall for," Dawn said with a disdainful laugh. "Will one of my sisters eat you or burn you alive? Such a mystery!"

"How do you know I won't choose you? Maybe blondes are my type," I shot back, feeling a twist of fear in my gut. As we got closer to the center of the glade, I could now see there was a raised dais waiting for us, where Gloriana herself sat clothed in brilliant white, on a wooden throne overseeing the party.

"You're not smart enough for that move," Dawn said with a tinkling laugh.

"That might be true," I allowed, "but you will just have to wait and see like everyone else."

A genuine Dawn smile flashed across her face and vanished. She squeezed my arm with her hand and whispered, "We're ready." Then with a loud scoff, she spun away from me and into the melee of the party.

"That seemed fun," Alex murmured to me as she left.

"I feel a little like Scrooge tonight. I've already been visited by two Fae today. Just one more and I get bingo."

"I hope she was the 'Ghost of Christmas No Way Jose.'"

I frowned, not as sure as Alex was. I knew why he didn't like her. Of all the Fae we had met, she had been the most dismissive of him for the content of his blood. That was a red flag, but was it the worst flag? Unfortunately, in this roster of single ladies, it might not be.

If Fae couldn't lie, then she had been telling the truth when she said I wasn't smart enough to choose her, right? But did that mean it was the truth or just her truth? Was Faerie truth relative or absolute? My heartburn sure wasn't relative. I felt like I was going to throw up.

The stage in the center was getting closer, looming like an iceberg looking to slice open an unsuspecting *Titanic*. Time to sink or swim. I felt cold, like I was already treading water in a hypothermic ocean. It was almost decision time. Tania, Ash, or Dawn? Ash or Dawn? Dawn? Ash? Ash. Dawn. Tania?

"You're panicking. Breathe," Orion murmured from behind me. "I can hear your heart racing, and so can half the beings in this clearing."

"Maybe I'm just excited to finally get a girlfriend," I gritted through a large exhale. But I followed my teacher's instruction, trying to find my center.

"I don't think even very excited people have pupils the size of dinner plates," Alex replied dryly.

Robin came to an abrupt stop, hitting the brakes as a wall of Fae blocked our path like a dam of flesh. There were thirteen of them. They all wore formfitting outfits accented in the green of the House of Spring. In the center stood a familiar face: Rogan. I had already made him look stupid once. It seemed he wanted to make it a double.

Remembering his altercation with Mav in the halls, I wondered if he was in on the plan or had another one of his own.

"You are blocking the way of the Queen's guest of honor," Robin intoned in a dark voice. "Make way for the will of the Queen of All Fae."

"We will not move," Rogan said.

"Move or be moved."

"We will not move."

"Once more, I ask you to allow us to pass." There was an air of ritual to the questions that Robin asked, like they were following some social script I hadn't studied.

"We will not move."

Robin turned and stepped aside with a sigh, holding out his hands to us both as if to say *have at it, then*, then crossed his arms with an impatient scowl.

"That's it?" I asked him with a dumbfounded stare. "The Queen is fine with her will being casually ignored?"

"The Queen believes in a spirited nobility," Robin said with a shrug. "If you are worthy of her protection, she will expect you to show it."

Dimly, I became aware of the party guests clustering around us in a loose circle like a playground fight was about to start.

Everywhere I looked, the alien faces of the Fae shone bright, high on drink or pheromones, I couldn't tell. All of them had the same feral light burning in their eyes as they watched for violence.

"Hi, Ro," I said in my most cheerful tone. "You seem to be doing your best impersonation of a wall, which is a great aspiration for someone as dumb as a rock. I just feel bad for all these other suckers you've conned into participating in your group costume. They deserve better."

"You don't belong here, mortal," Rogan snarled, ignoring my brilliant opening jab. He probably didn't understand it. "Leave now or be forced to leave."

"Okay, first of all, that is the lamest threat I've ever heard in my life. Seriously, read a book sometime. You should have said something like 'You can leave in one piece or many.' That would have been way better. Two, I never take threats from anyone in tights seriously. Sorry, those are the rules. And number three." I raised my right hand in a fist and showed him the ruby ring. "I seem to belong as much as you do."

As I spoke, I sent a mental whisper to Willow, and their flames leapt into being at my command. Now that I knew what to look for, I saw a similar ring on Rogan's finger with an emerald glistening in the center, which I guessed was the mark of a Lord of Earth. Appreciative murmurs rang through the crowd gathered around us. Rogan's eyes tightened as he heard it. Another piece of the puzzle clicked. This was another way that I was fulfilling my promise to the Queen without even meaning to.

Dawn and Ash had shown me that my very existence strengthened the power of the Fae. I had only scratched the surface of Willow's power, but it was dangerous. With the absence of the Lords of Fire, the other elements and the other courts had lost a competitor. This was someone who benefited from the quenching of the Flame the same way Mav did. The whole society was set up to profit on the setting of their own sun. It made me a little sick.

Rogan might not even care that I was a mortal. But it was a convenient complaint to cover his true motive. I was the return to a power balance he and people like him did not like, and this might be their last chance to stop it before I was untouchable.

I honestly didn't care about their internal political struggles; they meant nothing to me. But I don't like bullies and I really wanted my soul back. Those two ingredients combined to make a potent potion of inspiration.

I thrust both of my burning hands into the air, so all of the partygoers could see them. The murmurs grew to an excited tempo.

"My friends," I said, turning in a circle, unafraid to show Rogan and his earthy cronies my back because Orion stood next to me, looming like a redwood tree. I would love to see one of them try it. The Hunter was itching for an excuse to paint this glade a new shade of red. "Many of you have never met me, or even seen me. But you can see me now. My name is Matt Carver, and I bear the news of the returning flame. I am a Lord of Fire. Our Queen tells me that I am a lost son of this kingdom, and tonight this party is not just my birthday—it is a HOMECOMING!"

As I roared the last word, I sent my thoughts to Willow. *"Show them something they won't forget!"* I told them.

"THE RETURNING FLAME!" Willow screamed back at me.

I blinked in surprise. I hadn't expected my rhetoric to ignite something in the fire spirit's heart as well.

The fire around my hands erupted like twin volcanoes. Flames shot into the clearing of the sky and danced, sending sparks raining down in a display that would make Uncle Sam tear up on the Fourth of July. The assembled Fae cheered, some danced, and they scattered like cockroaches exposed to the light. The party resumed at breakneck speed.

"Try not to burn the place down, please," I muttered under my breath to Willow.

Willow didn't respond, but the eruption petered off like a fire hydrant running out of water pressure. I lowered my hands and turned my attention to Rogan and his friends, who hadn't gone back to partying. His aristocratic face boiled with rage; the attention of his peers was gone now. It felt like the entire species had already moved on to the next shiny thing. Whatever scene Rogan had hoped for was ruined. I felt a savage satisfaction in my chest at that.

"You've caused enough embarrassment for one night, Rogan." A woman's voice filled the space between us like a mountain. Tania had come to find me.

"Uh-oh," I called. "Mom's home."

Rogan's face paled, and he danced back a step as if the floor had suddenly turned to lava beneath his feet.

"Go, all of you," she snapped, and the blockage of Fae collapsed like a rotten wall. My path to the center was clear.

Robin clucked his tongue in disappointment at the retreating Spring Fae and shot me a grin before resuming his march toward the Queen. Tania fell in step beside me but didn't grab my arm. Her bodysuit was worked with rich browns and greens. The crown nestling in her dark hair was made from flowering blossoms. She looked like Mother Nature's favorite daughter. Her frown was as threatening as thunderstorm clouds building on the horizon.

"It seems that you've made a decision," she said after we took a few steps.

"It does?" I replied with a laugh. "If you know what it is, I would love to hear it, because I haven't even told myself yet."

"So, you are not Falling?" she asked with a surprised turn to face me. "I thought that—"

"I prefer to think of it as 'Turning to Autumn,' actually," I said sternly.

Tania was silent.

"Why did you send your idiot squad after me if you still wanted me to choose you?"

"I didn't send him after you. He's jealous."

"He's that bent out of shape about the Lord of Fire thing?"

"He's been trying to convince my sister to wed him for quite some time. He wants to be a member of the royal family, and Ash is the only one of my sisters who has given him an inch."

Aha.

It was possible that I was getting ahead of myself with the conspiracy theory of power and corruption stuff. Maybe me being a Lord of Fire had nothing to do with why Rogan hated me. I was just talking to the girl he liked. How depressingly juvenile. Even here in the Faerie Lands, it all boiled down to hormones and greed. It turns out that mortals and Fae aren't as different as they like to think they are, deep down they are moved by the same levers.

We made it to the center of the glade. Queen Gloriana noticed us from up on the dais; watching us approach with an unreadable expression. Mav and Ash sat on either side of her, as far apart from each other as they could get. A collection of servants carried more chairs and set them around her to make room for our approach.

"Matthew," Tania said softly, an urgent note in her voice. "Please."

I turned to face the princess walking next to me. Her brown eyes were pleading as she stared back at me. A strong pang of guilt hummed in my gut. Did I not have any sympathy for the Lady of Spring? Was my own situation really different? No, it wasn't. I had to stand before people more powerful than me and beg for my soul back. We both just wanted to be free.

But just because birds of a feather flock together doesn't mean it's a good idea. It just makes it easier for the shotgun pellets to hit both of them. Even if I got my soul back tonight, the Devil himself still had a bone to pick with me. If I was going to make it to thirty, I was going to need backup—not an apathetic royal partner.

"You don't know what you're getting into," she pleaded, her eyes glistening with barely restrained tears. "I don't want to do this."

I wondered if her mother had already told her about some creepy old king that she would have to marry if I didn't pick her. I gave her a gentle smile. "I really appreciate your honesty," I said, trying to be careful. "It's a major component of the decision I'm trying to make." Now, I thought that was a perfect Fae answer, completely true but promising nothing.

"You're a bigger fool than I thought if you choose to join that fallen court," she said as we parted at the front of the dais. I let her go without a word—the Queen was waiting for me.

Gloriana wore a brilliant golden crown in her dark hair. It seemed to glow like the moon with the reflection of her sun. Her gown looked like it had started life as a wedding dress before being fed to a wood-chipper. The front half had been ripped off and replaced with something that resembled a one-piece bathing suit, and the trail still hung off the back like a peacock's tail.

It was simultaneously ruined and perfect. She was breathtaking. It fit her like a glove, like snowcaps fit a mountain. In that moment, I understood how different the Fae were from us. No Hollywood celebrity's star could hold a candle to her sun.

Her golden eyes took me in at a glance, and I felt that she knew everything that had just happened. From the new ring on my finger to the showdown with Rogan, she was *aware* in a way that made my skin crawl and my brain feel like its personal space had been violated, like my apartment had after the ghouls broke in last year.

As Robin led us right to the front of the dais, Tania and Dawn sat with their sisters, arrayed behind their mother like guardians. The four seasons of the Dandelion Court were assembled in one place— probably for the last time.

Robin dropped to one knee. On instinct, I did the same. Mortal see, mortal do. Alex knelt at my side. I could barely make out Orion in the corner of my eye, but he was still standing—that made sense. He's special.

Gloriana rose from her seat and held up her hands. Silence rippled through the party like a wave. It wasn't like the crashing halt when the chamberlain announced our entrance, but a beautiful finale. If the party had been a concert, the composer would have picked that moment to be the perfect pause for intermission.

"My people!" The Queen's voice echoed from the treetops, filled with majesty and grace. "We are gathered here this evening to celebrate the ending of a life. Tonight, Matthew Carver the boy dies."

AS I'VE MENTIONED, my expectations for my birthday were pretty low, but even I wasn't ready for public execution. Startled by her pronouncement, I twitched, mentally preparing to leap to my feet and fight the entire Faerie race in a tuxedo, James Bond style.

"Stay still," Robin hissed, somehow sensing my panic.

I glanced at Alex, who gave me a blank look. Maybe I was missing something.

"Tonight heralds his twenty-fifth birthday. Among our kind, we consider a quarter century to be when a child arrives at their majority. After tonight, Squire Carver, you will no longer be a child, you will be a man."

Oh. Well, that was nice. I had already been able to vote and buy cigarettes and alcohol for years. It never occurred to me that this party was the supernatural equivalent of a twenty-one run, but as I glanced around at the definitely drunk Fae gathered around us, it suddenly seemed obvious.

"Rise, Matthew," the Queen called down to me. Slowly, I stood, my shoulders bearing the weight of a few hundred pairs of supernatural eyes. "Join me," she said, and I trotted to the stairs and up onto the dais. The assembled Fae looked hungry, staring at me like dogs waiting by their food bowl. They wanted something, and I still had only a few guesses as to what it was.

"It is traditional for a parent or guardian to give a gift on this monumental day," Gloriana pronounced to the crowd. "However, since you have neither present, it falls to me, your patron."

The glade was perfectly still, frozen in that immortal, inhuman way. Standing on the raised dais looking out at the sheer amount of Fae in attendance, I was a little stunned. Most of the ones clustered around us looked like they could be cousins to mortal humans, like I was used to seeing around the palace. But on the outer edges I saw shapes of inhuman creatures I didn't recognize. I felt heavier, like the sheer amount of attention focused on the Queen, and by proxy, me, increased the gravity in the glade by an order of magnitude.

"You are a man pulled between two worlds," the Queen said, turning to favor me with a smile brighter than anything else in the glade. "You are a squire of the Hunt and our returning Lord of Fire. Even though you have found your way back to your people, you are also of the mortal realm. It is only fitting that as you make your place among us, you have a key to your own home."

She held out a hand, and a white-and-gold-clad servant slipped a perfectly wrapped black box with an equally perfect golden bow into her waiting palm. Santa's best elves could not have done a better job.

Gloriana took a step closer to me and held out the box, her warm smile reflected in her shining golden eyes.

Heart racing, I took the box. When I told Robin what I wanted for my birthday, I hadn't really expected to get it. Slowly, I undid the bow, and it fluttered to the ground as I lifted the lid off the little black box. There, resting on a velvet cushion, was an old brass key. There were two masks etched into the top, one smiling and one frowning, facing in different directions. I reached out to touch it and let out a gasp as my fingers brushed the metal. It was cold as ice and buzzing with power like it was about to shock me.

"This is the Key of Portunus, forgotten master of doors. If you desire to travel between the mortal world and my home, put the key in any door and it will take you here or there."

My jaw dropped as I stared at the key. This was better than what I had asked for. I swiped the key and slid it into my pocket, terrified I would somehow drop it and lose it. I bowed deeply to Gloriana. Even I knew that this was a great gift. I was being honored in front of all of the Fae, and I had to make sure she knew I was grateful.

"Your Majesty is far too generous," I said, low enough that only those nearby could hear, even with their supernatural hearing.

"I am most assuredly not," the Queen replied. "You have earned that gift by keeping your faith to my people and to me. See that I do not have any cause to take it back." A tingle of that same electric power ran down my spine at her threat, but I only nodded.

"I keep my word, Your Majesty."

"I expect nothing less," she murmured with an almost frustrated tone.

She turned back to the crowd and beamed at them. Excited murmurs emerged from the crowd. My butterflies all dropped dead as my nerves turned into a stone of dread at the bottom of my gut.

"When the clock strikes midnight and his birthing day has ended, Squire Carver will be an adult by our reckoning. But not only will he be an adult, tonight we welcome him back to us as one who was lost. Tonight, our returning Lord of Fire will join my own household and be betrothed to one of my daughters."

"Mother, if I may interrupt you for just one moment," Dawn said, rising to her feet from her chair. "The squire is owed one more gift—justice, and if you will allow it, I would give it to him tonight."

Gloriana gave Dawn a long look, her golden eyes narrowing for a moment before she stepped to the side toward me, waving for the Lady of Summer to come to the front. "Indeed, he is," she agreed.

My heart began to beat its well-practiced drum solo of fear. This was it. Step one of the birthday party hat trick. Here in front of the entire court, I was going to prove my worth to the Queen and expose a traitor. I hoped Rogan was watching; he might be next. Last-minute panic ate away at my confidence, like I was back in college taking a final. Had I gotten something wrong? Dawn, Ash, Alex, and even Orion had agreed with my reading of the clues. Had we all been fooled? If we had, I had a feeling that Matthew Carver the adult might end up dying at his own birthday party too.

"As you may have heard," Dawn said, taking the reins of the party from her mother with fluid grace, "my mother has named me her executor in the search for justice. Squire Carver and the Hunt are our guests, and yet while under the roof of Goldhall, they were attacked by assassins."

She might have some... aggressive opinions about class and breeding, but there was no denying that the Lady of Summer was born to rule, from the moment she began speaking, the crowd was hooked on her words.

A low murmur ran through the assembled throng, a rumble of discontent that hinted at an avalanche of outrage. Dawn held up her hands like a maestro, silencing them.

"As my mother's executor, my word is her word, my will, her will.

An oath has been given to the Hunt, and it must be fulfilled. We are the Fae. We have never broken an oath, we have never broken a trust, and we will not begin now."

The crowd roared their enthusiastic agreement, like truth and faithfulness were their favorite football teams.

"I hope you know what you are doing," Gloriana murmured softly into my ear. Her voice was calm, but I didn't trust it.

"You told me to prove my worth," I replied, doing my best to keep my lips from moving while I spoke. "I found the source of your rats, and now we are cleaning house."

"As executor, I must now stand before the Iron Table in accusation. Today I bring before you in the name of the Queen, a traitor."

I risked a nervous glance at the far side of the throne, where Mav was seated. The Lady of Winter's face was impassive, frozen in a neutral mask. Her birthday ball rave outfit looked like it had started life as surplus combat gear. She wore a pair of shredded arctic camo cargo pants, with a matching top nestled under a long-sleeved fishnet. Her terrifying obsidian sword rested against her chair, just within reach.

"Tonight, we have celebrated the returning Flame and the strength it means for us. But, my people, we cannot progress into our future until we deal with our past! With the help of Squire Carver and the Hunt, I have uncovered a conspiracy, one that has been responsible for the systematic murdering of Lords and Ladies of Fire for the past four hundred years."

The crowd was silent, horror etched onto many of the Fae faces that stared up at Dawn, hanging on her every word like addicts.

"This conspiracy has been seeking to quench the flame of the Willow and extinguish the Path of Flames permanently, forever crippling the power of our people.

"I challenge my sister, Mav, Lady of Winter, to stand before the Iron Table and answer for her crimes against Fae and mortal alike!"

Dawn called in a crystal-clear voice.

I almost choked in surprise. I hadn't realized that Dawn would be willing to put her life on the line for this.

The glade was completely still, frozen in shock. Not a single person dared to move, or to breathe too hard. Gloriana's golden gaze turned to meet me, her twin suns boiling with rage. My throat went dry as I took in her baleful stare. Her wrath gave off a physical heat, making the air around her shimmer like a mirage on the horizon of a desert. Not for the first time, I was reminded that I had no idea how strong the Queen was—definitely more than me.

The Queen's fury moved past me to look over my shoulder. Slowly, so as not to make any sudden movements that might get me attacked by this furious, primal queen, I turned to check on how Mav was handling the accusation. The Lady of Winter was powerful. If she decided to throw herself at Dawn, I was uncomfortable with how close I was standing to the potential splash zone.

But Mav was not on the attack. The Lady of Winter remained frozen in her chair. A single tear traced its way down her cheek as she stared at Dawn. The Lady of Summer glanced at me and gestured for me to join her.

"You hired the Gilded Dancers to assassinate us on two different occasions, trying to kill us or break the treaty between Hunt and Fae," I recited, projecting my voice for the entire glade to hear. "You also sent them to kill your sister, the Lady of Autumn, and have been using them to execute Lords and Ladies of Fire for centuries."

Gloriana let out a disbelieving murmur behind me, which made me a little nervous. I kinda thought Dawn would break the news to her mother before we went full bore in front of everyone.

Despite my growing concern, I continued talking, getting even louder so I could hear my own voice over the rush of blood in my ears. "You tampered with the wards that would have notified the Royal

Guard of deaths during the attacks on both the Hunt and the Lady Ash."

"Well?" Dawn demanded, her voice cruel and strong. "Do you deny it? Speak now, sister. Will you refute my accusations for all to hear and send me to the Table?"

Mav's silence was the loudest thing I had ever heard. I almost felt bad for the Queen. I didn't think she was the best mother I had ever seen, but no matter what, having your daughter betray you and try to murder one of your other daughters has to hurt somewhere deep.

"Finally," I said, taking her silence as an opportunity to pile even more on her. "You gave the demons access to Goldhall to assist you in your quest to weaken the Dandelion Court."

Mav turned to look at me, her gray eyes flickering with an emotion I could not place. If I didn't know better, I would have said it was triumph.

Gloriana moved in a blur that was too fast for my eyes to track. One moment she was standing beside me, the next she was towering over her traitorous daughter. Her beautiful, sculpted face was twisted into a furious mask of rage.

"Do you confess?" she asked her daughter in a low, dangerous tone.

"I deny it!" Mav screamed boldly, the corner of her lips turning up in a vulture-like smile. Murmurs ran through the assembled crowd like the incoming tide.

It felt like the floor beneath me gave way and I was in a free fall a thousand miles up in the atmosphere. How could she deny it? It had to be true. But she *couldn't lie.* Dawn shot me a terrified glance before turning to her sister.

I could feel the Queen's displeasure growing like a thunderhead before me. If I didn't figure this out quickly, Dawn and I were both liable to get fried, birthday or no birthday. Think, Matt, think!

Fear gave my mind wings as I flew through the clues again. We knew too much. We couldn't be wrong. This was the only way it added up. But she had denied it. Somehow, she had denied it!

A wild thought occurred to me, like a single ray of light breaking through the clouds of my confusion. If I was going to catch her, I had to be as tricky as a Faerie. "What specifically do you deny?" I asked, narrowing my eyes.

I saw Mav's chin wiggle as her jaw clenched. My organs abruptly found themselves standing on solid ground. I hadn't been wrong about everything; something had been off just enough that she had tried to deny it and make it sound like she had been denying all the charges.

"What do you deny?" The Queen's voice was like hallowed ground, ancient and terrifying.

"I dealt with no demons, nor did I invite them in," Mav said at last, raising her chin stiffly, as if she still had some pride to retain.

Bingo.

"And the rest?" the Queen asked again in that terrible voice.

"I did all of those things," Mav said, staring into her mother's eyes, which might have been one of the bravest things I had ever seen. Except for the tears occasionally trickling down her cheeks, Mav looked as cool as a cucumber for someone who stood close to one of the great living Powers.

I was struck again by how much easier it was interrogating people who couldn't lie. I would have denied it until my dying moment. They could be walking me to the gallows, and I would never admit to having the slightest idea what anyone was talking about.

"Why?" Gloriana asked in a softer voice that did not carry throughout the glade. For the first time, I thought I saw a shadow of pain reflecting in her features, like an eclipse. "How could you do that to me, to your people?"

Mav's voice was cold and cruel as she answered her mother. "Don't act like you ever loved me. I was just your weapon. You were always going to throw me away and replace me with *her*." Her gray eyes flickered toward Ash. "All I ever wanted was for you to need me, but you were so obsessed with getting your precious Flame back that there wasn't anything, or anyone, you wouldn't do to rekindle it, even replace me with the Hunt."

"Oh, Mav, my daughter, my fierce falcon, I would have always needed you. I would never have thrown you away." Gloriana's voice was gentle and surprised, like the comforting words of a real mother.

Surprised by the change in her voice, I turned to glance at the queen. Where had all her rage gone? I noticed she didn't say love— only need.

"But now you've forced me to do just that." Her tone became hard once more. She glanced up and gave Robin a sharp nod, who in turn waved behind the dais. A squad of Royal Guards marched out from behind us, hands on their blades, golden eyes sharp. Murmurs ran through the crowd as they began to thaw out from their shock.

Several pairs of hands seized Mav and pulled her from her chair. Firmly, they forced her to kneel next to the Queen, who turned to look past me, to the hulking form of Orion.

"I have promised you justice, Hunter, and tonight you shall have it." The Queen gestured at the kneeling form of her daughter. "If you require her head, come and take it."

My own head whipped around to look at Orion. The Queen's promise had been made to the Hunt, so technically that meant it had been made to the Hunter. It was an oath between two rulers.

The Constellation strode forward, his right hand drawing the burning blade from over his shoulder. The sword's light washed over the dais, pushing back the natural darkness that filled the glade, like a city's light pollution corrupting nature.

The Hunter marched to stand beside the Queen, his black eyes fixed on the kneeling form of the princess. I could tell he was warring with the two aspects of his personality. The blood of demons and Immortals that flowed through his veins demanded he claim what was owed to him. But the mortal DNA whispered that there was a better way.

Our leader glanced over his shoulder at Alex and me, a frown set firmly on his face. The Fae had been one of his greatest enemies throughout the years, and while they had made a formal peace, I could tell that he itched to take this freebie.

Whatever permission he was searching for in our faces, he did not seem to find. With a frustrated huff, the Nephilim slid his burning blade back home into the sheath on his shoulder. "Throw her in your darkest dungeon and forget about her," he said, turning away from the Queen and princess and striding to stand next to Alex.

I breathed out a sigh of relief. Don't get me wrong, I wasn't a Mav fan by any stretch of the imagination. I had been the one to set this whole exposé up, after all. But I also wasn't sure I was ready to add "saw someone get decapitated" to the list of my birthday traumas. I already had more than enough.

Gloriana cocked her head, as if surprised by the Hunter's leniency. After a moment, she nodded. I couldn't tell if it was in acceptance or gratitude of his decision. She snapped her fingers, and the guards began to lead Mav away. This was already more awkward than most of my birthdays, and we were just getting started.

I glanced back at the two daughters who were still sitting. Ash sat straight back in her chair, face blank, like a scared student when another member of the class is being punished, or probably more accurately, like a child when their sibling has just been condemned to no TV for a month. Or the rest of their life, I guess?

Tania was in complete shock. Both her hands were over her mouth, and she stared at Mav with eyes the size of baseballs. It seemed that at least one daughter had been completely out of the loop.

Tension flowed out of my shoulders and neck as Mav was pulled off to the side, only to be replaced by the next stress in line. It was like each terrifying thing had taken a number and I was some sort of DMV for fear.

Gloriana stepped back up to the front of the platform, displacing me and Dawn with the effortlessness of a rising tide. She simply flowed into the space, and we were swept out like a pair of boats. The Queen of All Fae stared out at the expectant faces of her court, seemingly unbothered by the betrayal of her eldest daughter. She was a pillar of strength; she could have been carved from the very marble of her palace.

"Let it be known," she said in a conversational tone, as if she were speaking to a room of her closest friends and not the huddled mass of her subjects, "that we as a people owe a debt. It is fitting that tonight is a night to celebrate Matthew Carver, for he has done us a great service."

Chills walked down my spine as she spoke. To have the Queen declare that the entire Fae species was in my debt was something I couldn't wrap my head around.

"I gave Squire Carver a task. To prove himself worthy to join the royal family, I commanded him to root out the traitors in our midst. Not only did he obey my command, but he struck the head from a snake that I was too blind to see."

I struggled to swallow as Faerie after Faerie in the audience slowly turned their attention from their queen to me. Earlier, I had felt a little like a performing monkey in a suit. Everyone was excited to see me but didn't take me seriously, even with Willow's flames. Now their collective gazes were different. I felt like I was being measured by a thousand tailors at once, but instead of my inseam they were measuring my weaknesses. I was less like a circus animal and more like a steak being held out to a pack of wolves.

I think I preferred it when they saw me as an excuse to have a party.

"Come, Matthew," the Queen said, turning to face me, spreading her arms out in welcome. "You have been a good and faithful servant. It is time for the reward you were promised. It is time for you to choose one of my daughters and join my family."

Heart racing, I joined the Queen at what felt like the edge of the high dive. Now all I had to do was not belly flop.

GLORIANA GESTURED, AND the three remaining princesses filed out behind us, like they were
in a police lineup. Ash wore a bodysuit that fit the
dress code for all Fae. Hers was worked in two shades of orange, like
beautiful autumn leaves or a leaping flame. Unlike her sisters, she wore
no tiara. Her eyes were downcast, and she didn't meet my gaze. Dawn
and Tania gave me aggressive looks from either side of her.

"Matthew Carver, Squire of the Hunt, Lord of Fire, it is time
for you to fulfill the promise you made to me. Have you made your
choice?" the Queen asked.

I thought it was interesting that she kept calling it a gift and
then demanded I follow through on a promise, but I kept my mouth

shut. It was so dry I probably could have only croaked at her anyway. Tonight, I was getting my soul back, but there was a down payment to take care of.

A hush settled on the entire glade, like what I imagine it might be like if it had been covered in a foot of snow in the peak of winter... and empty. A crystalline clarity settled on me as I looked at the three sisters before me, each as lovely as a sunrise and dangerous as the sea. The silence stretched into one of those eternal moments as the entire kingdom waited to hear my answer.

Tania was not my friend. Tania wanted something from me and didn't mind if I profited at the same time. But she didn't care about me. She wasn't an ally; I was on sale, and she needed a Matt-sized piece of furniture to sit on. What would happen if I wasn't the key to the freedom she craved? She would turn on me in a heartbeat if it meant getting what she wanted. I know you're supposed to keep your friends close and enemies closer, but I'm not sure that rule applies to Fae wives.

Dawn also wanted something, but she confused me. I knew she wanted to rule, and saw herself as her mother's heir, but also, I was convinced there was more to it that I didn't know. I would have thought she was completely uninterested, but her conversation with me on the way to the dais had convinced me that she did want me to choose her. If I had to guess, she wanted to harness the first Lord of Fire in four hundred years to her house rather than let Ash rebuild. Yeah, that felt right.

I tried to catch Ash's eye in the still moment, but she would not look up. Her shoulders were slumped. She looked defeated. I knew that look well; it was one that had been at the forefront of my wardrobe most of my life. Of all of the princesses, Ash was the only one who had ever taken the time to speak to me as a person. She showed me her home and shared a piece of her life with me. I glanced down at the ruby ring on my finger and felt a faint tug of something on my conscience.

I turned to look at the Queen, time was beginning to pick up speed again, like a locomotive pulling its train from a standstill. My heart was racing, but it wasn't with fear anymore. It was the excitement an athlete gets right before the starting gun. This was it.

"Well, Matthew?" Gloriana said, her lips turned up in a slight smirk. "What is your decision?"

I let out a long exhale and stepped toward the princesses. There was no more think, only do. I held out my hand to Ash and waited a heartbeat. A legion of Fae collectively let out a quiet gasp as they saw my gesture.

"It seems to me," I said loudly, forcing my nervous voice to project across the glade, "that the House of Autumn has been without a Lord of Fire for far too long. If the Lady of Autumn will have me, I would fix that."

As I spoke, Ash's head snapped up in shock. Her radiant green eyes stared into mine, and for a moment, nothing else existed. We were transported to another plane that had no walls or light, only each other. It must have also had no oxygen, for I found I could not breathe.

Then she smiled.

It was a brilliant smile, like the coming of the sun after a storm. The kind that makes rainbows dance in the wake of fleeing clouds. As quickly as we had gone, we were back amongst the Fae in the wooded glade, and I could breathe again.

She took my hand. It was warm and soft in the best possible way. Without prompting, Willow's fire erupted from both of our hands, the flames dancing wildly with joy.

"Let it be so!" Gloriana spun to face the crowd and raised both her hands in the air. The Fae immediately let out a roar of noise, and the festivities resumed with a fury, like we had passed through the tranquil eye of a party hurricane and had been plunged right back into the thick of it. How quickly Mav and her treason were forgotten in the primal surge of the celebration.

I turned to look at Ash and gave her an embarrassed smile. Now that the decision was made, I found myself feeling bashful. The flock of stupid butterflies were back, this time impersonating the Blue Angels, doing wild acrobatics in my stomach. She laughed and squeezed my hand. Something inside my chest soared.

I had finally done something right. It had only taken twenty-five years, but I had done it. I almost wished I had cell phone service so I could call my father and tell him he was wrong about me. But then I came to my senses. There was no point in letting him ruin yet another moment for me.

Despite the general revelry, not everyone was celebrating.

I glanced out at the sea of Fae and noticed knots of them milling together, little islands of silence as the sea of the party raged around them. The members of the pockets of stillness all stared at the dais with obvious displeasure on their faces, glaring daggers at me or the Queen, or maybe both. As I studied the unhappy Fae, I noticed that most wore the earthy tones of spring. In the background, streams of figures in blue and black made their way toward the exit. That made sense, having the head of your house arrested for treason was probably a bit of a vibe killer.

The Queen clapped and shouted as the rest of her court partied, delighted by their celebrations the same way a parent delights at anything their toddler does, no matter how simple. The Lady of Summer made her way over to us, her imperious demeanor in full effect.

"An inevitable choice, I guess." She sighed dramatically, drawing up short before us. I felt Ash's hand stiffen in mine at her sister's words. I understood that. Dawn in this mode had a gift for getting under your skin, but just like with high school bullies, the trick was to not let her know when she landed a punch.

"It just felt thematically right," I said, gesturing at our flaming hands with a shrug. "Besides, I've never been any good at summer. Have you seen how pale I am? I burn super easily, and I hate how slimy sunscreen feels." I gave her my best smug smile, in parody of her own.

Dawn's grin only grew wider in response. Maybe she just appreciated good banter?

"Oh, you misunderstood me," Dawn replied, choking back a laugh. "I think the House of Fall is *perfect* for you."

"You mean the House of Autumn," I replied firmly.

A cackle escaped from Dawn's lips. "I cannot wait until her father hears about this. He already hates you so much I can't even begin to imagine the fury this will send him spiraling into. No one rages quite like the Devil."

My vision went stark and colorless, like I had just been hit with a flashbang. Dimly, I was aware of Dawn continuing her gloating, but I couldn't make out any of the words. My brain tried to give birth to any thought, but they wouldn't form.

Now I understood why her sisters called her the Lady of Fall.

Ash was the Devil's daughter. The same Devil whose girlfriend I had killed last year. The same Devil who was going to claim ownership of my soul in nine years. Who am I kidding? Everyone knows who he is.

Of course she was. I had already guessed that Gloriana chose to have children with powerful beings tied to the different elements of her houses. Ullr was a god of winter and had given her Mav. Dawn's father was a god, and she had power over the wind. Who better to bring the heat than the master of the fiery pits himself?

The Queen told me that she wanted to take Lucifer down a peg or two. Had I let myself be pulled into a jilted lovers' quarrel? Talk about coming out of the fire only to go into the bigger, hotter fire.

The first sound I heard as I got ahold of myself was the crack of Alex's palm smacking into his face. I thought that was a good response, so I did it too. Holy crapola.

"You're whose daughter now?" I asked my betrothed, voice an octave or two higher than usual.

"It's not like that," Ash said, her green eyes mirroring building tears.

Dawn chuckled a vicious, cruel laugh and walked away. "I tried to warn you," she sang, the damage from her conversational grenade already done.

"Oh, it isn't?" I demanded, my voice impossibly going even higher. "That's great to hear. Is it a different Lucifer? Different guy, someone I wouldn't know? What is this a Jesus, Jesús kind of situation?"

"No," Ash breathed with a defeated sigh. "He's the same one."

"Then how exactly is it different?" I almost shrieked.

"I've never met him," Ash snapped back, her own anger rising. "He left the moment my mother told him about me, and I've never so much as seen him. He may have given me some of his damned DNA, but he is no father of mine."

Oh.

I've always assumed that Hell was full of deadbeat dads, but it never occurred to me that one of them was running the place. I finally had the last piece of the puzzle I had been missing, but instead of a picture, it formed a mirror. I knew a little what that felt like. The heat of my anger flushed out of my body like steam escaping a vent and left me feeling cold and empty.

"I'm sorry. I know how much that hurts." I stared into my betrothed's—ugh, that felt so 1700s. I can't do it—I stared into Ash's eyes and saw them soften as she saw my anger dissipate.

"Why didn't you tell me?" I asked her.

"Mother made us swear not to tell you until after you made your choice. She was afraid that if you knew her connection to Hell, you wouldn't take the deal because you wouldn't trust us." Ash looked at the floor, unable to meet my eyes. The fall jokes hadn't been just snide barbs, I realized, but the Fae trying to hint what they physically weren't able to say. "That was why I've avoided you since the first time we spoke. I couldn't bear to lure you into a deal without telling you the truth. I was trying to exclude myself from Mother's game."

"Then why did you send me the ring?" I demanded. "Most lures are shiny. I'm definitely feeling a little lured right now!"

"The ring?" she asked, her brows furrowing in confusion. Her gaze tracked down to the Lord of Fire signet on my hand, and her eyes widened. "Matthew, I did *not* send you that," she breathed in horror.

I wondered if this was how all the children felt when the Pied Piper abruptly stopped playing his tune after leading them off into the wild. Someone had sent me the ring, implying it was from Ash, but if she hadn't done it, then who had?

"I'm so sorry," she whispered, tears forming in her eyes, hand over her mouth. "I know you can never forgive me, but this is not what I wanted to happen to you."

The look in her sad green eyes tugged on my heartstrings until they sang. It seemed that the Queen had been playing several games at once. If Ash had been forced to give her word to not tell me, then what could she have done? She and I were both just pieces of driftwood caught up in tides much bigger than us.

"What if... what if I did forgive you?" I managed a small smile as I stared at her.

"Oh brother," Alex muttered behind me, watching our entire exchange with something like amused outrage on his face. "We are so going to die."

I ignored him. I was busy snatching victory from the jaws of defeat. I had made it through two of the three hurdles tonight, and now all I had to do was get my soul back. El Diablo was already supposedly building a new circle downstairs for me, so realistically, how much more upset could he even get?

Things were finally looking up for Matthew Carver. I could get used to that.

From the back of the room, the chamberlain's staff boomed as it struck the stone, the sound echoing through the glade like a blast of thunder. A second time he struck, and then a third. My attention was pulled toward the disturbance. Even the Queen turned to stare.

"Presenting Damien Fireheart, Lord of Fire!" the chamberlain's voice echoed through the room.

The party vanished. It did not pause. It did not stop. It simply was and then it was not. One moment there was revelry and debauchery that would make Bacchus proud. In the blink of an eye, the party animals froze, like deer going still to hide from a predator.

The Fae parted to make way for the rapidly approaching Lord of Fire. It was easy to track his progress as the partiers scattered away from him like a disturbed school of fish. He moved at a crisp trot, straight as an arrow toward the dais. Somehow, I felt more stressed, but I didn't connect the dots until the front of the crowd parted to make space for him.

Into the clearing stormed my father, his solid gold eyes boiling with rage and his hands blazing with a familiar fire.

"*Hey, look, it's me!*" Willow squealed in our minds.

Somewhere in the background, a clock chime struck midnight.

THE RINGING OF the clock heralded the official end of my birthday. Which was the universal sign that things were about to go horribly wrong. My birthday is the metaphorical equivalent of someone saying "let's split up" in a horror movie—someone is about to die.

So, as I stared at my father—my *real* father, Damien Fireheart, not the mortal he had pretended to be my entire life—I tried to figure out why I was even a little bit surprised.

It had been right in front of me the whole time. The only way it could have been more obvious was if someone made a giant neon sign with an arrow pointing to a second, even larger sign that said, HEY, IDIOT, YOUR DAD IS THE LAST LORD OF FIRE. The Queen had told me that I had Faerie blood. I had assumed that she meant in some long-lost branch of my family tree, but she hadn't actually said that. Freaking Fae.

That was why Willow was able to bond with me without breaking the promise they had made to the last Lord of Fire. I was his son, a member of his family. The real reason the Queen had needed me was to unlock the Path of Flames and usher in a new era of fire-wielding Fae. All that nonsense about being a part of the Hunt was just the cherry on top. I had known I was getting played, but the sheer scope of it was staggering.

"Well if it isn't the prodigal Lord of Fire, returned once more to my hearth," the Queen crowed. "What was it you said? Something about your shadow never darkening my halls ever again?"

"I am taking my son, Gloriana," my father snarled. His golden eyes locked on to mine. "You. Come."

When I was a child, hell, even a few weeks ago, my father's voice had a physical force that I found almost impossible to disobey. My body twitched in response to his command, but my feet did not move.

"Now," Damien Fireheart growled. He pointed a flaming finger at the grass in front of him, like how a frustrated pet owner disciplines a rebellious dog.

"No," I said softly. I held up my own hands, burning with Willow's fire, and his golden eyes widened in surprise. I stood up straighter, bravery hardening my spine into rebar.

"What have you done?" he shouted. He was staring at me with more attention than he had given me in years. But it was too late for that. Matt was a free mortal. I didn't have to answer to him anymore.

"I don't need you anymore, Damien." The Queen cackled. "The Flame is rekindled with the son!"

How had this gone so sideways? Ten seconds ago, everything had made sense. Well, not complete sense, but a decent amount of sense. I wasn't the best poker player in the room, but I'd only needed to win a few hands to be happy. Now all of a sudden, I found out we were playing pinochle the whole time and I had no idea what any of the rules were.

"You're too late, Damien. The Flame has returned!" The Queen threw her hands up and her head back before letting out a terrifying cry that harkened back to primal days. "Celebrate, my children! Tonight is the new dawn of the Fae!" With a mighty cry, the Fae returned to their party at a tempo that would make even the mightiest of hurricanes feel insecure.

I stood still, letting the party swirl around me like the sea around a mountain. Unblinking, I held my father's golden gaze, sorting the new clues I had been given. Something felt wrong. Not just everything. Something very specific felt wrong. I just couldn't tell what it was. My subconscious was screaming at me to pick up the thread I had dropped, but my conscious mind couldn't even remember what it had forgotten.

I only saw what happened next because I was staring at my father. It all happened so quickly that if I had not been looking in the right direction, I would have missed it.

The Queen stood before her people with her arms raised and a roar of joy echoing back at her. She turned to look at me, her triumphant smile beaming like the moon. She was still smiling at me as Tania stepped behind her. The Lady of Spring drew a knife as black as the void of the Nothing from the folds of her outfit. I had just enough time to remember that Mav had denied working with the demons before the Lady of Spring slashed her mother's throat.

"I will be free!"

The party's cries of joy turned to despair like a single downward-sliding violin note. Gloriana crumpled to the floor, blood gushing from her neck. Her golden eyes were dim, the sun of her life setting—another Immortal fallen.

With the shriek of a banshee, Dawn tackled Tania like a linebacker. Robin rushed to the Queen's side, his face pale.

My father smiled a merciless, satisfied smile.

Then the killing started for real.

The first bloodcurdling cry came from my right. In the center of the party, someone had put on a mummer's mask, similar to the ones the Gilded Dancers wore, with one difference: This mask wasn't gold, but the same light-eating black as the dagger Tania had used to murder her mother. The assassin held a long knife in each hand, both dripping red with Fae blood. Under the mask, he was dressed in the colors of Spring.

Screams began to echo throughout the glade. Everywhere I looked I saw groups of Springers in shadowy masks slashing wildly into the party guests. My guests, at my birthday party... well, at my birthday *massacre* now, I guess.

It was enough to make anyone upset.

Alex and Orion converged on me like the points of a collapsing triangle.

"Well, this went better than I expected," Alex offered as we stared at the carnage unfolding in front of us. "I know it's your birthday party and all, but what are your thoughts on an Irish goodbye?"

"Matt," an urgent voice called behind me. I turned and twitched in surprise. The Devil's daughter was right next to me. That was going to take some getting used to.

"What the hell is happening here?" I asked her, doing my best to ignore that particular tangle in my life's thread at the moment. She was the nearest princess and the only one I even kind of trusted at this point so I hoped she could fill me on what I was missing.

Ash looked at the still form of her mother, at her sisters rolling on the floor like two kids in a playground tussle. Then she turned to me, green eyes distraught.

"Succession."

"Worse than that," Orion growled, staring at the masked assassins slaughtering their way through the middle of the room. "This is destabilization."

"Sorry, Poli Sci was one of the classes I skipped when I was getting my fake degree," I told them. "What are any of you talking about?"

"Think about it," Alex offered. "Gloriana was using her position as the Queen of All Fae to fight for you to get your soul back, right?"

I nodded.

"Where is she now?"

I looked at the Immortal's lifeless body lying only a few feet away and went cold.

The more I thought about it, the more it made sense. Tania had told me she would do *anything* to be free. That's what Samael had been doing while she visited the princesses: making backroom deals. The Devil would rather topple the monarch of a supernatural sovereign nation than give me my soul back. The CIA could learn a thing or two from him.

I felt like an idiot. We had figured out that Mav wanted to kill me and extinguish the Flame, and had *assumed* that the demons were connected to that because they would benefit in keeping the Dandelion Court weak. But the Flame had returned to the Dandelion Court, and there was more than one way to hobble a kingdom. A headless court was about as dangerous as a viper without teeth.

There wasn't a bad girl in this story. There were bad girls. We had forgotten about Tania. *I don't want to do this*, she had pleaded with me as we approached the dais. I had assumed she didn't want to be a princess for sale anymore.

She had been talking about matricide.

"Okay, so we're in the middle of a coup," I said, looking back out at the carnage. "It's my first time. What usually happens next?"

No one had time to answer my question before a bloody Faerie stumbled to the dais. He held a hand to a wound on his shoulder that was leaking blood everywhere.

"Lord of Fire, please!" he cried, his golden eyes unfocused with pain. "Save us."

Guilt flooded into me. Despite the trickery of the Fae, hadn't I just announced myself as the returning Flame? Here to protect and rebuild the glory of the Fae? And now here I was sitting on a stage watching people get slaughtered. Shame burned in the pit of my stomach, and the flames on my hand grew brighter as they fed on that powerful fuel.

I took a step forward, mouth open to promise deliverance.

"No," my father answered in a tone made of such iron that I was surprised they didn't burn his Faerie throat on the way out.

The wounded Faerie collapsed to his knees, face full of despair.

"Your people need you," he screamed. "Help us!"

My father's answer was a silence so stony that he might have been confused for a Lord of Earth instead of Fire. His golden eyes stared at the fallen form of the Queen of All Fae with a hungry expression. The black-masked Dancers continued slicing their way through the party. I looked down at the Fae flames flickering on my hands and felt the iron yoke of responsibility settle around my shoulders.

I had no interest in being like my father. I had seen enough of what he did or didn't do with the power he had been given. I wanted to be different—better. I *needed* to be better. Somehow, I knew that the passenger in my head, Willow the Flame Spirit, wanted the same thing.

My soul might be in danger of foreclosure, but it still cried out for the innocents dying that night.

"Orion," I asked softly, my eyes locked on the dancing flames surrounding my hands. "What does the Hunt think about assassins murdering my unarmed party guests?"

The big Nephilim growled. I could feel his primal hunger to hunt echoing in myself and Alex as his squires. This was *my* birthday. They were *my* guests. On a basic level, these assassins were poaching—a crime punishable by death. I know it's weird, but at least it's consistent.

"Okay, I vote we stop the massacre, capture the Lady of Spring, and stop this coup in its tracks," I said, lowering my hands.

"Then what?" Ash inquired, inserting herself into the triangle. "My mother will still be dead, and the throne will need a queen."

"That is way above my pay grade. I'm only a janitor, here to help take out the trash." I gestured at a group of black-masked assassins, whose attention had turned from the carnage to us. Their leader bore a pair of straight swords that he spun once in his hands as he marched toward us.

Alex sighed to no one in particular. "This is what I get for getting involved in your love life."

"I'm coming with you," Ash proclaimed, stepping up to stand by my right side. Her own hands burned with the flame of Willow.

"Absolutely not," I snapped. I still didn't know if I trusted Ash after... well, everything that had just happened. I know I'm one to talk about judging someone based on their father, but *come on.*

"I wasn't asking. I'm a princess, remember, darling?" The corner of Ash's mouth quirked upward in a sad smile. "I am the Lady of Fall. These are *my* people. That is *my* mother's body. These are *my* enemies, not yours."

"We could probably quibble about that last one," Alex muttered behind me.

"Fine," Orion snarled, cutting me off before I could argue with my whatever-Ash-was-now more. "We're out of time. Come if you wish, just stay out of my way."

Without another word, he sprinted to the edge of the stage and leapt at the approaching Fae assassins, flaming sword burning brightly. He belonged on a movie poster for his own action hero franchise.

The lead masked attacker raised his sword and caught Orion's bright blade as my friend landed on him. Then they were off, swords flashing at a speed I could barely follow. The assassins around him scattered like a school of fish startled by a shark, but immediately began to circle back, caging the Hunter in.

"Action, I guess," I said, when I managed to get my jaw working again after watching Orion's opening scene.

Alex, Ash, and I broke into a run of our own, racing toward the traitorous Fae sneaking up on my friend. I raised my left hand and sent a blast of Willow's flame leaping at one of the assassins, whose attention had been focused on Orion and had not spared a second thought for good old Matthew Carver & Co.

The ball of fire slammed into the back of the unsuspecting Faerie and launched him forward, smashing him into the ground as his fancy spring-rave attire burst into flames.

Quick as snakes, the four other assassins spun, turning to face me and the rest of the backup dancer troupe. A massive column of fire shot past me and devoured one of them so thoroughly nothing remained when it dissipated. Stunned, I turned to stare at Ash. The Lady of Fall was hovering several inches above the ground, her long red hair whipping around like dancing tongues of flame. Her golden eyes burned with the molten rage of an active volcano.

I might be a Lord of Fire, but the daughter of the Devil was one with *the* fire.

I turned back to face the assassins but found my way blocked by one of my nightmares. Damien Fireheart stood between me and the battle, his golden eyes frigid, like the cold metal of a gun barrel.

"Stop," he commanded in the voice of a father expecting absolute obedience.

On reflex, I drew up short, just a few steps away from my Faerie father. For a moment, we stared at each other. Everything else faded, the sounds of people fighting and dying. There was only the eternal struggle of two wills—a father expecting obedience and a son becoming a man.

"Get out of my way," I said softly.

"This is not your place," my father replied, cold anger simmering just below the surface, like a volcano swallowed by a glacier it was thawing its way out of. I knew from personal experience it was only a matter of time before it erupted.

"It's the only place I got," I snarled.

"You idiot. You have no idea what you have undone. I forbid you."

The fiery serpent of rage that lived in my guts writhed in fury at his words. I didn't even process what he said. It didn't matter. He did not control me anymore. He hadn't wanted to be my father a year ago, why start now?

"Get out of my way," I said again, doing my best to echo his frozen tone.

"I will not protect you," he warned.

"That won't be any different from the rest of my life," I snapped.

My father flinched slightly, something moving across his face like a ripple on a still pond. Was it anger? Shame? I didn't care. My friends needed help and he was in my way.

"They don't deserve your help," he tried, switching tactics.

"I say they do." I jutted my chin out in defiance. This was the most I had ever argued with my father. If I had still been living my old, boring Matthew Carver life and not standing in the shadow of a collapsing supernatural civilization, I think I might have been soaring on an adrenaline high unlike anything I had ever experienced. Instead, all I wanted to do was go fight Faerie assassins wearing demon masks.

"You don't know them like I do," he pressed.

"And I don't know you at all!" I shouted. "Your whole life is a lie."

"Who do you think murdered your mother?" he snarled, his anger bubbling through his cool, a classic Damien Carver warning sign.

I didn't notice. I didn't notice anything. My brain didn't work anymore. It was on vacation. There had been quite enough revelations for one night, thank you very much. If anyone else had any secrets to reveal, they should send me an email, and I would leave it unread until I felt like dealing with it.

Was that a coping mechanism to cover up the fact that I was completely hysterical? Yes. Why do they call it being hysterical when you lose your marbles but also being funny hysterical? Do you have to be weird to be funny? Oh no, does that mean I'm weird?

What was I not thinking about again?

My breath was coming in ragged gasps. I was hyperventilating. I was like an oxygen-starved fire, fading, fading, fading. It was my fault. I had convinced my mother and sisters to make the drive to come see me. They were washed out in a flash flood. I did it. It was me. I killed my mother.

"Matthew," my father snapped, "listen to me. You don't know what they took from you."

My father's voice yanked me out of my spiral. My identity felt like it was crumbling, but I was able to stop leaning on it for a moment. With enough therapy and duct tape, I could probably stitch it back together later.

I had enough of the threads to start sewing an idea together. Gloriana had been breeding super children to fill the roles of her court and rebuild the bloodline of the Fae. The youngest one was Ash. My father was the most powerful Lord of Fire. When it came to fire, he would have been the preferred stud, so to horribly speak.

He must have turned down the Queen's advances, and that did not go over well. So Damien left and took his toys with him, locking the power of the Flame away from the Dandelion Court, forcing the

Queen to look elsewhere—and by elsewhere, I mean straight down, to the fiery pits.

"You were supposed to be Ash's father," I breathed.

Both of my father's eyebrows shot straight up. I knew he always thought I was the dumb child. He was probably right about that, but that didn't mean I didn't have my moments. My sisters were just really smart, okay?

"You locked away her access to Willow and then went into hiding," I continued, "and she found a way to make you pay."

I think at that moment, my father saw me for the first time. His head tilted and his eyes studied me, surprised at what they found. I didn't care what he thought he saw. *He* had gotten our family killed, not me. That made me angry.

"You're the reason they're dead." I clenched my fists, Willow's flames burning brighter in response. "They never even knew they were in danger."

A vicious shriek sounded from behind me. I spun, expecting to see Dawn or Tania standing victorious over the other.

What I found was way worse.

Mav stood on the dais, free from the guards that had been taking her away. In her right hand was her naked obsidian blade, stained red. Her gray eyes were fixed on the still form of her mother in horror. A bubble of rage began to form in my stomach. She didn't get to be devastated by that.

"They drowned," my father said in a dark voice. "Who do you suppose she would send to do that?"

There was no way that she could have heard him over the din of the battle raging all around us, but the Lady of Winter, follower of the Path of Water, turned, her enraged gaze settling on us.

Damien moved next to me, and together we squared up across from her. My father and I were not good, but given the circumstances,

I was more than happy to shelve our issues for a few minutes for the sake of justice—served at boiling temperatures.

"Extinguish the Flame!" Mav screamed, a fanatical light burning in her eyes. She slashed her free hand in our direction, and a dozen razor-sharp knives of ice whistled toward us like frozen bullets.

TRY NOT TO slow me down," my father growled as
the knives shot at us like homing missiles. In one fluid
motion, he slammed both of his hands to the ground,
shooting flames as he leapt, doing his best impersonation of a rocket
trying to achieve liftoff. He shot toward Mav at Mach Damien, right
knee extended like a blade.

Leaving me all alone to deal with the icy projectiles.

"Ack!" I yelled in a very manly voice, swinging both of my hands
from right to left, willing Willow to form a wall of flames between me
and the daggers. Ice slammed into the front of my shield and came
out the other side as steam.

I extinguished the wall in time to see Mav drop into a roll, dodging my father's assault. He landed gracefully, trotting a few steps to bleed off his momentum. The princess instantly lashed out with a creeping carpet of ice, trying to snare his feet, like she did when she "rescued" us.

With a contemptuous gesture, my father carved a line of flames on the ground, cutting off the ice's approach. Watching the two experts battle with their spirits, I felt like a kindergartener watching the NFL for the first time. I didn't even know you could *do* that.

But this wouldn't be my first time being the new kid on the block in a fight. I had plenty of experience with that. Not trusting my ability to rocket myself to the dais, I broke into a sprint, trying to flank the icy princess while she focused on fighting my father.

Without even glancing my way, she flung out her right hand and sent a frozen spear hurtling at me at the speed of sound, or what felt like pretty close to it. Hoping there wasn't any secret sauce to my father's fancy move, I thrust both of my hands in front of me and willed the fire to push me backward.

It felt like after a lifetime of doing pushups, the earth had finally decided to push back. My arms slammed into my chest and sent me hurtling back with the force of a full-body tackle, performed by me on me. I tripped over my own feet and fell, giving myself a great view of the hurtling ice weapon as it shot over me.

It wasn't pretty, but it got the job done. I will gladly take a pile of bruises over an icicle through my spleen any day of the week. But this was no time to stay on the ground. I had a family to avenge. I sprang back to my feet in time to watch Mav summon a curved shell of ice, blocking a furious burst of flames from my father.

Damien performed a smaller super leap, using one hand to throw himself over the princess. Passing above Mav, he rotated, sending a pair of fireballs shooting down at her. Continuing his flip, he landed on his feet behind her with a small flourish. Mav sent out another sheet of ice, slicking the dais where he landed, sending him skidding like a car without snow tires while she dodged his attack.

Yeah, I was definitely the rookie here.

A year's worth of being Orion's sidekick gave me an idea. I didn't have to land a heavy blow on her to win. All I had to do was be so annoying that she couldn't protect herself from the big cheese Lord of Fire she was facing. I could do that. I'm very good at being annoying—just ask my father.

With that in mind, I willed the flames on both my hands to flow into long, sinuous whips. They surged with heat as I raised my right hand to flick its flaming tongue at Mav. Some sixth sense must have warned her, because she jerked to the side, narrowly dodging my attack. The flaming whip still cracked with a satisfyingly vicious sound. I'm not sure how the physics on that worked. What was making the cracking sound? I decided not to question it.

Mav whirled around to fix me with her gray-eyed glare. I gave her my best Hunter's grin, full of teeth and hunger, and sent the whip in my left hand toward her like a striking snake.

Ice coalesced around Mav's hand like a frozen gauntlet, all the way up to her elbow. Faster than I could track, her hand shot out and caught my whip in a frigid grasp. With a superhuman jerk, she yanked me off my feet, as if my whip had gotten snagged on a runaway freight train.

As I fell, I sent my will surging down the whip she was holding, commanding it to burn even brighter. Willow began to glow with a white-hot heat, and steam poured off Mav's icy gauntlets. The Lady of Winter gritted her teeth and poured her own strength into reinforcing her ice, adding extra layers to her protection as quickly as my flames ate through them. I could feel my focus fading; whatever muscles I needed to train to increase the strength of a spirit like Willow were severely underdeveloped compared to Mav's.

But I didn't have to be stronger—just strong enough. My father regained his feet behind the Lady of Winter, his flames burning with the raging power of jet fuel. With a snarl on his face, the missing Lord of Fire drew his hands back and sent a thick beam of fire lancing directly at Mav like an arrow. She whirled to face it, a look of horror crossing her face as the blast sped toward her.

A vicious wind that must have had a hurricane for a mother swept in between the two combatants. It snagged the beam of fire and bent it, curving it to shoot off into the night sky.

Dawn, the Lady of Summer, strode onto the dais. Behind her, she dragged the still body of her sister, Tania, by the heel. Her normally perfectly coifed hair was wild, shooting in every direction. Her eyes had turned to solid gold, and the rage on her face was enough to make my father and Mav look like they were in good moods.

"Sorry, Damien," Dawn called to my father as she stepped between the two of them, releasing the limp form of Tania as she did. "I will still have need of my frigid elder sister if I am to rule."

"Who says you are?" Mav demanded, turning to face her sister. Dawn didn't even glance at the Lady of Winter. Invisible streams of air picked up Mav and slammed her to the ground with the ease of a giant toddler throwing a toy.

"I do," she responded firmly.

I barely managed to keep my jaw from slamming into the dais next to her. The little I had seen of the Path of Wind had not shown me the kind of power it could have. I wondered who her father was to give her access to such power.

"She took everything from me," my father snarled, taking a step toward the Lady of Summer. "I will not be denied what I am owed."

I resisted the urge to point out that I was still alive, so technically it wasn't "everything." I didn't think he'd appreciate it—or agree.

"I forgot you were always so *forceful*," the Lady of Summer said, shivering with mock fear at my father's demands. "I will determine exactly what it is you are owed." Echoes of her mother's authority rang through her voice like a bell.

"I don't answer to you." My father's flames swelled with his frustration. He took an aggressive step toward Dawn.

"Oh, but you will." The heir apparent's wild hair began to dance in warning as a vicious wind whipped up around her, like she was the eye of her own cyclone. "I am not my mother," Dawn said softly. Fire and Air stared at each other for what felt like an hour.

Just when I was certain that my father was going to steel his resolve and attack, the queen-to-be spoke again. "I didn't know, Damien. I would have stopped her if I had. I swear this to you on the marble and gold of the Dandelion Throne."

Her oath took some of the heat out of my father's flames. After another moment, he lowered his hands and nodded once. The winds that whistled around us died down immediately.

"Welcome home, Lord Damien." Dawn inclined her head politely to him, in a way that reminded me of how her mother had once greeted me.

"I will require certain assurances," my father said, folding his burning hands in front of him.

"And you shall have them," Dawn said. "I will need a strong right hand to help me rebuild this place."

Mav let out a feral growl from where she was crumpled up like a forgotten piece of paper.

"Silence, wretched sister of mine." Dawn gave Mav a firm kick without looking at her. "You're lucky I don't feed you to the Hunter after all."

The queen-to-be turned her golden-eyed gaze on the massacre still happening at my birthday party. "I think that is enough of all this." She gave her floored sister another kick. "Give me ice," she commanded.

Groaning weakly, Mav raised the arm that was still wrapped in the remnants of her ice glove into the air. With the sound of a crystal goblet shattering, the glove exploded into a hundred pieces of frozen shrapnel and shot into the air.

Dawn raised both her hands, a glare of intensity settling on her face like the grim wall of an approaching cold front. Wind roared around us, seizing the wickedly sharp pieces of ice and sending them out into the glade like the north pole's version of hornets. I turned in horror, expecting to see dozens fall like wheat before a scythe, but each piece of shrapnel wove its away around the innocent partygoers, homing in on the black-masked Fae and cutting them to ribbons.

All around the glade, the demonic masked Fae dropped like flies. The cold wind of razor-sharp ice moved as quick as a thought and had no mercy in it. The judgment of the Lady of Summer was final and terrifying. Her execution of the traitors was more brutal and absolute than Orion could ever be.

Her deadly missiles sheared the weeds of every single black-masked assassin in the garden glade—except for one. In the center of the clearing, Orion faced off against the lean Faerie with two blades. Their swords flashed as they circled each other. Orion's tuxedo was shredded. As I watched, the lean Faerie blurred forward, moving faster than I could believe. Orion blocked a blade and twisted but was too slow. The second thin sword traced a line across his left shoulder, tearing another hole in his suit. Orion grunted but kept moving, his sword flashing as he did his best to hold his own.

The two swordsmen were staring at each other with such intensity that I suspected neither of them knew the battle around them was over. It was obvious that Orion was facing a master with the blade; even their footsteps were beyond perfect.

Dawn circled the combatants with her ill wind once, before letting the ice fall to the ground like a hailstorm that had run out of gas. Surprised, I glanced at her. Why had she spared this one? She noticed my questioning look and shrugged, still watching the two combatants circle each other with a sharp eye.

Her miniature storm seemed to alert them to the outside world watching their duel. The masked sword master looked around the glade and saw his comrades were dead. He tilted his head to the side as he turned from the carnage back to Orion. With a casual shrug, he reached up with one hand and pulled the mask off. Black lines filled the veins on his face like liquid shadow, pooling around his eyes. As I watched, the dark veins began to fade as if they were burnt away by the light. The Faerie swordsman tossed the black mask aside with a grimace of disgust.

I blinked in surprise. It was Raynar, the master swordsman who had been teaching Ash her lessons with the blade. The one with the old, weathered face, which went against every rule of immortality that I knew. The Hunter didn't seem surprised in the slightest to see the old Fae. Raynar had given Orion a gnarly scar the last time they fought, I guess there's only so many people who could do that.

The ancient duelist gave Orion a small, tired smile and saluted him with one of his blades. "I suppose it was meant to be that we would meet here, at the end," he said with a soft sigh.

"I would have thought you knew better," Orion replied.

"The old ways are broken." The swordsman shrugged. "I have seen the desires of the Flame burn the wick of my people's candle until it is barely a nub. What would I be if I did not try to safeguard what little of my people's glory remains?"

"Living past tonight," I muttered under my breath. I thought I heard Dawn snicker behind me.

"But that dream is already dead," Raynar continued, ignoring the rest of the gathered Fae. "If I cannot save my people, at least let me avenge those whose wicks you cut short, Hunter."

Orion didn't bother to answer the Faerie sword master. But then again, self-control is kind of his thing and not mine. He merely shrugged in his tattered tuxedo and launched himself forward, flaming blade seeking a hole in Raynar's double-sword defense.

As smooth as a dancer, the old Faerie brought up one blade to divert Orion's attack, while going on the offensive with his other one.

I've mentioned footwork before. It sounds ridiculous, but footwork is the thing that wins sword fights. Yes, of course you need to have the strength to lift a blade and the coordination to do things like block and parry. Those are the basics, the ink outlines of the art. But footwork is the colored paint you fill it in with. It is where sword fighting goes from brutish to elegant, right until someone's stomach gets run through.

Orion sidestepped into the incoming attack and spun between Raynar's two swords before dropping below the one trapped with his and pirouetting out of reach of the old Faerie's blade. Mercury himself would have been impressed, and I've heard his feet are as fast as it gets.

But Raynar was made of the same stuff as Orion, and his footwork was equally immaculate. Without a pause, he flowed around my teacher's attacks, twin swords ringing as they countered and struck. Something was different. His blades were perfect, his skill undeniable, yet he seemed slower than he had been. His attacks didn't land on the Hunter anymore. The black veins had all but vanished from his face. I glanced at the mask that he had thrown away, suspicious about what gifts the demons had given Tania.

"Lord Damien," Dawn drawled, never taking her eyes off the legendary fight occurring in front of our eyes. "Do be a lovely Lord of Fire and do me a favor? Would you take my beloved sister Ash into protective custody? Use whoever you need to make that happen." She gestured at some of the guards milling around the dais, dressed in the Dandelion gold and white.

"What are you doing?" I demanded, turning to stare at her. She gave me a small, sad smile.

"Successions are never a pretty thing, darling. I need to consolidate my authority and demonstrate my ability to rule, or the court will never accept me. I can't have my sister running around giving people *options*. What kind of message would that send? You're lucky I like you so much, or I might do the same to you."

Not for the first time, I wondered if supernatural societies learn politics from us or the other way around. I realized now why she had left Raynar alive—he and Orion were providing a wonderful distraction. Sure enough, I saw Alex and Ash among the onlookers clustered around what was probably the duel of the century. I glanced over my shoulder, watching my father marshal the guard like he had never left. Of course he loved giving orders to good little soldiers that would just fall in line.

Deep in my chest, my conscience grumbled. I had chosen Ash. I had chosen her because I had dared to hope she would fight for me, help me get my soul back. When I made that choice, she had the power, and I was the one who needed help. I had never dreamed that within thirty minutes, our positions might be reversed.

Ash might not be able to help me anymore, now that Dawn had won. All I had to do was step aside and let everything that was outside of my control happen how it was going to happen. I didn't work here. I had a magical key—I could walk out the door and go home right now.

I should walk out the door and go home right now.

But was that who I was? Content with taking what I could from others but not offering my help in return? Was that who Orion or Alex were? No, my two friends hated my plan and hated being here, but they had done so because I needed them. That is about as selfless as you can be. Would I be worthy of having friends like that if I only helped someone else when it benefited me?

No. No, I wouldn't be.

I guess there's a reason the easy path and the high road never seem to be going in the same direction.

I let out a frustrated little sigh and turned to face Dawn. She stared at me with a bemused smile, her golden eyes dancing. Why had they suddenly changed? A mystery for another day.

"Yes, Squire Carver?" Dawn asked. Her voice sounded oddly encouraging, like she knew what I was going to say next. Was I really that predictable?

"I can't let you do that," I replied, shocked at how smooth my voice sounded.

"You?" She raised a royal finger to point at me, her bemused smile growing. "You cannot *let* me." She quirked an eyebrow, daring me to answer her challenge.

"No," I sighed.

"Oh, what could have been, Matthew Carver." She laughed a genuine Dawn laugh, one that made her seem like a real person.

I gave her a helpless shrug. The hands had been dealt and played; all we could do now was collect our chips.

"Good luck." She beamed at me before snapping her fingers to get the nearby guard's attention. My father's head spun around, eyes narrowing as he saw me standing across from the queen-to-be. I'm not predictable; he's just known me my whole life, which is totally cheating.

"Gentlemen, please make sure the squire here doesn't feel the need to get involved." Dawn arched an eyebrow at me as she gave the order.

I was confused. If I didn't know better, I would say she wasn't upset with me for standing up to her. If anything, she seemed pleased? What kind of queen encouraged… Then again, Robin himself told me Gloriana preferred a "spirited nobility." Maybe Dawn was much the same.

Whatever game she was playing, I didn't have time to sit and do the math. The liveried Royal Guards strode toward me, hands on their faerie steel blades. The flame of teenage rebellion that still thrived in my heart flared as I stared at my father right in his eyes and gave him a tight smile, pointed both of my hands at the floor, and ordered

Willow to give me a little jet fuel.

"*Wheeeee!*" the little spirit shouted in my head as they hit the gas pedal.

I had the distinct pleasure of seeing my father's face twist in frustration as I shot backward off the dais and toward my friends like an airplane lifting off the runway. Unfortunately, I was still staring at him as my feet landed on the ground and I fell over backward, landing on my rump and skidding a few paces in the blood-slicked grass.

If I was going to keep trying that move, I really needed to learn how to stick the landing. The embarrassment stung more than the ground, but they were both worth it to give Damien Fireheart a little sass. What a stupid last name, by the way.

With no time to check for bruised pride or broken bones, I sprang to my feet and raced to the edge of the circle, where Ash and Alex were watching two steel tornadoes try to kill each other.

It was cool, but I'd had a ringside view of the Zagan versus Orion rematch, so I guess you could say I had seen it all before. No sooner had that thought crossed my mind than Raynar threw one of his swords like a spear at Orion. The Hunter dodged nimbly, twisting at the hip to let the blade shoot by like a missile. Alex and I let out a simultaneous squeak as we ducked under the weapon as it whistled by.

"Hey, be careful!" Alex shouted at Raynar with a look of indignation on his face. "You could take somebody's eye out with that!"

"I kind of think that was the point," I hissed, tapping on his shoulder with urgency. My friend's tuxedo looked a little ruffled, but he didn't seem to be hurt. In his right hand he clutched a long dagger that he had snatched from some poor masked assassin. In his other hand, he held a pair of the black mummers' masks, like grisly trophies. Before I could ask, a warm hand settled on my shoulder, interrupting me. With a jolt, I turned to face my... betrothed. My Faerie princess, also half-demon, betrothed. That was going to take some getting used to.

My gaze slipped down to the hand she had on my shoulder, before snapping back up to her concerned green eyes. I could deal with my love life later; the first order of business was to not get thrown into a Goldhall prison cell. Somehow I doubted they were as luxurious as the mansion I had been staying in. Oh, who am I kidding? In this place, the jail probably had toilets made out of solid gold.

"We, uh, we gotta go," I whispered to the two of them, eyes still on our dueling boss. "Dawn has some big plans about how she would like to lay out the living quarters in the palace, and Ash's new ones are not the most ideal."

"What?" Alex asked, staring at me like I was an idiot. To be fair, I kind of felt like one.

"Those guys," I said, pointing at the approaching detachment of soldiers led by my father, "are coming to take Ash and put her under 'protective custody.'"

"Why didn't you just say that in the first place?" my friend asked. Immediately he began shoving his way to the center of the ring.

"It's time to go," I said, turning to look at Ash. My heart was beating all funny, and I didn't know why. Maybe I had a murmur or something. "I don't suppose you'd like to come check out the mortal world for a while?" I asked, holding out a hand like I saw a prince do once in a movie.

The Lady of Autumn turned and stared at her triumphant sister with an iron look on her face. For a moment, I thought she was going to refuse and charge at her sister all by herself. Hopefully all by herself. I really didn't want to fight Dawn. I had just left there, and going back would be awkward. But whatever stubbornness the princess was feeling faded like the setting sun.

Ash dazzled me with a bright smile that shone like a beacon amidst all the death and destruction surrounding us. "I thought you'd never ask," she said, and took my hand.

A SHRILL WHISTLE SPLIT the glade, and Alex made it to the front of the ring. "Orion, zip him up, we gotta go!" the younger Nephilim roared before turning back and moving toward Ash and me.

The Hunter glanced over his shoulder. His black eyes narrowed as he took in the three of us and the approaching soldiers. He spun back to Raynar and swung three savage blows, driving the wiry sword master back with each step. He only paused his reckless advance as the Faerie ended up at the very edge of the spectators.

Without a moment's hesitation, the Nephilim spun on his heel and sprinted toward us, simply leaping over the front row of Fae gathered around the ring, landing behind them.

Holy crap.

I was never going to be that cool.

"Show-off," Alex muttered next to me as we broke into a jog. Behind us, the ring erupted into shouts as Raynar struggled to get through the crowd. Frustrated, the ancient sword master roared, and they scattered like Fae with their Queen's head cut off.

"What's the plan?" Robin asked, falling into step next to me as we hustled through the glade that was supposed to be the site of my birthday party but had been *so* overbooked with other events.

"Are you coming with us?" I asked in surprise. Robin had been a favorite of the Queen. I would have thought he would stick around and try to insert himself into the new administration. As far as I knew, Dawn and he had no issues.

"Regime changes are usually pretty hard on the old staff members," he said with a casual smile, as if we weren't sprinting through the site of a massacre, running from Royal Guards. "Besides, I have a feeling the adventure is going to be much more interesting with you."

I didn't like how he put that. I was very afraid he was going to be correct.

"We just need to find a door!" I shouted, fishing my hand around in my stupid tuxedo's pockets until I found the Key of Portunus, which the Queen had promised would take me back to the mortal world.

"There's no place like home, there's no place like home," Alex panted from my other side.

I glanced at our little group, upset that it was so easy to assign the roles of Tin Man, Cowardly Lion, and Scarecrow. That didn't leave a lot of character options for me.

"Please tell me I'm not Dorothy," I complained.

"Oh no, Ash is Dorothy. She has red hair," Alex reassured me. "You're the dog."

I don't know what I expected.

We raced past the chamberlain's rock, with the sound of soldiers in rattling armor chasing us. Orion led the charge, bursting out the doors into the mazeways of Goldhall. I stared at the thick golden carpet waiting for us on the other side in thematic horror.

"Well, I guess all we have to do is follow the yellow—"

"Don't," I cut Alex off, pointing at the nearest door. "This way."

We ran up to the big oaken door set in the side of the hall. Orion tried to open it, but it was locked. Everyone moved to the side, leaving me to figure out how the heck this magical key worked. It didn't come with an instruction manual, but I've opened a door or two in my life before. The door had a big round door handle with a keyhole in it. I took my best guess and shoved the key in. It fit perfectly, though it should not have.

There was a loud whoosh of air behind us, and the doors to the forest glade banged against the wall several times, caught in an indoor hurricane. Dawn, the uncrowned Queen, hurtled down the hallway, carried by the winds of her own personal storm. I guess she wasn't content to let her guards have all the fun. How very Dawn.

"That's my cue," I shouted, twisting the giant brass key into the doorknob. There was an echoing click that resounded even over the whistling winds of the approaching Dawnstorm.

"Here goes nothing!" I yelled, and shoved on the now-unlocked door. It opened into an office building hallway with faded mustard-yellow wallpaper. "Go, go, go!" I shouted, waiting for my friends to get through the doorway while I tried to free the key from the door.

Dawn was getting closer now, the poor carpet was being torn to shreds by the rage of her passing. One by one my friends raced through the open door. With a frantic twist, I managed to pull old Porty's key out of the handle and leap through the doorframe, pulling the door shut as I went.

I swear I saw Dawn toss me a wink as the door closed.

The moment it clicked shut, the sound of Dawn's maelstrom was cut off as abruptly as if I had hung up on her. Willow's flames immediately went out on Ash's hands. I checked my own and saw they were extinguished too.

Right. Now that I was no longer in the Faerie Lands, I bet Willow wasn't able to draw on their power the same way anymore. I hoped the little spirit had taken a deep breath before we left. I wasn't sure how soon I was going to be invited back for them to get another.

I turned to make sure everyone was accounted for. Ash was staring at the closed door. I wondered what it felt like to have the door to the only life you had ever known slammed in your face. Probably a little like going to college.

I turned to investigate the door we had escaped through. On this side, it looked very different than it had in the Faerie Lands. Instead of being tall and made of oak with gold detailing, it was short and white with a frosted window. The paint was peeling, and it looked like it hadn't been cleaned in a long time. Shadowy shapes moved on the other side of the glass, but strangely, first they were too fast, then too slow.

An old metal sign, rusting on the corners and covered in flaking paint, read FAERIE LANDS—NO TRESPASSING.

As I glanced around, I saw similar doors on either side of the long hallway that went on for what seemed like forever. I checked the other way, the hairs on my arm already starting to stand on end. A second eternity sprawled in that direction, dotted with doors. The whole building had a musty smell, like it hadn't been used in a long time. Fluorescent lights hummed at regular intervals, illuminating everything with the same yellow tint. It looked like an office building that had been built in the seventies and then abandoned.

"Dorothy, I don't think we're in Kansas anymore," Alex said. I couldn't even be mad at him. He was right.

"Okay," I breathed, looking around the everlasting hallway. It would have been perfect for one of those classic Scooby Doo–style chase scenes. "Where in the world are we?"

"We are Between," Robin murmured with a breath of awe in his voice.

Orion grunted his agreement. The big Nephilim had sheathed his sword once we were through the doorway and was looking around with open curiosity. Seeing him relax—as much as he was capable of it—made me feel a little better.

"Between what?" Alex asked.

"Between everything," Orion replied, staring up at the ceiling. I glanced up, half expecting to see yet another never-ending hallway, but it was a normal ceiling, white fissured tiles fading to a gross yellow.

"There should be a door that will take us back to the mortal world." Orion gestured down one of the hallways. "All we have to do is find it."

"Okay, gang," I said, rubbing my hands together, "let's split up!"

"No!" The force of four people's refusal hit me like a wave, and I staggered back a step. I guess it was too soon for a horror movie joke.

"I *mean* let's split up to cover both sides of the hallway as we go in the same direction," I grumbled. I glanced at Ash, who was standing next to me, still looking at the door we had left. Gently, I poked her shoulder to get her attention. "Any preference on which direction we go?"

The Lady of Autumn looked down both hallways before turning back to me with a shrug. "Left," she said.

So we went left.

Each door we passed was like the Faerie one, but they varied in levels of disrepair. One particularly rotten-looking door had iron chains across it, holding it shut. The sign that hung from it read Xi-BALBA—Devoured. No Entry. I saw signs on doors for places I had never heard of, and ones that were familiar, like Olympus and Asgard.

The farther we walked, the more chained-off doors we found.

I thought of the Nothing that Gloriana had shown me devouring her kingdom. Had the worlds behind those doors suffered similar fates?

I found myself walking next to my mentor as we journeyed through the infinite hallway. Orion was silent, his gaze focused on the carpeted horizon. I didn't mind the silence; it gave me time to process what we'd just survived.

Just because I had learned how to swim a little in the last year didn't mean I was ready for the deep waters. I hadn't listened to Orion's wisdom, and it had almost gotten us all killed. Shame burned a hot brand on my cheeks as I felt myself blush. I had been a jerk.

"You were right," I said.

"I know," he rumbled. I turned my head to glare at him but stopped when I saw the small smile chiseled into his stone jaw. I took that to mean we were okay. I have far better friends than I deserve.

"I'm sorry I dragged you both into this mess." I sighed. "I thought I knew what I was doing, but I had no idea about my father." I glanced over at Ash, who was trailing just behind me. "Did you?" I asked.

Ash shook her head. "No, she kept me in the dark about that too. I never met Damien. He and my mother had their falling out before I was born."

"She wanted him to be the father of her Autumnal daughter," I told her. Maybe royals were more used to this kind of conversation, but it still felt super gross to me to talk about siring children like planning a dog breed.

Ash simply nodded. "I guessed as much. She would only have gone after my father if she was desperate."

I'm no therapist, but that is an incredibly messed-up thing for a child to have to think about their parents.

Ash reached out and grabbed my wrist, pulling me to a stop. I turned to find her green eyes burning with intensity. "I'm sorry I didn't tell you about my father. I know that might make you never trust me again. But you don't have to be your father, and I don't have to be mine. Blood doesn't always tell."

I found myself smiling as she spoke. The stupid freaking butterflies needed to leave me alone. I nodded once. Maybe she was right.

"I've got something!" Alex called from farther down the hall.

We gathered around a door that looked healthier than a lot of the other ones we had passed, if a door could be said to have health. The metal sign read TERRA—MORTAL REALM—PROCEED WITH CAUTION. I had never seen anything so beautiful. I had gone too long without TV and air conditioning.

I held out the Key of Portunus and reached for the handle. "Any guesses where we are going to pop out?" I asked the group. "Good old Mother Earth is a bit bigger than Goldhall. We don't have passports, so if we're anywhere that isn't America, we're in big trouble."

"The key is more than just a simple door opener," Robin said. "Focus your mind, tell it to take you home. There are many doors in the mortal realm that it can open. Tell it which one you want."

"Los Angeles!" I shouted at the key, holding it up to my face—hopefully it understood English. Slowly, I slid the key into the lock and did my best to visualize LA. I thought about the smog, the traffic, and eternal sunshine. I thought about street tacos and ramen.

With a thundering click, the key turned, and the door opened, squealing on rusty hinges. The fluorescent lights in the hallway flickered, their incessant hum cutting out for a second before resuming with a fury. Somewhere down the hall, I thought I heard another door creak, but when I looked, I didn't see anything moving.

The door to ye old terra firma opened into a dark room. I could make out some holes in the wall and a ceiling that showed a faint light streaming in from outside. I thought I smelled a hint of char over everything.

"Well, not quite what I had in mind," I said.

Orion held up his hand for silence and strode through the door, his palm hovering near the hilt of his sword. Slowly, the rest of our band followed him through. Alex paused as he drew next to me and gave me a wicked smile.

"I quit as your manservant. I expect a written apology and a hamburger, *and* I want to be the first to congratulate you."

"Congratulate me on what?" I asked, letting him enthusiastically shake my hand.

"Getting your soul back!" My friend gave me a beaming smile and stepped through the door to our world, leaving me the last in between worlds.

He was right. I had done it—I had done it! With all the murdering, couping, and running, I had almost forgotten. The contract was breached. *I had my soul back.* A giant smile spread across my face as I looked at my friends through the door, who were all smiling back.

It had worked.

The lights in the hallway flickered again. This time I *definitely* heard a door creak open and slam shut in the hallway. "Time to go!" I said, stepping through the door, holding the key and slamming it shut behind me.

We were in an empty warehouse. The door that the key had chosen to push us out of was a broom closet or something. The building was in extreme disrepair. In the faint light, it looked like there had been a serious fire a while ago and no one had bothered to repair it since.

In fact, it kind of looked familiar...

Someone deeper in the darkness ahead of us began a slow clap.

"Uh-oh," Alex breathed.

Orion's sword leapt free of its scabbard, casting a brilliant light around us and illuminating the bones of the empty warehouse that Alex and I had accidentally summoned Lilith in, almost a year prior.

Standing in the center, on the peeling and charred paint that we had used to make the circle, was Zagan. At his feet were two large black duffel bags. His fell katana was belted at his waist, and his ever-present smirk was twice as large as usual.

"Matthew Carver," he said with a sneer. "Happy birthday."

WHAT DO YOU want?" I demanded as my
friends fanned out around me. Orion didn't
bother with any words, only a low, feral growl
as he stepped toward the CFO of Hell.

"Give it a rest, Hunter." Zagan sighed, nudging one of the bulging
bags before him with his foot. "I'm not here for yet another boring
sword fight. I think we've quite worn that out for a while, don't you?
How was the party, by the way?"

Looking at Zagan, I remembered where I had seen a blade that
ate the light before. Tania had killed her mother with a knife made
from a similar metal as the katana he carried. It had been a message
for me. The entire coup was personal.

"Your plan failed," I blurted, staring at the fallen angel. "Tania won't be the next Queen of All Fae, Dawn will."

"I suspect you underestimate the webs that the Seducer weaves," Zagan replied with a chuckle. "I would never dream of taking credit for her work. No matter, either way, you're still here."

Dawn's wink as the door closed in her face suddenly seemed much more mocking. Maybe this was payback for exposing Tania to Samael.

"I assume you're here to give Matt his soul back," Alex said, crossing his arms. He was still carrying those black masks from the battle. Zagan's eyes glittered as he noticed them, but he didn't comment.

"On the contrary, I'm here to make a delivery." He scooped up the two bags and tossed them at my feet.

"Surprise! I can read a contract too. Five million dollars, as promised." He gave me a vicious little smile.

"I think you're a little late. Midnight was like an hour ago; my birthday is over and done with," I countered, giving the bags a kick, trying to send them back toward the demon. They didn't move, and I stubbed my toe on something hard. What was in there, bricks?

A rich laugh bubbled out of Zagan. "Midnight in the Faerie Lands, maybe," he said with a broad smile. "Did you really think that the Faerie world runs on mortal Pacific Daylight Time? They don't even have a sun anymore, the poor bastards. No, no, Squire Carver, it is currently…" He pulled out a silver pocket watch on a chain and checked the time. "Ten seventeen p.m. on your birthday. A perfectly acceptable delivery time within the bounds of our contract."

I glanced at Robin, who gave me a small frown but nodded. I couldn't remember the exact time that Dan had signed the contract in my name, but the cutoff time had to be only a matter of minutes. We were so close.

"What happens if I run? You can't finish your delivery to me if you can't catch me."

Zagan rolled his eyes—or tried his best. "Yes, you could *run*," he allowed in a bored tone. "In fact, if you do, I won't even chase you."

"Why do I doubt that?" I asked, narrowing my eyes in suspicion.

"Because you are going to take that money, and you are going to thank me for it," Zagan replied, examining his fingernails.

"That's not going to happen."

"Have you *considered*, Matthew Carver, what will happen to your sister if your deal is broken like this?"

Terror froze me in its icy grip. My worst fear was unfolding before me.

"If you don't take this money tonight, you will be free. The contract will be broken, and we cannot claim you." Zagan shrugged. "Can you imagine the horrors that will await her when my master gets his hands fully on your sister? We will *eat* her. She will bear every torment in your name."

What kind of man, what kind of brother would I be if I sold my sister to my enemies to be free? I glanced at my Faerie lawyer again, who gave me a sad nod, confirming what he had told me before.

"Or," Zagan continued with a casual gesture at the five million dollars spread at my feet, "you can take the money and keep your sister safe." His cruel smile broadened. "There's always next year."

"Do you mind if I confer with my legal team for a moment?" I asked through a cotton mouth. The jaws of the trap were clear to me. Either I let the deal stay in place or the scions of Hell would take their rage out on my sister.

"Tick-tock, Matthew, we are on a schedule here," Zagan drawled, checking his pocket watch again.

I had no good choices to make. Either I sent my sister packing into an eternal hornet's nest that I had riled up, or I gave up on this chance to get my soul back. Even though there was always next year, I doubted they would drop the ball on this particular loophole again.

I glanced around the room at my friends. Each of them met my eyes, a somber understanding on their faces. Even Orion showed an expression for once. This wasn't a choice any of them could make for me, but their hearts were just as broken.

All of this work. All of the danger that my friends and I had survived—for nothing.

"Thirty seconds," Zagan hummed, tucking his pocket watch away in his pants. The CFO of Hell stood there, with his hands in his pockets, casually waiting without a care in the world.

I stared into his black eyes with my own. They weren't as intimidating as I had once thought. I had seen the true void of the Nothing. He was but a shadow. A big shadow with pointy teeth, but a shadow nonetheless.

"Twenty now," Zagan warned.

Come on, Matt! I needed to focus. All I could hear were Meg's screams when we woke her up in Lazarus's lab. How could I let her go back to an eternity of that? My older sister had always looked out for me. Now it was my turn.

"Five."

But was I falling into the trap? Of course I was. What a stupid question. Was there any way to save myself and her, or was I just locking myself in the cell next to her?

"Four."

It didn't matter, I realized. It didn't matter whether or not there was a way. I had to try. That was who I wanted to be. That was the brother my sister deserved to have.

"Three."

"Fine," I snapped, interrupting Hell's CFO proving that he knew how to count. "You've made your delivery." My words came out thick, through choked-back tears. "Now scram." Tension bled out of the room as everyone exhaled.

"One more item of business," Zagan said, turning his gaze on Ash. "Your father summons you." The departing tension must have hit a roundabout because it came piling back into the room as quickly as it left.

I glanced at Ash, nervous.

The Lady of Autumn, drew herself up to her full height. Even though she was dressed in bright colors that would be more at home at a rave, her dignity was as sharp as a razor. She showed no fear hearing her father's wishes, only the strength of her royal upbringing. Gloriana might have been an impossible mother to please, but I thought she would be proud of her fiery daughter in this moment.

"No, I think not," she told the demon.

"It's not really a request," Zagan admitted with a smirk.

"And yet it should be," Ash replied coolly. "I am accompanying my betrothed, Squire Carver, to the mortal realm. I have no time for a detour."

"Your *what?*" Zagan hissed, taking a step closer. Orion's blade leapt forward, point hovering just short of the fallen angel. Zagan seethed but took a step back. "Your father will never allow this."

"I have no father." Ash shrugged, crossing her arms. "If you see the one who gave me my bloodline, thank him for the heritage, but his opportunity to be my father came and went a long time ago."

Zagan gnashed his teeth in frustration but kept his eyes on Orion's sword, ready to strike. For some reason, the demon didn't seem eager to start a fight in this warehouse. Maybe this place was a stark reminder that the last demon who crossed us died.

"We'll see about that." He glowered at Ash before turning to face me with a wicked smile. "Be seeing you," he promised. He crouched low and leapt straight up, smashing through the rotten low ceiling of the warehouse and into the night, leaving me a soulless millionaire.

Happy birthday to Matthew Carver.

The five of us stared at the bags of cash sitting at my feet like they were venomous snakes. No one wanted to be the first one to touch them.

"Oh, for crying out loud," Ash growled after a few seconds passed, reaching down to wrench open one of the bags. As my toes had reported, it was filled to the brim with cash. Stacks and stacks of fifty- and hundred-dollar bills stared at me, each as crisp as a winter morning.

"What are the odds that these are all counterfeit and I go to jail?" I asked, staring at the mountain of pristine money before me. "How on earth did they get brand-new bills like this?"

"Oh, come on." Alex laughed, squatting down to pick up a band of money. "Who do you think runs the Federal Reserve?"

I really hate it here sometimes.

"Matthew," Robin interjected, stepping up to my shoulder. "It occurs to me that you have some expenses we should discuss."

I glared at the Faerie for a long, long moment. He stared back, a guileless smile on his face. "Do I now?" I said with a sigh. I could only imagine where this was going. The bill always comes due with the Fae.

"Your betrothed, the Lady of Autumn, is a guest at your invitation. She has never been to the mortal realm before. She has nowhere to stay, and no way to provide for herself."

"Well, we were betrothed," I protested, "but, uh, Gloriana isn't really around anymore to hold up her end of the bargain." I didn't look at Ash. "I don't know if that still counts…"

"You made a deal with the Dandelion Throne," Robin reminded, his golden eyes heavy with a sadness that I didn't understand. "There may be a new queen resting upon it, but the throne remains, as does your deal. As long as you uphold your end, Dawn will have no choice but to do the same."

Well, crap. making a deal with Gloriana was dangerous enough. I was not thrilled to find out that my least favorite cheerleader captain,

Dawn would now be holding the reigns.

"You are her host. Surely you weren't planning on having her stay at your apartment? That would be *most* improper."

I hadn't really gotten that far. I had been busy trying not to die. But I had to admit he had a point. Just because she was my betrothed didn't mean I wanted her staying with me. I barely knew the lady, for crying out loud. I glanced at Orion, who gave me a pained nod. The Hunter hates agreeing with the Fae, but when they're right, they're right.

"Okay, fair enough," I sighed, eyeing my small fortune with a bad feeling. "What do you suggest?"

"She is a princess, and used to a certain level of... comfort." Robin visibly shuddered as he glanced around the burned-out warehouse we had appeared in.

I rolled my eyes.

"I take it you are acting as her body servant?" I asked.

"Only if Her Highness wishes," Robin insisted, bowing in Ash's direction.

I glanced at my betrothed, only to find a matching giant grin on her face. Of course the two Fae thought this was hilarious.

"You always served my mother faithfully, Robin. It would be my honor to have you in my household."

"How much, Robin?" I grumbled, pinching the bridge of my nose with my finger and thumb. Hearing Alex choking on his own laughter in the background did not help either.

"Los Angeles is quite expensive. I'm sure you understand," he began.

"Just give me a number," I demanded in an exasperated tone. This was worse than taxes.

"One million," he said firmly, "with another million dollars in six months, if the lady finds she enjoys the mortal realm and wishes to reside here longer."

"Am I paying her to stay?" I demanded incredulously. "This is highway robbery."

"This is providing for a *guest*, Squire. You are on your way to being a noble of the Dandelion Court. You have responsibilities that come with your betrothed and your rise in station. Or did you think there were only perks and no real work to being nobility?"

Alex was bent over with his hands on his knees, wheezing with laughter. Even Orion looked like he was fighting with a smile. I did my best to ignore them.

"Fine," I groaned. "Deal. Can we go now?"

"Then there's the matter of my legal fees. I assume you will want to put me on retainer to help you find another way to get your soul back?"

"Isn't that part of the deal I made with the Dandelion Court?" I asked, feeling indignant.

"Yes, but this is the court in exile. We are dandelions floating in the wind. If you wish to leave the work entirely in the hands of Dawn, you are welcome to take it up with the new queen when she has time to deal with you."

I had to admit he had a point. There is a difference between someone being legally required to help you, and someone who wants to help you. I had faith that Robin would be much more motivated to get results instead of doing the bare minimum.

"How much for a retainer?" I asked. I needed all the help I could get. I might as well invest some of the Devil's money in fighting against him.

"A million seems fair," Robin mused with a mischievous smile. "Besides, you owe me for all the previous help."

Honestly, if it only cost me a million dollars to get out of owing a proper favor to a Faerie, I suspected I was getting a discount. But that didn't mean it didn't sound like a ridiculous amount of money.

"You're just making up numbers," I sputtered. "What lawyer is worth a million dollars?"

"Plenty of them, actually," Alex managed from across the room.

"Quiet, you," I snarled, pointing an accusing finger at my friend. He and Orion only laughed harder.

"I am worth more," Robin said with a shrug. "I'm giving you a discount and you know it."

Whatever. I didn't care anymore. It was all made-up money anyway. Even after my Fae expenses, I still had two million more dollars than I had started today with. That was more than enough to keep me fed and clothed for a year. What else did I need?

"Fine, you are now on retainer." I gestured at the money bag. "Have at it."

Robin dropped down to his knees and began sorting the money, his eyes moving impossibly fast as he counted the bills. His speed-reading ability was a good trick. That alone probably made him worth more than most lawyers.

I glanced at Alex, whose face was as red as a tomato, and I scooped up a couple bands of hundreds and tossed them at my friend. He stopped laughing as he caught the cash. "What's this for?"

"I know you're not supposed to tip manservants, but I couldn't help myself," I taunted.

"That's it? I was your servant for like a *month*," Alex complained as I turned away.

"Do a better job next time," I barked back.

Everyone laughed. That made me feel a little better.

After Robin finished sorting the cash, we marched to the exit of the warehouse, to the same door Alex and I had dashed out of to escape Lilith's fire almost a year ago. It felt oddly right to be bringing a new flame into the mortal realm through this door. I turned to look at my betrothed, who stood in the back of our group with both hands over her mouth, green eyes sparkling with excitement. Almost everything had gone wrong, but I didn't hate this. Not completely.

"My lady Ash," I said, giving her a deep bow from the waist. She giggled behind her hands, the sound of muffled delight barely making it through. "Welcome to the mortal world."

With a hearty kick, Alex opened the warped iron door to reveal a warehouse district in LA. We could have done better for a first look, but at least the only way to go from here was up.

With a gasp, Ash rushed outside to look at everything. The rest of the gang followed, chuckling as they watched a Faerie princess see an industrial zone for the first time in her life. I guess if you had only ever lived in a gold-and-marble prison floating in a black void, construction equipment has its own sort of magic to it.

Robin was the last one to walk past me. As he did, he leaned in close, golden eyes twinkling with his usual mischief. Softly, ever so softly, so that only I could hear him, he whispered:

"Don't despair yet, my friend. There's still a way."

STAR SUMMIT
BOOK THREE OF THE DEBT COLLECTION
AVAILABLE NOW:

Scan the QR Code below, or go to: andrewgivler.com/books

Thanks for reading Dandelion Audit!

I hope you enjoyed it. If you did as always, please leave a review on Amazon, Goodreads, and anywhere else that you review books. It helps new readers find the series, and me pay my bills!

If you want to keep up with me, go to: andrewgivler.com/links or scan this (different) QR code on your phone!

ACKNOWLEDGEMENTS

Writing SOUL FRAUD was the hardest thing I've ever done, but somehow DANDELION AUDIT was even harder. I can't thank you all enough for the kind words and excitement that you have showed over the Debt Collection in the year since the first book's release.

That energy pushed me to make this book even better. I hope I succeeded. I can't wait to see what you think and am excited for you guys to see where the story goes in STAR SUMMIT.

Thanks to my brilliant friends and Alpha Readers: Aki, Caleb, and Molly. You guys had to read the worst version of this book, but your enthusiasm shaped it tremendously. The Beta Readers who had to help me refine it even more: Alex, Britanni, Casey, Chrissy, Chris, Galen, Katie, Seb, Ryan, SM, and as always –Taylor. Also, a huge shoutout to Austin and Rich from the 2ToRamble podcast who tore this to shreds. They're excellent reviewers, so go check out their stuff.

A massive thanks also to Seth Ring, Jamie Castle, James Hunter, and Bryce O'Connor who have taught me so much about being an author and self-publishing. I couldn't have done it without them. Go read their books, they're very good.

Thanks to my incredible artist Chris McGrath for the cover. I hope the book lives up to you art. Thanks also to Shawn T. King for the incredible cover and design work, and Crystal Watanabe as always for her tireless work editing my nonsense into something coherent.

I hope you are having as much fun as I am. Buckle up, there's more to come.

Printed in the USA
CPSIA information can be obtained
at www.ICGtesting.com
LVHW090339081123
763115LV00042B/1299/J